PRESTON & CHILD

VERSES FOR THE DEAD

HEAD of ZEUS

First published in the USA in 2018 by Grand Central Publishing,
a division of Hachette Book Group, Inc.

First published in the UK in 2018 by Head of Zeus, Ltd

9 7 5 3 1 2 4 6 8

A catalogue record for this book is available from
the British Library.

ISBN (HB): 9781788546768
ISBN (XTPB): 9781788546775
ISBN (E): 9781788546751

Printed and bound in Great Britain by
CPI Group (UK) Ltd, Croydon CR0 4YY

Head of Zeus Ltd
First Floor East
5–8 Hardwick Street
London EC1R 4RG
WWW.HEADOFZEUS.COM

VERSES FOR THE DEAD

DOUGLAS PRESTON and LINCOLN CHILD are the number one bestselling co-authors of the celebrated Pendergast novels, as well as the Gideon Crew books. Preston and Child's *Relic* and *The Cabinet of Curiosities* were chosen by readers in a National Public Radio poll as being among the one hundred greatest thrillers ever written, and *Relic* was made into a number one box-office hit movie. Readers can sign up for their monthly newsletter, The Pendergast File, at www.PrestonChild.com and follow them on Facebook.

Lincoln Child dedicates this book to
his daughter, Veronica

Douglas Preston dedicates this book to
Gussie and Joe Stanislaw

VERSES
FOR THE DEAD

I

ISABELLA GUERRERO—KNOWN to her friends and fellow bridge club members as Iris—made her way demurely through the palms of Bayside Cemetery. Overhead stretched an infinite sky of pale azure. It was seven thirty in the morning, the temperature hovered at seventy-eight degrees, and the dew that still clung to the broad-bladed St. Augustine grass drenched the leather of her sandals. One plump hand clutched a Fendi bag; the other gripped the leash against which Twinkle, her Pekingese, strained ineffectually. Iris walked gingerly through the graves and coleus plantings—only three weeks ago Grace Manizetti, laden with groceries, had lost her balance while coming back from the local Publix and broken her pelvis.

The cemetery had opened half an hour before, and Iris had the place to herself. She liked it that way—Miami Beach seemed to get more congested with every passing year. Even here in Bal Harbour, at the north end of the island, traffic was worse than she remembered from the congested New York of her childhood, growing up on Queens Boulevard. And that dreadful mall they'd built a few years back north of Ninety-Sixth had only made things worse. Not only that, but an undesirable element had begun to creep up from the south, with their bodegas and *casa* this and *tienda* that. Thank goodness Francis had had the foresight to buy the condominium in Grande Palms Atlantic, right on the beach in Surfside and safe from encroachment.

Francis. She could see his grave ahead now, the headstone a trifle bleached by the Florida sun but the plot clean and neat— she had seen to that. Twinkle, aware their destination was approaching, had ceased tugging on the leash.

She had so much to be thankful to Francis for. Since he'd been taken from her three years ago, she'd only grown more aware of her gratitude. It had been Francis who'd had the foresight to move his father's butcher business from New York City to the Florida coast, back when this section of Collins Avenue was still sleepy and inexpensive. It had been Francis who'd carefully built up the establishment over the years, teaching her how to use the weighing scales and cash register and the names and qualities of the various cuts. And it had been Francis who'd sensed just the right time to sell the business—in 2007, before real estate fell apart. The huge profit they'd made had not only allowed them to buy the Grande Palms condo (at a rock-bottom price a year later) but also ensured they could enjoy many years of comfortable retirement. Who would have guessed he'd be dead of pancreatic cancer so soon?

Iris had reached the grave now, and she paused a moment to look beyond the cemetery and admire the view. Despite the crowding and traffic, it was still a tranquil sight in its own way: the Kane Concourse arching over the Harbor Islands toward the mainland, the white triangles of sailboats tacking up Biscayne Bay. And everything drenched in warm, tropical pastels. The cemetery was an oasis of calm, never more so than early in the morning, when even in March—at the height of the tourist season—Iris knew she could spend some reflective time at the grave of her departed husband.

The little vase of artificial flowers she'd placed by the headstone was somewhat askew—no doubt thanks to the tropical storm that had blown through the day before yesterday. Knees protesting, she knelt on the grave. She righted the vase, plucked a handkerchief from her handbag, wiped off the flowers, and began to tidy them. She felt Twinkle tugging on the leash again, harder than before.

"Twinkle!" she scolded. "No!" Francis had hated the name Twinkle—short for Twinkle Toes—and had always called the dog Tyler, after the street where he'd grown up. But Iris preferred Twinkle, and somehow now that he was gone she didn't think Francis would mind.

She pressed the vase into the turf to anchor it, patted the grass all around, and leaned back to admire her work. Out of the corner of her eye she saw movement—the groundskeeper maybe, or another mourner come to pay their respects to the dead. It was almost eight now, and after all, Bayside Cemetery was the only graveyard on the whole island: she couldn't expect to have it all to herself. She'd say a prayer, the one she and Francis had always said together before retiring to bed, and then head back to Grande Palms. There was a board meeting at ten, and she had some very definite things to say about the state of the plantings around the condo's entrance loop.

Twinkle was still tugging insistently at the leash, and now he was yapping, too. She scolded him again. This wasn't like him—normally the Pekingese was relatively well behaved. Except when that awful Russian blue in 7B set him off. As she rose to her feet, mentally preparing the prayer in her mind, Twinkle seized the moment to bolt, the leash slipping off Iris's wrist. He went flying away across the damp grass, dragging the leash and barking.

"Twinkle!" she said sharply. "Come back here this instant!"

The dog came to a frantic halt at a headstone in the next row. Even at this distance she could tell the stone was older than Francis's, but not by much. There was a scattering of fresh flowers at the base and what appeared to be a handwritten note. But this was not what caught Iris's attention; flowers and notes, as well as a variety of cherished mementos, could be found on half the graves in Bayside. No: it was Twinkle himself. He'd apparently found something lying at the base of the headstone—and was making a fuss over it. She couldn't see what it was, as the object was blocked by his body, but he was hunched over it, busily sniffing and licking.

"Twinkle!" This was unseemly. The last thing Iris wanted was to make a scene in this place of repose. Had he found an old dog toy? A piece of candy, perhaps, dropped by some passing child?

The prayer would have to wait until she'd grabbed the dog's leash.

Stuffing the handkerchief back into her handbag, she strode toward Twinkle. But as she approached, scolding and tut-tutting, the dog grabbed his newfound prize and scampered off. With a mixture of dismay and embarrassment she saw him disappear into a grove of cabbage palms.

She sighed with vexation. Francis would not have approved; he'd always maintained that dogs should be well disciplined. "Fluffy little cur," he would have said. Well, Twinkle would get some discipline tonight: no Fig Newton with his Purina.

Muttering to herself, Iris followed in the direction the dog had run, stopping when she reached the stand of palms. She looked around. Twinkle was nowhere to be seen. She opened her mouth to call his name, then thought better of it—she was in a cemetery, after all. Chasing after a dog that had gotten loose was bad enough. Besides, the movement she'd noticed earlier had now resolved itself into a group of three people, two girls and a middle-aged man, standing in a semicircle around a grave to her left. It wouldn't do to make a scene.

Just then, a flurry of movement caught her eye: it was Twinkle. He was some twenty yards ahead, down near where the graveyard met the water, and he was digging frantically in an amaryllis bed. Dirt was flying everywhere.

This was *terrible*. Iris hustled forward as quickly as she could, clutching her bag. The dog was so engrossed in his digging that he did not notice as she came up behind, grasped the leash, and gave him a tug. Surprised, Twinkle did a half somersault, but despite being dragged away by the collar he refused to let go of his prize.

"Bad dog!" Iris scolded as loudly as she dared. *"Bad dog!"* She tried to grab whatever it was that Twinkle had found, intending to yank it away, but he evaded her swipe. It was the size of a miniature toy football, but it was so covered by dirt and dog slobber that she could not tell what it was.

"Drop that, do you hear me?" Twinkle growled as Iris reached for it again, and this time she managed to grab one end. She knew he wouldn't bite her—it was just a question of pulling the thing out of his jaws. But the dog's prize was disgustingly slippery, and he was holding on to it with tenacity. The two struggled, Iris dragging the dog toward her, Twinkle resisting, digging his paws in the grass. She glanced over her shoulder apprehensively, but the group at the other grave site had not noticed.

The nasty tug-of-war lasted nearly thirty seconds, but in the end the thing was just too big for the dog's small jaws to maintain a firm grip, and with one determined tug Iris managed to yank it away. As she straightened up, checking that both her handbag and leash were secure on her wrists, she registered that the thing was a piece of meat. A gluey, reddish ooze had seeped out of it during the struggle, staining her hand and dirtying Twinkle's muzzle. At the same time, she realized how unusual a piece of meat it was—tough and leathery. Her first instinct was to let go in disgust, but Twinkle would only have seized it again.

With Twinkle yapping and leaping, trying to reclaim his find, Iris reached into her handbag, pulled out the handkerchief, and began wiping the thing off. What on earth was it doing lying on a grave?

She cleaned one side, and a short, thick crimson tube—like the end of a radiator hose—sprang into view. Suddenly she stopped, frozen in horror. She had been a butcher's wife long enough to know now exactly what was in her hand. It had to be a dream, a nightmare; it could not possibly be real.

The sense of unreality lasted only a split second. With a shriek of revulsion she dropped the thing as if it had burned her. Instantly, the dog grabbed it in his gore-drenched jaws and once again slipped free, running off in triumph, leash flapping. But Iris did not notice. There was a strange roaring in her ears, and she suddenly felt a wave of heat come over her. Black spots danced around the edges of her vision. The roaring grew louder, then louder still, and the last thing she saw before crumpling to the ground in a dead faint was the group around the other grave running in her direction.

2

Assistant Director in Charge Walter Pickett, clad only in a damp towel wrapped around his waist, relaxed in the cedar-walled sauna. It was large, with two racks of benches, and it was empty save for one other man—young and tall, with a swimmer's build—sitting at the far end near the door. Pickett himself had taken a position beside the dipper of water that helped control the sauna's heat and humidity. Pickett preferred to be in control of any situation in which he found himself.

A single sheet of paper, protected in a sheath of clear plastic, sat on the bench beside him.

He glanced over at the thermometer set into the wall, beads of moisture partly obscuring its face: a pleasant 165 degrees.

The sauna adjoined the men's dressing room and shower complex deep inside the Federal Auxiliary Support building, on Worth Street. "Auxiliary Support" contained not only a variety of satellite offices, but also a shooting range and such amenities as squash courts, a pool, and of course this sauna—and it was just around the corner from his office in 26 Federal Plaza. It was a far cry from the spartan Denver FBI office where he'd been special agent in charge until three months ago.

Since graduating from the Academy, Pickett had moved up quickly through the ranks, making a name for himself in the counterespionage and criminal enterprise divisions, as well as the Office of Professional Responsibility. All along he'd had his eye on this job: head of New York City operations. It was one of the truly top positions in the Bureau and the logical stepping-stone to Washington. Everything depended now on running a tight ship and scoring big on high-profile cases...and Pickett had no doubt of his ability to do both.

He settled back against the wall, pressing his bare shoulders to the hot wood. He could feel his pores opening in the moist heat. It was a pleasant sensation. He let his eyes half close as he ruminated. Pickett was supremely confident in his abilities, and he assiduously avoided what he had seen derail many other talented agents—he was not a blowhard, an obvious careerist, or a martinet. One of his most valuable posts had been in High-Value Detainee Interrogation, where he'd spent several formative years after the Academy. That, along with his stint in OPR, had given him a degree of psychological insight rare in an FBI supervisor. Ever since, he had put to good use what he'd learned about human behavior and the nature of persuasion.

When he'd taken over the New York Field Office, he'd found it in a state of disarray. Morale was low and case clearance rates were below average. The office felt top-heavy with desk jockeys. He had solved the latter problem via a series of transfers and early retirements. He wasn't a micromanager by nature, but he'd taken the time to look at each division, find the most promising individuals, and entrust them with positions of greater responsibility—even if it meant elevating them above

their longer-serving peers. Turning the office into a true mer-
itocracy had solved the morale issue. Despite his tenure in
OPR—like all law enforcement, FBI agents distrusted people
who'd worked in internal affairs—he'd earned the respect and
loyalty of his subordinates. And now the New York office had
become a humming, well-oiled machine. Even the case clearance rate was starting to take care of itself. He'd managed to
turn things around, and do it in a single season. It was a job
well done, but he was careful to conceal any trace of self-
congratulation.

Despite all this, there was one issue left to deal with. It was a
thorny personnel matter inherited from his predecessor. He had
left this particular issue for last.

Over the years, Pickett had dealt with his share of trouble-
some agents. In his experience, such people were either
antisocial loners or chip-on-the-shoulder types who'd come into
the Bureau with a lot of personal baggage. If they were dead-
weights, he did not hesitate to transfer them the hell out—after
all, Nebraska needed its share of field agents, too. If they showed
promise, or boasted impressive records, then it came down to
reconditioning. He would thrust them out of their comfort
zone; dump them into an unexpected environment; give them a
wholly unfamiliar task. Make sure they knew a bright light was
shining on them. The technique had been effective in interroga-
tions and internal misconduct investigations—and it was just as
effective in bringing rogue agents back into the FBI family.

If this agent's file was anything to go on, the man was about
as rogue as they came. But Pickett had parsed his personnel
jacket—at least, its unclassified sections—and outlined a course
of action designed to address the problem.

He looked up at the clock: 1:00 PM exactly. As if on cue, the sauna door opened and a man stepped in. Pickett glanced over with practiced casualness and had to restrain himself from doing a double take. The man was tall and thin, and so blond that his carefully trimmed hair was almost white. His eyes were a glacial hue and as cold and unreadable as the ice they resembled. But instead of being stripped and wearing a towel around his waist, the man wore a black suit, impeccably tailored and buttoned, along with a starched white shirt sporting a perfectly dimpled knot at the collar. His shoes were polished to a brilliant shine and were of the expensive, handmade sort. Of all the thoughts that could have wandered into Pickett's temporarily stunned mind, the foremost was: *Did he actually walk through the locker room, showers, and pool dressed like that?* He could only imagine the fuss it must have caused as the agent broke all the rules on his way to the sauna.

The other man in the sauna, sitting near the door, looked up, frowned in brief surprise, and glanced down again.

Pickett recovered immediately. He knew this agent had a reputation for being epically eccentric. That was why he'd chosen not only to change up the man's duty orders, but this location to discuss them. In his experience, atypical situations—such as meeting naked in a sauna—helped throw challenging subjects off balance, giving him the upper hand.

He'd let things play out.

Before speaking, he picked up the wooden dipper from the water barrel, filled it, then poured it over the sauna stones. A satisfyingly thick gush of steam wafted through the room.

"Agent Pendergast," he said in a level voice.

The man in black nodded. "Sir."

"There are several banks of lockers beyond the showers. Would you care to change out of your clothes?"

"That won't be necessary. The heat agrees with me."

Pickett looked the man up and down. "Take a seat, then."

Agent Pendergast plucked a towel from a pile near the door, walked over, wiped the bench next to Pickett free of moisture, then folded it neatly and sat down.

Pickett was careful not to show any surprise. "First," he said, "I want you to accept my condolences on the death of Howard Longstreet. He was a superb intelligence director, and I understand something of a mentor to you."

"He was the finest man I ever knew, save one."

This was not the reply Pickett had expected, but he nodded and stuck to his agenda. "I've been meaning to speak with you for some time. I hope you won't mind my being blunt."

"On the contrary. Unlike knives, blunt conversations make for the quickest work."

Pickett looked at Pendergast's face for any hint of insubordination, but the agent's expression was utterly neutral. He went on. "I'm sure it won't surprise you to learn that, in my few months as head of the New York Field Office, I've heard a lot about you—both official and unofficial. To put it frankly, you have a reputation of being a lone wolf—but one who enjoys an exceptionally high percentage of successful cases."

Pendergast accepted this compliment with a little nod, such as one might make to a partner at the beginning of a waltz. All his movements, like his speech, were measured and catlike, as if he were stalking prey.

Now Pickett delivered the backhand of the compliment. "You also have one of the highest rates of suspects not going to trial because, in the FBI vernacular, they were *deceased during the course of investigation.*"

Another graceful nod.

"Executive Associate Director Longstreet was not only your mentor. He was also your guardian angel in the Bureau. From what I understand, he seems to have kept the inquiry boards off you; defended your more unorthodox actions; shielded you from blowback. But now that Longstreet is gone, the top brass is in something of a quandary—when it comes to dealing with you, I mean."

By now, Pickett had expected to see a degree of concern flickering in the agent's eyes. There was none. He reached for the dipper, poured more water on the stones. The temperature in the sauna rose to a toasty 180 degrees.

Pendergast straightened his tie, refolded one leg over the other. He did not even appear to be sweating.

"What we've decided to do, in short, is give you rein to continue with what you do best: pursue psychologically unorthodox killers, using the methods that have brought you success. With a few caveats, naturally."

"Naturally," Pendergast said.

"Which brings us to your next assignment. Just this morning, a human heart was found left on a grave in Miami Beach. The grave belonged to one Elise Baxter, who strangled herself with a bedsheet in Katahdin, Maine, eleven years ago. On the grave—"

"Why was Ms. Baxter buried in Florida?" Pendergast interrupted smoothly.

Pickett paused. He did not like to be interrupted. "She lived in Miami. She was in Maine on vacation. Her family had her body flown home to be interred." He paused to make sure there were no other interjections, then he picked up the sheet of plastic-enclosed paper. "On the grave was a note. It read—" he consulted the paper— "'Dear Elise, I am so sorry for what happened to you. The thought of how you must have suffered has haunted me for years. I hope you will accept this gift with my sincere condolences. So let us go then, you and I—others are awaiting gifts as well.' It was signed, 'Mister Brokenhearts.'"

Pickett paused to let this sink in.

"Very obliging of Mister Brokenhearts," Pendergast said after a moment, "although the gift does seem in rather poor taste."

Pickett frowned through the sweat gathering around his eyes, but he still caught not the slightest whiff of insubordination. The man sat there, cool as a cucumber despite the heat.

"The heart was found by a cemetery visitor at around seven forty-five this morning. At ten thirty, the body of a woman was discovered beneath some shrubbery on the Miami Beach Boardwalk, about ten miles to the south. Her heart had been cut out. Miami Beach PD is still working the scene, but we already know one thing: the victim's heart was the one found on the grave."

Now, for the first time, Pickett saw something flash in Pendergast's eyes—a gleam, like a diamond being turned toward the light.

"We don't know the connection between Elise Baxter and the woman killed today. But it seems evident there must be one. And if this mention of 'others' in the note can be trusted, more killings might be in the offing. Elise Baxter died in Maine, so even though it was a suicide, interstate jurisdiction means we're involved." He put the piece of paper down on the bench and slid it toward Pendergast. "You're heading for Miami to investigate this murder, first thing tomorrow morning."

The gleam remained in Pendergast's eyes. "Excellent. Most excellent."

Pickett's fingers tightened on the sheet as Pendergast reached for it. "There's just one thing. You'll be working with a partner."

Pendergast went still.

"I mentioned there would be a few caveats. This is the biggest. Howard Longstreet isn't around to watch your back anymore, Agent Pendergast, or to bring you home after you've gone off the reservation. The Bureau can't ignore your remarkable record of success. But neither can it ignore the high mortality rate you racked up achieving it. So we're partnering you up, which of course is normal FBI protocol. I've assigned you one of our sharpest young agents. You'll be lead agent on the case, naturally, but he'll assist—every step of the way. He'll function as both a sounding board...and, if necessary, a gut check. And who knows? You may come to appreciate the arrangement."

"I should think that my record speaks for itself," Pendergast said, in the same silky antebellum drawl. "I function best on my own. A partner can interfere with that process."

"You seemed to work well enough with that New York City cop, what's his name—D'Agosta?"

"He is exceptional."

"The man I'm giving you is also exceptional. More to the point, it's a deal breaker. Either you accept a partner, or we give the case to someone else." *And let you twist in the wind until you come around*, Pickett thought privately.

During this brief speech, an expression had come over Pendergast's features: a most peculiar expression, one that Pickett could not, for all his long psychological experience, identify. For a moment, the only sound was the hissing of the sauna stones.

"I'll take your silence as assent. And now's as good a time as any to meet your new partner. Agent Coldmoon, would you mind joining us?"

At this, the silent young man sitting in the far corner stood up, snugged the towel around his waist, and—bathed in a sheen of sweat—came over to stand before them. His skin was a light olive brown, and his features were fine and, in some respects, almost Asiatic. He glanced dispassionately at the men seated before him. Trim and erect, he looked almost a model agent. Only his hair—jet black, worn rather long, and parted in the middle—did not fit the image. Pickett smiled inwardly. His pairing of these two was a masterstroke. Pendergast would be in for a surprise.

"This is Special Agent Coldmoon," Pickett said. "He's been with the agency eight years, and already he's distinguished himself in both the Cyber Division and the Criminal Investigative Division. The fitness reports submitted by his superiors have never been short of exemplary. Eighteen months ago, he was awarded the FBI Shield of Bravery for meritorious service during an undercover operation in Philadelphia. I wouldn't be surprised if someday he collects as many commendations as you have. I think you'll find him a quick study."

Agent Coldmoon remained expressionless under this panegyric. Meanwhile, Pickett noticed, the strange look had left Pendergast's face, to be replaced with a genuine smile.

"Agent Coldmoon," Pendergast said, extending his hand. "A pleasure to make your acquaintance."

"Likewise." Coldmoon shook the proffered hand.

"If your credentials are anything like ADC Pickett here describes," Pendergast continued, "I'm sure you will prove a great asset to what promises to be a most interesting case."

"I'll do all I can to assist," Coldmoon said.

"Then we shall get along famously," Pendergast said. He glanced back at Pickett. Except for a single bead of moisture on Pendergast's forehead, the heat didn't seem to have affected him in the slightest: the man's shirt and suit looked as crisp as ever. "We leave for Miami first thing tomorrow morning, you say?"

Pickett nodded. "Ticket and a summary of your orders are waiting on your desk as we speak."

"In that case, I had better prepare. Thank you, sir, for considering me for this case. Agent Coldmoon, I shall see you on the morrow." He nodded at each in turn, then stood and exited the sauna—with the same light, easy movements with which he had entered.

Both men watched the sauna door close behind him. Pickett waited a full minute before speaking again. Then, when he was sure Pendergast was not coming back, he cleared his throat. "Okay," he said to Coldmoon. "You've just heard me outline your cover. You're going to play second fiddle on this case."

Coldmoon nodded.

"Any questions about what your *real* assignment is regarding Pendergast?"

"None."

"Very good. I'll expect regular reports."

"Yes, sir."

"That will be all."

Without another word, Special Agent Coldmoon turned and left the sauna. Pickett picked up another dipperful of water, poured it over the cherry-colored stones, then leaned back once again, sighing contentedly as another blast of steam filled the cedar-lined room.

3

Mrs. Trask wheeled the tea cart carefully down the shadowy hall leading from the kitchens of the mansion at 891 Riverside Drive, New York City. It was unusual, serving tea at this time of the afternoon, not quite three o'clock—normally, Pendergast preferred it late rather than early. But such had been his request, along with a lavish presentation: instead of the usual ascetic green tea and ginger biscuits, today there were Bath buns with lemon curd, scones, clotted cream, madeleines—even miniature Battenberg cakes. As a result, it was the first time in ages she'd had to serve afternoon tea on a cart instead of a simple silver tray. She felt fairly certain this was all meant to please his ward, Constance—despite the fact she ate like a bird and would probably touch little of it.

Indeed, since their rather abrupt return to the mansion just over a week before, Pendergast had seemed especially attentive to Constance. Even Proctor, Pendergast's stoic chauffeur-*cum*-bodyguard, had mentioned it to Mrs. Trask. Pendergast had been more than usually talkative, drawing Constance out on her favorite subjects late into the night. He had assisted with her

long-term task of researching the complex and—it seemed—
often mysterious Pendergast family tree. He had even professed
an interest in her latest project: a terrarium devoted to the prop-
agation of imperiled carnivorous plants.

Mrs. Trask moved from the corridor into the reception hall,
the wheels of the tea cart creaking over the marble floor. From
the direction of the library, she could hear the low tones of Pendergast and Constance in conversation. Just this quiet sound
gladdened her heart. She didn't know why Constance had left so
suddenly for India last December, or what had occasioned Pendergast's own recent trip to bring her home. That affair was between Pendergast and his ward: Mrs. Trask was simply pleased
the household was together again. And though even *that* was
about to be interrupted—with Pendergast's abrupt news that he
was bound for Florida—Mrs. Trask took comfort in knowing
the journey was merely business.

It was true she rather disapproved of Pendergast's "business"—
but that was something she kept to herself.

Now she wheeled the cart into the library, with its deep mahogany tones; cabinets laden with rare fossils, minerals, and
artifacts; and walls of leather-bound books rising to a coffered
ceiling. A large fire was blazing on the hearth, and two wing
chairs had been pulled up close to it. They were empty, however,
and Mrs. Trask searched for the room's occupants. As her eyes
adjusted to the flickering light, she made them out. They were
together in a far corner, heads almost touching as they bent over
something of evident interest. Of course—it must be the new
terrarium. Even now, Mrs. Trask could hear Constance speaking of it, her contralto voice just audible over the crackle of the
flames. "...I find it ironic that *Nepenthes campanulata*—which
for fifteen years was believed extinct—is now merely considered

threatened, while *Nepenthes aristolochioides*, then barely recognized as a species, is presently critically endangered."

"Ironic indeed," Pendergast murmured.

"Note the peculiar morphology of the *aristolochioides*. The peristome is almost vertical—rare among pitcher plants. Its feeding mechanism is most interesting. I'm still awaiting a shipment of native insects from Sumatra, but local rhinoceros beetles seem a satisfactory diet. Would you care to feed it?" And Constance held out a pair of forceps, almost a foot long, which glinted in the firelight, with a wriggling beetle at the end.

There was the briefest of hesitations. "I'd much prefer to watch your more practiced hand at work."

Mrs. Trask chose this moment to clear her throat and trundle the tea cart forward. Both occupants turned toward her.

"Ah, Mrs. Trask!" Pendergast said, turning from the glass-walled terrarium and approaching her. "Punctual as always."

"Rather more than punctual," Constance said, coming up behind Pendergast, her violet eyes scanning the cart. "It's just gone three. Aloysius, did you request this cornucopia?"

"I did indeed."

"Are we having the Trojan army for tea?"

"I'm giving myself a sending-off party."

Constance frowned.

"Besides," Pendergast went on, sitting down and helping himself to a madeleine, "you look thinner, subsisting on that monastic diet."

"I ate very well, thank you." Constance took a seat in the opposite wing chair, bobbed hair swinging at the motion. "You know, I really wish you'd let me come to Florida. This case that's suddenly been dropped in your lap—it sounds intriguing."

"And *I* really wish I had not had a partner forced upon me. But there it is. Constance, I promise you shall be both my sounding board and my oracle, *à la distance*."

Mrs. Trask chuckled as she poured out two cups of tea. "Can you imagine, our Mr. Pendergast with a partner underfoot? It'll never do. When it comes to working with others, he's a lost cause—if you'll pardon my saying so."

"I'll pardon your saying so," Pendergast replied, "if you'll be good enough to bundle a few of these madeleines in with the rest of my packing. I understand that certain airplane food can be hazardous—if not worse."

"Is he indeed a lost cause?" Constance said, turning to Mrs. Trask. "One can always hope."

Mrs. Trask had already turned to leave, and so she missed the look that—so fleetingly—passed between Pendergast and the woman seated opposite him.

4

AT PRECISELY TWENTY minutes to seven that same evening, Special Agent Pendergast—having checked into the Fontainebleau Hotel and ensured that the La Mer Presidential Suite he'd booked was to his liking—strolled through the echoing lobby in the direction of the Atlantic. The sprawling, marbled space—with its "Stairway to Nowhere," flocks of chattering guests, and labyrinthine entrances and exits—felt more like a first-class departure lounge than a hotel. Glass doors whispered open as he approached, and he exited into the expansive grounds. Navigating among several sparkling pools, he passed bars, spas, and lush plantings on his way to the South Tropez Lawn. Sunbathers, glancing up at him through their Oakleys or Tom Fords, were not surprised by the black suit he wore; they assumed he was some sort of hotel lackey headed to one of the private poolside cabanas. Other butlers in black could be seen making their way among the cabanas, bringing their guests everything from fruit smoothies to fifteen-hundred-dollar bottles of Dom Pérignon.

Crossing the lawn, Pendergast strolled along a path that

wound through manicured grounds until it reached a set of steps, which rose to intersect a walkway of wooden planks, lined with royal palms. This was the Miami Beach Boardwalk, a pedestrian boulevard that hugged the oceanfront from Indian Beach Park down almost to the port of Miami.

Pendergast turned southward, then paused. To his left ran a narrow strip of shrubbery and sea oats, beyond which lay the beach; to his right stretched an unbroken procession of hotels, condominiums, and pleasure domes of various types, brilliant white against the cobalt sky. There was the faintest of breezes; the temperature was eighty degrees and the air pleasantly humid. A septuagenarian woman walked past wearing huge round sunglasses and a pink thong bathing suit, balancing carefully on Italian sandals with stiletto heels.

Pendergast gazed thoughtfully about for a few moments more. Then he straightened the knot of his necktie, shot his cuffs, and joined the scantily clad throng of pedestrians walking along the promenade. A leisurely half an hour's stroll took him as far south as Twenty-Third Street, by which time the boardwalk had descended to a paved surface. Another few blocks, and the crowd of pedestrians thickened and milled about. The reason was obvious: a hundred yards ahead, the boardwalk was roped off by yellow crime scene tape.

Now the strip of shrubbery to his left had widened into a series of hedges and clipped topiary shrubs—each section maintained by a swanky hotel on the opposite side of the boardwalk. Beyond the elegant plantings ran a long berm. Turning down a narrow lane, Pendergast climbed the concrete steps to the top of the berm, his silvery eyes taking in everything. Here was another path, this one slender and sandy. Ahead and below stretched the beach itself, lined with rows of umbrellas and chaise longues, punctuated by the occasional lifeguard stand. Beyond lay the Atlantic, its brilliant cerulean turning a pale aquamarine as it neared the coastline.

He gazed seaward for a long moment, then he turned west, taking in the stunning display of wealth that made up this part of the island. Beyond he could make out Biscayne Bay and, still farther west, the spires of downtown Miami. It was now seven thirty, and the sun was preparing to dip below the horizon: something it had already done ninety minutes earlier, back in New York. Pink opalescent clouds gathered in the distance.

For a time Pendergast stood motionless, the light breeze riffling his hair. At last, he looked back down toward the section of shrubbery and boardwalk set off by yellow tape. A number of rubberneckers in the hotels opposite were doing the same. The murder had already hit the news feeds, but the police had managed to keep the stolen heart out of it.

Now, at the same leisurely pace, he descended the stairs again and approached the tape. Most of the cordoned area was made up of what appeared to be a chest-high hedge maze, meticulously pruned, set between the boardwalk and the sea berm. Pendergast stepped forward until the lower button of his suit jacket was just touching the tape. Clearly, the main event was over: the only people he could see within the cordon were a Crime Scene Unit worker—still wearing his mask and booties— and a police officer sitting on a nearby bench, evidently keeping the scene secure.

Pendergast had approached so quietly that the policeman remained unaware of his presence. It was only when he began to duck beneath the tape that the man looked over. The vacant expression on his face changed to one of annoyance, and he rose from the bench and began walking over, hiking up his pants and straightening the duty belt around his waist. He was in his late forties, with thinning chestnut hair, widely set eyes, and a florid face. Despite his relatively thin limbs, a noticeable paunch pushed against his shirt.

"Hey!" he said roughly. "You! Stop!"

Pendergast obliged—but not until he had slipped under the tape and straightened up once again.

The cop came up, frowning. Tiny blood vessels were sprinkled liberally over his cheeks. Below his shoulders were stitched the blue-and-gold patches of the Miami Beach PD. "What the hell do you think you're doing? This is a restricted area. Get back behind the tape!"

"Excuse me, Officer," Pendergast said in his most engaging voice, "but I believe my presence here is authorized."

The cop looked him up and down. "What are you—an undertaker? They took the body away hours ago."

"I am not, I fear, an undertaker, although you can be forgiven the misconception. I'm a special agent with the FBI."

"FBI?" The cop's wide-set eyes narrowed. "Let's see your creds."

"Certainly." Pendergast reached into his suit pocket, removed a slim leather wallet, and raised it, letting it slip open. The top part contained his ID, with rank and photo; below was his shield.

The local cop scrutinized it carefully. Then he gazed back at Pendergast with less suspicion but increased animosity. "FBI," he repeated. "I did hear something about you boys coming down. Something about *liaising* with us on this case."

"That's right," Pendergast said. "How good of you to recall, Officer—" he glanced at the nameplate— "Officer Kleinwessel. Now if you don't mind, I'll just take a look for myself."

But as he stepped forward, the cop put a hand on his chest to stop him. "You're not going anywhere, pal."

Pendergast did not like being touched. "I beg your pardon?"

"Like I said—I heard about you boys coming down. What I heard from my sergeant was the FBI would be here tomorrow. Not today. The paperwork hasn't cleared our end. Unless you can produce a letter of authorization, I can't let you onto this crime scene."

Pendergast paused. He recalled a certain level of grumbling in the FBI about Miami law enforcement. They seemed to have a collective chip on their shoulders when it came to the FBI, dating back to the tenure of an overly zealous SAC of the Miami Field Office. There had been one especially unpleasant contretemps a few years back in which the FBI attempted to cuff an MBPD bicycle officer and remove him from the scene of a crime. Now, it seemed, the favor was being returned.

Pendergast closed his shield but kept it in hand. "I have my orders," he said, "and they state that my task is to examine the site of this homicide."

"And I have *my* orders. And they say not to let anyone onto this crime scene until I hear differently from my sergeant. Now get back on the other side of that tape...*sir*."

"Officer," Pendergast said in a tone of infinite patience, "you have seen my credentials. You yourself acknowledge that the FBI will be assisting. I would be most obliged if you'd kindly step aside and allow me to investigate."

"*Investigate?*" The cop laughed. "I guess you think you're some kind of Sherlock Holmes."

"Officer Kleinwessel, there is no reason to be insulting."

"I'm just stating a fact. And that fact is, you and your *deduc-*

tions will just have to wait until tomorrow—that is, unless you have written authorization saying otherwise."

Pendergast considered this. He had his orders from Pickett, of course—but they sat, along with tomorrow's plane ticket, on his office desk, which he had not visited in several days. Now he leaned forward against the restraining hand.

"You mentioned Sherlock Holmes," he said in a mellifluous drawl. "I never much cared for the fellow myself—he always seemed so needlessly melodramatic. But very well; if it's Sherlock Holmes you want, then Holmes you shall have." He paused a moment. "Officer Kleinwessel, I see no reason that we should not be friends. Do you?"

Kleinwessel's response was to give Pendergast a small push toward the tape.

"And as your *friend*, I feel honor-bound to warn you that you are putting your career, your marriage—and possibly your life— in jeopardy."

"I don't know what kind of bullshit you're talking. But I'll only tell you once more. Move away from this crime scene or I'll handcuff your ass."

"I fear it is not bullshit at all. Since your retirement is approaching, and you no doubt wish to retain that meager pension you have coming, you might consider doing a better job of concealing your drinking habit. Although perhaps it's academic— that Cuban Hound brand of rum you favor is not only high-proof, but rife with damaging aldehydes and esters. Unless you start abstaining immediately, it seems likely that cirrhosis of the liver will make your retirement one of short duration."

He paused. Kleinwessel opened his mouth. "What the hell—?"

"Your wife must be a patient woman, having to endure your drinking all these years. If she knew you had a mistress as well—

a rather down-market mistress in Opa-Locka, too—it would undoubtedly be the final straw. And so you see, Officer Klein-wessel, I *do* care about you. I've just explained how your job, marriage, and life are in jeopardy—hidden jeopardy, for the time being. Of course, it's always possible that your indiscretions might come to light." And with this, Pendergast replaced his ID wallet in his suit pocket—making a show of removing his cell phone at the same time.

The color had drained from the policeman's face, leaving him deathly pale. He looked around, as if appealing for invisible aid. "How could you—" He almost choked. "How could you—" he spluttered, face aflame, unable to finish.

"Are you asking me, sir, how I have made my, as you called them, 'deductions'?"

Pendergast waited in silence, but Officer Kleinwessel seemed unable to formulate a reply.

"Well then: I observe from the ring on your right little finger that you graduated from the police academy nineteen years ago—the date is graven for all to see—meaning that your twenty is almost up. Yet for all your time on the force, you wear neither insignia nor chevrons, meaning that you remain of low rank: the very fact you were assigned to guard an inactive crime scene speaks volumes. Hence the minimal pension. And while we're on the subject of rings, I see you are not wearing your wedding ring. The pale band of skin around your ring finger, however, suggests it has recently been removed—and the callus on your knuckle implies that taking it off and putting it on again is a common procedure. As for the nature of your mistress, a mere glance at your clothing is sufficient. When the Opa-Locka neighborhood northwest of here was incorporated early in the twentieth century, its founders famously employed a Moorish architectural theme. As part of this theme, an exotic ground cover from the Middle East, known as *Erodium glandiatum*, was planted in the public areas. The seed of that *Erodium* species has a most characteristic appearance: long and thin, one end like a corkscrew and the other feathery, like the gills of a lobster. Opa-Locka happens to be this plant's *unique and only* habitat in the United States—that, plus its odd-looking seed, has anchored the fact in my memory. You currently have at least two specimens of said seed clinging to your person: one behind your right knee, and another peeping from the cuff of your trousers. The former is fresh, the latter rather bedraggled—indicating that you have been in the vicinity of Opa-Locka at least twice in recent days, and probably more, while in uniform. Alas, Opa-Locka has not prospered over the years. If that were not enough to establish the social stratum of your paramour, then the very faint odor of cheap perfume—Night of Desire, if I'm not mistaken—wafting from your person would suffice."

The cop had lowered his arms and retreated several steps, looking at Pendergast as if he had some kind of contagious disease. "How the *fuck* do you know all that?" he asked, his voice high.

"Elementary, my dear Kleinwessel."

"I haven't had a drink in ten years," the man said in a whining tone. "You can't prove that I have. What's this shit about Cuban Hound rum?"

"There is no point lying to me, Officer. As I said, I'm trying to help. The protruding abdomen evident from the strained buttons of your shirt, taken with the overall gauntness of your physique, is indicative of advanced ascites. The phymatous rosacea evident on your face is also suggestive. As for the type of alcohol, not only is Cuban Hound the cheapest, most potent, and most readily available brand of spirits in the region, but its distinctive pint bottle is most convenient for carrying discreetly...and apart from the aroma, I note that the rear right pocket of your trousers has grown rather shiny in precisely that shape. Now, Officer, may I proceed with my work? Or—?" He raised his cell phone with a smile.

For a moment, the officer's jaw worked futilely, the muscles of his face alternately clenching and relaxing. And then, without a word, he stepped aside.

"Much obliged," Pendergast said. As he glided past, he paused to put a hand lightly on Kleinwessel's shoulder. "I shall be sure to have a word with your sergeant, telling him how very useful you have been. Perhaps we can get you that chevron, after all." Then he leaned in, as if to impart a secret. "By the way," he said in a low tone, "poor Conan Doyle got it all wrong: Sherlock Holmes used the process of *induction*—not deduction."

He then moved on unimpeded through the hedge maze, occasionally pausing here and there to kneel, take a loupe from his pocket, and examine something in the mulch that lined the path. At one point he removed a pair of tweezers from his suit jacket, plucked a tiny item from the undergrowth, and placed it in a small test tube.

Dusk was gathering by the time he reached the far side of the hedge, where the lone CSU worker was packing up and preparing to leave. Pendergast showed him his FBI shield, and the man proved far more helpful than the officer had been. He pointed to an area beneath the hedge wall where numerous marker flags had been placed. The mulch was almost black here, and very damp—soaked with a great deal of blood. Pendergast knelt once again and pressed the ground lightly with his fingertips, noting its sponginess.

He removed a small penlight and shone it around. "What can you tell me about the killing?"

"It seems the initial attack was a knife wound across the neck," the technician said, pulling down his mask. "She was dragged from the path into this isolated spot, her throat cut from behind with a very sharp knife, her chest chopped open with the edge of some large instrument—probably a hatchet—and her heart removed. The M.E. believes she was already unconscious at the time of excision—it was loss of blood that killed her. The body was rolled beneath the hedge—here—and mulch kicked loosely over it."

"Blood spatter?"

"What you'd expect. Primarily projection spatter onto the underside of the hedge and in the surrounding mulch."

"When was the proximate time of death?"

"Around four o'clock this morning, give or take."

"And she was found by—?"

"A couple of newlyweds from Seattle. They chose that spot to fool around." The man nodded toward a nearby bench.

"This was around ten thirty, I believe?"

"Ten fifteen, yes."

From his kneeling position, Pendergast looked around. The hedge was thick, and at four in the morning on a moonless night the spot would be very dark indeed. The boardwalk and beach would be deserted, or nearly so. He glanced upward; the view of the nearby hotels was obscured by palm trees and ornamental bushes. Given the populous nature of the barrier island, it was a well-chosen location for a murder.

"May I have a moment?" he asked. "I'm not gowned up."

"No worries, we're all done here," the CSU worker replied.

Pendergast searched the area carefully for fifteen minutes,

occasionally employing his loupe, tweezers, flashlight, and cell phone camera. But it was as Kleinwessel had said—there was very little to see.

At last he stood. "Thank you for your patience."

"Of course." The man picked up his case and began walking toward the exit to the hedge maze.

Pendergast fell in beside him. "Is there anything else of note about the murder?"

"Nothing, except that we found a couple of bloody footprints leading away from the scene."

"Footprints?" Pendergast raised his eyebrows. "That would seem worthy of note."

"They were made by a pair of cheap men's sandals, size large. Available in any store, easily disposed of. Can't get more generic than that. Good luck tracing those—everyone wears them, day and night."

"Everyone?"

"All the tourists, and probably half the residents." They were approaching the crime scene tape. "This is the Florida coast, right? You plan to go sunbathing in those?" And he nodded toward Pendergast's bespoke John Lobb shoes, the leather shining dully even in the dying light.

"I see your point." Pendergast paused. "Day and night, you say?"

"That's right."

"Ah." And Pendergast stopped a moment to gaze off into the distance. "What quaint customs you have here, my friend."

5

THE FOLLOWING MORNING, a white Nissan Altima pulled up in front of a house on Tigertail Avenue in the northeast section of Coconut Grove. It sat there idling at the curb for a minute while the driver fiddled with various knobs, buttons, and display screens. At last the engine died, the driver's door opened, and Special Agent Pendergast emerged. He dusted himself off, gave the vehicle a baleful glance, then crossed onto the pavement and approached the house.

It was a well-maintained Mission-style dwelling of white stucco, perhaps fifty years old, and surrounded by the heavy "hammock" of trees the town was known for. Although it was located in a bustling residential neighborhood—Pendergast could hear the drone of lawn mowers and the chatter of children on their way to school—this particular house seemed to be asleep. He mounted the front steps, paused for a moment, then pressed the doorbell.

There was a sound of chimes within, and ten seconds later came the soft sound of approaching steps. The door opened and an elderly man appeared. He was almost as tall as Pendergast,

dressed in a crisp polo shirt and Bermuda shorts. A thin covering of white hair was roughly combed across his sunburnt pate.
He gazed at Pendergast in mute inquiry.

"Good morning," Pendergast said. "Harold Baxter, I believe?"

"What can I do for you?"

"My name is Special Agent Pendergast, FBI." He removed his
shield and showed it to the man. "I'm very sorry to intrude on
your privacy, but I wonder if I might have just a few minutes of
your time."

The man blinked. "The police were here yesterday afternoon."

"Yes, I'm sure they were. I promise I won't be here as long as
they were."

"Very well. Come in." Baxter stood aside while Pendergast
opened the screen door and slipped into the house.

The man led him through a living room and dining area—
both spotless and smelling faintly of mothballs—out onto a
tiled lanai at the rear of the house. Cushioned deck chairs were
placed around a glass table, and Baxter motioned the agent toward one. As Pendergast was sitting down, a woman of similarly
advanced age appeared at the sliding doors. She held a dish
towel in one hand.

"Harold?" she asked, although her gaze was on Pendergast.
"Is this another—?"

But Pendergast had already risen again and come forward.
"Mrs. Baxter? My name is Pendergast, and I'm with the FBI.
Would you mind if I spoke with you and your husband for just a
moment?"

"Well…no, I guess not." The woman walked toward one of
the chairs, remembered the dish towel in her hand, then folded
it neatly over the back of the chair and sat down.

Pendergast looked at the old man and woman in turn. "First, let me thank you. I know this is difficult, and I'm the last one who'd want to reopen old wounds. So perhaps the easiest thing would be for you to tell me how much you know about the business the detectives were here on yesterday."

Baxter glanced at his wife. "They didn't say much. Asked questions, mostly. It had to do with some...*thing* that was found on Elise's grave."

Pendergast nodded for him to continue.

"And they wanted to know if we had any knowledge of that woman who was murdered yesterday, Miss...Miss..." He glanced again at his wife.

"Montera," the woman said. "Felice Montera."

"I see," Pendergast said in his most sympathetic tone. "And may I ask what you told them in response?"

"We said that, as far as we know, Elise had never met or even heard of that poor girl. *We* certainly had not. I mean, Elise met a lot of people, but she always told us about them. Every night, over dinner, she'd tell us about her day..." The old woman's mouth twitched, and she reached unconsciously for the dish towel.

"So your daughter lived with you."

The man nodded. "It was convenient for her. She worked close by, in Coral Gables. Elise was saving up for a place of her own, but she was very particular—not surprising, I suppose, in her line of work."

"And what line was that?"

"She was a real estate agent. Very promising one, too, given how young she was. On the fast track."

The mother dabbed at one eye with the dish towel. "The police asked us all these questions yesterday."

"I'm sorry; I'll try to be brief. I understand that your daughter died in Katahdin, Maine."

A silence. Then Mr. Baxter nodded.

"Did she have relatives up there? Friends?"

"No," the father said. "It was a conference for Sun and Shore—the realty company she worked for. Basically a getaway, a reward for the top-selling agents."

"Sun and Shore Realty has offices all over the state," the wife added as she refolded the dish towel.

"And did Elise have anybody she was close to at that time? A boyfriend, for example?"

The father nodded. "Matt. A good kid. In the submarine service—at least, he was at the time. Boomers."

"Do you know if they had recently disagreed about anything?"

"They got along fine. Matt saw her whenever he rotated out. He was in the middle of a two-month tour when it happened."

"And you say that she was happy in her work?"

"That job meant everything to her. Along with us, of course. And . . . and Matt."

"Would you call her an optimistic person, in general?"

"You can stop right there," Mr. Baxter said. "The cops wanted to know the same thing, so let me save you a little time. If our Lizzy was unhappy, she was an awful good actress. Job. Boyfriend. She'd even finished a course in personal safety the month before. You know: self-defense, intruder prevention, that kind of thing. Why would somebody planning to end their life take a course like that?" He shook his head. "It makes no sense."

"I understand that's how it must seem—and the senselessness must make it all the harder to bear." Pendergast paused a moment. "Just one more question. You say Elise lived here at home. Is her room currently occupied?"

The elderly couple exchanged glances. Then the husband shook his head.

"Would you mind if I took a look?"

A short silence. Then Harold Baxter rose. "I'll show you the way."

As the three were climbing the stairs, there was a sudden burst of childish squealing and shouting from outside. "The neighborhood's changing," Baxter said. "Lots of young folk moving in. We've talked about it, but we just don't have the heart to leave the Grove . . . and this house."

He stopped partway along the upstairs hall, opened a door, and waved his hand. "We haven't changed anything."

Pendergast stepped into the room. It was a bright, friendly space, painted canary yellow, with a canopy bed and blond wood furniture. There were two watercolors of beach scenes on the walls and some framed photographs on the dresser. As he glanced around, he noticed that the mother of the dead girl was hovering in the doorway.

He turned toward them. "Thank you most kindly," he said. "I'll only be a minute."

As her husband went downstairs, Mrs. Baxter pointed at a plastic evidence bag sitting on the bedside table. "Those are the personal effects they returned to us after Lizzy . . . from Maine. The police asked to take a look yesterday. I guess they left them on the nightstand."

Pendergast walked over and picked up the bag. Inside were a small leather wallet, a ring of braided silver, and a gold chain with a medallion bearing the image of a saint with a wooden staff.

"That's Saint Jude Thaddeus," the woman said.

Pendergast turned it over in his hands. "The patron saint of lost causes."

"She wore that necklace ever since her junior year of college. Never would tell us the reason." Mrs. Baxter's voice turned quiet and strange. "I ask myself why she ended her life every day. Every single day. But I never get an answer." A sob. "She had so much to live for."

Pendergast looked at her. "I know you still grieve," he said quietly. "And you believe there must have been signs or clues you or your husband missed. But as difficult as it is, you should know: suicides that come without warning are the hardest to cope with—and with the only voice that can explain them gone, the ones that most defy comprehension. What you must not do is blame yourselves."

As he spoke, the woman watched him closely. Then, as if on impulse, she stepped forward and, with both of her hands, closed his fingers around the medallion.

"Keep it," she said.

Pendergast looked at her inquiringly. "Mrs. Baxter, I—"

She silenced him with a curt gesture. "Please. I think you're someone who knows a little about lost causes."

Then she turned away and followed her husband downstairs.

Pendergast remained motionless for a moment. Then he slipped the medallion into a suit pocket and, at the same time, pulled out a pair of latex gloves. He replaced the evidence bag, then began moving quickly around the room, examining knick-knacks and toiletries and the volumes in the small bookcase. As Elise Baxter's mother had said, the police had been up here already—he could see the confusing marks of their shoe prints on the floor and the disturbed dust on the bureau. This was vexing—even after all these years, he would have preferred the room as fresh as possible—but expected. Distantly, he heard the chimes of the doorbell from downstairs. Now he began opening various drawers—the dresser, the nightstand, the vanity—searching quickly through their contents, careful not to disturb anything.

Footsteps, quieter this time, sounded on the staircase once again. Pendergast removed the gloves and slipped them back into his pocket just before Agent Coldmoon—wearing a dark-gray suit—arrived in the doorway. He seemed a little out of breath, and beads of sweat had gathered on his temples. Arriving along with him was an odor foreign to Pendergast—something like singed cat hair mixed with butyric acid.

"Agent Coldmoon," he said, stepping forward. "Dressed this time, I observe. How nice to see you again."

"Likewise," Coldmoon replied, shaking the proffered hand. "Although I'd expected to see you earlier."

"You mean, on the six AM plane from LaGuardia? Yes. Well, given the nature of the case I thought it best to come down here without delay. I arranged for a flight late yesterday afternoon." Pendergast sampled the air again. "Beg pardon, but would you consider it rude of me to ask what that unusual smell is?"

"What smell?"

"I don't know. The smell that might linger on the clothes of someone who'd, say, just walked through a malodorous chemical refinery."

Coldmoon said coldly, "I don't smell anything. Now, do you think you could please get me up to speed?"

"Of course. Felice Montera, aged twenty-nine, was killed at roughly four AM yesterday, apparently while jogging before work—she was a nurse at Mount Sinai Medical Center, and her shift began at six. Her body was hidden beneath some shrubbery near the Miami Beach Boardwalk and found several hours later by a honeymooning couple. There was little good evidence at the crime scene. The local police have already interviewed numerous people—hotel workers, sanitation crews, nearby residents and vacationers—but no witnesses have come forward yet, and nobody heard anything: no scuffle, no cry. Ms. Montera had recently broken up with her boyfriend, but apparently he was not in Miami Beach at the time."

"Have you seen the body?"

Pendergast nodded. "First thing this morning. It, too, afforded few clues. Apparently, the throat was cut by a knife, then the breastbone split with the single blow of a hatchet. There was no sign of rape or molestation—the killing was done quickly. Nothing appears to have been taken…except, of course, the heart. Beyond the note on Elise Baxter's grave, and its mention of a gift, there seems to be no motive for Ms. Montera's death. A few bloody sandal prints were found leading away from the scene, but given the preponderance of that style of footwear here, the police have little hope of it providing any useful evidence."

"How expert was the knife or hatchet work?"

"The hatchet showed determination rather than any particular anatomical or surgical expertise. It struck slightly off center in the manubrium bone. On the other hand, the throat cut was either proficient or lucky—the right carotid was neatly severed, causing the victim to bleed out quickly."

Coldmoon nodded slowly. "Any theories?"

"No."

A silence gathered. Then Coldmoon began to speak again in his monotonic voice. "What about a link between the victim and the suicide whose grave it was?"

"None that I can find. No common acquaintances, interests, careers, or personal intersections. It's possible the victim was chosen at random. And then there is the odd literary reference in the note."

Pendergast paused, but Coldmoon did not ask the expected question.

Instead, he said, "The note also stated others were awaiting gifts."

His eyes were not brown, but rather a golden green. Pendergast noticed they wandered about the room, like a bored schoolboy's.

"Which suggests there's a link somewhere." Pendergast paused. "And it means we have a ticking clock—and a great deal of work to do. As a result, I'd suggest we pursue separate lines of inquiry."

"Separate?"

"You, for example, could continue to look into the circumstances of Montera's death—there is still much to go over, after all—while I investigate the Baxter suicide."

"In other words, I should go over ground you've already covered."

"Not at all. I only paid the briefest of visits to the crime scene. There is still a great deal to be learned about Ms. Montera's life, her background, her acquaintances, an interview with the ex-boyfriend. With any luck, the Miami Beach PD will have already done some of the heavy lifting for you by now. Besides, I'd benefit from a second perspective."

Coldmoon's eyes stopped their transit of the room and came back into focus on Pendergast. "I'd prefer to stay with you."

A look of professional surprise came over Pendergast's features. "That would be a duplication of manpower."

"We're partners, and our orders are to work together. Speaking of orders, ADC Pickett asked me to give you this memorandum." He pulled one hand from his pockets and held out a sealed envelope, folded and slightly travel-worn.

Wordlessly, Pendergast took the envelope, tore it open, and removed the single sheet within.

SA Pendergast:

Pursuant to my orders of yesterday afternoon, you will work closely and directly with Agent A. B. Coldmoon, including him personally in all lines of investigation, wherever they lead, and keeping him privy to all your conclusions or suppositions resulting from said investigation. Any deviation from this mode of operation will be considered insubordination.

ADC Pickett
New York Field Office

Pendergast carefully refolded the note, replaced it in the envelope, and slipped it into a pocket of his black suit, his face expressionless.

6

As THEY LEFT the house together, Coldmoon asked, "How did you get here? Did you rent a car?"

Pendergast indicated a white Nissan parked in front of the house. "Alas, yes. Isn't it my good fortune you came along when you did—the streets around here are absolutely overflowing with traffic, and so labyrinthine as to be Kafkaesque. There's somewhere we need to be in forty-five minutes, and, really, I'm such a poor driver—I'm sure you'll do a better job of navigating than I could. Would you mind? Besides, your car looks more to my liking." He nodded at the dinged-up Mustang Shelby GT500 Coldmoon had parked by the curb.

"I tried to requisition a pool car from the local FBI, who sent me to the DEA, and after a lot of paperwork they gave me this confiscated vehicle. Said it was the best they could do on short notice. Not sure if it was a favor, or a joke."

"Perhaps they thought it would blend into the surroundings."

Coldmoon glanced at the rented Nissan. It appeared that Pendergast was abandoning it. He shrugged and walked around to the Mustang's driver's seat. Pendergast started to reach for a rear door—in, apparently, a habitual motion—saw the vehicle had none, then opened the passenger door instead.

"Where to?" Coldmoon asked.

"Bayside Cemetery, please. Bal Harbour."

While Coldmoon was plugging this into his cell phone, Pendergast made himself as comfortable as possible in the bucket seat. Then he glanced at Coldmoon, with a loud sniff. "Do you mind if we open the windows? Air-conditioning irritates my nasal passages."

"Don't mind."

"Thank you." He lowered the passenger window. "Since we're to be partners," he went on, "I assume you'd prefer to proceed on a first-name basis. My first name is—"

"Coldmoon will be fine," the agent said as he pulled away from the curb.

"Excellent. Of course," replied Pendergast.

The Mustang drove like a low-rider; its engine howled rather than purred, and every bump or crack they passed over seemed to be magnified a hundredfold. As they drove, Pendergast briefed him on what the Miami Beach PD had done. He had liaised with one Lieutenant Sandoval, a chief homicide detective in charge of the case, and the man had already provided a sheaf of evidence on the Montera murder, with more lab reports on the way. The killing seemed to be both random and hasty, but the MO was abnormal: the "blitz" style of attack was indicative of a disorganized killer, but the high level of control and lack of evidence left at the crime scene suggested the opposite.

Coldmoon found that Pendergast's description of the traffic was also accurate. He was able to avoid the worst of downtown by sticking to Route 1, using the traffic-avoidance features of his smartphone app, but once he crossed the Intracoastal Waterway onto the island it became an unavoidable nightmare of valet cars triple-parked outside waterfront hotels, clueless tourists, and elderly drivers who had no business behind the wheel. It took the entire forty-five minutes Pendergast had allotted to cover the twenty miles to Bayside Cemetery.

At last, Coldmoon turned off Collins Avenue and headed west. Bayside Cemetery was small and relatively quiet: about a dozen acres of palm, magnolia, and gumbo-limbo trees, with ranks of headstones pleasantly arrayed in the fretted shade beneath. Coldmoon pulled through the gates and parked in a small dirt lot surrounded by white birds-of-paradise. There were a number of vehicles in the lot, a few of them official.

Pendergast got out of the car and nodded to a police officer sitting in one of the vehicles, who looked curiously at the Shelby. But then, instead of walking directly to the grave where Montera's heart had been placed—which Coldmoon could see in the distance as a large square of yellow—Pendergast began to take a seemingly random stroll through the grounds, pausing here and there to gaze at the surrounding landscape or scrutinize something in the grass. Coldmoon followed, saying nothing. Pendergast meandered through the gravestones in his black suit, nodding like a resident undertaker to the occasional visitor, eventually making his way to a small groundskeeper's shed. He skirted its rear, still looking casually around, then continued his stroll. At last he headed toward the grave of Elise Baxter. Now that they were closer, Coldmoon could make out a small knot of people huddled together near the crime scene tape. There were five in all, looking confused and upset. Their attire and demeanor seemed local: Coldmoon was already learning to differentiate tourists from residents. On the far side of the tape, two duty policemen were standing together, talking in low tones and occasionally casting an eye toward the group.

"Good morning," Pendergast said to the gathering. "My name is Special Agent Pendergast, and my associate is Special Agent Coldmoon. Thank you for coming."

There were some nods and shifting of feet. Coldmoon could tell from their body language these people did not know each other, and he guessed they hadn't expected to be a part of a group.

"The reason I asked you to come," Pendergast said, "—beyond, of course, the opportunity to pay your respects to Ms. Baxter—was because I understand you're the people in the immediate area, outside her family, that knew her best. I wanted to see if any of you could think of a reason her grave was, ah, *chosen* in this way, and to hear why you think Ms. Baxter took her own life." He turned to the closest person: a stout, middle-aged woman in a floral dress with blond highlights. "If you wouldn't mind introducing yourself, ma'am?"

The woman looked around at the others. "I'm Claire Hungerford."

"And how did you know Ms. Baxter?"

"I worked with her at Sun and Shore Realty."

Pendergast said, "Thank you." His voice was an almost tangible unguent of southern gentility and charm. "How did you become acquainted?"

"We both specialized in Coral Gables real estate. I still do. We were the two real estate agents in the office who got the Silver Palm in back-to-back years."

"The Silver Palm?"

"It's an award from the franchise for the agents with that year's highest increase in sales volume."

"I see. And is that why the two of you were chosen for the Maine conference?"

The woman nodded.

"Looking back on it now, what was your impression of Elise Baxter's state of mind at the time of the convention?"

The woman played nervously with her hair. "Nothing stood out. She was just her usual self."

"She didn't act unusual in any way? Especially quiet or moody, for example?"

"No. But she was always rather quiet. I mean, I worked in the same office with her for two years, but I still didn't know her that well. She was never what you'd call the life of the party, although—"

"Yes?" Pendergast pounced.

"Well... I think she might have had a little too much to drink that night."

"What makes you think that?"

"Because she left the banquet a little early. Before the final presentations. She spoke to me a moment as she was leaving, and I noticed her walk was a little unsteady."

"What did she speak to you about?"

The woman blinked at the question. "She asked if I'd be joining her on the bus trip to L.L. Bean in the morning."

"I see. And that was the last time you saw her?"

"Yes."

The next three inquiries proceeded in a similar fashion. A college roommate; a childhood friend from the neighborhood; a man she'd often partnered with at Arthur Murray. They all, Coldmoon observed, had relatively vague and unremarkable memories of Elise Baxter: she'd been a pleasant young woman, ambitious but reserved. She'd demonstrated nothing to indicate suicidal behavior, but nothing to rule it out, either.

At last, Pendergast thanked them profusely and bid them good day. As the group began to break up, he raised a hand to stop the fifth person, who had so far been silent: a man of perhaps sixty, a bit scruffier than the rest, wearing a weather-beaten sun hat, a white T-shirt, and faded green pants.

"Carl Welter?" Pendergast asked.

"Yes," the man replied. He had a husky voice that bespoke years of unfiltered cigarettes.

"Do you know why you were asked here?"

The man kept looking from Pendergast to Coldmoon and back again. "I wasn't no friend of the dead woman."

"No. But you were the watchman on the midnight-to-eight shift the night before last—when the object was left on her grave."

"I already spoke to the police about that yesterday. Twice."

"I'm aware of your statement. And you told them—" here Pendergast reached into his suit pocket, took out an official-looking piece of paper, and consulted it— "that you were in the vicinity of the groundskeeper's shed, sharpening a lawn mower blade, when you heard the creak of metal, as if a gate was being opened. This was—" another exaggerated examination of the paper— "between two and two fifteen AM. You naturally investigated, but it was a dark night, the moon was veiled, the front gate was closed and, in short, you found nothing amiss."

"That's what I told them," the man said a little belligerently, nodding to underscore the statement.

"And it was a lie," Pendergast said in the same buttery voice.

"What in—?" the old man croaked, then fell silent.

"A transparent lie, easily exposed. In fact, I'm surprised you haven't received a *third* visit from the authorities as a result. But, Mr. Welter, if you're honest with me, I can promise that we will all overlook your indiscretion."

The man opened his mouth to protest, but Pendergast folded the paper, returned it to his pocket, and continued. "Please don't waste our time with protests. I bring it up at all only as a formality—to make sure this graveyard has nothing more to tell us. The item was not left on Elise Baxter's grave at two AM, you see—for the simple fact that, at that time, it was still in its owner's chest. Ms. Montera was not killed until four." He paused, watching the groundskeeper's reaction. "In truth, Mr. Welter, you heard nothing that night. The only real question is: why did you lie about it?"

The man began looking between them again, only now his expression had become hunted.

Pendergast let the pregnant silence grow. Then, just as he drew in breath to speak, Coldmoon suddenly interjected. "You were sleeping one off," he told the groundskeeper.

Now both Welter and Agent Pendergast turned toward him.

Coldmoon went on. "Your shift began at midnight. Given the two six-packs of Pabst Blue Ribbon you drank, I'd say that by midshift your blood alcohol concentration must have been around 0.2 percent, leaving you in no condition to notice any disturbance, much less investigate it."

"You—" the groundskeeper began again, then fell silent one more time.

"The fact is, you lied about hearing something because you didn't want the management to know you were drunk on duty. Isn't that right?"

Nobody moved.

"Just nod your head if that's right, Mr. Welter," Coldmoon said. "Once will be enough."

After a moment, the groundskeeper gave an almost imperceptible nod.

"Very good," said Coldmoon. He glanced at Pendergast. "Anything else you want to ask?"

"No, thank you," said Pendergast.

The car was quiet while they drove south. As they passed through North Beach, Coldmoon finally asked: "Where are you staying?"

"The Fontainebleau. And you?"

"Holiday Inn."

"You have my sympathies."

"So, I gotta ask, the Bureau's picking up your tab—?"

"No, it is not. Since I believe your hotel is farther along than my own, would you mind dropping me off? I'll have Lieutenant Sandoval send over a second copy of the case file for your review, along with any new lab reports. We can reconvene this afternoon. Will that suit you?"

"Sure."

After another minute or two, Coldmoon felt Pendergast's pale eyes swivel toward him. "Do you know why I asked those people to speak to us as a group, rather than individually, and at the grave site?"

"No."

"Ah." Pendergast settled back in his seat.

"But if *I* had organized such a gathering," Coldmoon said, "I'd have done it for two reasons. First, it would throw them off balance, having to make a statement in front of witnesses— and beside the grave of their old friend, too. Kind of works on a person's superstitions, lying about a friend at their grave site.

Second, if I'd decided that those people had little to add to the investigation, I wouldn't want to waste more time interviewing them than necessary."

"Very good," Pendergast said, and remained silent for about a mile before speaking again. "How did you know the groundskeeper was—as you put it—sleeping one off?"

"The same way you knew: those dozen empties stashed behind his hut. After the murder, in all the excitement, he obviously didn't have time to get rid of them—just stuff them back there and hope nobody noticed. And he decided to make up something vague to tell the cops. Imply he was awake."

Silence from the passenger seat.

"That *is* how you knew—right?" Coldmoon asked.

"Ah, here we are!" Pendergast cried abruptly as the expansive sweep of the Fontainebleau's arrivals drive came into view. Coldmoon pulled in and Pendergast exited the vehicle.

"Shall we say three PM in the pool area?" he asked.

"Fine."

Pendergast closed the door. Then he walked around to the driver's window and put his elbows on it. "About those empty beer cans," he said, leaning in slightly. "It would appear that roving eye of yours indicates attention to detail, rather than lack of interest. How lucky for me."

"What—?" Coldmoon began to ask. But Pendergast had already turned away, and without another word he disappeared into the crowds milling around the hotel entrance.

7

At a quarter past three, Agent Aloysius Pendergast sat in a private cabana just beyond the vast, comma-shaped shadow of the Fontainebleau's Chateau Tower. The cabana's privacy walls—thin canvas—were rolled down on either side, limiting his view to those palm trees and sunbathers facing the Atlantic. Pendergast was not interested in the view; although his padded chair was angled toward the light, his eyes were closed and half hidden by a Montecristi Panama hat of exceptionally fine weave.

There was a rustle just outside, then a waiter appeared. "Sir?" he said over the fugue of nearby conversation.

Pendergast opened his eyes.

"I'm so sorry to disturb you. Would you care for another julep?"

"Thank you. Please ask the bartender to use Woodford Reserve this time, and to muddle in less sugar and more mint."

"Sir." And the waiter vanished. Pendergast raised one hand to lower the brim of his hat a little farther, then settled back into motionlessness. He had replaced his usual dead black suit with one of crisp white linen; one leg was crossed casually over the other, and the horsebits of his alligator slip-ons gleamed gold in the sun.

He remained unmoving while the waiter refreshed his drink, taking the old glass away. He did not stir at the cries and shouts that occasionally erupted from the swimming pools around him. When a particular shadow crossed the canvas wall of his cabana, however, he opened his eyes.

"Agent Coldmoon," he said. "How nice to see you again."

Coldmoon, appearing at the entrance, nodded.

"Please, have a seat. Would you care for one of these morsels?" And with a languid wave, Pendergast indicated a small tray of dates, stuffed with chèvre and wrapped in crisp strips of bacon.

Coldmoon stepped in and perched awkwardly on one of the cabana's deck chairs. "No thanks."

Pendergast flagged down a passing waiter. "Something to drink, then?"

"Not right now." Coldmoon, too, had changed and was now wearing faded jeans, worn square-toed roper boots, a leather belt with a Navajo sand-cast buckle, and a long-sleeved denim work shirt. A sheaf of papers was tucked under one arm.

"Ah," Pendergast said, indicating the papers. "Homework."

Coldmoon said nothing.

Pendergast picked up one of the dates and popped it into his mouth with a dainty motion. "I'm curious. Do you—as you asked me this morning—have any theories?"

Coldmoon put the folder on the chair. "The autopsy added nothing new. Forensic toxicology results won't be in for some time, but I doubt we'll find anything there. Background checks and initial interviews don't raise any red flags—so far, no persons of interest, nobody who had a particular reason to want her dead."

Pendergast nodded.

"And it's like you said. Superficially, the Montera killing shows indications of both organized and disorganized behavior."

"Curious, isn't it?"

Coldmoon pursed his lips. "On the one hand, it would appear to be the random, impulsive action of a sociopath. On the other, the crime scene was carefully controlled and reveals no useful evidence beyond what the perp wanted us to find."

A scream sounded nearby, followed by a splash, then laughter and a quick burst of Italian. Coldmoon, Pendergast noted with interest, was possessed of unusual inscrutability. He sat stiffly on the edge of the reclining chair, as if determined to resist the comfort it promised. As usual, the man's green eyes were never still.

"Why 'superficially'?" Pendergast asked.

"Because sociopaths don't feel remorse. Their defining characteristic is lack of empathy for other people. There's a contradiction there."

"Which is?"

"The note on the grave."

"*Acta est fabula, plaudite!*" Pendergast said. "Precisely what troubles me. Why would a sociopath kill somebody at random, with a spectacular degree of violence, in order to leave a present on a grave with a note full of sorrow and contrition? And how did he make his choice, Agent Coldmoon? Killing Ms. Montera where he did meant getting her heart to a cemetery more than a dozen miles away, with precious little time to spare. Why not choose a victim closer at hand?"

"He could be playing with us. The note, even the grave, could be a diversion."

"Yes. And that is precisely why we have to go to Maine."

Coldmoon raised an eyebrow. On his impassive face, the small gesture spoke volumes.

"Ah. Do I sense an objection?"

Coldmoon's answer, when it came, seemed carefully chosen. "Going to investigate Elise Baxter's suicide—I'm assuming that's your idea—would seem a low priority right now."

"Consider: the evidence we've seen in Ms. Montera's murder has led nowhere."

"But that evidence is still coming in. The crime's only thirty-six hours old."

"All the more reason for haste. It can wait another thirty-six while the Miami Beach PD finish their lab work. More killings might be in the offing."

"With respect, Agent Pendergast, that's not how the Bureau prosecutes this kind of case. The crime was committed here. This is where we're supposed to look for the killer, *especially* if he might strike again."

Pendergast was silent for a moment. Then he took a contemplative sip from his mint julep. "I was afraid you'd say that. But there's a great difference between *looking* for a killer and *finding* him. Who knows where he will strike again? The next *here*, if there is one, may be Alaska. No—the best place to pick up his trail is at the beginning, with the suicide of Elise Baxter. We must be like David Livingstone, searching for the source of our own Nile."

"Nice metaphor. But even if I agreed with you, there's a problem."

Agent Pendergast uncrossed his feet. "I assume you mean our friend Pickett."

Coldmoon nodded.

"Do forgive me—I'm not used to being leashed." Pendergast took another sip of his julep. "Ah, well, it was simply a suggestion. Perhaps you should call him and get his refusal immediately. Any later and it might interfere with my dinner appetite."

Coldmoon looked around the cabana exterior for a moment. Then he took out his phone, dialed, and put it on low-volume speaker.

The call was answered on the third ring. "Pickett."

"Sir, this is SA Coldmoon. I have SA Pendergast listening in."

"Very well. Progress?"

Coldmoon wasted no time on preliminaries. "Sir, Agent Pendergast believes we should go to Maine."

"Maine? What the hell for?"

In one lithe movement, Pendergast's loafers were off the deck chair and on the tiles. "Sir," he said, leaning toward the phone, "I believe the local authorities have the investigation well in hand, and I'd like to investigate the link between the two women."

"Link? From what I've seen, the killer chose that grave site at random."

"How can we be certain of that?"

"What link could there possibly be?" Pickett asked impatiently.

"We don't know yet. I put in a request to have Ms. Baxter's body exhumed, but her parents are objecting. And—"

"And I'm not surprised. What are you implying: that she wasn't a suicide? That she was murdered? Is this your 'link'?"

"As I said, there's no way to know—not without an exhumation."

"All you need to know would be in the pathologist's report and the original autopsy. Stop focusing on this suicide and forget the idea of a second autopsy. What you're supposed to be investigating is a murder that took place in Miami. Have you spoken to the family of the dead girl, what's her name, Montoya?"

"Montera. No, we have not. However, Agent Coldmoon and I have both read the transcripts of their interviews with the Miami Beach police, and they are—"

"Frankly, Agent Pendergast, this is precisely the kind of out-of-left-field move coming from you I worried about. Like chartering a private jet to get down to Miami twelve hours early."

A pause. Pendergast said nothing.

"Even assuming you're right, your first priority is clearly with a fresh homicide—not a suicide that happened a decade ago and fifteen hundred miles away. I can't sign off on this. You can get whatever files you need from Maine shipped down. If you find something—*then* go."

"The Maine files are likely to be useless—"

"Agent Pendergast, this is one investigation that's going to be run by the book. Now—"

"Sir," Coldmoon interrupted. "I agree with Agent Pendergast."

There was a long moment of dead silence. And then the voice from New York said: "You do?"

"The MBPD appears to be doing a thorough job, with great backup from the Miami PD. There's a window of opportunity. I think we should take it to check out this avenue of investigation."

"But I told you—the selection of victim and grave site could well be random."

"I agree one of them is most likely random, sir," Coldmoon said. "But I don't think we should assume *both* are random. The letter seems specifically addressed to Baxter."

The next silence was even longer. "You'll leave first thing in the morning," Pickett said crisply. "And you'll use commercial transportation. But before you leave, you are to interview the Montera family, *in person*."

"Understood, sir."

"And Agent Coldmoon? I don't want boots on the ground in Maine any longer than twenty-four hours before you head back to Florida." There was a click and the phone went still.

Slowly, Pendergast looked over at Coldmoon. "I didn't think you agreed with my suggestion."

"Who says I do?"

"Then why—?"

"I go with my partner."

"Agent Coldmoon, I do believe you have unexpected depth."

The agent shrugged. Then he put his hand out to stop a passing waiter. "Bring me a bottle of Grain Belt, please. Room temperature, not chilled." And he sat back in the deck chair and laced his fingers together. "Since we're supposedly off duty, I guess I'm thirsty, after all."

8

N*O PUEDO DORMIR*," Mrs. Montera said, dabbing at her eyes with a ragged handkerchief. She had been dabbing, virtually nonstop, since Coldmoon arrived at the little apartment on Southwest Eleventh Terrace an hour before, as the sun was sinking into a pink atmosphere. Now everyone was sitting around the well-used kitchen table: Coldmoon, heavyset Mrs. Montera, and her two surviving children, Nicolás and Aracela.

Although Coldmoon had been mistaken for Hispanic on a few occasions, he knew no Spanish and even less about Miami's Cuban culture. He was relieved when, despite the stream of detectives that had come through the apartment earlier in the day, the Monteras had welcomed him in, patiently answered his questions, and offered him dinner. He'd refused once, twice, then finally allowed himself to be served congri and tamales.

He had never been in a residence painted so many bright colors, or with so many crucifixes and statuettes in evidence. It made his own childhood home seem monochromatic by comparison. The place was compact but neat, and he sensed pride in the smallest details: the way the frying pans were carefully stacked on a shelf above the counter, the spotless collection of faded photographs of family now long dead. Mrs. Montera's parents, old and frail, were both asleep in a back bedroom, exhausted from grief, and Coldmoon had not asked to speak with them: he'd grown up with the Oglala tradition of *tiospaye* and did not wish to intrude himself on Felice Montera's extended family. He knew there was nothing they could tell him, anyway.

Unfortunately, there was little anyone could tell him. The family had already answered the same questions for the Miami PD, but they patiently went over the facts again. Nicolás worked as a mechanic in a nearby auto shop, and Aracela, who had lost her bookkeeping job when a neighborhood bodega closed, supplemented the family income by babysitting. Felice, the most ambitious of the children, had been an LPN, already well into the coursework necessary to become a registered nurse. While she had friends both here in Miami and back in Cuba, most of her time was taken up either at the hospital or with coursework. The few free hours she had were spent with family or, until they broke up, with her boyfriend, Lance.

When the subject of Lance came up, the atmosphere around the table darkened. Nicolás muttered something in Spanish under his breath.

Despite the family's obvious animosity toward Lance, they knew little about him. Apparently, Felice had been guarded about the details of their relationship and had brought him to the apartment only once: the chemistry had been bad enough that she hadn't tried a second time. She'd met Lance six months earlier, not far from Mount Sinai, at a club where he'd worked as "door staff"—in other words, a bouncer. He'd been fired from the club two months ago, and Felice broke up with him a couple of weeks after that. Again, she'd been vague with specifics—

she'd mentioned money problems, but Nicolás believed it was Lance's temper that ultimately scared her off.

"He would call," Nicolás said as he washed dishes. "Money—always money. Sometimes he wanted to borrow some. Other times, he wanted some back. Even after they broke up, this *comemierda* would call." He spat into the sink.

"Do you know when they last met?" Coldmoon asked.

"She told me, maybe three, four weeks ago. He stopped her outside the hospital."

"Why?"

"Same thing. Claimed she owed him money. They argued, she threatened to call the cops." Nicolás shook his head.

"What's his last name?"

"Corbin."

"Corvin," the sister corrected.

"Any idea what he's doing now?"

"Felice said he got a job at another club. Edge, I think it was called."

"Where's that?"

Nicolás thought a moment. "Cape Coral."

"I suppose you told all this to the Miami PD?"

Both Nicolás and Aracela nodded.

Coldmoon stood up. "Thanks for going through this with me again. I'm very sorry for your loss, and we'll do all we can to bring the perpetrator to justice."

Mrs. Montera, still dabbing at her eyes, tried to wrap up some tamales for Coldmoon to take along, but he gently declined. "*Encuentre al hombre que hizo esto,*" she said, pressing his hand.

Down on the pavement, Coldmoon looked up Edge on his cell phone. He called and asked for Lance Corvin.

"He's kind of busy right now," a voice shouted back over the sound of throbbing music. "Try later."

"When do you close?"

"Three."

Coldmoon glanced at his watch as he got into the Mustang. A few minutes past eight. As a suspect, this Lance Corvin sounded too good to be true...which meant he probably was. Cape Coral, he recalled, was pretty close. With any luck, he'd interview this Corvin, get a statement, and be back in his hotel room by nine.

It was turning into another beautiful night. Only half paying attention, he punched the nightclub's name into the traffic app of his phone, then dropped it on the passenger seat and pulled away from the curb. Although he hadn't told Pendergast, not being on hand to examine the scene of Felice Montera's homicide had irked him. This talk with her family had, if nothing else, helped create a human being from the victim—something that was very important to him, and which made the tragedy of her death that much greater.

Guided by the soothing voice of the GPS, Coldmoon made his way out of the crowded side streets of Little Havana and onto a main thoroughfare, where after a few miles the traffic grew mercifully thin. In retrospect, he was pleased he'd agreed to divide the evening's investigative responsibilities with Pendergast. The senior agent had remained in his suite at the Fontainebleau, tracking down by phone old acquaintances of Elise Baxter. Coldmoon knew how that worked; one acquaintance would lead to another, then another. Pendergast would be up calling half the night, long after Coldmoon had hit the sack.

Lulled into tranquility by these thoughts, Coldmoon only became aware something was amiss when the GPS guided him onto the westbound ramp for I-75. What the *hell?* The freeway stretched ahead of him, a divided highway disappearing into utter darkness, with only the occasional pair of headlights to relieve the monotony.

He quickly pulled onto the shoulder, consulted his cell phone, then let out a string of particularly graphic Lakota curses. Cape Coral wasn't near Coral Gables, or Coral Springs, which he had confused it with—it was way the hell over on the west coast of the state, at the far end of an arrow-straight ribbon of freeway known as Alligator Alley.

Alligator Alley. "Sweet mother of fuck," Coldmoon murmured. A hundred and forty-five miles. Two and a half hours. Each way.

Briefly, he considered pulling through a break in the highway meridian and heading back to his motel. But he immediately realized that would never work. The interview with the boyfriend was critical, even if it was ground already covered by Miami PD. He'd already promised Pendergast he'd interview the ex-boyfriend. No way could he give any possible suspect a pass—even if his conscience allowed it.

With a sigh, he hit the gas, turned back onto the freeway, and headed west. Within minutes, even the other headlights had vanished, and there was nothing but high-mast lighting poles for company. Unrelieved blackness lay to his left and right. He let the speedometer drift up to eighty, then ninety, before inching above one hundred. If a state trooper stopped him, hopefully the fellow law officer would give him a pass. If not—well, it was turning into that kind of a night anyway.

It was ten thirty when he pulled the Shelby into the empty valet spot directly in front of The Edge. To Coldmoon, the building looked like an abandoned processing plant that had been gussied up with a bit of neon. A line of people, dressed to party, were waiting behind a velvet rope leading to the entrance. Two burly men in jeans and leather vests flanked the door, through which came the muffled thump of dance music. His mood had not been improved by passing through Alligator Alley.

A valet approached his window. "Keys?"

"Where's Lance Corvin?" Coldmoon asked.

"That's him," the valet said, pointing at one of the men in leather vests.

"I want to talk to him." He grabbed his phone, opened the car door, and got out.

"Sir, you can't leave your car—"

"I said, tell him I want to talk to him."

But Corvin had picked up on the exchange and was already coming over. He pushed the valet aside—none too gently. "Yeah?"

"Lance Corvin?"

"What about it?"

"I'm Agent Coldmoon of the FBI." Coldmoon considered digging his shield out of his back pocket, but decided he wouldn't bother. He leaned back on the car. "I have some questions about Felice Montera."

The bouncer's expression hardened. "The cops have already asked me all about that."

"Good for them. Now I'm asking you."

"I was working here night before last. A million people must have seen me."

"Maybe. But the club closes at three. Ms. Montera wasn't killed until four."

"Corvin!" the other bouncer said, gesturing at him. "Tell that jackass to move his car and get back here!"

"That's one hour to cross the state. You think I grew wings or something?" Corvin said.

"Maybe you left work a little early that night."

Corvin crossed his heavily muscled arms. "Look," he said, "I didn't kill that bitch. Okay? Question answered. Now move your fucking car."

The events of the evening—the sense of loss in the Montera apartment; the inconsolable expression on the face of the victim's mother; the wearisome drive through a trackless landscape—came together. The normally phlegmatic Coldmoon took a step toward Corvin, so close his chest was actually touching the bouncer's crossed arms. He leaned into his face and spoke in a whisper.

"Did you just say *'fucking'* car? About my *Shelby*?"

Although the bouncer was taller than Coldmoon and had at least fifty pounds on him, some instinct of self-preservation caused Corvin to slowly ease his arms down to his sides. But he did not step back. "It isn't against the law to swear," he said, his voice faltering.

Still staring at Corvin, inches from his face, Coldmoon slid out his cell phone. "While we're considering how the law applies to my eight-hundred-fifty-horsepower Super Snake, I'm going to call a magistrate judge and get a warrant. And then we'll go back to Miami, where you and I will spend all night together in a little room with a very bright light."

"I, um, wait. I have proof." Corvin finally took a step back and reached into the front pocket of his jeans. He pulled out a piece of paper, unfolded it, and held it out. "I got this driving home the night Felice was killed."

Coldmoon examined the paper. It was a traffic summons. Corvin had received a ticket from the Cape Coral police for speeding, two nights before. The time on the summons was 3:50 AM.

He looked at it a moment longer, then used his cell phone to take a photo of the summons. Staring wordlessly into Corvin's face, he relaxed his fingers and let the ticket fall, where it fluttered down onto the bouncer's shoes. Then, getting back into the Shelby, he started the engine, pulled away from the curb, and mentally prepared himself for the long, dark, featureless drive back to Miami.

9

THE LODGE AT Katahdin was not actually near the mountain bearing the same name. It was many miles outside of Baxter State Park, on what looked like the edge of an endless forest, not far off the interstate. Coldmoon could imagine few places more different from Miami Beach. Maine had seen a lot of snow that winter, and though it was late March everything was still obscured by drifts of white: mailboxes, woodsheds, even cars and trailers were hardly more than protuberances in the snow cover. The only patches of color came from the sand on the plowed streets, which turned the snow an evil reddish color. The late-morning scene reminded him of the long winters he'd spent growing up in Porcupine, South Dakota.

He pulled the car they'd rented at the airport into the parking lot of the lodge. It had been plowed halfheartedly, and a large signpost announcing the resort was half obscured by wind-blown snow. A total of three cars sat in the lot. One was a police cruiser.

Agent Pendergast, sitting in the passenger seat, unbuckled his seat belt. "Shall we?"

Coldmoon eased out into the frigid air: five below, not counting the windchill.

They had spoken little on the flight up that morning, and even less in the drive from the airport. Coldmoon got Pendergast up to speed on his movements of the night before—a subject he didn't particularly care to dwell on. In turn, Pendergast briefly described tracking down an additional half a dozen of Elise Baxter's acquaintances and co-workers in the Miami area. All of the people he'd phoned remembered Elise Baxter as a quiet young woman whose suicide had come as a total surprise.

The two walked down the treacherous sidewalk toward the entrance. Pendergast was encased in a gigantic parka that made him look like the Michelin Man. Coldmoon recognized it as a Canada Goose Snow Mantra, stuffed with down and sporting a tunnel hood lined in coyote fur. It was billed as the warmest coat on earth and sold for upward of fifteen hundred dollars. Coldmoon wondered where in Miami Pendergast had managed to acquire one so quickly. For his part, Coldmoon was comfortable in a twenty-year-old Walmart down jacket, shiny and faded with use, patched in places with duct tape.

As if reading his thoughts, Pendergast turned back, face invisible within the snorkel-like hood. "You're a man of cold climes, I assume?"

Coldmoon shrugged.

"You really should invest in one of these." Pendergast patted his reflectorized chest. "A favorite of South Pole scientists. And even I couldn't ask for more pockets."

He stepped forward and pulled the main door open, and a blast of warmth blew out from the interior. They entered a dark lobby in which every piece of furniture—even the front desk—

was covered with drop cloths. The air was redolent of sawdust and mothballs. The lobby was expansive, Coldmoon noticed, but—judging by the scuffed frames of the landscapes on the walls and the slightly shabby carpet—the lodge had seen better days. A low drone of conversation could be heard from an open door behind the front desk.

At the sound of the front door closing, the conversation abruptly ceased. A moment later, three people came out of the back room. The first was an overweight man in his late fifties, wearing a red button-front sweater and worn corduroys. The next was a woman about the same age, as bony as the man was fat, with wiry forearms. She wore a dress cut like a maid's. The last to emerge was a uniformed policeman, bald and very short, with a manila folder in one hand.

The man and woman smiled at the new arrivals a little uncertainly. The policeman simply nodded.

"Horace Young?" Pendergast said, his voice muffled by the parka. "Carol Young?" He stepped forward, drawing off a massive mitten, hand extended. "I'm Special Agent Pendergast and this is my associate, Special Agent Coldmoon."

They shook the proffered hand. Then Pendergast unzipped his hood, pushed it back, and turned to the police officer. "And you are—?"

"Sergeant Waintree," the cop said. He glanced in Coldmoon's direction. "I spoke with Agent, ah, Coldmoon on the phone yesterday afternoon."

"Thank you all for being so accommodating on short notice." Pendergast glanced around the lobby. "I see you aren't anticipating guests."

"We're taking advantage of the winter to spruce up the lodge," Horace explained.

Despite the warmth of the lobby, Coldmoon noticed that Pendergast had not unzipped his parka.

"Well, let us not waste more of your time than necessary. If you wouldn't mind getting the others, we'll get started right away."

"There are no others," Horace said.

Pendergast glanced toward Coldmoon.

Sergeant Waintree answered the implied question. "Your partner here asked me to assemble everybody who was working at the lodge when the Baxter woman took her life."

"Just the Youngs?" Pendergast asked. "And the staff? The cooks and waiters?"

The woman answered. "Bolton—he was our cook at the time—got a new job in a North Carolina resort years ago. Donna and Mattie—the waitresses, that is—they're both retired. Moved in with their children somewhere, best I know."

"Maintenance?"

Mr. Young shifted his girth from one foot to the other. "Willy died year before last. Cancer got him."

"Maids?"

"I was the head maid," the woman said. "Before I married Mr. Young." She smiled coquettishly.

Coldmoon found himself staring at her ropy neck. Somehow, it made him think of a seagull.

"Our primary business is in the summer and fall," Young told Pendergast. "Hikers, bird-watchers, nature lovers, leaf-peepers. We shut down for the winter and spring. Hard to keep full-time folk on a part-time job. We usually make do with students. They're not bad once you train them up. Some stay just one summer, others for a couple."

"Business has slacked off a bit, too," the woman said. "Flights to Europe are so cheap these days."

If Pendergast was disappointed by the meager showing, it was not obvious. "I understand," he said with the ghost of a smile. "If it's all right with you, then, may we start with your records?"

The Youngs exchanged glances. "Be our guest," Mr. Young said. "Unfortunately, the registration ledgers and books were lost in a fire a few years ago. We've very little left but old computer files." He tapped a pile of printouts.

Pendergast raised his eyebrows. "What sort of fire?"

"Grease fire that started in the kitchen. We quickly got it under control, but the old files were stored in a shed next to the kitchen vents and burned down."

"And you?" Pendergast turned to the police officer.

He held out the folder. "Here's the case file. Interviews, photographs, and the rest."

Over the next half hour, Pendergast and Coldmoon looked through the hotel's records, such as they were, for the two-month period surrounding Elise Baxter's suicide. Pendergast used his phone camera to document every page. The Youngs waited nearby, answering questions when necessary. Their faces had expressions of curiosity mixed with a kind of embarrassment. Sergeant Waintree watched from a distance, arms folded, offering nothing. He seemed to Coldmoon a typical Mainer, insular by nature, independent, taciturn. On top of that, he was suspicious and a little defensive—as well he should be, given how thin the police file looked. Coldmoon knew that suicides often got scant attention, but even by that metric it seemed the bare minimum had been done here, even for a small, understaffed department.

Pendergast began asking questions of the owners themselves. Both remembered the night Elise Baxter died, but only vaguely, and only because of the suicide. The Sun and Shore real estate agents had gathered for a dinner party in the lodge's small banquet room, at the tail end of the season. To the best of the Youngs' recollection, they'd had an excellent time. Neither remembered anything out of the ordinary—no arguments, no voices raised except in laughter. Nobody seemed to get intoxicated. Neither remembered seeing Elise Baxter; but then, there was no reason for them to have noticed.

Carol Young, on the other hand, had a very clear recollection of the following morning. She had been the maid who discovered the body, hanging from the shower curtain rod in her bathroom. The woman was clearly dead, eyes open, tongue protruding. Carol uttered a shriek, then fainted. The shriek alerted nearby guests. Horace Young had sense enough—after seeing that Elise Baxter was deceased—to close the door and leave everything alone until police arrived.

At this point in the conversation, Sergeant Waintree took over. The first responders were a patrol cop—now retired and living in Arizona—and an ambulance driver, who'd died in a car wreck just a few months back. Next came a small Crime Scene Unit, who took down the body, performed an initial forensic evaluation, took samples and photographs—now in Coldmoon's possession—and then handed the body off to the coroner. The coroner was still around, no longer practicing but living down the coast in a town called Bristol.

"Were you on the force at the time?" Coldmoon asked Waintree as he opened the police folder.

The cop nodded. "Ayuh."

"Part of the investigation?"

"Wasn't that much to investigate. Went through all the details, though."

"Such as?" Pendergast asked, looking at the folder as Coldmoon paged through it.

"Nobody heard or saw anything out of the ordinary. Some of the guests in the surrounding rooms, and the staff on duty that evening, were interviewed. So were a few of the co-workers of the deceased."

"Where are the transcriptions of the interviews?" Pendergast asked.

"These were just informal interviews, no reason to suspect anyone of anything. There are summaries in there."

Pendergast pulled out a sheet of paper with two sentences on it. "Such as this?"

"Yep."

Pendergast dropped the paper back into the folder. "Any security cameras or video feeds?"

"This is Maine, Agent Pendergast," Mr. Young said, as if that explained everything.

"Were there reports of any strangers in town? Anything that seemed unusual or out of place?"

"There are always strangers—tourists—in town that time of year," replied Waintree. "Right up to the last leaf falling. But no complaints, fights, incident reports during the week she hanged herself."

"What about the scene of death itself? Any evidence of an unusual or suspicious nature?"

Both the manager and the policeman shook their heads.

"And no suicide note?" Coldmoon said.

"None," said Waintree.

"What about the coroner's report?"

"It's there."

"You mean, this three-page photocopy of typed notes?" said Coldmoon. "There aren't even any X-rays."

"It's like I told you on the phone yesterday," the sergeant said.

"There's not a lot to learn from the file. You could have gotten it sent to Miami and stayed a lot warmer," he added in a stolid voice.

Coldmoon and Pendergast glanced at the brief coroner's report. *"The usual ligature marks associated with a suspension hanging,"* Coldmoon read aloud. *"Death was caused by asphyxiation."*

"She hanged herself from the curtain rod," Pendergast said. "In my experience, curtain rods—especially in hotels—are not the sturdiest of platforms. Frequently, they are attached by suction cups."

"Not in the lodge, they're not," said Young. "Ours are fixed with mounting brackets. Three screws apiece, right into the studs." He smiled proudly.

Pendergast took another glance around the lobby. "Well, then. Perhaps we should take a look at the room."

Young nodded. "You're in luck. That's one spot we're not renovating this winter."

The place where Elise Baxter took her life looked like countless other motel rooms Coldmoon had seen. Dense carpeting, iron-hard and patterned in a design intended to hide stains. A double set of heavy curtains to ensure the morning sun wouldn't disturb late sleepers. A duvet cover that probably hadn't been washed since the start of the last season. Coldmoon had read somewhere the dirtiest thing in a motel room was the TV remote, sometimes covered with *E. coli* or even contagious, antibiotic-resistant MRSA. He looked around. There it was, lying on the table beside some flyers advertising local attractions.

The bathroom was small, with a porcelain tub and yellow floor tiles. The curtain rod—fixed securely, as Young had said, to mounting brackets—hung a few inches below the upper molding. Coldmoon eyed the distance from the floor to the faintly mildewed ceiling, guessed it was the standard eight feet. More than enough headroom to get the job done.

Pendergast turned to him. "May I see the photographs, please?"

Coldmoon opened the folder again and together they looked through the glossy, well-thumbed prints. At least the photographer had done a thorough job, getting all the right angles as well as a full sequence of the body. Elise Baxter hung from the shower rail by a knotted bedsheet. The woman was wearing a terry-cloth dressing gown that had come loose at the top, exposing one breast. She was much less attractive than she had been in the portrait in her parents' living room: the dried, protruding tongue; staring eyes; and mottled petechiae spreading up from her neck like overripe blueberries—all indications of asphyxiation—were textbook in a suicide like this.

Pendergast pointed to a close-up of the dead woman's legs. Despite the settling of blood in her lower extremities, Coldmoon could make out a sheen on her toes and ankles, as well as on the porcelain lip of the tub.

"She, um, soaped her feet," Young said.

"So she couldn't change her mind?" Coldmoon asked.

"It is not uncommon," said Pendergast.

Young shook his head.

Pendergast looked around the room. "Mr. Young, the tiles here are different from the photographs. And the curtain rod appears to be of relatively recent vintage."

"Yes," the man replied. "I mean, we had to change everything. And not just the bathroom: new bed, wallpaper, carpet—the whole nine yards." He paused. "Hotel workers are even more superstitious than hotel guests."

"Very good," Pendergast said, not looking as if it was good at all. He replaced the glossy photographs into the manila folder. "We're going to look around the room for a bit, if you don't mind."

"Not at all," the Youngs said in unison.

"And Sergeant Waintree, we can go over the other aspects of the suicide back at the station once we've finished here."

The cop's expression became, if anything, more stolid. "I'm sorry, Agent Pendergast, but that won't be possible."

"Why not?"

"Well..." Waintree hesitated a moment. "Chief Pelletier told me to convey his apologies, but we're awfully busy at the moment."

"Is that so?"

"Yes, sir. See, we've had a real epidemic of opioid-related crimes and overdoses swamping our office. That, and the usual domestic stuff we always get around now, when the winter gets long. The case files you already have contain everything relevant, and I'm the only eyewitness to the suicide still on the force. There's no point in going into the station."

Pendergast's face had grown opaque during this recitation. When Waintree finished, Pendergast let a lengthy silence build. Just as he was about to reply, Coldmoon—acting on some internal warning he didn't quite understand—jumped in. "Speaking of that," he said to the Youngs, "which rooms have you put aside for us?"

The couple exchanged glances. "Oh my," said Carol Young. "But there's none available. We're closed."

"No rooms? I thought the entire lodge is empty."

"Sure it is," said her husband. "Like everyplace around here. Population drops like a stone once the leaf-peepers are gone. Perfect time for renovations."

"I thought you said this part of the hotel wasn't being renovated."

"This *room* isn't being renovated. Like I told you, it already was. All the other rooms..." Young gave a helpless shrug.

Coldmoon absorbed this. "Can you recommend anywhere in town?"

"Town's boarded up tight, I'm afraid. All the skiers are over around Big Squaw. Won't find a place within an hour's drive that's open this time of year."

"No room at the inn," Pendergast murmured as he exited the bathroom.

"There's the Lowly Mackerel," Sergeant Waintree offered.

"That's right!" Young said. "They do keep a few rooms open year-round, don't they? I've always wondered why."

"It's just this side of Millinocket," Waintree said. He turned and headed for the door, then stopped. "As regards dinner, you might want to stop at the SaveMart on your way to the motel."

"No restaurants open, either?" Coldmoon said. But Waintree had already followed the owners into the hall and out of sight.

"I'm not surprised there's a local opioid problem," Pendergast murmured. Then, rubbing his hands together, he undertook the most meticulous examination of the room Coldmoon could ever recall seeing: using a magnifying glass to inspect the edges of the carpet from one end of the bedroom to another; disassembling both the phone and the radio and examining their interiors; applying a tiny, fine-bristled comb to the mounting brackets of the bathroom shower rod. Now and then, small plastic envelopes would appear as if by magic from the innumerable pockets of his parka; he would pluck up an item from the scene with a pair of jeweler's tweezers, then replace the envelope and continue.

Coldmoon watched with mounting amazement for a while before he spoke. "The owner said the room was redecorated. And Elise Baxter committed suicide here over eleven years ago. Hundreds of guests have used this room since then."

As he spoke, Pendergast had produced a small multi-tool from the parka and was unscrewing a heating register at the base of the wall. "Very true," he said. "Nevertheless—" he probed the duct-work he'd just exposed with a light, took up the tweezers again, and removed something stuck to a metal burr— "Elise Baxter *was* in this room. And it was here that she took her life."

"What exactly do you hope to find? Hoping she'll speak to you from the Wanagi Tacanku?"

"That's one possibility." Pendergast stood up and brushed himself off. "Agent Coldmoon, as I'm sure you've noted, the files we received were virtually useless. Without the hotel registers indicating who else stayed here the night of the suicide, we have precious little to go on. That is why I am anxious to glean what I can, if anything, from this room. No doubt you'd prefer to occupy your time in some other way. Shall we meet in the lobby?"

He shrugged. "Sure." And without further ceremony he left the room.

Coldmoon was long accustomed to waiting: in BIA offices and tribal courts; on the Quantico parade grounds; in unmarked cars. He'd grown to like it. Besides, he'd been up most of the previous night and felt rather weary. Finding the lobby empty, he pulled the drop cloth from one of the sofas—despite the preparations, no workmen were on site—picked up a couple of magazines from a nearby table, and settled in to read.

Sometime later, he woke. The wall clock read ten to three. The lobby was as empty as when he'd first returned to it; there had been no sign of either Horace or Carol Young. He paused to listen. The lodge was still as a tomb. What the hell was Pendergast doing?

He replaced the magazines on the table, stood up, and began walking down the carpeted corridor, toward what had been Elise Baxter's room. The door, which he'd left open, was shut and locked. Stepping up to it, he paused to listen. There was no sound from beyond.

The rooms in the lodge did not use magnetic passcards but old-fashioned keys. Making no noise, Coldmoon crouched to peer through the open keyhole.

At first, he saw nothing. Then he noticed Pendergast. The man was lying on the bed, still wrapped in the parka, hands folded across his chest. The photos Sergeant Waintree had brought were arranged on the bed around him, almost like offerings encircling an idol. Something was in one of his hands: a gold chain, attached to a medallion whose details Coldmoon could not make out.

For a moment, Coldmoon wondered if the senior agent of the investigation had suffered a heart attack or stroke. But then he saw that Pendergast's chest was rising and falling in a faint but regular rhythm. He must be asleep, though even that seemed unlikely—not even sleepers lay that still.

Coldmoon watched through the keyhole for another moment. Then, rising, he turned and went back in the direction of the lobby.

10

JENNY ROSEN FOLLOWED her friends Beth and Megan around the corner of Seventh Street and onto Ocean Drive. Then she stopped. Stretching ahead of her, suddenly, was an endless Babylon. Encountering the boulevard was like mainlining a shot of adrenaline directly into the central cortex: an overwhelming and seemingly impenetrable wall of competing backbeats, billows of perfume mixed with the smell of grilled fish, car exhaust, and mojo-marinated meat, with the occasional whiff of weed. And the lights: candy-cane strings of white that wound up every palm trunk; garish neon signs in the windows of tattoo parlors and beachwear shops; and—blazing from every marquee and sign that ran ahead for at least a dozen blocks—a confusion of floodlamps and strobes and multicolored lasers, swinging about and vying madly for her attention.

"Come on," Beth shouted over the calls and laughter of the crowd surging along the sidewalk. "It's just up here."

Jenny and Megan walked after Beth as she made her way—pushed her way, actually—through the throng. Most were young, Jenny's age or a few years older, vaping and screaming at the top of their lungs to each other over the cacophony, half of them drunk and the other half high. Jenny had wandered through her share of trendy neighborhoods—the Lower East Side, the Mission, LA's Venice and Silver Lake—but she'd never before experienced such a motley assortment of hipsters, punks, cybergoths, gang-bangers, surfers, losers, stoners, posers, and countless other subspecies, all mingled together into one volatile soup.

Jenny and Megan hurried past a hookah lounge, a narrow service alley, then a brilliantly lit store selling trendy sunglasses, trying their best to keep up with Beth. As usual, she had taken charge, acting the control freak. Just because Beth's home was in nearby Georgia, and she'd spent "like, forever" in Miami two years ago—actually, just one night—she'd assumed the mantle of veteran clubber, taking her two friends under her wing and promising to show them a memorable night out.

Now the two of them caught up to Beth, who had stopped, hands on her hips, and was looking at one of the few shopfronts that was closed, its metal shutters down. "... The *fuck?*" she said. "This is the place I was telling you about. I can't believe it's closed. Maybe they just moved to a bigger space." And she took out her phone and started tapping the screen, rocking obliviously this way and that as people shoved past her.

Jenny plucked at the neck of the top she was wearing. Late March, but already Miami was unbelievably humid, and this crush of hot, sticky bodies only made it worse. If she'd had her way, they would have gone to a place like LIV—still one of the top megaclubs in the country, let alone Miami Beach—but Beth was tight with money and didn't want to have to spend for table service. Besides (and this was the clincher), LIV hadn't been Beth's idea. *Her* idea—just like it had been her idea to book the trashy, funky-smelling Airbnb condo miles from anywhere—had been to walk a dozen blocks down Washington, fake-remembering several awesome bars along the way, all of which turned out to be expensive or lame or both. Nevertheless, they'd dutifully had a drink in each: tequila sunrises for Megan, some fruity cocktail for Beth. Jenny, who wasn't much of a drinker, had ordered vodka-crans at each stop.

Now Beth had put the phone away and was in motion again. "Come on, Meg," she yelled over her shoulder. "Jen-girl."

Jenny resisted the impulse to shoot a glance at Megan. That wouldn't be smart: Megan was Beth's best friend, and had been for two years, since sophomore year at Macalester. Megan had even decided to follow a vaguely similar career path. Beth was hoping to get an advanced degree in communications, specializing in public engagement. Megan was talking about doing graduate work in sociology, with a primary interest in ethnic relations. Jenny herself had been considering some kind of medical research, but a semester of organic chem had cured her of that. Now she was drifting instead toward an MFA in ceramics.

She pushed her way through the crowd a little morosely. The yelling that surrounded her made her head ache—and the three drinks under her belt weren't helping any.

They passed the Colony Hotel, its white-and-blue arc deco façade gleaming in the artificial light, and continued northward. Theirs, Jenny mused, was an unlikely threesome. She knew, though no one had said it to her face, that she was the odd one out. But she didn't make friends easily, and she'd invested too much time in Beth and Meg to just toss the relationships aside. That was why, when the other two had been offered interviews at the U of Miami Graduate School—travel expenses paid—she'd tagged along for the weekend. Although she didn't like to show it, money wasn't a problem in her family, and she'd bought the ticket herself. It wasn't that she was all that eager to see Miami Beach, really—it's just that she didn't want to spend a long weekend alone in her Kirk Hall single. And who knew? It might be fun. Maybe Beth wouldn't be her usual bossy self. Maybe it would be a fun, stress-free getaway.

Yeah. Good luck with that.

They crossed the street and passed a number of restaurants, one after another after another, all with bikini-clad seductresses or leather-lunged barkers standing out front, doing their best to entice tourists in for a meal. Then, suddenly, Beth veered toward a set of metal double doors, outlined in black light, with a leather-clad bouncer standing nearby. She looked back at them excitedly.

"Here we go!" she said as the man checked her ID.

Megan began pushing her way through the crowd with evident enthusiasm, ID already out for inspection. "Come on, Jen-girl!" Beth cried, gesticulating wildly.

Jenny hated being called "Jen-girl." But she gamely followed her friends into the club. She caught a brief glance of a spotlit sign above the doorway: ELECTRIC OCEAN.

Inside, it was incredibly dark, and the atmosphere vibrated with the pulsing beat of merengue records a DJ was spinning. As her eyes adjusted, Jenny could make out a large dance floor in the center, with booths along the left-hand wall and a bar along the right. She could see that Beth and Megan were already on the crowded dance floor. Jenny began walking toward them, then turned instead and made her way toward the bar. Although she'd caught a buzz already, she needed a little more courage if she was going to dance.

The bartender took her twenty, pushed a tall vodka-cran toward her, then laid five ones on the counter. Jenny leaned against the bar, sipping her drink, watching the vague forms of the dancers as the flickering lights brought them in and out of view. Already she'd lost sight of her friends in the gyrating crowd.

Almost before she knew it the bartender had taken her empty glass and replaced it with another. *Damn, they really push the booze in this place.* She fished out a second twenty and handed it to him. Something even louder than the music blasted one of her eardrums; she looked over to see a skinny, goateed guy in a post-punk outfit yelling at her.

She turned to him. *"What?"*

"I said, are you *a parking ticket?"* he yelled back.

"Parking ticket? What are you talking about?"

"Because *you've got fine written all over you!"* He laughed wildly, eyes wide. His limbs were moving about constantly, the martini in his hand sloshing, and even in this light she could see his pupils were mere pinpricks. *And here I thought guys in the Twin Cities were lame.* The last thing she wanted at the moment was to be picked up by a creep.

She downed her drink and pushed away from the bar. In the hazy middle distance, illuminated by brief, flickering pulses of light, she could see a staircase lined in blue neon. People were filing up and down in a steady stream. The creep started yelling at her again, and to get away she forced her way over to the staircase and began to climb. She found herself in front of a second dance floor, just as dark, but instead of salsa music the air was full of techno-house. She walked over to the dance floor and stood at its edge, wondering if she should join in and try to make eye contact with somebody. As she did, she realized she wasn't feeling that well. The floor seemed to be swaying a little under the assault of a thousand feet—but then she realized *she* was the one that was swaying. Five drinks was way beyond her usual limit—and those last two had been strong as fuck.

All of a sudden, she realized she had to get out. The suffocating blackness; the press of sweaty bodies; the inescapable pulse of lasers and throbbing electronic beats and wild screams—it was all too much. Panicky now despite all the booze, she forced her way out of the scrum and down the stairs—she might have fallen had there not been so many people descending ahead of her—and staggered toward the double doors that led to Ocean Drive.

Even the sidewalk crowds seemed a relief after the club. She walked a few feet, then leaned against the façade of the building, taking deep breaths. The panic was passing.

At that moment, two shapes came dashing up. Squinting against the bright neon, she made out her friends.

"Thought that was you I saw running by," said Beth. "What's up?"

"Nothing," Jenny said. "Sorry. You want to go back?"

"Naw, there's just a bunch of fuck-boys in there. Hey, listen: I heard about a club that's really lit. It's not far, just a block or two."

Jenny took a deep breath. "You know what? You two go ahead. I think I'm going to catch an Uber back to the condo."

Beth looked crestfallen. "Don't crap out on us now, Jen-girl."

"Really, I'm kind of wiped. Go ahead, have fun. I'll see you later." She reached for her phone.

But Beth was too quick: she already had hers out and was pulling up the Uber app. "It'll take fifteen minutes, maybe double that, to reach you in this traffic. You've got time to at *least* check this other place out." And without waiting for a reply, she finished scheduling the pickup and then began making her way up Ocean Drive, shoving her phone back into her fake Dolce & Gabbana bag as she did so.

Automatically, Jenny started to follow. But as quickly as the panic had gone away, something else started rising to take its place: the sick feeling she'd noticed earlier. It was coming back, big time. Damn, she thought: it was that fifth vodka-cran. Chugging it had been a mistake.

She stopped again, looking around at the infinitude of glittering lights. They blurred; came into focus; blurred again.

"Guys," she said. "I'm really not feeling well. I think I'm gonna vom."

But Beth and Megan were walking on, unable to hear her over the noise.

Jenny looked around quickly. The world was tilting in a sickening way, and her stomach was feeling worse by the second. She couldn't just toss up a sidewalk pizza here, in front of a million people...but she felt a saliva faucet, which could only mean one thing, start up at the back of her throat.

There: just one building down was one of those service alleys that poked out in random spots along the boulevard. Without another thought she raced for it. As she ran into the sudden, narrow darkness, past foul-smelling dumpsters and doorways that opened onto greasy kitchens, the light and noise receded until she could actually hear her own feet on the bricks. There was only blackness before her, and—far away, it seemed—the glow of light from Ocean Court and, still farther, Collins Avenue. Amazing how things could change from being so overcrowded to so empty in just a few seconds.

Suddenly, nature would let her go no farther. She leaned toward the closest wall, steadied herself with one hand, and let the scallop shu-mai, crispy duck, and black rice dumplings exit her stomach and return once again to the outside world. It went on and on, until nothing was left but dry heaves.

Slowly, the awful sensation of nausea passed. Jenny was still buzzed—and her sides had started to ache—but at least she felt human again. She took a deep, cleansing breath. It was almost cozy here in the dark; she felt a strange affection for the temporary privacy it had afforded. But Beth would probably have an APB out for her by now. A light breeze rustled the scraps of litter behind her as she turned back toward the boulevard. She'd call off the Uber and show her friends that she could party like—

And it was then that the rustling grew suddenly louder—louder than any breeze; a hand clamped down hard over her mouth; a strange sensation ran quickly across her neck; and then her throat abruptly filled with warm, gushing, choking blood.

11

IT WAS ALMOST four thirty when Pendergast returned to the lobby. He didn't say exactly what he'd been doing in Elise Baxter's room, and Coldmoon didn't ask, although he noticed the man still had his parka on, zipped up tight; given the hothouse air of the hotel, perhaps he'd been undergoing his own version of a sweat lodge.

At the sound of activity, Young, the manager, waddled out of the back office, made sure there was nothing else they needed, again expressed regret that he couldn't put them up, and gave them directions to Millinocket.

They stepped out into the bitter cold and got into the rented car, Coldmoon once again behind the wheel. Following Young's directions and the car's GPS, they began driving southeast over increasingly remote and poorly plowed roads. Now and then they passed a farm or commercial building, half buried in snow. Already it was getting dark, but Coldmoon didn't mind; the night couldn't be any bleaker than the day.

Ahead he saw a yellow-and-red sign peeking out from above the trees: the SaveMart that Sergeant Waintree had mentioned.

A lower piece of the sign was missing, apparently blown away by a shotgun, exposing the fluorescent bulbs within.

"We'd better stop," Coldmoon said.

Pendergast, who had been perusing the suicide photographs, glanced up. "Pardon?"

"We should pick up some food. Waintree warned us there might not be any restaurants open this time of year."

"Ah, yes. Of course." And Pendergast put the photos to one side and followed Coldmoon out of the car.

They were the only two customers in the dingy little market, which was about to close. Pendergast seemed strangely at a loss in the place: in the tiny produce area, he picked up a head of lettuce, turned it this way and that, put it back; he wandered up one aisle and down another, finally stopping at the herbal tea shelf.

He picked up a box with two fingers. "Coconut chamomile passion fruit?"

"Don't look at me." Coldmoon quickly made his own choices: a tin of sardines, a protein bar, ramen noodles, four packs of Twinkies, and a bag of the cheapest ground coffee he could find. Then he moved to the checkout. Pendergast followed a minute later, empty-handed.

When they got back in the car, Pendergast pulled the photos from the police folder again. The agent seemed to be lingering over one shot in particular: a full-frame view of the woman hanging from the curtain rod, the top of one ankle resting on the edge of the tub, head askew, tangled hair not quite able to mask the bulging eyes.

"What about it?" Coldmoon asked.

It took Pendergast a moment to reply. "I was just thinking."

"About?"

"What you said to Pickett yesterday—that it seemed unlikely Ms. Montera and Elise Baxter were *both* randomly chosen."

"Doesn't it seem that way to you? That one of them must have been chosen deliberately?"

"Indeed." Pendergast put the photo aside. "I agree the likelihood of both women being randomly selected is practically nil. But there is a third possibility."

Coldmoon thought a moment. "You mean that both women, not just one, were deliberately chosen."

"Yes. And if that's the case, I fear it makes our task either much easier—or much harder."

Already, Coldmoon was growing used to Pendergast's Buddha-like pronouncements. As of yet, there was zero sign that Baxter's death had been anything but a suicide, or that—to be honest—there was any real connection between the deaths at all. He gave a neutral grunt. He felt, more than saw, the agent glance at him a moment before turning his attention to the road.

There were a surprising number of cars parked in the lot that doglegged the Lowly Mackerel. When they went inside the lobby, the reason became apparent: in a blizzard the previous week, a fallen tree had taken out an electrical substation, leaving a few dozen homes without electricity. The families who had no relatives in the area had been forced to come here for accommodation. No, the owner said, there were no more rooms: he'd even opened up the second floor, which was usually mothballed for the winter.

Coldmoon watched while, in a feat of combined persuasion, threat, supplication, and bribery, Pendergast talked the owner out of his own room: 101, with two double beds, a color TV, and no Wi-Fi. "Guess I can always stay with my cousin Tom," the man said as he pocketed a thick wad of folded bills. "You just wait in the lounge while I make up the beds and get my things stowed. Won't be but a minute."

The lounge was a sad-looking room with curling linoleum floors, a small kitchen, and a bumper pool table, currently unused. The manager went off to fix the room while Pendergast and Coldmoon approached one of the tables.

"Let's divide the police material," Pendergast said, tapping Waintree's folder. "Then compare notes."

"What's there to compare? The autopsy and forensic reports total five pages. The interviews about the same. And the photos speak for themselves."

"It is precisely because of the paucity of the report that we must think—to use a peculiar expression—'outside the box.' Reviewing the material from a fresh, even random, perspective may result in unsuspected discoveries."

Resisting an urge to shake his head, Coldmoon gestured at the folder. "Have at it."

Pendergast quickly sorted the papers into two small piles, then took a seat at the table, drew one pile toward him, and began silently leafing through it. Coldmoon meanwhile made a circuit of the room, inspecting the beat-up board games, shelves of paperback books, and other time-wasting detritus typically found in such a place. Going through the kitchen cabinets, he was happy to find a hot pot sitting on one of the shelves.

At that moment, the manager came in. "Room's ready," he said. "Want to take a look?"

"Sure," said Coldmoon, scooping up a random paperback, the hot pot, and his share of the papers.

Pendergast didn't look up from his reading. "I'll follow later, thank you."

The manager opened the door to 101 and Coldmoon walked in. It seemed clean enough—Coldmoon wasn't particular—and the manager bid him good night. Dumping his satchel and windbreaker on the floor, Coldmoon gratefully slipped off his holster and service piece and dropped them on one of the beds. He plugged in the hot pot to make sure it worked. While he'd picked up ramen for dinner, that could wait—what he felt right now was seriously undercaffeinated. He filled the dinged-up pot with water, let it come to a boil, and threw in a couple handfuls of coffee grounds. Then he turned it down to a simmer, grabbed the papers and the Twinkies, and lay down on the empty bed, pushing off his boots with a sigh.

It was two hours and three packs of Twinkies later that a key sounded in the lock. Then Pendergast appeared in the doorway. He stepped inside, closed the door behind him, then stopped again. He looked around the room—at the double beds with their stained coverlets; at the faded wallpaper, marked here and there with crayon; at the tiny bathroom with its single towel—then glanced at Coldmoon, who was lying on the bed in his socks, paperback in his lap, a scattering of photocopies and Twinkie wrappers around him. Pendergast's nostrils flared.

"There it is again," he said.

"What?"

"That peculiar aroma. Something between a burnt cigarette filter and Drano."

Coldmoon sniffed. It wasn't his feet—at least, he didn't think so. "You mean the coffee?"

"Coffee?"

Coldmoon nodded toward the hot pot. "Coffee. I made it when I got in."

Pendergast looked over and waved his hand through the air as if to clear it. "Unfortunately, you've allowed it to boil, and now it's ruined."

"Well, that's how I make it. I boil it for a couple of hours." It was the way Coldmoon's father, and grandfather, and great-grandfather had made coffee, and it was the only way he liked it. Growing up on Pine Ridge Reservation, there had always been a blue-flecked enamel pot of coffee simmering on the woodstove. As necessary, more grounds were thrown in and additional water added. The idea of filters or percolators was ridiculous. To his palate, a batch of coffee wasn't really good until the grounds had been simmering at least a week.

Pendergast shuddered. He looked around once more, and as he did so a strange expression passed across his face almost too quickly for Coldmoon to register. Then the pale visage went neutral again. He unzipped his parka, hung it on the hanger screwed into the door, then sat down on the other bed, where Coldmoon had dropped his service piece. To Coldmoon's vast surprise, Pendergast picked up the holster. Then, even more surprisingly, he pulled out the handgun.

"Browning Hi-Power," he said as he hefted Coldmoon's 9mm gun. "Nice balance. John Browning's last design before his death, I believe. Not so different in functionality from my own Les Baer." He fingered the cartridge disconnect, and the loaded magazine slid out into the palm of his left hand. "It appears to have seen a lot of action. A family heirloom, perhaps?"

It had in fact belonged to Coldmoon's great-uncle, who'd carried it through the Second World War. But Coldmoon wasn't thinking of this. He sat up in sudden outrage, a shower of papers falling away as he did so. A person's gun, especially a law officer's gun, was his most personal possession. Nobody else touched it—certainly not without asking, and not in this casual way.

"What the hell are you doing?" he demanded.

Pendergast looked at him. "I'd have thought it obvious. I'm inspecting your weapon."

Coldmoon held out his hand. "Give me that. Right now."

Pendergast's gaze fell on the hand for a moment before returning to Coldmoon's face. Something in those cold cat's eyes set off an instinctual alarm in the younger agent.

The two stared at each other in silence for a long moment. Then Pendergast slid the magazine back into its chamber. "Agent Coldmoon," he said. "We find ourselves in this remote and barren region, forced against our will to share unpleasantly close quarters. Under the circumstances, this bed—with its lone pillow—is the only spot in the entire state of Maine that I can call my own. You and your paperwork have taken up residence on the other bed. Now, since you have deliberately left your handgun on *my* bed—and since we, as gun owners and enthusiasts, know there is no greater transgression than handling another's weapon without permission—your placing it here can only mean one thing: that you wished me to examine and appreciate it. I have now done so. And a fine vintage firearm it is."

And with this he slipped the weapon back into its holster and, saying nothing more, held it out to Coldmoon.

Coldmoon took it and, equally silent, put it on the nightstand on the far side of the bed. It occurred to him that he had just been given a righteous dressing-down by his senior partner. As he got up to refill his coffee cup from the bubbling pot, it further occurred to him that he deserved it. Not only was Pendergast dealing with an obstinate boss and uncomfortable surroundings, but the case wasn't going exactly as planned. The last thing he needed was being disrespected by his own partner.

He picked up one of the case files and sat back down on his bed with a soft grunt. He supposed he should cut the guy a little slack.

Coldmoon woke suddenly out of a dreamless sleep. The first thing he felt was confusion: it was not dark, but light. Then, blinking, he realized where he was: in room 101 of the Lowly Mackerel. He'd fallen asleep, fully dressed, while reading from the case file of the Katahdin police: a piece of paper was still clutched in one of his hands. Blinking, he could see Pendergast, sitting on the edge of the other bed, back to him. He was apparently still ruminating over the photographs of the death scene.

Another ring, and Coldmoon realized it was his phone that had woken him. He dug it out of his pocket, noticed the time was quarter past twelve. "Yes?"

"Agent Coldmoon?"

Coldmoon's remaining sleepiness vanished as he recognized the voice. "Yes, sir."

"Where are you?"

"In a motel outside Millinocket."

"Okay," came the brisk voice of Pickett. "Listen to me very carefully. I want you both to pack up your stuff. And then I want you to get on the earliest plane back down to Miami. I don't care if you have to drive to Boston to catch it—you find that plane and get on it."

From his perch on the edge of the bed, Pendergast had swiveled around and was listening intently.

"Will do," Coldmoon said as he sat up and began pushing his feet into his boots. "What's up?"

"What's *up*?" Pickett echoed with a furious iciness. "There's just been a second murder in Miami—and my lead investigators are over a thousand miles away, chasing a wild goose. Now get the hell out of that motel and onto the road."

The phone went dead.

12

COLDMOON HAD NEVER been to South Beach in person; he'd only seen images of it on postcards, or shots of its nightlife splashed across websites advertising exotic vacations. Now, as their taxi from Miami International finished the slow, eight-block crawl across the island and turned from Fifth Street onto Ocean, he was confronted with quite a different picture. In the merciless early-morning glare, without benefit of neon and softening darkness, the famous boulevard looked tired and shabby, its hotel awnings and alfresco restaurant umbrellas sun-faded beneath the palms.

One thing that was not different was the crowds. Even at nine in the morning, they were out in force, wearing shorts and T-shirts, bikinis and sun hats, cell phones almost invariably clutched and ready for any selfie opportunity. Several blocks ahead, Coldmoon could make out an even denser knot of people that could mean only one thing.

As the cab began creeping northward, Pendergast—who, other than discussing the contents of the Katahdin police file, had remained mostly silent during their frenetic attempts to get from Maine to Miami—turned to him. "In case I neglected to mention it," he said, "I want to thank you for endorsing my suggestion that we go to the site of Elise Baxter's death. Without a pattern established, there was no way to know in advance that the killer would strike again, strike so soon, or strike in the same city. Nevertheless, I regret our absence prevented us from being here at the time of the killing."

Coldmoon shrugged. "I go with my partner," he said once again. And then he added: "Right...or wrong."

Pendergast's only response was to turn his ice-chip eyes back to the hubbub ahead of them.

The taxi managed to proceed a few blocks before hitting a dead stop, blocked by pedestrians, police cars, and other cabs. Coldmoon and Pendergast opened their doors. Pendergast gave the cabdriver a generous tip, along with instructions to drop their luggage off at his hotel, then the two made their way through the throng to the congested spot that—as Coldmoon had anticipated—surrounded a large area marked off with crime scene tape. For the first time, he noticed members of the press among them, fruitlessly shouting questions and pointing mikes.

Pushing their way past the gawkers, they presented their IDs and ducked under the tape. Coldmoon gave the scene a quick once-over. They were facing a narrow alley that ran west between a Vietnamese restaurant on one side and an über-trendy art deco hotel on the other. Scattered along the inside periphery of the tape were various knots of police officers, both in uniform and in plainclothes, either talking to witnesses or simply standing guard. Farther down the alley, a couple of CSU workers were standing around what was obviously the spot where the body had been found. The other end of the grimy alley was blocked

by police cars and emergency vehicles, flashing light bars striping the surrounding façades.

Despite the unfamiliar surroundings, Coldmoon recognized
the tableau itself. This was an advanced homicide scene. As he
looked around at all the police, ranks made evident by various
lapel pins and shoulder badges, he was reminded of the words
of Joseph, legendary leader of the Nez Percé: *White men have too
many chiefs.*

A person sorted himself out from the bustle and came forward. Coldmoon took in the details: short, lean, middle-aged,
Hispanic with brilliant black hair, dressed in light-colored pants
and a tie but no jacket. He seemed to know Pendergast—at
least, he was not surprised to see a man wearing a full-on black
suit and somber tie, like some Secret Service agent parachuted
down here into the middle of Sodom.

Pendergast stepped forward, extending his hand. "Lieutenant
Sandoval," he said. "Allow me to introduce my partner, Special
Agent Coldmoon."

Sandoval shook Pendergast's hand, then Coldmoon's.

"I read the brief you prepared for us on the Montera killing,"
Coldmoon said over the cacophony. "Comprehensive, thanks."

Sandoval nodded. "You just got here," he said to Pendergast
with the faintest of accents. It was a statement, not a question.

"Alas, yes."

If Sandoval was surprised, he didn't show it.

"Let me bring you up to speed." He motioned them away
from the mob, farther into the service alley. "Time of the homicide was around eleven thirty PM. The victim is Jennifer Rosen of
Edina, Minnesota. She was spending a long weekend here with
two college friends."

"Who found the body?" Pendergast asked.

"A dishwasher working in the restaurant adjoining the alley." Sandoval had a funny habit of wiping his index finger across his upper lip, as if to smooth a nonexistent mustache. Now he used the finger to point toward a greasy-looking door beside a dumpster. "The friends weren't far behind him, though—they got here maybe four, five minutes later."

"How much time passed between the murder and the discovery of the body?" Coldmoon asked.

"Not long. According to the M.E., she'd recently bled out when the dishwasher found her, lying there." And Sandoval pointed past the dumpster toward a patch of concrete busy with chalk outlines, evidence flags, and ponded blood.

"And what did he see?"

"Nothing. At least, so far as we know. He only speaks Vietnamese, so we had to get an interpreter for the statement." Sandoval looked over his shoulder at a dazed-looking Asian man in a dirty white smock, sitting on a trash can and flanked by two cops with digital recorders. "He went out with a few bags of garbage and found Rosen on the ground, motionless. For a moment, he was too shocked to notice anything else. When he did look around, the alley was empty."

"What about Ocean Drive?" Pendergast asked. "Any eyewitnesses?"

"Yeah. Too many. It took the EMTs and the first squad car about eight minutes to respond, and when they got here there were already a hundred people hovering around, who all claimed they'd seen the killer—including Ms. Rosen's two friends, who are still over at Eleven Hundred Washington giving statements. You think it's crazy here now? You should have seen it last night." Sandoval shook his head.

"Any of the eyewitnesses check out?" Coldmoon asked.

"Not so far. I mean, their stories all contradict each other, and given the state of the victim..." The lieutenant fell silent.

"Please go on," Pendergast urged.

"The MO was similar to the Montera woman. Throat cut expertly with a knife, then the chest hacked open with a hatchet or some similar heavy, single-bladed instrument. It was an efficient job, done quickly. The perp or perps took the girl's heart and vanished immediately, leaving her dead on the pavement." Sandoval shook his head. "Of all the would-be witnesses out last night, not one mentioned seeing a blood-spattered man carrying a hatchet and a human heart."

"Was she forced into the alley?"

"Apparently not. She seems to have come in here with the intention of—well, being sick. Copious amounts of vomit were found near the body, and it matches traces of partially digested food from her stomach."

"Security cameras?" Coldmoon asked.

"None in the alley. As for evidence, all the onlookers who came rushing in to see the body after its discovery, trampling over everything—well, you can guess how that complicates our job."

"Photos?"

"Got a whole bunch. And that's about it, so far."

"Thank you, Lieutenant."

Sandoval turned away, disappearing into the noisy throng that lined the tape cordoning off the boulevard. Coldmoon watched him go. Then he looked at Pendergast. "Similar MO, different setting. The killer had an objective, and he accomplished it quickly and without drawing attention to himself."

"Yes," Pendergast murmured. He glanced away, toward the

grimy, sad-looking spot behind the dumpster where the young girl's life had ended. "The logistics are impressive."

Coldmoon considered this. "You mean, that he was able to kill and cut out a human heart, and then escape?"

"Precisely. Passing through an area with heavy pedestrian traffic—not unlike Jack the Ripper in its own way. Why choose such a busy location, with such a high risk of being seen?" He turned toward Lieutenant Sandoval, who was coming back with a handful of photographs. "Are there any cemeteries in the vicinity?" he asked.

Sandoval handed over the photographs, thought a moment. Then he shook his head. "None except Bayside, but in Miami proper, quite a few."

"Then I would advise—" Pendergast was interrupted by a tumult behind them, voices raised in pitch and urgency. An officer in uniform pushed through, went up to Sandoval, and spoke in his ear.

"A heart's just been found," Sandoval told them as the uniform retreated. "On a grave in the city of Miami. Excuse me." And the lieutenant turned and vanished into a scrum of uniformed police.

Pendergast came up behind Coldmoon as the babble increased and said: "My blood alone remains. Take it, but don't let me suffer long."

Coldmoon turned to him in surprise. "Was that Crazy Horse, at Camp Sheridan?"

"Marie Antoinette, actually. In Paris." Pendergast turned back and gestured in the direction of Miami. "Shall we go see what present Mister Brokenhearts has left us this time?"

13

THE SPASM OF activity increased in intensity—and then, quite suddenly, Coldmoon sensed a change. Cops began to disappear. One minute they were talking in small groups, gesturing into phones—and then they were gone. The uniforms remained, manning the taped barriers and guarding the evidence, but the plainclothes seemed to vanish as if into thin air. At the same time, he started hearing the *whoop whoop* of sirens. Unmarked cars that had been hidden among the throngs of onlookers now started to detach themselves and force their way into the street, driving on sandy meridians and against the flow of traffic in order to make headway. Behind him came another series of whoops, and he turned to see one of the police cars that had been blocking the rear alley shoot off with a squeal of rubber. But the two of them, Coldmoon realized, weren't going anywhere—they'd taken a taxi to and from the airport, and Coldmoon's requisitioned Mustang was parked back at his hotel. He felt like the kid stranded at the end of musical chairs. "What the hell are we going to do for a car?" he asked. "And where's the crime scene? 'City of Miami' is kind of vague."

Pendergast ducked under the tape and away from the crime scene, moving fast, threading his way through the onlookers. Coldmoon hurried to follow. Pendergast stopped outside a souvenir shop, plucked a map of Miami from a rack near the entrance, and, with a whiplike movement, opened it. Together they peered at the map. He pointed to a rectangle of green amid a sprawling grid of printed streets. *"Ecce!"*

Coldmoon squinted in the bright sunlight. "City of Miami *Cemetery.*"

"Approximately four miles from our present location."

Coldmoon glanced around again. Plenty of cars, barely crawling—but no cabs, no limos, no cop cars offering empty seats.

The proprietor of the store had spotted them and was making her way out from behind the cash register. Pendergast stuffed the map back into its rack and took off down Ocean Drive at a brisk walk. Coldmoon swung in behind him. Ahead loomed one of South Beach's omnipresent art deco hotels. Pendergast jogged up the curving drive to the bellman's station, dodging parked cars and passersby. A lone taxi idled at the hotel's front steps, its yellow paint job faded almost white by the sun. Its trunk was open and the driver was shoving suitcases into it, while a heavyset elderly man was helping an equally elderly woman prepare to get into the backseat.

Pendergast introduced himself to the white-haired man, shaking his hand and giving a courtly bow to the woman. Coldmoon began to approach, but something told him he'd have better luck hanging back. Other people started to appear: valets, bellmen, someone who looked like a concierge. For a minute, this small knot surrounded Pendergast and the elderly couple, hiding the three from Coldmoon's sight. And then the group began to break up, the bellmen taking the luggage from the trunk and lugging it back to the hotel. Now it was the white-haired gent who was shaking Pendergast's hand, nodding and beaming. As the couple began to ascend the steps toward the hotel entrance, Coldmoon—coming forward—caught the old man's parting words: "Thanks again, mate!"

"Good day." Pendergast slammed the trunk closed, then ushered Coldmoon into the still-open rear door. "After you."

Coldmoon slid in. The cabdriver, who had watched all this transpire with bewilderment, frowned. "What the hell, *ese*? That was a forty-dollar ride, man."

"I think you'll find this ride more profitable," Pendergast said, getting in beside Coldmoon and closing the door. He opened his FBI shield, showed it to the driver. "You know the best way to Miami City Cemetery?"

The man—late thirties, with a tiny ponytail and a Cuban flag tattooed on one arm—didn't seem impressed. "Yeah."

Pendergast reached into the pocket of his suit and pulled out a thick sheaf of folded banknotes. "How fast can you get us there?"

The driver was still standing on the pavement. "In this traffic? Shit, maybe twenty, thirty minutes."

Pendergast threw a fifty-dollar bill into the front seat. "How about ten?"

The driver got in and grabbed the bill. "I haven't got wings, man—"

Another fifty went into the front seat. "Then perhaps you could grow a pair. Of wings, I mean."

The cabbie scowled. "Listen, I've already got three points on my license, and—"

"You're forgetting that we're FBI. Just get us there the fastest way—the *fastest* way—you can."

"Yeah," Coldmoon added for emphasis. He figured the man might even be up to the task—he looked more like a getaway driver than a cabbie. He peered into the front seat, trying to make out the man's taxi license. "Put the hammer down—Axel."

The driver slammed his door and peeled out of the hotel parking loop, almost immediately getting stuck on Ocean Drive.

Pendergast turned to Coldmoon. "Do you have a preferred traffic app on your phone?"

"Waze."

"Open it, please. Check the traffic to the cemetery. Open a backup app as well, in case the suggested routes differ."

The cab veered onto the shoulder, avoiding the stalled traffic, then swerved sharply left at Ninth Street.

"Mind explaining what went on back there?" Coldmoon asked as he woke up his phone and dialed in the Miami City Cemetery.

"Just a moment." Pendergast leaned forward. "What route are you taking?" he asked the driver.

The man braked violently at the intersection of Collins Avenue, forcing Coldmoon to grab the oh-shit handle above his window. "The causeway, then Biscayne."

Pendergast looked inquiringly at Coldmoon, who looked in turn at his phone. MacArthur Causeway was a solid red line of traffic, stretching all the way from Miami Beach to the mainland. He shook his head.

"No," said Pendergast.

"What do you mean, no?" came the reply from the front seat. "You want to get there or not?"

"Venetian Way looks like a better bet," said Coldmoon, jumping back and forth between traffic apps.

"Over the *islands*? You crazy, man, or—"

"I'll make you a deal," Pendergast interrupted. "My friend here will provide the directions; you will follow them, breaking any and all traffic laws necessary to keep us moving; and I'll keep handing you money. What do you say?" And he peeled off another fifty and tossed it into the front seat.

The driver, Axel, glanced at it, then—jamming his foot on the gas again—shot across Collins Avenue to the screaming protest of oncoming horns. For a busted-up old taxi, Axel's ride had plenty of juice.

"Flashers on, please, and take the median strip to the light," said Pendergast.

"Whatever." The cab mounted the curb and tore along the grass, fishtailing slightly.

"Right on Meridian, left on Seventeenth," Coldmoon told the cabbie.

Pendergast settled back as the cab swerved back onto the roadway and shot along Meridian to a symphony of blaring horns.

"So what happened back there?" Coldmoon asked.

Pendergast settled into the seat. "A charming couple from Brisbane, on their way to Orlando. I advised against it and pointed out the wisdom of staying another day at their hotel—in an upgraded room, of course, at no charge to them."

"Why not just flash your gold and take the damn cab away from them?"

"To such a lovely elderly couple? How uncouth."

"So you conned them out of their taxi."

"I did them a favor. No civilized person should have to set foot willingly in Orlando. I suggested the World Erotic Art Museum would be a better choice, just around the corner from the hotel."

The cab turned onto Seventeenth, then accelerated dramatically, pinning the two agents to their seats. The driver threaded his way expertly between cars, honking and swerving, finally driving over the edge of a sidewalk.

"Run the light, please." With this comment, another fifty landed in the front seat.

The cabbie ran the light and continued on. Coldmoon checked the apps again. No route was traffic-free, but this one was the least of many evils.

Ahead of them, a vista of intense blue suddenly appeared—Biscayne Bay. Thirty seconds later the road became a bridge, bisecting a parallel series of lozenge-shaped isles, glittering green and white in the cerulean, like jewels set into a Fabergé egg. Coldmoon stared at the gleaming high-rise condos and marinas before him, fringed by countless palm trees and seeming to rise out of the tropical water like dream castles. It occurred to him that had he been shown a picture of such a place during his childhood on the Pine Ridge Reservation, he would have assumed it was something out of a fairy tale.

His thoughts were interrupted by a violent screech of brakes that threw him against the driver's headrest. Recovering, he saw a long line of brake lights ahead and what appeared to be an accident. He realized that Pendergast—and the driver, via the rearview mirror—was looking at him expectantly.

"Well?" Axel asked. "What now, Davy Crockett?"

Coldmoon glanced at his phone. They were on the eastern edge of Rivo Alto Island. "Make a left, two rights, then back onto Venetian Way."

Without another word, the driver twisted the steering wheel, gunned into the oncoming lane, drove along it for a hundred yards, then made a left, the rear end fishtailing. Pendergast let another fifty-dollar bill drop gently into the front seat.

"You know, it would probably have been easier to just rent a chopper," Coldmoon said.

To his surprise, Pendergast took the suggestion seriously. "Anything would be an improvement on this abominable traffic." He was silent a moment. "This is the second time I've been late to a crime scene. I won't be late to a third."

The taxi, once again weaving in and out across both directions of traffic, now veered over the final island in the chain and approached the breastwork of hotels lining the mainland shore. "Right on Second Avenue," Coldmoon said, observing that Route 1, too, was little better than a parking lot, thanks to construction ahead.

By way of answer, the cab shot across one intersection, then another, narrowly missing being T-boned by a moving van, then made a harrowing right onto Second, the rear tires smoking, again using the median strip, weaving among palm trees as if on a slalom course. And then the car lurched once again to a stop. This time, it looked more or less final: all lanes ahead were at a standstill, apparently blocked by the construction and spillover from Route 1.

"Damn," he muttered.

But even as he spoke he saw Pendergast throw another bill into the front seat and get out. Coldmoon followed suit. Three blocks ahead, he could make out a patch of green: the cemetery.

"Eleven minutes," Pendergast said. "Excellent. Perhaps we'll even beat our friend the lieutenant." And threading his way between the cars to the sidewalk, he began moving north at a smooth but rapid walk.

14

SPECIAL AGENT COLDMOON nodded to the two cops manning the gate as he passed into the City of Miami Cemetery. More cop cars were arriving, and activity was ramping up. He paused to cast a cold eye over the scene even as Pendergast skipped lightly ahead. An asphalt lane bisected the cemetery: a large grassy area surrounded by a green-painted fence and shaded by gnarled oaks. Lining the central lane were tombstones and mausoleums of various styles and shapes, some decrepit, others well kept. The cemetery looked venerable, and—judging by the vaults—was home to some pretty wealthy corpses. Strange place for a burial ground, though: almost in the shadow of downtown Miami.

When he had taken in the spirit of the place, he strode toward the mausoleum where the heart had apparently been found, a grim temple of granite roped off with crime scene tape, surrounded by a growing crowd of police and forensic teams. Pendergast was nowhere to be seen. He spoke to one of the local cops and learned the interior would be cleared and ready for their entry in about thirty minutes.

Coldmoon took a leisurely stroll beyond the crime scene tape, committing to memory all he could of the scene. This particular mausoleum was built from massive blocks, with two stone urns flanking the entrance and a heavy copper door covered with verdigris. The name carved above the lintel was FLAYLEY. As he passed the open front doors, he could see the shabby interior, brilliantly lit, where two CSU investigators in white suits moved about. They reminded Coldmoon of ancestral spirits, confused and wandering, seeking release from their earthly shackles.

On the far side, a distant figure caught his eye: a mourner in black, kneeling, head bowed in sorrow. Then he realized it was Pendergast. He ambled over to find his partner examining the grass, nose practically buried in the ground. A pair of tweezers was in his hand.

"Find anything?"

"Not yet." Still, he slipped a test tube out of somewhere, put something invisible into it with the tweezers, and stood up. He continued to work his way in a circle around the mausoleum, as if, Coldmoon thought, "cutting for sign"—a tracking trick he had learned during his childhood.

"I would appreciate a second pair of eyes on the ground," Pendergast said. "I'm looking for ingress and egress."

"Since last night was a full moon, with a cloudless sky, you're assuming he didn't walk in by the service road."

"Precisely."

They made an excruciatingly slow loop, picking up every trace they could. Finally, when they got back to where they had started—with no success, it seemed—Pendergast squinted toward the mausoleum. "Ah. The chamber of the dead is now ready."

Members of the Crime Scene Unit—under the watchful gaze of Lieutenant Sandoval—were packing up their gear and taking off their suits. Following Pendergast, Coldmoon ducked under the tape and entered the mausoleum.

Both right and left walls were lined with niches, three rows of five, making thirty crypts total, all sealed over save for one at the far left. A plaque of marble covered each crypt, carved with a name and dates, but some of the coverings had cracked and fallen to the floor, revealing the rotten coffins within. The floor was thick with dust and evidence of rat activity, while the walls were massively stained from roof leaks.

While Pendergast prowled around silently, Coldmoon focused his gaze on the niche in question. It was one of the newest.

AGATHA BRODEUR FLAYLEY

SEPTEMBER 3, 1975

MARCH 12, 2007

Its marble plaque had been removed and set aside. Hanging before the coffin on a string, like a Christmas ornament, was a human heart, swinging ever so slightly, cradled in a crude net made of roasting twine. A single drop of clotted blood hung from the bottom like an icicle. A sticky pool had formed on the floor below it.

Fastened to the heart with a large diaper pin was a note. Coldmoon approached it with caution, photographed it with his cell phone, and then stepped back to read it.

My lovely Agatha,

Your end was the most horrifying of all and for that I am so very sorry. Death lies on you like an untimely frost. Because I

*am a man of Action and not just words, I have brought you a
gift by way of atonement.*

*With fond wishes,
Mister Brokenhearts*

"Brokenhearts fancies himself a man of literary parts," said
Pendergast, coming up behind him.

"You mean the quote from *Romeo and Juliet*?"

To Coldmoon's gratification, Pendergast's brows rose slightly
in surprise. "Indeed. We can add that to the line from T. S. Eliot
in the previous note."

"'Let us go then, you and I, when the evening is spread out
against the sky,'" Coldmoon intoned. "I took a bunch of English
lit classes my freshman year," he said by way of explanation.

"Indeed. Although I can't imagine what J. Alfred Prufrock has
to do with *this*—" Pendergast gestured at the oversize diaper
pin, its lime-green plastic head molded in the shape of a Teenage
Mutant Ninja Turtle— "except to indicate our killer might have
a droll sense of humor."

While Coldmoon took photographs, Pendergast went down
again on his hands and knees to examine the floor, plucking
more invisible items here and there with the tweezers. As he
worked, Coldmoon heard an excited voice in a thick Florida
drawl outside, along with the more measured tones of Lieutenant Sandoval.

"Ah, the man who found the heart," said Pendergast as he
rose. "Shall we have a word?"

The man was retelling the story of his discovery to Sandoval.
Coldmoon turned on his recorder and slipped it into his front
pocket.

"My good man," said Pendergast, "we haven't heard your story yet. May we listen in?"

"You bet. I was just telling the policeman here—"

"Your name?" Coldmoon interrupted.

"Joe Marty. I'm the day caretaker. So anyway, after I arrive, I'm doing my rounds and I see them copper doors open. I think to myself, it wasn't like that yesterday. Nossir. I keep a close eye, gentlemen, on these tombs. A lot of famous people are interred here, and we don't want anyone messing with them, or taking souvenirs. So I see them doors open and I poke my head in. Don't see nothing. So I push the door open a little more and go inside. Still nothing."

His voice was rising in pitch, building to a climax.

"But there's this funny smell. Off, you know. So I turn around and bump this thing with my head, setting it swinging back and forth, you know? And I says to myself, there shouldn't be anything hanging in here like that. So I reach out to grab it and it's all wet and sticky, and there's this piece of paper pinned to it, and I let go real fast. And I see my hand is all covered with something, so I hold it out into the daylight and it looks like blood and that's when I start yelling. Yessir, I yelled like you wouldn't believe. Then I call the manager and he calls the police, and here we are! Let me tell you—"

Pendergast adroitly inserted a question into this torrent of words. "What time did you arrive at work?"

"Seven. That's when I start. Nothing like this ever happened here—"

"When you touched the heart," Pendergast asked, "did you notice if it was still warm?"

"Why, shoot, I never thought of that. But now that you mention it, it *was* a bit on the warmish side." He shuddered.

"Any ideas how the killer might have entered and left the cemetery?"

"Hell, that fence ain't tall enough to keep anybody out. We get kids coming in here, drinking beer, urinating—very disrespectful."

"Often?"

"Damned often enough."

"Thank you. Agent Coldmoon, any questions?"

Coldmoon saw Marty turn his small, wet eyes to him. "Do people ever come to visit this tomb? Lay flowers?"

"No, this is one of them that don't seem to have nobody."

"Who's responsible for upkeep?"

"We do the grounds. But the plots themselves belong to each family, and they're supposed to do it. Lot of them don't, and it's a goddamned shame—"

"Are you familiar with the Flayley family?"

"Never heard of them. Not famous like some in here. Maybe they've died off, or live far away. It happens. I don't mind telling you, when I saw that heart swinging back and forth, it just about froze my blood."

"I'm sure it did," said Coldmoon. "Thank you."

Joe Marty walked off, casting about, looking for someone else to tell his story to. Coldmoon could see that at the cemetery entrance the press was starting to arrive in force, kept back by the police.

A homicide detective approached, wearing a seersucker suit and brandishing a pair of files. He handed them to Sandoval, who flipped through one quickly, then passed it to Pendergast. "Here's the initial backgrounder on Agatha Flayley. Another suicide. Found hanging from a bridge in Ithaca, New York."

"Thank you." As Pendergast took the file, Coldmoon caught

a quick movement out of the corner of his eye: a tall, lanky man in a Hawaiian shirt and skinny jeans, a hipster porkpie on his head, was approaching swiftly. When he saw them turn toward him, he called out: "Could I have just a brief word with you gentlemen—?"

A reporter. Sandoval's face blossomed with annoyance. "Jesus, look who's here. Don't you know this is off limits?"

The lanky man waved some sort of card. "Come on, Lieutenant, think of all the favors I've done you guys! Please: one question, two, that's all."

"Get back behind the perimeter."

"Wait, just a—" The reporter suddenly froze, staring at Pendergast. "*You!*"

Coldmoon looked at his partner. The agent's face, usually expressionless, showed a rare surprise.

"What are you doing here?" the reporter asked.

Sandoval sighed in exasperation. "Smithback, get behind the perimeter before I have my men escort you out. You know this is a restricted area."

"Hold on, please." The reporter took a step toward Pendergast and stuck out his hand. "Agent Pendergast. How are you?"

Pendergast was still for a moment. "Fine. Thank you." He reluctantly took the hand, and Smithback gave his a vigorous shake.

"You *know* this guy?" Sandoval asked Pendergast.

But Smithback swung around and answered the question. "Of course he knows me."

"All right, you've said hello. Now back behind the perimeter." Sandoval beckoned to some uniforms. "Sergeant Morrell," he called out. "Will you and Gomez show this guy out?"

"Pendergast, *please!*"

Pendergast seemed to recover himself. "Mr. Smithback, I'm surprised to see you. I hope you are well?"

"Great, thanks." The reporter glanced toward the swiftly approaching officers and lowered his voice. "Um, why is the FBI involved?"

"Two reasons. The case presents unusual psychological aspects that have interested our Behavioral Analysis Unit. And the targeted graves are out-of-state suicides, triggering federal involvement."

"Targeted how?"

"I regret we can't get into details."

"Okay, but—" By now the two cops had hooked the man by the arms and were leading him away. *"Is this a serial killer?"*

Instead of replying, Pendergast turned to Coldmoon, who was looking at him questioningly. Sandoval was doing the same.

"In case you are wondering," Pendergast said, "I knew his brother well. A tragic story. Someday I shall tell you about it."

Coldmoon nodded. He doubted he would ever hear the story, but then again, he wasn't sure he particularly wanted to.

15

THE MIAMI FIELD Office of the Federal Bureau of Investigation was one of the more prominent in the country, given its role in covering not just nine counties of Florida, but also Mexico, the Caribbean, and all of Central and South America. It was housed in a new, high-tech building of bluish glass that soared above the streets of Miramar, northwest of Miami, and it was the most spectacular field office Coldmoon had ever seen: more like a postmodernist sculpture than a federal building. He tried to tell himself he wasn't the least intimidated.

He followed Pendergast into a second-floor conference room dominated by a mahogany table and leather chairs, interactive whiteboards and 5K flatscreens—the very latest in technology. Coldmoon wished he had his comforting thermos of camp coffee at hand. The image of the hanging heart, with its icicle of blood, had unexpectedly stayed with him since that morning.

They were early. Other agents arrived—most from the Miami office—with nods and murmurs and took their places. After everyone was accounted for and the clock crept past three minutes to the hour, the door opened and Assistant Director in

Charge Walter Pickett strode in, followed by a curious, shuffling man in horn-rimmed glasses and a baggy suit, more like a librarian than an FBI agent. Pickett went directly to the head of the table, dropped a stack of folders and, not bothering to sit, said: "Greetings, ladies and gentlemen."

The man was, as usual, impeccably dressed and groomed, the very picture of an FBI agent. He radiated confidence, coolness, and enough self-assurance to fill a room.

"I'd like to introduce you to Dr. Milton Mars, specialist in charge of Behavioral Analysis Unit Four. He will shortly present a psychological profile of the perpetrator. But first, I want to run through what we have on the latest killing."

With admirable efficiency he briefed them on the murder of Jennifer Rosen. Based on the forensic analysis, it appeared to be a homicide of opportunity, quickly and expertly accomplished, with almost nothing in terms of real evidence left behind. He then moved on to the receiver of the heart.

"Agatha Brodeur Flayley was found hanging from a bridge in Ithaca, New York, on a visit to Cornell University, where she was applying for a job. It seems the interview did not go especially well; all evidence pointed to suicide, and it was ruled such by the local coroner's office. We have his report to this effect. She was unmarried, and her body was interred in the Flayley vault here in Miami, under the provisions of a long-established family trust. We're still assembling background on her." He paused. "Miami Homicide has, naturally, been looking for any links between the new murder victims and the prior suicides. We have found none. I think we can proceed under the assumption that the killer may be selecting suicide victims, but at random, with no other connection, historical or otherwise."

A low chorus of agreement; several nods. Coldmoon, too, couldn't imagine how the decade-old suicides could be related to the recent murders. He glanced at Pendergast, but saw nothing save the usual masklike expression.

"And now, Dr. Mars?"

The man in the horn-rims stood up and gave a friendly nod around the room. "You are all no doubt familiar with ViCAP, the FBI's Violent Criminal Apprehension Program. It houses the Behavioral Analysis Unit's main database." The man's nasal voice was curiously strong even in the large room.

"Human behavior falls into patterns. No behavior is truly unique. The ViCAP database covers all known serial killers: MO, victim data, crime scene descriptions, laboratory reports, criminal history records, statements, psychological analyses— in short, everything associated with every crime. By plugging the facts we know about a given serial killer into the database, we can often extrapolate the facts we don't know. We've done this with Brokenhearts—who, admittedly, is one death short of technically being labeled a serial killer—and I will now present you with the results. Please feel free to interrupt me with questions."

There was a rustling, notebooks coming out and tablets being woken up. This was where the rubber met the road.

"Our psychological analysis indicates that, despite surface impressions to the contrary, Brokenhearts is a highly organized killer. He selects the place, not the victims. He waits in that place, having mapped out his actions in detail beforehand. To frustrate video-camera identification, he chooses areas where many people are coming and going. When a victim arrives at the location, he completes the pre-choreographed crime with notable boldness. He is confident enough to kill in high-traffic areas, and to travel some distance to the site where he intends to place the heart.

"The killing is done swiftly, with two different bladed instruments. The throat is cut; the breastbone is split; and the heart is severed from the arteries—all with a notable lack of tentativeness. This implies a practiced action.

"This type of killer is of what we call the ritualistic type. The motivation usually involves a religious fixation, often with the Devil, Satan, God, or Jesus. The killer is likely schizophrenic, hearing voices that he interprets to be from a good or evil divinity, urging specific action. The killer has grandiose visions of his place in the world, and thus feels compelled to perform certain actions. He is almost invariably physically fit and, in this case, very likely under the age of twenty-five. He is male. Contrary to popular belief, he is in control of his actions. He is not compelled to kill; he does it voluntarily, and could stop if he found reason to do so."

The man pushed his glasses up his nose. "The murderer uses the same implements for each killing, which he guards carefully when not in use. While the victims are female, there is no evidence the killing was done for libidinous purposes."

There was a short silence at this bit of information.

"There are other characteristics we can infer. He lives alone. He owns a car. He has no girlfriends or sexual partners. He most likely has no criminal record. He appears more or less normal to his neighbors. Significantly, killers of this type almost invariably suffered severe childhood abuse—sexual, psychological, and/or physical—at the hands of a close relative, usually a father. Maternal abandonment is also a strong background characteristic. Sometimes, the killer comes from an unusually severe religious or cultish family background involving forced, ritual-like actions that must be performed with great precision—otherwise, punishment will result. The killings then reprise these early experiences."

"And such killers often thrive on attention," Pickett added, "so let's not give him any. It's bad enough that gossip about his leaving the hearts on suicide graves is starting to leak out— we're not sure, but we think we have the City of Miami caretaker to thank for that. So let's keep a lid on other details: the content of his notes, his name, everything."

"I agree." Dr. Mars paused and looked around owlishly. "So. Any questions?"

Pendergast spoke: "Is it common for a murderer such as this to regularly employ two weapons?"

"No."

"I thought not. Our killer first sneaks up from behind and cuts the throat—rather expertly, too, ensuring a quick death from exsanguination—then removes the heart, the possession of which seems to be his primary object."

"That fits the profile," Dr. Mars said.

"Would you care to speculate on why the killer doesn't simply chop out his victim's heart? Why waste time cutting her throat?"

There was a pause. "To silence his victim, perhaps," Dr. Mars said at last.

"There are other ways to ensure that without resorting to the extra work, and risk, involved in using two weapons. Might it not be that the killer—who, as I think we agree, is more interested in obtaining the heart itself than in committing a murder—is trying to cause the victim as little suffering as possible?"

"That...that would not fit the standard profile."

"But you would agree it is possible?"

Dr. Mars frowned. "Yes. Now, if there's nothing else—"

"Just one other question," Pendergast interrupted smoothly. "Earlier, ADC Pickett mentioned the killer's self-ascribed moniker: Mister Brokenhearts. This seems to imply a connection to the novel by Nathanael West, *Miss Lonelyhearts*, or perhaps to the agony columns of newspapers. Have you explored that connection?"

"Er, I'm not familiar with the novel."

"You would be wise to acquaint yourself with it. It's a novel about alienation from the modern world…and murder. The Miss Lonelyhearts character in the novel—who, by the way, is a man—is plagued by a suffering he's all too aware of, but cannot seem to ameliorate."

"That novel isn't in our database," said the man.

Pendergast evidently did not like this answer, and he fixed Mars with a glittering stare. "There are many things in heaven and earth that are not in your database, Dr. Mars."

"I doubt our killer is much of a reader," said Pickett, with irritation.

"On the contrary, he quoted T. S. Eliot in his first note and paraphrased the Bard in his second."

"All right, all right, the BAU will look into that angle. Are there any other questions or comments?"

The discussion went on for a while. Coldmoon kept quiet. He hated meetings like this, where people spoke not to exchange information but to impress their superiors or hear themselves talk.

At last Pickett rose. "If there's nothing else—?" he said, finality in his voice.

"One small matter," said Pendergast, raising a white finger.

Coldmoon felt a spike of adrenaline. There was something he

was starting to recognize in Pendergast's smooth tones—an occasional, secret undercurrent of pugnaciousness.

"Yes?"

"I request authorization to exhume the Flayley corpse."

"We already discussed this in relation to Baxter," said Pickett. "What purpose could it possibly serve? It was an open-and-shut suicide that took place eleven years ago...and as many states away."

"And yet, I should still like an autopsy."

"Might I remind you the body was *already* subjected to an autopsy—as is common with suicides?"

"I'm aware of that. I just saw the coroner's report on Ms. Flayley. And it was as vague and unhelpful as the autopsy on Elise Baxter."

Pickett sighed. "What, exactly, do you hope to find?"

"I'm not certain. That's precisely why I want to look. The remains are easily accessible. And this time, there appears to be no family in a position to object."

Pickett looked at Coldmoon, and for an uncomfortable moment the agent thought he might ask his opinion. But that would obviously be improper, and Pickett finally said: "Very well, Agent Pendergast—if you feel that strongly about it, and as you are the agent of record in the case, I'll put through the authorization."

"I am much obliged," said Pendergast. "And I would be even further obliged if it could be done at the earliest opportunity."

16

Pickett was as good as his word. *"At the earliest opportunity,"* to Coldmoon's amusement, turned out to be in the middle of that very night. Coldmoon was pretty sure Pickett had arranged things that way to make it as inconvenient as possible. But if Pendergast was annoyed, he did not show it. In fact, just the opposite: he appeared pleased, if you could call a man as sphinx-like as Pendergast "pleased." On the other hand, the cemetery staff were deeply put out, and as they gathered at the mausoleum Coldmoon could feel a chill that had little to do with the night air.

"A lovely evening," said Pendergast. "What an impressive array of stars. This is not the first time I've noticed that the empyrean seems closer here than it does in New York."

This rapture-in-miniature surprised Coldmoon. The sky had cleared and, despite the moon and the city that surrounded them, a vast river of midnight stars did in fact arch overhead. Even as Coldmoon glanced at them, a shooting star flashed across the darkness. When he was a boy, his grandmother had explained that at birth a person received the life-breath from

Wakan Tanka, which at death flew back to the spirit world in a flash of light. Perhaps this *wichahpi* streaking across the heavens was Jennifer Rosen, her breath of life returning to the eternal.

The cemetery director himself was on hand to supervise, a roly-poly man with dimpled cheeks and pursed lips framed by jowls. His name Coldmoon hadn't quite caught, but it sounded something like Fatterhead. A machine for transporting coffins had been driven to the door of the mausoleum, but because of the granite steps it couldn't enter. A total of four laborers with canvas slings would extract the coffin from the niche, carry it out, and slide it onto the transport cart. An ambulance waited in the lane to take the remains to the morgue in the medical examiner's building. The vehicle's headlights threw long shadows among the burial niches.

"All right," said Fatterhead, "let's get going."

The workmen crowded into the mausoleum, arranging themselves around the dark slot, while Coldmoon and Pendergast stood outside. The pendulum heart had been removed. The brass handle of the coffin, visible on the end, was not used; instead, they employed a long pole to arrange one of the canvas straps around the end of the coffin. The men gave a gentle heave, and the coffin slid partway out. A second canvas strap was slung beneath it, the coffin edged out another few feet, another strap added, and so on until only the far end of the coffin remained in the niche.

"Looks like these guys have done this before," murmured Coldmoon.

As the far end of the coffin slid out, all four laborers, two on each side, strained under the weight, muscles popping beneath their T-shirts. Now that it was fully in view, Coldmoon could see that the coffin, despite being relatively new, was nevertheless

a wreck—the leaking roof had evidently dripped on it continu-
ously and the wood had expanded, popping off the hinges and
brass fittings and causing significant rot along the rear side.

In a practiced motion, the four men swung the coffin around.
After a pause, all took a step at once, and then another, slow-
marching the coffin toward the door as if participating in a
funeral cortege.

As the coffin passed through the door, the workers prepared
to descend the stone steps to ground level. When the lead men
took the first step, there was a sound like paper being crumpled,
and a vertical crack suddenly appeared in the coffin's rotten section. It began to sag in the middle.

"Easy now!" the director shouted. "Hold on!"

The men halted, faces covered with sweat. But ominously,
with a crumbling sound, the crack continued to work its way
along the bottom and up around the other side.

"Quickly! Another sling around the middle!" the man cried as
more workmen came rushing up. But it was too late: the two
halves of the coffin separated down the center, and then something inside began peeping out through the widening gap—the
midsection of a corpse.

"*Close up the gap!*" Fatterhead screamed.

But the two halves of the coffin appeared to have taken on lives
of their own. They now swung open sideways, like a candy bar broken in half—and the body, itself cracking into two pieces, slid out
in a cloud of rotten silk and decayed clothing, landing on the damp
ground with a hollow sound. The corpse, pickled from a decade
of water leaks, belonged to a woman with a mass of brown hair,
wearing what might have been a black dress and pearls.

Coldmoon was deeply shocked. He had been raised to have
the utmost respect for the dead.

"Son of a *bitch!*" Fatterhead shouted as everyone else stared in horrified fascination.

Silence. Then the director recovered himself and spoke more calmly. "Please get the body shroud and transfer the remains of the deceased into it."

The workmen took the body bag that had been lying on the cart, laid it out parallel to the corpse, and together, hands under the remains, shifted the two pieces into the bag, zipped it up, and placed it on the coffin transport.

"What about the coffin?" asked one of the workers.

"We'll get that on the next trip," said Fatterhead. He turned to Pendergast. "I am so sorry, sir. This is the very first time . . . exceptional circumstances . . ." He wrung his hands, words failing him.

"I wouldn't worry," said Pendergast, laying a comforting hand on his shoulder. "I doubt if either half of Ms. Flayley will bear you any grudge."

17

D<small>R</small>. C<small>HARLOTTE</small> F<small>AUCHET</small> did not like to work with rubber-neckers around, be they cops or feds. The green ones often made involuntary noises, breathed loudly, or even vomited. Worse, the experienced ones tried to show off their nonchalance with jokes and asinine comments.

She waited, arms crossed, by the gurney, with the subject still zipped in a body transport bag. The chief FBI agent entered first. He was a typical fed, crisp blue suit peeking from under his scrubs, salt-and-pepper hair trimmed short, square jaw, broad shoulders. He was followed by a strikingly pale man in a black suit who looked uncommonly like many of the undertakers she dealt with—except no undertaker she'd ever met had quite such piercing silver-blue eyes. Clearly these two were big fish, indicative of the case's high profile. Important or not, they'd get no privileges in her morgue. Nor would there be chummy introductions or shaking of hands, which, at any rate, was forbidden in the autopsy chamber.

This duo was followed by a younger man, with longish black hair parted in the middle, whose ethnicity she was uncertain of. They all looked gratifyingly uncomfortable in their scrubs, and she gave them an unfriendly stare as they lined up. "Gentlemen," she said as soon as they'd introduced themselves, "the rules are simple." She looked at them in turn. "Rule number one: no talking or questions unless absolutely necessary. Rule number two: silence. That means no whispering or rustling. Rule number three: no sucking on menthol drops. If you start to feel sick, please leave immediately."

Nodded acquiescence.

"I will be speaking out loud during the procedure. Please understand that I am not talking to you; I am talking to the videorecorder."

More nods. They seemed agreeably cooperative—at least, so far.

"Thank you. Now I will begin."

She turned to the body, lying on a trolley next to the gurney. It was an unusual shape. Her supervisor, Chief Forensic Pathologist Dent Moberly, had warned her the remains were in poor condition and would be challenging to work with. So much the better. Fauchet, an assistant M.E. only five years out of medical school, had ambitions of running her own department in a great city—preferably New York. It was the difficult, the celebrated cases that would get her where she wanted to go. She was glad that, for once, Dr. Moberly had not insisted on seizing the spotlight.

She began by reading off the information on the medical card—the subject's name, personal data, date and recorded cause of death. Then she unzipped the body bag and nodded to the diener waiting in the background. The morgue assistant came forward and expertly transferred the remains from the bag to the gurney.

She began her general observations. "I note that the corpse has sustained significant deterioration," she said. "This includes what is evidently a series of wet-dry cycles, decomposition followed by desiccation." There was still a smell of embalming fluid, but it had not been able to hold back the ravages of decay. The corpse was in two pieces, and examining it grossly, she saw that the poor state of the body rendered the original—and evidently hasty—autopsy almost academic. She would essentially be starting from scratch.

All the better.

She began with a new Y-incision, and the diener handed her shears to open the chest cavity. The bones were brittle and snapped like dry twigs. The organs had already been removed in the autopsy eleven years before, then returned to the body cavity—now they were little more than shriveled black lumps adhering to the peritoneal wall, in an advanced state of decomposition. Soon she was "in the zone," as she called that moment when her entire attention became focused on the body and all else faded away. She slowed down when she reached the genital area and performed a very careful dissection. This was a forensic autopsy, and as such there was always the possibility of sexual assault. But this body was too far gone to see much beyond the original M.E.'s work and the grossest of injuries.

The clock ticked. The three spectators remained gratifyingly silent. And her boss, thank God, remained elsewhere.

Finally she moved up to the head. According to the records, the decedent had hanged herself. She saw with a frown that the doctor who'd performed the initial autopsy had barely examined the neck, beyond confirming its role in the woman's death. She made a U-shaped incision in the frontal aspect of the neck and began a meticulous dissection, freeing the sternocleidomastoid muscle from its lower attachments, exposing the carotid sheath and artery, the vagus nerve, and the omohyoid and sternothyroid. She finally exposed the cervical spine and noted the trauma still visible from the hanging.

"Dr. Fauchet, a question?"

She turned. It was the pale one, the one she believed was named Pendergast, who spoke. She was about to reiterate her rules, but something in his eye—soft and entreating—caused her to hesitate. "Yes."

"Do you see any evidence of strangulation *prior* to hanging?"

"No."

"None? From what I saw, the neck showed considerable abrasive trauma."

"According to the coroner's report, it was what we call an incomplete hanging—one where there wasn't a long drop involved. Typical in a suicide. The abrasion and trauma you see here...and here—" she pointed with a scalpel— "was caused by the subject thrashing about during the period of suffocation. There is no traumatic spondylolisthesis of C2, that is, a fracture of the spine, between cervical one and two, because the drop was not long enough. For the same reasons, I do not observe any severe ligature injuries. Again, all of this is consistent with a suicidal hanging."

"Thank you."

She turned to continue her work when a sensor chimed and the door was flung open by her boss.

"Ah, Charlotte, I see you are well along!" The chief forensic pathologist spoke loudly as he strode into the room, filling it with the scent of Old Spice. "This is Charlotte," he added condescendingly to the chief fed. "Our first African American pathologist. Top notch." He turned back to her. "May I?"

"Go ahead, sir," said Fauchet, keeping her voice studiously neutral.

She should have expected this. Naturally, he was all gowned up and ready to go, and he quickly moved in, crowding her back from the body, picking up a scalpel with a flourish, and starting to poke and prick and cut here and there, making disapproving noises—mostly, whether he realized it or not, relating to the hastily done 2007 autopsy.

"The dissection of the carotid should be diagonal," he told her. Naturally, he was wrong—that technique was twenty years old—but Fauchet had learned never to contradict her boss while the tape was running.

He fussed and poked, slicing away in the neck area she had already half finished. She winced as she saw his scalpel make a hash of her work. "You forgot to fully expose the first cervical," he said. "Let me do it."

She was about to say that she was in the middle of doing so, but again held her tongue.

He worked for a few minutes as everyone watched. "I was speaking earlier about this case with ADC Pickett, here," he said, "and it seems to me there are no surprises. Everything I see here is consistent with death by hanging. Do you agree, Charlotte?"

"Yes." And she did in fact agree.

Moberly poked at the corpse a bit more, and then straightened up and looked around, pulling down his mask. "Agent Pickett warned me this would be a waste of our time, and it appears he was correct." He looked around. "So, Charlotte—are we done with the gross examination?"

She glanced at the neck. Her dissection was still not complete, even though Moberly had done his best to ruin an already-spoiled cadaver with his fancywork. "Just a few minutes more," she said.

To her surprise, the silvery-eyed fed leaned in toward her. "Dr. Fauchet, would you do me the favor of examining the hyoid bone?"

"I've exposed most of it." She stepped up and pointed her scalpel, using forceps to deftly expose the rest. "It's fractured, if that's your question."

"Is that normal in such a hanging?"

"It depends. The hanging itself doesn't normally fracture the hyoid, but in an incomplete hanging such as this, the violent struggles of the subject will sometimes result in such a fracture."

"But you see no reason to question the cause of death?" interjected the senior agent—the one named Pickett. "Suicide by hanging?"

"No."

She could see Pickett shoot a poisonous glance at Pendergast. She was sorry her findings didn't support whatever he was looking for—he seemed like a kind enough man.

"Well, well," said Moberly, "thank you, Charlotte, for your assistance." He waved a hand. "You can wrap up here."

He led the group of feds toward the door. Just before leaving, the one named Pendergast glanced back at her with a sympathetic expression, and—if she hadn't known better—she would have felt sure that he'd winked.

Coldmoon did not enjoy autopsies, and this one had left him a little queasy. He followed Pendergast and Pickett out the hospital door. Once in the fresh air he breathed deeply, trying to flush the smell of formalin and death from his lungs.

As they waited for a driver, Pickett turned to Pendergast. "Satisfied?"

"I'm rarely satisfied."

"Well, *I'm* satisfied. Moberly is one of the top forensic pathologists in the country, and that assistant of his looked pretty sharp, too."

Pendergast paused. "I should like to go to Ithaca."

Pickett stared at him. "I'm sorry—what did you say?"

"The Baxter death occurred on November seventh, 2006. The Flayley death on March twelfth, 2007. Four months apart."

"Meaning what?"

"The timing appears unusually close. And both were Florida residents, killed outside of the state."

"Coincidence. You've been around long enough to know that cases like this throw up meaningless coincidences. Agent Pendergast, it's crystal clear that both victims committed suicide. *That's* the connection. Our guy has a *fixation* with suicide. Look how sorry he feels for them. Besides, the women didn't know each other. A trip to Ithaca isn't going to shed light on anything of relevance."

"Nevertheless, I would like to go."

Coldmoon listened to all this with an impassive face. He had to agree with Pickett. It was a waste of time to go to Ithaca, and he wasn't about to go out on a limb again after getting burned the last time.

"I can complete my investigation in a day," Pendergast went on. "There and back."

Pickett hesitated, as if considering something. Then he shook his head in disbelief. "Very well. If you feel that strongly, go ahead. No overnight—if Brokenhearts strikes again, you need to be here when it happens. But before you go, I want you to check in with the forensic lab to see if anything worthwhile has come up."

"Thank you, sir."

"Agent Coldmoon, you'll accompany Pendergast to Ithaca, of course."

"Yes, sir." Coldmoon silently indulged in a lengthy, and highly descriptive, Lakota curse.

Pickett's car arrived and he got in. "I'm heading back to New York. It should go without saying I don't want to have to come down here again."

He slammed the door without another word, and the car immediately sped off.

18

THEY MADE THEIR way down the icy East Avenue sidewalk, passing grim-looking administrative buildings, heading toward the Thurston Avenue bridge. Although upstate New York was not as cold as Maine had been a few days before, there were still plow-mountains of snow at the street intersections and in the corners of parking lots. Pendergast was again clad in his Snow Mantra coat, while Coldmoon was wearing his old down jacket, unzipped. He readjusted the satchel hanging off his right shoulder. Even for a chilly day in late March, the streets seemed quiet—apparently, it was spring break. Coldmoon had been through this town once or twice, several years back, and except for the Starbucks on the approaching street corner the place looked unchanged: gray and dejected, waiting for spring.

They reached the intersection and stopped briefly beside a flagman for a crew fixing a water main break. Coldmoon took advantage of this pause to reach into his satchel, pull out a battered thermos decorated in red-and-black plaid, remove the cover that also served as a cup, and pour some of his camp coffee into it. One of the nice things about being a fed was not having to deal with TSA bullshit—they could show their creds at the airport security station, board with the pilots and flight attendants, and bring whatever they felt like in their carry-ons.

As the delicious aroma of the burnt coffee wafted up, Coldmoon's two companions turned toward him: Marv Solomon, a Cornell University security officer, in surprise, and Pendergast in displeased recognition. Coldmoon ignored them as he placidly sipped the tepid coffee; he had long since grown accustomed to such reactions.

It looked like they'd be delayed at the intersection another minute or so. "One moment, please," Pendergast said. Then he disappeared into the nearby Starbucks. He came out shortly holding a cardboard cup with a white plastic lid, which he handed to Coldmoon.

Coldmoon took it in his free hand and examined it, turning the cup around.

"Espresso doppio," Pendergast told him. "Two shots of pure French roast, freshly ground. Not quite Caffe Reggio, but more than adequate for a civilized brew." There was the faintest emphasis on the word *civilized*.

Now Coldmoon had his hands full. He took another sip from his thermos lid.

"Try the other," urged Pendergast, kindly.

He tasted—gingerly—the drink Pendergast had given him. He'd never had a Starbucks coffee before—it was too damn expensive. He quickly took another gulp of camp coffee, rinsing the taste from his mouth. Then he poured the espresso into a nearby snow pile and dropped the empty cup into a waste can.

"Too civilized," he said.

The flagman waved them past and they continued down the hill. Now, directly ahead, lay the bridge. It was not especially impressive—just a pair of green steel arches rising gently toward the sky, the two-lane road between them passing over Fall Creek Gorge and disappearing into the snowy landscape beyond. Coldmoon could hear a faint rushing sound, almost like wind.

"There she is," Solomon, the security officer, said, waving toward the bridge as proudly as if he'd built it himself.

They paused again and Coldmoon glanced at the man. He found it interesting that Pendergast had requested this Cornell security officer instead of a local cop to act as guide. Perhaps he'd been unimpressed by their reception in Katahdin. Or perhaps it was the fact that Solomon had been with the university two dozen years and had seen three bridge suicides firsthand. In any case, they'd already retrieved the case files from the Ithaca PD. They were now crammed into his satchel with the thermos, ready for examination on the flight home.

He glanced at his watch. Twelve thirty. If they wanted to catch the plane home that evening, they'd better scramble. Even with the earliest Miami-to-Syracuse flight, it had still taken them almost four hours to get here. In addition, Coldmoon had requested they make an hour's detour on the way back to the airport so he could take care of some personal business, and that further limited their time.

"Let's take a look," he said.

They crossed the street, Solomon leading, and went another hundred yards to the pedestrian walkway that spanned the eastern flank of the bridge. The Fall Creek Gorge fell steeply away beneath their feet, its prominences and stratifications fanged by long, menacing icicles. The base of the gorge lay far below, covered with flat boulders punctuated here and there by menhirs sculpted by water. Upstream, the falls were half-frozen, but gray-black cataracts of water, spurting defiantly from its middle passage, turned the rushing sound he'd noticed earlier into a roar. From this distance, it was clear the bridge supports were flanked by decorative iron fencing in the same green and, beyond that, sturdy netting, elaborately rigged, to catch any falling bodies.

"Happened right there," Solomon said, hitching up his pants and pointing just ahead. "I was doing perimeter tours that night and happened to be very near when the call came in. Got here within two minutes, before even the cops. Didn't touch anything, of course. It was too late. I knew there was nothing I could do to save her."

Pendergast pulled a thin folder, which he'd appropriated from the stack of Ithaca PD case files, out of his parka. "Two students found her, I understand. Were they still there when you arrived?"

Solomon nodded. "Yep. Both sitting down. Stunned. Guess I can't blame them." He paused. "It was a warm evening for March. Real pleasant. Coming on a new moon, too."

"You've got a good memory," said Coldmoon.

"I'm not likely to forget that night. Not the way *she* died." And Solomon cast them a significant look. "This bridge is pretty famous for the so-called Cornell gorge suicides. Before they put up that netting, more than two dozen people—many of them students—jumped into the gorge. Flayley's the only person that I know of who hanged herself instead of jumping."

"What else do you remember?" Pendergast asked.

"She used yellow polypropylene rope. You know, the kind they rig boats and things with. Real strong for its weight. Tied one end around the railing, here—" He pointed. "Of course, the netting wasn't in place at the time. They put that in a few years later."

Pendergast opened the folder and paged through it for a moment. "A very common brand of rope, I see. Available in most states." He glanced up at Solomon. "Was she dead by the time you arrived?"

The man hesitated. "Well, that's hard to say."

"What do you mean?"

"She was...well, I saw her limbs twitch for a couple of seconds. Legs, mostly. Don't think she was still alive, it was just..." He fell silent again for a moment. "The ones that called it in, they said she was struggling when they first got there. They were too freaked out to do anything. Hadn't made the rope long enough to break her own neck, I guess." He licked his lips. "Poor woman. What a way to go."

"Nobody saw her approach the bridge or jump off?"

"No, sir. Like I said, it was a dark night. Quiet. Little traffic that late."

"How late?"

"Ten past midnight."

Pendergast went back to the folder. Coldmoon wondered why he was asking these questions; most, if not all, of the answers would be in the case files. It was almost as if the man had to absorb something from eyewitnesses, or the scene itself—as if he were waiting for the very landscape to murmur its secrets to him.

"And it was determined that Ms. Flayley knew none of the university students or any Ithaca residents," Pendergast said without looking up.

"She knew nobody. Was just in town for one night. Had an interview at Cornell in the afternoon."

A so-so interview, too, Coldmoon knew; an expression of interest, but not a definite job offer. That's what Pickett had said, and the HR department at Cornell backed him up. Agatha Flayley, thirty-one at the time of her suicide. Parents long deceased, no siblings or significant others. Place of residence: Miami. Place of employment: Outpatient Consulting, Mercy Miami Hospital. Interested in a position as patient advocate at Cornell Health. *Who the hell moves voluntarily from Miami to upstate New York?* Felice Montera, the first woman to have her heart rudely chopped out, had been in the health field, too, he remembered—a nurse at Mount Sinai. Connection?

As Coldmoon mused, Pendergast had walked down the bridge alone, hands in his pockets. At the far end, he abruptly stopped and looked around. Again, Coldmoon was struck with the odd notion that the man was waiting for something. He mentally shrugged it off: whatever it was, it wasn't any more peculiar than lying motionless on a hotel bed in Maine for a couple of hours. The agent's eccentric behavior, the "Pendergast mystique" Pickett had warned him of, was something Coldmoon felt impervious to.

Solomon, the security officer, was saying something. Coldmoon tuned in; realized he was talking about snow in the forecast; tuned it out again. Now Pendergast was coming back. Just before he reached them, he faced the bridge once more. For a split second, he seemed to freeze, and Coldmoon was certain he heard the agent draw in a sharp breath. But then he turned back, his expression as inscrutable as ever, and the moment—whatever it was—had passed.

Pendergast nodded to the security officer. "Thank you, Mr. Solomon," he said, slipping the file back into his parka. "I don't think we need to take up any more of your time."

On the way back to the Syracuse airport, Coldmoon—as he'd requested—made a detour for personal reasons. His destination was the federal penitentiary at Jamesville, New York. He kept the visit brief—about half an hour—and the deviation from their planned route took no more than an hour. They made their flight to Miami with time to spare. After the cramped and noisy flight up that morning, Pendergast insisted on upgrading them both to first class for the flight back, at his own expense. Coldmoon was too tired to object.

Coldmoon had never flown first class except once as a sky marshal, and after an initial period of uneasiness began to enjoy the legroom, the attentive service, the free dinner. He especially liked the flight attendant who had refilled his Dewar's on the rocks twice and asked for nothing but a thank-you in return.

He glanced over at Pendergast, who was paging listlessly through another of the evidence folders. The man had said little during the drive back, beyond fielding a call from Sandoval to inform them there were too many Miami cemeteries to surveil effectively. But the man had been unfailingly polite. Sipping his third scotch, Coldmoon felt a certain uncharacteristic generosity of spirit settle over him. Pendergast hadn't made a fuss about his unexplained stop at the pen; hadn't even asked him about it. He'd gone out of his way to make a friendly gesture by bringing him an espresso. Dumping it in the snow, on reflection, had been rather mean of him.

"You never asked why I wanted to stop at Jamesville," Coldmoon said.

Pendergast looked over. "Conjugal visit?"

"No. It has to do with why I became an FBI agent."

Pendergast closed the folder.

"I grew up on a reservation in South Dakota. When I was eleven, my father was murdered in a bar fight. My mother and I were almost certain who did it. But the killer was in tight with the tribal police. There was no investigation. We had nobody to appeal to—local and state police have no jurisdiction on the rez. The feds did, but they couldn't be bothered. To them, it was just a fight between two drunken Indians. So the case was shelved. I was lost for a while, went to college, and then after a lackluster start it suddenly clicked. I worked my ass off to get that degree, graduate at the top of my class, and earn a spot at Quantico. Once I left the Academy, I made sure I got rotated into the satellite field office in Aberdeen. I investigated my father's murder and found all the evidence needed to convict the killer. That was my first case."

There was a brief silence. Coldmoon took a sip of his Dewar's.

"So you became an FBI agent out of a desire for revenge."

"No. I became an agent to help ensure that kind of injustice doesn't happen again."

"I see." Pendergast paused. "And the perp is currently housed in Jamesville?"

"I like to visit him when I'm in the area."

"Naturally. A reunion of sorts." Pendergast nodded. "Which of the council fires is yours, by the way?"

"What?"

"The seven council fires of the Lakota."

"Oh. Teton. Oglala."

"And yet your eyes are pale green."

"My mother was Italian."

"Indeed? I've spent a great deal of time in Italy. What was her family name?"

"It doesn't matter." While Coldmoon loved his mother, he couldn't help but feel she'd tainted his otherwise unadulterated Sioux bloodline. He'd taken her last name for his own middle one, but never told anybody what it was—he'd even kept it to a mere initial on his FBI application.

"Forgive me for prying. In any case, I hope your, ah, visit was a success." And with that Pendergast went back to his reading.

Coldmoon regarded the agent with private amusement. It seemed the grim justice of the situation appealed to him.

At least they agreed about something.

19

Roger Smithback drained his bottle of porter and placed it on the scarred wooden table. Moments later, the barmaid—blond, fortyish, with spandex shorts worn over a swimsuit—came over. "Another, sugar?"

"Hell, yes."

She plucked her order pad from a pocket of her shorts. "You boys ready?"

"I'll have a grouper sandwich," Smithback said. "Extra banana peppers, please."

She turned to Smithback's companion.

"The usual," he said. The waitress smiled, scribbled on her pad, then turned away.

Smithback glanced across the table. The man who stared moodily back at him was ordinary in almost every way: average height, tanned, mouse-brown hair with a two-day stubble, wearing a Ron Jon T-shirt and baggy Bermudas. It was one of the getups Miami undercover cops favored—if you knew what to look for.

And Roger Smithback knew what to look for. He'd been

working the town for six years now, starting as a lowly researcher at the *Miami Herald* and battling his way up to full-fledged assignment reporter. And Casey Morse had, more or less, risen along with him. They'd met during Smithback's second week at the *Herald*. Back then, Morse was a newly minted patrol officer, assigned to Little Haiti. He put in his time pounding the pavement, spent two years on a narco rotation, and now he was a vice sergeant in the central district. And Smithback had been buying him cheeseburgers—rare, fried onions, no lettuce—once a week for the whole ride.

The waitress put a fresh bottle of Morning Wood on the table. Smithback grabbed it and took a long pull. The strong flavors of coffee, maple, and—yes, there it was—bacon that washed over his taste buds were stimulating and comforting. The beer was brewed just up the coast by Funky Buddha, and it was usually available only seasonally. But the Sunset Tavern always seemed to have a supply on hand, and that was the main reason Smithback frequented the place—that, and because it was a typical cop bar, where he knew Morse could chill out and relax.

They shot the usual shit for a while—the depressing prospects for the Marlins' upcoming season; the new Zika outbreak in Liberty City; the tyrannical behavior of Morse's new lieutenant. Morse was a pretty decent cop, but he never seemed to get along with his immediate superiors. Smithback wondered if that said more about the bosses or about Morse himself.

Smithback let the small talk continue, fiddling aimlessly with his porkpie now and then, until their dinners arrived. He'd done this for so long, he had it choreographed down almost to the individual dance steps. It wasn't that he played Morse or his one or two other cop friends, exactly—it was more of a give-and-take in which both sides benefited. Police never liked to be thought of as leakers to the press, except of course when it benefited them directly—but they were as gossipy as anybody else. If they thought you *already* knew something, they wouldn't change the subject...as long as they could rationalize they hadn't been the first one to give up any dirt. But naturally, they were as curious as the next guy. So if you, as a reporter, had picked up an interesting tidbit of your own here or there...well, you could barter. That's one reason Smithback often frequented neighborhoods like this one, where he might uncover tips that would interest a sergeant on the vice squad.

Smithback knew his style wasn't flashy, but he didn't care. He'd known plenty of reporters who lived just for the big leads. His older brother, Bill, had been one of them—always looking for an angle, antennae never at rest, pissing people off, a bull in a china shop who'd do almost anything to get another story above the fold. It wasn't that he was a bad guy—Bill had been a great big brother, with a heart as big as a house, and Roger missed him and mourned his untimely death every day—it's just that their work styles were as different as their personalities. Bill had liked jazz and poetry and Damon Runyon, while Roger preferred mathematics, Marvel comics, and classical music.

Their father had been a newspaperman, too, and in a funny way Bill and Roger had grown up mirroring two different sides of his personality. On the one hand, as a reporter their father had been the terror of their quiet Boston suburb, chasing down leads and local scandals with the determination of an ink-stained harpy. On the other, once he took over the reins of the *Beverly Evening Transcript*, he'd become more nuanced and strategic in his thinking: planning for the long term, seeing beyond the next big scoop, and carefully grooming both his paper and his sources. Roger understood that approach. The *Transcript* had been his dad's first and last love—and he'd died at the tiller, so to speak, suffering a massive heart attack while sitting hunched over the phototypesetter.

Outside on Northwest Eighth, traffic hummed. The cars would slow down later, when the hookers came out. Morse was enjoying his burger, giving it his full attention. That was good, Smithback mused. Funny how cops always seemed to prefer comfort food when they went off shift—just like they seemed to prefer bars with the word *Tavern* in their names.

"How'd you make out with that commissioner?" he asked nonchalantly. He'd gotten a tip that a certain Miami commissioner had been hiring escorts using county money, and he'd passed it on to Morse.

"It's looking good." Morse licked ketchup from his fingers. "Damn good, in fact. Of course, the fucking lieutenant is going to snag a piece of the collar if we do bring him in."

"That sucks ass." Smithback watched as Morse drained his gin and tonic, signaled the waitress for another. "Sounds like my life story."

"Yeah? That editor—what's his name, Kraski—still riding you?"

"Always." This was a bit of an exaggeration, but it never hurt to get in some brotherly bonding over shared sufferance.

"Wish I had a bone I could throw your way in return," Morse said. "But it's been pretty quiet. Except for those two killings, of course."

"Yeah." Smithback took another sip of his beer. He was faced with a bit of a dilemma. It was true he normally didn't handle homicides—and Morse knew it. On the other hand, the two *Herald* reporters who usually monopolized the murder beat were presently on vacation. His father had always harped on the importance of instinct—"trust your gut," he liked to say—and even though the cops were being unusually tight-lipped about the recent killings in Miami Beach, it was obvious they were linked. Both victims were women who had their chests hacked open with "a heavy, bladed instrument." That was all the cops would say, but he'd happened to be in the right neighborhood two days before, when half of the law enforcement of South Beach suddenly peeled off for Miami City Cemetery. It was no secret there'd been a big fuss at another cemetery just a few days earlier. He'd kept his ear to the ground, heard rumors that a body part—a heart, supposedly—had been found. Didn't take a rocket scientist to put the pieces together. And Smithback's own gut was telling him he should take advantage of his colleagues' vacations before some stringer did.

He wanted this story. But he didn't want to alienate Morse, lose him as a source. So he'd surprise the sergeant with a nugget of information that not only was tasty, but would imply he knew more than he actually did—a version of what, in game theory, was called the "ultimatum game." If he played it right, maybe he'd learn something.

"Yeah," he said. "The killings. Someone must be going ballistic." He finished his Morning Wood. "Otherwise, why call in the feds?"

Morse looked at him with surprise and suspicion. "You know about that?"

Smithback shrugged as if it weren't important. After all, he wasn't a homicide reporter. "Sure. Pendergast wouldn't be down here otherwise."

"Pendergast?"

"Yeah. Special Agent Pendergast and I go way back." This was the nugget; and it was, in fact, partially true. His brother had spoken of Pendergast many times, in a tone alternating among frustration, admiration, and fear. Roger had even met the agent a few times: first, at Bill's wedding, and again when Bill was murdered and Pendergast handled the case. The last time he saw the FBI agent was at Bill's funeral. So when he'd spied the gaunt, black-clad man at the city cemetery two days before, it had not only been a huge surprise but also confirmed his own suspicions—serial murder. The agent hadn't answered his question on the subject, but then, he hadn't needed to.

The suspicion in Morse's expression receded, but the surprise remained. "This Pendergast tell you much?"

Smithback had guessed right: the sergeant seemed almost as curious about the case as he was. But he'd have to tread carefully. *Trust your gut.* "Not all that much. Just that weird shit at the cemeteries."

To his relief, Morse nodded. "*Weird* isn't the word," the cop said as a fresh G&T was placed before him. "Those notes are definitely from a psycho. I mean, who'd use a candy-ass name like that?"

Damn. Time to improvise. "Yeah," Smithback said, still hitting the nonchalance hard. "When I first heard about that, I figured the guy was, you know, messing with you. Like Jack the Ripper or something."

Morse snorted. "At least *Jack the Ripper* has some balls. But *Mister Brokenhearts*? How fucked up is that?"

"Seriously fucked up." And Smithback looked down as quickly as he dared, picking up his sandwich and taking a bite to conceal a look of triumph. Not only had he just confirmed some suspicions and made a huge score—that the killer called himself Mister Brokenhearts—but he also hadn't burned his bridges. Morse would think he'd gotten everything from Pendergast.

He'd lied, but only to get the truth. And he'd done it subtly, successfully employing the ultimatum game. Both sides of his dad would be proud of him.

"How's the burger?" he asked the sergeant through a mouthful of grouper.

20

THE TWO NOTES, smeared with blood, lay between sheets of glass on the stage of a stereo zoom microscope under bright light. To Agent Coldmoon they looked like pages from a rare manuscript. The forensic document examiner—the FBI field office in Miami employed an expert who did nothing but analyze pieces of paper—was a short guy of about forty, massive, with a shaved head, a weight lifter's body, and a wrist tattoo just peeking out from under the cuff of his lab coat. His name was Bruce Ianetti. Despite the slightly gangsterish look, he also managed to exude the nerdy air of a man who treasured the arcane knowledge of a field most people didn't even know existed.

Pendergast took the lead, and Coldmoon—still bleary from that day's rushed trip to Ithaca and back—once again had to conceal his admiration for the man's chameleonlike ability to handle people from all walks of life, roughly or kindly, adopting various temporary guises of his own as the situation demanded.

"It was hell prying these two letters away from Miami PD," Ianetti was saying, or rather bragging, after Pendergast had asked him for a tour of his lab and listened with great attentiveness as the man gushed on and on about the latest technology.

"So I understand," said Pendergast, his voice oozing sympathy. "I'm delighted these letters are now in the hands of someone with your competence. Tell us, Dr. Ianetti—what have you discovered?"

"It's mister, not doctor, but thanks for the promotion." He laughed. "Anyway, we found no DNA, fingerprints, or any sort of physical evidence. It's a very fine paper, 100 percent cotton fiber mill, cut with a razor or X-Acto knife from a much larger sheet. Thirty-two-pound weight, linen finish. Ideal for writing: smooth, almost buttery, with minimal feathering or bleed. Chemical analysis of the paper and its coating indicates it is almost certainly of the Arches brand, cold-pressed, made in the Vosges region of France."

"Most interesting," said Pendergast. "A rare paper, then?"

"Unfortunately not. Arches is one of the most famous and widely used watercolor papers in the world. Tracing it may be impossible, since the user clearly cut it in such a way as to avoid including the watermark or edges. He handled it with great care, not leaving a speck of DNA or any other physical trace."

"But the stock itself is recently made?"

"I'd say within the last few years."

"I see. And the pen and ink?"

"The note was written with an old-fashioned fountain pen—you can tell from the almost calligraphic effect of the lettering that the pen had a very flexible, iridium-tipped nib of the kind commonly manufactured in the 1920s and '30s. The nib is wide, but not a stub. The ink is triarylmethane blue, and naturally it's of much more recent vintage than the pen. Most likely it's Quink—high quality, but widely available. Shame, really, given all the boutique inks available today, which would be easier to narrow down."

More nodding from Pendergast.

"And the handwriting?" Coldmoon asked. Handwriting analysis was one of his pet interests.

"Here's where it gets interesting. Normally, in handwritten notes such as these, the writer makes an attempt to disguise their handwriting—sometimes by writing with the nondominant hand, sometimes by using block letters. It's quite easy to tell genuine handwriting from disguised—on many levels. But the writer here has not tried to disguise his handwriting. As you can see, it's a nice cursive, easy and natural, not labored, pleasing to the eye. As for the nature of the handwriting itself—"

At this point the phone on Ianetti's desk chimed, and he held up a finger to excuse himself. A moment later he was back. "We've got a visitor," he said. And as he spoke a man entered the lab, dressed in a gray suit.

"Commander Gordon Grove," the man said, extending his hand to Pendergast. He was of average height, with a thoughtful face, gray eyes, and long gray hair brushed back. He had a bit of a paunch, Coldmoon noticed, but the suit was cut well enough to keep it hidden. If he was armed, the weapon was hidden as well. "And you must be Special Agent Pendergast. Given what a busy day it's apparently been for you, I wasn't sure I'd find you here this late."

Pendergast took the hand.

The gray-haired man turned to Coldmoon. "And Agent Coldmoon." The man clasped his hand in a large, cool grasp and gave it a pleasing shake. He then turned to the document examiner. "Bruce and I go way back to his days in Miami PD. He's the best forensic document examiner in the country."

Ianetti blushed, tattoo and all. Coldmoon exchanged a glance with Pendergast. *Who's this guy?* he wondered.

"I don't know if you gentlemen remember the Two Bridges murder about six years back? I was still a homicide detective then, and it was Bruce who cracked the case by proving that a certain will's signature page was a different kind of paper from the rest of the document and must have been forged."

"There was more to it than that," said Ianetti modestly.

"Don't sell yourself short," Grove told him. "Anyway, the reason I'm here is because—not to put too fine a word on it—the MPD and Miami FBI have a difficult history. Sometimes a little pressure is necessary to make them play nice together. These two key pieces of evidence are a perfect example."

"Thanks for shaking them free of the MPD so quickly," Ianetti said. And then he added hastily: "Sir."

"Happy to help." Grove turned to Pendergast. "ADC Pickett asked the Miami PD for a liaison, and I'm that man. There was a regrettable misunderstanding between a Miami officer and an FBI agent a few years back, and in the wake of that it's become my job to smooth over relations between local and federal authorities. You'd be surprised how much red tape this lets us avoid. I'm here to make sure you get what you need, when you need it."

"Thank you very much indeed," said Pendergast.

"Enough about me." Grove turned to the document examiner. "Mr. Ianetti, I believe you were about to share with us your findings on the handwriting?"

Ianetti cleared his throat. "The question always comes up: what can you tell about the perp from the handwriting? I'm afraid that in the past twenty to thirty years, the 'science' of handwriting analysis—graphology—has been thoroughly debunked."

"Debunked?" Coldmoon couldn't believe what he was hearing. "What do you mean?"

"It's a pseudoscience. Graphology is on the same level as astrology, palmistry, and crystal ball gazing."

"I don't buy it," Coldmoon said. "You can tell a lot about a person from how they write. Messy handwriting means a messy person, a bold signature indicates a big ego, and so on."

"It's very attractive to think that," said Ianetti. "But a 1982 meta-study—a study of studies—proved beyond doubt that graphology was hopeless when it came to predicting personality traits. It turns out, for example, that many extremely well-organized people have illegible handwriting and vice versa." He arched an eyebrow. "Surely *you* don't believe in astrology or the power of crystals?"

Coldmoon didn't answer. What he'd been taught to believe growing up was nobody's business. He glanced at the commander, who was nodding. "Local police forensic labs have mostly abandoned graphology," he said.

Throughout this Pendergast's face had remained studiously neutral. Coldmoon looked once again at his partner, who placed a pensive finger to his lips, then lowered it again and spoke. "And yet," he said quietly, "there's a great deal about the killer's *psychology* we can learn from these notes. We're dealing with a highly organized individual who quotes Shakespeare and Eliot, uses fine paper and rare vintage pens—in short, a man of literary pretensions. You point out that searching for the paper or ink would prove difficult—especially in this day of online purchasing—but your people might want to look into book clubs, libraries, and other haunts where a self-identified literary gentleman might hang out."

"Excellent suggestion," said Grove. "I'll put our people on that."

"Anyway," Ianetti said, "that's about all I can tell you—except that that the perp is almost certainly left-handed."

"Indeed?" Pendergast raised his eyebrows.

"It's much harder to tell than people think. However, this writer definitely employs what we call the sarcasm stroke: on the handwritten t's, the finishing cross ends with a sharp cut from right to left, rather than the other way around."

This bit of erudition was absorbed in silence.

"My report will be ready first thing tomorrow morning," Ianetti said. "I'll email you a copy."

"You've been most helpful," Pendergast replied. "Thank you."

They headed out of the lab, Grove accompanying them. As they reached the door, the commander glanced at his watch, then turned to them. "My goodness—seven thirty already. I have to run, but I'm glad I caught up with you. I just wanted to make your acquaintance and ensure you're getting everything you need." Cards came out and he pressed one into each of their hands. "Call me if you have any problems."

"Much obliged," said Pendergast drily, tucking the card into his black suit pocket.

As Grove headed down the corridor, Coldmoon looked at the card. It read: *Gordon Grove, Commander, Liaison for External Affairs, Miami Police Department.*

"Liaison," murmured Coldmoon. "In other words, Ass Covering 101. Nice way to ease into your pension. If we fuck up, it's our fault. If they fuck up, it's our fault."

"There are many essential police skills they don't teach you at the Academy," said Pendergast. "Ass covering, as it is so charmingly termed, being the most important."

21

Hᴇ sᴛᴏᴏᴅ ᴍᴏᴛɪᴏɴʟᴇss in the humid darkness, all senses alert. He was aware of the faint breeze, now at last turning cool, as twilight became night, drying the perspiration on the nape of his neck. He was aware of various smells, some sharp and close, others farther away: crushed grass, roasting pork, diesel, salt water, cigar smoke. His mind tuned in the fragments of sound that enveloped him: the *blatt* of a boat horn, distant laughter, thumping bachata from a discotheque, angry acceleration of a motorcycle, screech of brakes. Most of all, he was aware of the light: at night, it seemed rare, precious—more real. You didn't notice light during the day; you were immersed in it; you put on your sunglasses and ignored it. But at night it was different. Darkness was like the setting of a gemstone, and the qualities of light were as numerous as its colors: soft, low, intense, gauzy, tremulous. The sodium streetlamps; the high-rise stacks of light that were the hotels; the yachts whose mooring lights gleamed out of the velvety darkness of the creek. He was most comfortable in the dark, because he could become safe, invisible, and unnoticed. This anonymity was a cloak that deserted him in the day, and he had to guard against the resulting exposure. He had learned this long ago, through painful experience and through the Lessons. It was the dark, and the nonexistence it conferred, that made it possible to do his sacred duty—to complete the Action that was as necessary to him as breathing. *Action*...this moment of being a nobody wrapped in the night was the best time, when he could forget the shame and regret and be in the moment, his senses heightened without fear. While preparation was meticulous, the Action itself could never truly be predicted. Always there were variations, surprises. It was like poetry in that way; you never knew where a great poem would lead. It was like a battle in which the outcome was obscured in fog and smoke—the "poem as a field of action," as William Carlos Williams wrote.

The running lights of a passing boat swept through the tree branches, and he pressed himself against the trunk, melting farther into the whispering darkness. The approaching Action made him think of Archy and Mehitabel, who lived in the deep, reinforced pockets of his cargo pants. As a child, before the Death and the Journey, he had read and loved the little books about Archy and Mehitabel, their humorous verses and stories—Archy, a free-verse poet who'd been reincarnated as a cockroach, and Mehitabel, a scruffy alley cat. He identified with them both. They were nobodies, too; vermin, despised by the world. But they had nobility, and it was right that he named his tools after them. They were his only friends. They never let him down. And in return he kept them clean and sharp, just as he had been taught in the Lessons, honing them until they could cut a hair. They would have gleamed brightly in the moonlight if he did not take care to blacken them after sharpening. Action would dull them soon enough, the warm gush of liquid rinsing away the black. Mehitabel usually came out first, her lone claw cutting so fast and smooth and deep there was no pain, only swift and merciful sleep. And then Archy would make his appearance. His wooden handle felt as much a part of him as his own arm. Archy, lowly though he was, carried the power of expiation. He could forget almost anything with Archy in his hand, even the Journey. As he grew older, his truth had become clearer and more bitter—and that was good, because bitterness and truth were the only reality. *Because it is bitter.* Just as his own heart had grown bitter with remorse.

But this was not a time to dwell on the past, but rather to stay in the present, to be as keen as Mehitabel; to be conscious of the sweat drying on his neck and the cigar smoke drifting in the breeze and the strange mechanical conversations of distant traffic: because now he realized the waiting was almost over and the Action was approaching; he could hear it and see it and he would soon even smell it and feel it. It would happen so quickly. There would be the Action first, and then next would come the thing, the sole thing that, one day, could—he hoped—make the pain and guilt and shame go away forever:

Atonement.

22

Agent Coldmoon was lounging on the queen bed of his room at the Holiday Inn Miami Beach, watching a rerun of *The Dick Van Dyke Show* and eating four packets of chocolate chip cookies he'd picked up from the vending machine in the lobby, when the telephone rang.

Coldmoon was not particularly a fan of the show—he had about as much in common with Rob Petrie and his '60s suburban family as he did with a colony of Martians—but he always enjoyed predicting whether or not Van Dyke would trip over the ottoman during the opening credits. He waited a few seconds—ottoman successfully navigated this episode, just as he'd predicted—before picking up the phone.

"Yeah?"

"Special Agent Coldmoon?" It was Assistant Director Pickett.

Coldmoon reached over and muted the TV. "Yes, sir."

"I've been expecting a call from you."

Pickett liked having people phone him, rather than the other way around. Making Pickett reach out now and then was one of Coldmoon's little private mutinies. "The flight was late getting in," he said. "Then we had a meeting with the document examiner."

"What happened in Ithaca?"

"We stopped by the local PD, picked up the case files, spoke to the woman at Cornell who'd interviewed Agatha Flayley, then got a tour of the scene from the first responder."

"What about the motel she stayed in the night before she killed herself?"

"Torn down half a dozen years ago. Staff scattered to the winds. No records."

"So basically it was the waste of time I predicted."

"We haven't finished going through the files."

"You didn't need to leave Miami to do that." An exasperated sigh. "So you didn't get *any* takeaway from the trip? Nothing at all?"

"No, sir, I—" Coldmoon hesitated, recalling Pendergast's odd behavior on the bridge. That sudden catching of breath, as if he'd seen something, or put two pieces of a puzzle together.

Pickett jumped on the hesitation instantly. "What? What is it?"

"I think Pendergast is holding something back from me."

"Such as?"

"I don't know. Some theory. A plan of action, maybe. Something crystallized for him today, up in Ithaca. At least, that's how it looked to me. I can't tell you any more than that."

"Have you asked him about it?"

This was a stupid question, and Coldmoon didn't particularly try to hide it. "You know Pendergast better than that. If he senses me doing any probing, he's just going to withdraw further."

"All right. Any sense of how this theory, or whatever, is going to manifest itself?"

"I just...sense that a storm is coming."

"A storm? Good. In fact, it's perfect." There was a pause. "You're right—I know Pendergast. Sooner or later he's going to do something crazy. Something out of left field, or of questionable ethics, or even specifically against orders. So I want you to watch him, Agent Coldmoon. And when you think this storm is about to break, I want you to report back to me."

Coldmoon moved restlessly on the bed. "Can I ask why, sir?"

"I thought we discussed this at the time you agreed to be his partner. I'm going to shut it down before it happens."

"Even if whatever it is might help the case?"

"What will help the case is *accomplishing* things. We both know that if Pendergast can be relied on to do anything, it's to veer off on some wild goose chase that wastes time and makes everyone look bad. That's you and me, Agent Coldmoon. Look what happened with the Maine trip."

"Yes, sir."

Pickett's voice had uncharacteristically risen in volume. "I've been frank with you. The truth is, Pendergast's like a serpent in the garden. *My* garden. I've seen how he's dealt with superiors before." He stopped abruptly, as if catching himself, and there was a short silence before he began again, his voice lower. "Here at the FBI, we do things by the book because that's how we collar our perps and defend our actions in court. We protect ourselves, our cases, and our chain of evidence—and we maintain our reputation for integrity. That's why I need you to keep a close eye on your partner, and report to me if he starts going off the rails."

Coldmoon frowned. "I'm no snitch. Sir."

"Oh for chrissakes, nobody's asking you to be." His voice was rising again. "This is about best practices. We talked about this—remember? Neither you nor I want this case to blow up in our faces due to insubordinate or unethical action by your partner. This case is important to *both* our careers. Pendergast is a bomb waiting to go off, and it's up to you to defuse it. This has nothing to do with snitching."

"Yes, sir."

"Good." Pickett's voice softened. "Listen. You're a promising agent. You've already come far, against some damned long odds. I admire your ambition. And I shouldn't need to spell it out, but you have more to lose here than anyone. You do understand, Agent Coldmoon?"

"Yes, sir."

"Then I needn't take up any more of your evening. I'll expect to hear from you soon."

The phone went dead with a soft click, and picking up the remote, Coldmoon turned his attention back to the TV. Shit, he'd seen this episode—it was the one where Rob Petrie spends the night in a haunted cabin.

With a sigh and a muttered curse, he started channel flipping.

23

YOU CAN LET me off here," Misty Carpenter said, leaning forward slightly and touching the headrest of the front seat. As the Uber pulled over, she noticed—in the rearview mirror—the driver's nostrils flare slightly as he caught her perfume.

She got out and stepped onto the sidewalk, slipping her phone back into the Miu Miu clutch that hung from her shoulder. The black car slid away from the curb and merged with the southbound traffic on Collins Avenue. She paused a moment, breathing in the pleasant night air. To her left, across the wide avenue, ran a procession of luxury hotels and high-rise condos, bathed in gentle pastel lights. To her right, beyond a dark ribbon of grass, lay Indian Creek, with its display of yachts and superyachts, motionless on the still water. Just another perfect evening in Miami Beach.

Misty began walking along the pavement, aware of the sleek tightness of her black cocktail dress, the faint click of her Louboutin sandals on the concrete. Harry, she knew, liked this dress best of all.

"Harry" was J. Harold Lawrence III, chairman emeritus of the largest privately held bank in Palm Beach County and owner of the 120-foot cruising yacht *Liquidity*. Even today, when he no longer ran the executive suite, everyone called him "sir" or "Mr. Lawrence." Everyone, that is, except Misty. Misty always called her clients by their first names.

Not that she would ever call them "clients" to their faces. That would imply there was more than one. Misty wanted each of her special friends to think they were her *only* special friend. It was almost true: she confined her attention to a select group of less than a dozen refined and wealthy people, most but not all elderly. The thing they all had in common was an appreciation for Misty's rare combination of beauty, elegance, empathy, and youthful erudition.

She slowed for a moment, looking toward Indian Creek, her perfectly plucked eyebrows knitting in a frown. She'd gotten out of the Uber too early. This was the low-rent district: the yachts here were all berthed together, stern in, tucked into their slips like so many floating brownstones. The larger vessels like *Liquidity* lay just beyond, moored parallel to the waterfront.

She glanced at her watch: quarter past nine. Harry would be waiting for her by now, sitting in the salon, the bottle of his favorite vintage champagne chilling in a bucket of ice. They would probably dine on board—he preferred that this time of year—and he might be a trifle melancholy. Almost a decade ago to the day, his wife had succumbed to cancer. It was Misty's job to help him forget this, of course; to make him smile with her sparkling wit, to engage him in conversation on the topics he enjoyed most. For three or four hours, she would ensure he forgot his cares and his loneliness. And then she would leave—and five thousand dollars would be wired into her bank account by morning.

Misty—actually, Louisa May Abernathy from Point of Rocks, Montana, both parents deceased—had what she believed to be a unique vocation. It did not involve sex—at least not anymore, now that her select list of special friends had been established. It was safe: since she did not take on new clients, there was no need for verification, references, or screening agencies like P411. She provided a laudable and worthy service. It paid extremely well. It was probably even legal.

She moved on, heels clicking in the dark pools between the streetlights. Knots of traffic would come and go as the signals changed: busy one minute, quiet the next. The lights of the hotels threw dim, multicolored shadows over the palm trees, Indian Creek itself, and—on the far side—Pinetree Park. She had passed the regular boat slips now; she would see the sleek lines of *Liquidity* not far ahead.

It always surprised her how many of the yachts were dark and seemingly uninhabited, even by crew, as if they were just extravagant art meant only for display. The scene, its darkness softened by the tapestry of light filtering down from the east, reminded her irresistibly of Magritte's series of paintings *L'empire des lumières*.

Growing up, Misty had always been smarter and better looking than her classmates, and as a result she'd endured a childhood of resentment and isolation. This all changed when she went to Wellesley, and her hungry intellect suddenly found full flower. There, she learned the art of conversation and the ways to use her good looks as an asset—or, if necessary, a weapon. She ultimately graduated with a triple major in art history, classical languages, and music: a fascinating stockpile of arcane knowledge that, she realized upon receiving her diploma, she had absolutely no idea what to do with.

She had money from a part-time college job, and—with no other plans—decided to blow it on a grand tour before taking her next step. She found she enjoyed sneaking into casinos and private parties, mingling with the highest European circles she could bluff her way into. Nine months later, she ended up in Key Biscayne, where a Jaguar XK nearly ran her over as she was crossing Crandon Boulevard.

The car was driven by sixty-year-old Carmen Held, distracted and distraught from the death of her husband four months earlier. The woman, horrified by what she'd almost done, insisted on helping Misty into the nearest building: as it turned out, an upscale restaurant. Over a long lunch, the two women bonded. Ms. Held—Carmen—unburdened herself to Misty. She was lonely, and sad, and most of all resentful: finally, she had money and time to truly explore life, but no longer anyone to explore it with.

Misty very much enjoyed her lunch. She already knew she appreciated, even preferred, the company of older people. In turn, they clearly relished her ability to talk intelligently about many subjects; the way she made it so easy to confide in her. Students were perpetually hard up, and it was always nice to dine out as a guest of someone who didn't care how much money they spent. Carmen was sixty, but she'd taken very good care of herself and—if you looked past the incipient wrinkles—was actually attractive. Quite attractive.

A strange and yet perfectly reasonable idea began to take form in Misty's mind.

She really had no plans for the evening, and when Carmen said she was driving back to Miami Beach and offered Misty a ride, she accepted. In short order, Carmen became her first special friend—and the strange yet reasonable idea of hers soon became a career.

A temporary career, Misty reminded herself as she left the side-walk and began wending her way beneath the dark palms toward Harry's yacht. It was fulfilling, it kept her well fed and well dressed, but it wasn't something you could do forever. Recently, she'd been thinking about applying to law school. She'd saved up two hundred thousand already; that was more than enough. Another six months, and she'd get serious about those applications.

She slowed, frowning again. The yacht whose mooring lights gleamed out of the velvety darkness was unfamiliar. The *Liquidity* must be moored just beyond it. Harry would be setting out the champagne glasses; she'd better hurry. She quickened her pace, annoyed at how her heels sank into the damp grass. Maybe six months was too soon. She couldn't just abandon her special friends—certainly not out of the blue. The applications could wait another year. She wasn't quite ready to give up drinking cru classé Bordeaux, and...

From out of the insect-heavy darkness of the palms, a sharp rustling sound intruded on Misty's thoughts. She turned toward it, but even as she did so something flashed deep across her neck with horrifying speed but a strange lack of pain. There was a brief involuntary sound and then it was almost like going to sleep.

On the expansive balcony of his presidential suite in the Fontainebleau's Versailles Tower, Pendergast gingerly took a sip of the tea his waiter had brought him, then nodded his approval. True first-flush Darjeeling, harvested from one of the high-altitude plantations in West Bengal: the grassy notes of its delicate, aromatic bouquet were unmistakable. He watched as the waiter left; took another sip; then replaced the cup beside the teapot, sat back on the padded lounge chair, and closed his eyes.

The chair was flanked by two piles of case folders, each held in place from stray ocean breezes by makeshift paperweights: his Les Baer 1911 on one, and his backup weapon, a Glock 27 Gen4, atop the other. He had read through the folders with minute care; they had nothing further to offer him.

Slowly, he wove the various strands of the recent murders and distant suicides together in his mind: those that fit and, more interestingly, the one that did not. As he did so, the sounds and sensations of the South Florida night gradually receded: the faint smell of the ocean; the murmur of conversations from the bars and alfresco restaurants far below; the delightfully warm, humid atmosphere that mirrored his own skin temperature so exactly.

Now he set the mental weaving aside. He knew what he must do next. The key was to accomplish it while breaking the least amount of crockery in the process.

"If it were done, when 'tis done," he murmured to himself, *"then 'twere well it were done quickly."* And with that he opened his eyes, sat up, and picked up his cup of tea.

As he did so, his keen ears picked up a sound, faint yet discernible—an abrupt, gargling shriek, not at all like the laughter from below, instantly cut off.

Pendergast froze, cup halfway to his lips. He waited, but the sound was not repeated. With the bulk of the hotel curving around him, it was impossible to tell precisely where it had come from. Nevertheless, Pendergast raised the cup to his lips—took a sip, this time regretfully, knowing the tea would be tepid or worse by the time he returned—then replaced the cup, stood, swept up both firearms, and exited.

24

Sᴛᴀɴᴅɪɴɢ ɪɴ ᴛʜᴇ vast, cool space, Coldmoon couldn't help but experience a strong feeling of déjà vu. Understandable: it was just recently they'd been inside a moldy mausoleum, and now they were visiting another home for the dead. They called this one a "columbarium." He hadn't known what the word meant until Pendergast explained that it was a building where the jars holding a person's ashes were placed in niches for eternal rest. It was much nicer than the Flayley mausoleum: there was a rotunda with a dome, all gold leaf and white marble, and the niches were fronted with glass. You could see the jars inside, along with small statues and porcelain or engraved silver plaques on which were written the names and dates of the deceased. Nevertheless, it seemed cruel and barbaric to Coldmoon. What was the point of keeping your ancestor's ashes around, after the disrespect of burning the body and, thus, impeding their journey to the spirit world?

His eye strayed past the police tape to the niche that was now a crime scene. It contained a jar of pure white marble. But it was white no more; a single streak of blood had issued from underneath the lid and run down the jar's side, along the glass base of the niche, and from there sent a few small drops to the white marble floor.

"It appears," Pendergast murmured, gazing at the scene, "that a portion of ashes were taken from the jar." He indicated a gray pile on the floor, marked with a crime scene flag. "This made room for the heart to fit inside. The note was laid in the niche, propped up between that porcelain figurine of Saint Francis and the deceased's name." He turned to Coldmoon. "Do you see anything odd?"

"The whole thing is odd."

Pendergast looked at him as he might a backward student. "I, on the contrary, find a virtually perfect reprise of the previous *modus operandi*. What is odd, or at least telling, is the *consistency* of Brokenhearts's tableaux."

"You think this was staged?"

"Exactly. Not for our benefit; but for private reasons. Brokenhearts is not a man of drama. He lives inside his own mind and cares little for us or the investigation. Ah: here comes the note."

Sandoval was still at the Indian Creek site where Pendergast—along with others—had discovered the latest body. Nevertheless, CSU had wasted no time once the location of the heart was reported. Now a CS investigator plucked the note from its resting place and brought it over. Coldmoon photographed it with his cell phone, while Pendergast read aloud:

My dearest Mary,

The angels weep for you, and I weep with them. Please accept this gift with my most profound regrets.

With much affection,
Mister Brokenhearts

P.S. The stars move still, time runs, and Mister Brokenhearts will atone again.

Pendergast nodded and the investigator took the note away. Coldmoon could see a light in Pendergast's face, a suppressed glow of excitement.

"What do you think?" Coldmoon ventured to ask.

"The note is most revealing."

"I'm all ears."

"First, we have another literary quotation, this time from *Doctor Faustus*. The original reads: 'The stars move still, time runs, the clock will strike.' I assume you're as familiar with Christopher Marlowe as you are with Eliot and Shakespeare?"

"Sorry, I didn't go to Oxford," Coldmoon said, annoyed despite himself.

"My sympathies. The play is about a man of learning who, in pursuit of greater knowledge, sells his soul to the devil. The clock striking is an allusion to Mephistopheles coming to fetch Faustus and drag him down into hell."

"And the significance?"

"Hell is the ultimate atonement."

Coldmoon waited for further explanation, but it wasn't forthcoming. Typical of Pendergast: he stated that the note was revelatory, but would only dance around the perimeter of why. He decided to offer up an observation of his own. "The P.S. seems to be addressed to us, you realize. That's a change."

"Indeed. Although I don't think he's stirring the pot—I believe he's trying to explain."

Coldmoon almost said *Explain what?* but decided he didn't want to give Pendergast another opportunity to be coy.

They watched in silence as CSU continued to comb the scene. Coldmoon could hear, in the distance, the low roar of the media that had gathered at the edge of the columbarium grounds, beyond the police cordon. This third murder had burst the dam; the Brokenhearts story had gone national and everyone was out there, clamoring for information: CNN, *Dateline NBC*, the whole shebang.

"I wonder how that reporter, Smithback, got the Brokenhearts name," he said. "Wasn't that information privileged?"

Instead of answering, Pendergast approached the niche. "Mary S. Adler," he said, reading the name engraved on the plaque. "April fourteenth, 1980, to July seventh, 2006. We already know she died in Rocky Mount, North Carolina, of suicide by strangulation. And that the date of her suicide is four months before Baxter's and eight months before Flayley's."

"I don't see how the records are going to tell us anything. Brokenhearts has obviously selected these people *because* they're suicides. All we'll find out from them is what we already know. What I'd ask instead is: why is the killer apparently selecting suicides that occurred within a certain narrow time frame?"

Pendergast turned to him, a not unkindly look in his eye. "Agent Coldmoon, that question is indeed highly germane, and does need to be asked. Yet I sense our killer is operating on a higher plane of logic."

"What does that mean?"

"Recall my allusion to the *Doctor Faustus* quote. I sense our killer feels personally responsible for these deaths, which by the way may—or may *not*—be suicides."

Coldmoon repressed an urge to roll his eyes. "If they're not suicides, what are they? According to the profile our guy was, like, fourteen years old at most when those deaths occurred."

"I'm aware of that."

"Then what possible link could he have?"

"I'm not necessarily saying he's *physically* linked. But the question you just raised about the time line is, in fact, a mystery at the very heart of this case. Our man has been killing with alarming regularity and rapidity. We need to exhume Elise Baxter."

Oh no. Not again. "Pickett's going to have a fit if you ask him to do that a second time."

"We have higher loyalties than a man's ill temper, do we not, Agent Coldmoon?"

"You really want to piss him off like that?"

"What choice do we have? The only other option is to wait for Mary Adler's autopsy records. And I would guess they will be about as helpful as the previous ones—which is, not at all. Once the police conclude suicide, that's all the medical examiner can see."

Pendergast waited until they got back to their temporary office at Miami FBI before he made the call. Coldmoon could hear only one side of the conversation, but it was short and contained no surprises. Pendergast lowered his phone.

"Pickett has refused—again."

"So much for that idea."

"Quite the contrary. I'm the agent in charge, and as such I

have the authority to exhume Baxter—despite Pickett, and despite the parents' wishes."

"Are you serious? That's direct insubordination."

To Coldmoon's vast surprise, Pendergast smiled. "You shall learn, if you haven't already, that in life insubordination is not only necessary but even, at times, exhilarating."

Later that evening, while alone in his hotel room, Coldmoon got the message he'd been both expecting and dreading: *Call me now.*

He made the call, sweeping empty Twinkie wrappers off the bed, and found Pickett in a state of irritation. "Coldmoon? I've been waiting to hear from you ever since my conversation with Pendergast."

Fact was, Coldmoon had been intending, all afternoon, to make just such a call. He knew he had to inform Pickett about Pendergast's intentions. And he had every reason to do it. Pendergast's idea was just another harebrained scheme that would yield nothing and end in disaster. He remembered Pickett's warning: *You're a promising agent. You've already come far, against some damned long odds. I admire your ambition. But you have more to lose here than anyone.*

"Sir, I—" Coldmoon began.

"No need to explain." Pickett's tone softened. "Look, I know you're in a tough position. I get it: loyalty to your partner and all that. But that last time we talked, you told me that a storm was coming—and now I think I can guess what it is. Did you get the autopsy records from North Carolina on that latest suicide? What's her name—Mary Adler?"

"Not yet. It seems they're having trouble locating them. Something about a mix-up while everything was being digitized."

"So he's going for the Baxter exhumation, despite my orders. Isn't he?"

"Yes."

"I *knew* it. Okay. Now, don't try to talk him out of it. Understand?"

Coldmoon didn't answer.

"Look. It's all on him—nothing's going to blow back on you as junior partner. With this clear insubordination, I can transfer the guy out of my hair, send him to some nice, quiet midwestern backwater—and you'll be *senior* partner in the case. So just go along with his plan—all right?"

Coldmoon swallowed. "All right."

25

THE ELISE BAXTER exhumation, while not as disastrous as Agatha Flayley's, presented its own difficulties. It was scheduled for 6:00 AM, so as not to disturb normal visiting hours, and Coldmoon woke to the sound of rain drumming on his hotel window. Bayside Cemetery was soggy beneath a torrential downpour, and despite all precautions—high-tech lifting equipment, waterproof tarp, a temporary tent erected over the worksite— the hole began flooding and Coldmoon ended up sliding around in the mud, ruining his Walmart suit. By the time they had loaded the coffin into the back of the hearse, Pendergast also was a fright: his black suit soaked, shoes and pant cuffs caked with mud, and a streak of mud on his face that made him look like a freshly exhumed corpse himself. What was worse, Pendergast insisted they accompany the coffin to the morgue and begin the autopsy immediately, without allowing time to change. For some reason, he was in a god-awful hurry. Coldmoon, feeling guiltier than he'd expected, wondered if perhaps some sixth sense of Pendergast's anticipated the betrayal he was walking into.

They arrived in the basement receiving area of the morgue, rain still pounding on the car roof. The morgue assistants worked quickly, sliding the coffin out of the hearse, getting it on an electric rolling rack, moving it to a special receiving bay, washing and cleaning the coffin, then at last opening it and transferring the corpse onto a gurney. The entire process took less than half an hour and Coldmoon watched, fascinated at the efficiency. The corpse, moreover, was the opposite of Flayley's: aside from being a strange color, it looked as if Baxter might have died a week ago.

They followed the remains into the morgue and into an autopsy room. Once inside, Pendergast turned to Coldmoon. "I've called ahead to make sure Dr. Fauchet was assigned to the case, and not her supervisor—Moberly."

Coldmoon nodded his approval. While he didn't know much about forensic pathology, he knew a first-rate asshole when he met one.

Two dieners began prepping for the autopsy, laying out instruments, readying the video camera, adjusting the lights, and cutting the clothes off the corpse. A strong smell of formalin, wet earth, and rotting flesh filled the room, and Coldmoon found himself studying the walls and ceiling. This entire business was a wild goose chase—but that didn't make him any happier about how Pickett had maneuvered him into playing Judas. He reminded himself once more that it was Pendergast who seemed determined to sabotage his own career with flagrant insubordination. What could he do? He'd worked too hard, against very long odds, to commit hara-kiri now.

When the corpse was ready, the door opened and Fauchet stepped in.

"Gentlemen," she said, with a curt nod. "Do we remember the rules?"

"Indeed, Dr. Fauchet," said Pendergast, with a courteous bow.

"Then I'll begin."

She went into a lengthy and precise description of the body, having the dieners turn it over and back again. This completed, she had barely started the Y-incision when the door opened and Moberly entered, all gowned up, trailed once again by the smell of Old Spice.

"Ah, Charlotte," he said. "I'm glad to see I'm just in time!" He moved in, then turned to Pendergast and Coldmoon. "There was some sort of communication problem—word of the autopsy only reached my office a few minutes ago. I called ADC Pickett and he says he never authorized it. Who did?"

"I have that honor," Pendergast said coolly.

"Well, it seems you're at odds with your superior, Agent Pendergast, but that's none of my affair. What I'm concerned about is that, in an important case like this, the chief of pathology needs to be involved. In fact, I don't understand what Charlotte is doing here."

"I specifically asked her to conduct the autopsy," said Pendergast.

"And who gave you the authority to make a decision like that? We can't leave any room for inexperience or mistakes." He turned toward one of the dieners, simultaneously pointing at the video camera. "I'm taking over. Are we running?"

"Yes, Dr. Moberly."

"Good. Charlotte, you may remain and watch. It'll be a valuable learning experience for you."

A series of expressions, none of them happy, passed across

Fauchet's face as she pulled down her mask. She opened her mouth to speak, evidently thought better of it, then stepped back and replaced the mask.

"The snips, please."

A diener handed the snips to the chief.

"Excuse me, Dr. Moberly?" Pendergast said in a low voice.

Unexpectedly, Coldmoon felt the hairs on the back of his neck prickle. There was that same something in Pendergast's tone he had heard before—only worse.

"Yes, Agent Pendergast?" Moberly spoke over his shoulder.

"Put the instruments down, turn around, and look at me."

The command was made in a low, honeyed voice, but somehow it did not sound the slightest bit pleasant.

Moberly straightened up and turned, his face uncomprehending. "I beg your pardon?"

"Dr. Fauchet will do the autopsy. You are welcome to stay and watch, and perhaps *you* will find it a valuable learning experience."

Moberly stared a moment longer, his face darkening as he took in the affront. "What do you mean by speaking to me that way?"

Pendergast fixed his glittering silver eyes on the chief of pathology. "I asked Dr. Fauchet to conduct this medicolegal autopsy, and conduct it she will."

"This is outrageous," Moberly said, his voice rising. "How dare you give orders in my own pathology department?"

A pause. Then Pendergast asked: "Dr. Moberly, are you sure you want me to answer that question?"

"What the hell is that supposed to mean?" he said angrily. "Is this some sort of threat? You know, Pickett warned me about you. Who do you think you are?"

"I'm an FBI agent with access to excellent resources."

"I don't give a damn about that. Remove yourself from my morgue."

"I have used those resources to look into your past. It is— what is that term?—*checkered*."

He paused. Moberly stared at him, as if frozen.

"For example, your 2008 autopsy of sixteen-year-old Ana Gutierrez, in which you determined she died of a blood infection, was overturned by a court-ordered second autopsy, which showed she had been the victim of rape and strangulation. Or your 2010 autopsy of eight-month-old Gretchen Worley, in which you concluded she died of shaken baby syndrome, when—"

"That's *enough*," said Moberly, red-faced. "Every pathologist makes mistakes."

"Do they?" Pendergast said, his smooth voice continuing. "I note from your Miami personnel file that, on your application for chief forensic pathologist, you did not disclose that you had been fired in Indianapolis in 1993."

A silence.

"Fired, I might add, after being arrested and convicted of drunken driving…on your way to work."

The silence that followed was electric.

"There's more, of course," said Pendergast, ever so quietly. "Shall I go on?"

The unbearable silence continued for a moment. Then Moberly simply shook his head. Coldmoon, startled at this sudden turn of events, noticed the man's face had lost all its color. The doctor's eyes swiveled toward the upper corner of the room. Coldmoon followed the gaze to see a gleaming lens.

"Ah!" Pendergast cried. "The video camera! Good heavens,

was what I just said captured on tape? How *awkward*. I imagine it will have to be officially investigated. In the meantime, Dr. Moberly, we've chatted long enough. I think you might want to leave, after all. Good morning to you."

With trembling hands, Moberly slowly removed his mask and scrubs, dropped them in the bin, and shuffled out the door. The door hissed shut. The two dieners stood motionless, their mouths open. No one spoke.

Finally, Coldmoon, still stunned by the sudden reversal of Moberly's fortunes, said: "I can't believe how you just crushed that guy. I mean, you left him speechless."

"When one detonates a nuclear bomb," Pendergast said, "the shadows left behind on the walls are rarely able to protest." He turned to Dr. Fauchet, who herself looked shell-shocked. "I regret disturbing your procedure with such drama. Please proceed."

Fauchet took a long, deep breath, then without a word picked up the instruments and began to work.

26

Eᴌɪsᴇ Bᴀxᴛᴇʀ's ʙᴏᴅʏ was far better preserved than Agatha Flayley's, and as such, the autopsy was far more bearable. Coldmoon endured it with his usual stoicism, glad he'd had nothing but camp coffee that morning. Fauchet proceeded with exceptional care, it seemed, with a steady stream of comments addressed to the video camera as she worked. Pendergast, for his part, remained silent. Ten o'clock came and still Fauchet worked on, slowly disassembling the body, removing the organs and putting them in containers. There were no surprises. Baxter gave every indication of being a suicide, like Flayley.

Shortly before eleven, Coldmoon felt the cell phone in his pocket vibrate. He pulled it out so quickly that coins spilled everywhere. Pickett. Fauchet had already warned them to not answer their phones in her presence, so he quickly ducked outside into the anteroom.

"Yeah?"

"I've been calling Pendergast's phone," said Pickett. "He's not answering. I heard a while ago from the chief M.E., Moberly, that he's exhumed the Baxter remains against my orders. I want to talk to both of you, *now*."

"Pendergast's still observing the autopsy."

"Coldmoon? Did you not hear what I said?"

"I'll go get him."

"You do that."

"Hold on."

Coldmoon slipped back into the autopsy room. Fauchet was finishing up now, working on the head and shoulders, and Pendergast was watching carefully. Coldmoon signaled and he came over, frowning.

"Agent Pickett's on the phone. He wants to talk to us."

Pendergast almost looked like he was going to refuse, but then nodded. They slipped out into the anteroom, and Pendergast handed him the change he'd dropped on the autopsy room floor.

"Your thirty pieces of silver," he said.

Coldmoon didn't answer this. He put the phone on speaker.

"Agent Pendergast?" came Pickett's voice. "Are you there?"

"Yes."

"Agent Coldmoon?"

"Here, too."

"Good, because you both need to hear this. SA Pendergast, I understand you authorized the exhumation of Baxter's remains, obtained a warrant, and are conducting an autopsy."

"Correct."

"So instead of pursuing a valuable line of inquiry such as the call-girl murder—which took place right across the street from your hotel, I understand—you've gone ahead with this autopsy contrary to my orders. My *direct* orders."

"I did."

A pause. "I just heard from the Baxter family lawyer. You did the exhumation over their objections. They're going to sue."

"That is unfortunate."

"Is that all you can say? 'Unfortunate'?"

"Since this is a federal law enforcement matter, their permission was not required."

"I know that. But this is the real world, and a lawsuit like this doesn't look good. So—has the autopsy revealed any vital new evidence?" There was a heavy dose of sarcasm in the voice.

Nobody answered.

"Agent Coldmoon?"

"No, sir, it didn't," said Coldmoon.

"Is it completed?"

"Just about."

"I see. Agent Pendergast, I told you on more than one occasion that this would be a waste of time, and you still disobeyed my orders. Your insubordination has done nothing but generate a lawsuit and a public relations problem."

"I'm sorry to hear it," Pendergast replied.

"I am, too. Because you must certainly understand that such behavior by a federal officer is unacceptable. You're aware that the FBI views insubordination in the strongest negative light. I'm taking you off the case. I've already set the wheels in motion. Coldmoon's going to be the new lead agent, with three junior agents, two from Miami and another from New York. And as it turns out, Agent Pendergast, we have an opening in the Salt Lake City Field Office."

Silence.

"Let me emphasize this is not a demotion or a punishment. It's not even a matter for OPR. The Salt Lake Field Office covers all of Utah, Idaho, and Montana. It will be a major responsibility, equal to what you're doing here."

Pickett paused. The silence continued.

"The bottom line, Agent Pendergast, is that your sense of ethics conflicts with mine. I simply can't manage an office with a freelancer such as yourself doing whatever the hell you please, with no regard for the chain of command. Do you understand?"

"I do."

"Do you have anything to say for yourself?"

"No."

"Agent Coldmoon, if you have any thoughts on what I've just said, let's hear them."

Coldmoon was surprised at Pendergast's mild acquiescence. If it was, in fact, mild: what was that crack a minute before about the thirty pieces of silver? But as he'd been listening to this triumphant tirade of Pickett's, Coldmoon was even more surprised to find that something was happening to *him*. He was beginning to grow angry: at himself, for getting maneuvered into this situation; at Pendergast, for his secretive and unorthodox methods; but most of all at Pickett—for encouraging him to violate one of the FBI's most sacred codes... that of loyalty to your partner. It was not right. Pressure or no pressure, he should never have agreed to Pickett's agenda, and he could only blame himself for that. But Pickett should never have put him in the position in the first place.

"I do have a thought," Coldmoon said.

"I'm listening."

"My thought is that I'm 100 percent behind my partner. You take him off the case, you take me off."

"What? Have you lost your mind?"

"I think what I just said was both clear and logical."

"Well, I'll be..." There was a moment of silence before Pickett's voice came rasping out again through the cell phone speaker. "You've disagreed with Pendergast's entire investigative approach. You said he was wasting your time on irrelevant tangents. You got burned going to Maine, Ithaca was a bust, and now you're burned a third time with this useless autopsy. And yet here you are, sticking up for him with a misplaced sense of loyalty. Well, if that's how you want it, I'll transfer the both of you to Salt Lake City. This is a high-profile case and I'll have no trouble finding top-notch agents to take it over. Is that really how you want it?"

"Yes, sir, that's really how I want it."

"So be it. I'm flying down to make things official." The phone went dead.

Coldmoon turned and found Pendergast's eyes on him. "You didn't have to do that."

"Yes, I did. I deserved it. I agreed to spy on my partner—I guess you probably figured out that's what's been going on."

"I suspected it from the start."

Coldmoon gave a mirthless laugh. "Of course you did."

"You're a good man, Agent Coldmoon."

"Hell, Salt Lake City won't be so bad. I've always liked the West. Florida is too flat. And too green."

After a silent moment, Pendergast indicated the autopsy room door. "We might as well hear Dr. Fauchet's conclusions before we pack our proverbial bags."

They filed into the room just as Fauchet turned and put down her instruments. "Gentlemen, I'd like to show you something. Please come this way."

Coldmoon and Pendergast stood on either side of the gurney

as Fauchet adjusted the overhead light to illuminate the frontal portion of the neck.

"I'll try to describe this in layman's terms," she said. "But first, let me point out that—as with the corpse of Ms. Flayley—the initial autopsy this body received was perfunctory, at best. Now, bearing that in mind: do you see these marks here, here, and here?"

She pointed to several very faint bruises.

"These were caused by ligature strangulation—according to the coroner's report, a knotted bedsheet, which she allegedly used to hang herself from a curtain rod. In a hanging like this, these bruises would be expected. Do you follow me so far?"

Coldmoon nodded.

"Now, here—" she indicated a horseshoe-shaped bone she had exposed in the upper neck— "is the hyoid. This bone was fractured in the Flayley corpse, as you know. In that case it was fractured in the middle, what we call the body of the bone—as it is here. Again, typical of a self-hanging." She paused. "In *addition*, there are fractures in the two greater horns, here and here, which form the wings of the hyoid."

She rolled a portable magnifying glass on a stand into place. "You can see better with this."

Coldmoon looked, then Pendergast did the same.

"Both horns are fractured in a fairly symmetrical fashion." She pushed the stand away. "This type of double fracture cannot be caused by ligature strangulation. It's typically caused by what we call a push-choke. That is, two hands are wrapped around the upper larynx and great pressure is brought to bear with the thumbs, a squeeze combined with a push or shake. It takes a person with powerful hands to do this—almost invariably a man. Right-handed in this case, judging by the differing degree of trauma to the two wings. Such choking cannot be self-administered."

"So you're saying—" Coldmoon began, then fell silent.

"I'm saying the victim did *not* die of a ligature strangulation. She died of a choke hold. The ligature strangulation was done immediately after death, when bruising was still possible, as a way of covering up the push-choke and making the death appear a suicide." She paused. "But this was *not* a suicide. This person was most definitely the victim of a homicide."

27

Roger Smithback paused to blow his nose on a real estate gazetteer, crumple it into a ball of newsprint, and then toss it in the trash before entering Bronner Psychiatric Group PA, a low white-brick building on Northwest Fifteenth Avenue. The pollen season—actually, not a season but a year-round threat in Florida—was in full swing and his allergies were acting up as usual.

He took a moment to breathe deeply and practice mindfulness, centering himself for what was to come. He wasn't an investigative reporter, but the last few days he'd started wondering if maybe he should switch his focus: he seemed to have the nose of a good one. The nose—presently runny—had brought him here, for example.

With a pair of binoculars it had been easy to get the names and dates of the decedents off the two roped-off graves where Mister Brokenhearts had left his grisly offerings—Baxter and Flayley. Other journalists, of course, had done the same thing and now the names were publicly known. Same with yesterday's recipient, Mary Adler, the one whose ashes were kept in a columbarium.

But he'd taken it further than the rest of his half-assed journalistic brethren. He'd retrieved Baxter's and Flayley's obituaries from his paper's digital morgue—he hadn't been able to find Adler's—and learned they were both suicides. And then he'd dug up their former addresses from old phone books and figured out that—though they'd died out of state— they'd lived in Miami, just a few miles from each other. From there he was able to fit together bits and pieces of their personal histories.

No doubt Miami PD and Pendergast had trod the same path. But then he'd had a stroke of genius. He flushed even now, thinking about his amazing cleverness. Here were suicides of two young women full of promise. He wondered: Did either of them go to a shrink? And if so, which ones, and could he prize any information from them?

Then it got even better. As he went through archived web pages, he was able to pull up sixteen psychiatrist and psychotherapist offices within a reasonable radius of each residence. He cleared his throat, worked up a shtick, and began making calls, using a variety of ruses, including posing as a long-bereaved brother seeking closure on his sister's inexplicable suicide. He knew that he wasn't going to pry any medical records out of these clinics over the phone, but he might be able to learn if anyone had at least treated a patient named Baxter or Flayley.

And this was where he hit pay dirt. Baxter and Flayley had indeed both seen shrinks—*the same one*. A guy named Peterson Bronner. Now, this was an incredible connection—yet one so improbable he doubted whether the police or even Pendergast had made it. Or had they, and they were just keeping it secret? Either way, it didn't matter—*he* had the scoop.

So who was this Bronner, and what did he know about

Baxter and Flayley? Smithback had a vague idea—or maybe it was a hope—that Bronner himself might be involved in nefarious doings. Mind working feverishly, he had posited a number of scenarios: Baxter and Flayley had discovered Bronner was cheating Medicare, or he was a cash-hungry Dr. Feelgood, or he was doing something else of an illegal nature...and he had killed them to cover it up. Who better than a shrink to know exactly how to stage a suicide? Or maybe Mister Brokenhearts himself had been—or still was—a patient of Bronner's? Christ, maybe Bronner *was* Brokenhearts, apologizing for their suicides, which would be an obvious treatment failure for a psychiatrist...!

Smithback took another deep breath and tried to rein in his imagination. First, he had to meet this Dr. Bronner.

Smoothing down his unruly hair, he put on the hangdog look that he imagined a severely depressed person might exhibit and pushed open the glass door to Bronner Psychiatric Group PA. He shuffled up to the receptionist. A plump man in his thirties greeted him cheerfully, asked his name, then inquired as to whether he had an appointment.

"Um, I don't," Smithback said in a monotone. "I'm—" He stifled a sob. "I've tried everything. I've got no hope left. I just want to end it all. I need to see Dr. Bronner right away—it's an emergency."

The receptionist seemed flustered, especially for someone working in a shrink's office. "I'm so sorry, but we don't handle walk-ins. You need to go to an emergency room." He picked up the phone. "Here, I'll dial nine-one-one and get you an ambulance."

"Wait! No. I won't go. I want to see Dr. Bronner and no one else! He helped my sister years ago—she said he worked miracles. I won't see anyone but him!" He raised his voice, hoping to become enough of a nuisance to flush out the doctor.

The receptionist, now thoroughly alarmed, said, "I'll get you a nurse right away." He pressed a button.

"I want the doctor!" Smithback wailed. This was a little embarrassing—his brother Bill had always enjoyed staging shows like this, but then he was an extrovert. Roger wasn't nearly as good at it himself.

A nurse rushed out into the reception area: a gaunt older woman with the demeanor of a battle-ax.

"I need to see Dr. Bronner!" Smithback cried. "Don't you understand? I'm desperate!"

The woman fixed him with a stern but compassionate look. "What is your name, sir?"

"Smithback. Ro...Robert Smithback."

The nurse nodded briskly. "Dr. Bronner is retired. I will bring you in to see Dr. Shadid."

Smithback hadn't considered the possibility Bronner was retired. The clinic still bore his name. He stared, stupefied, trying to think what to do next.

"Mr. Smithback? Please come with me."

If Bronner was retired, he didn't need to go through all this rigmarole. He'd better get the hell out. "Um, you know what? I'm feeling *much* better."

Apparently, this was a bad sign, because her voice immediately softened. "I think you should see the doctor right away. Really I do."

Oh God. "No, no. I'm good!" He turned and fled the office, the nurse's voice calling him back as he hurried out the door and sprinted across the parking lot to his car.

Inside the car, he glanced back. No one was following him.

Thank God. He pulled out his phone and—using his newspaper's information gateway—quickly located a Dr. Peterson Bronner. But he lived way the hell down in Key Largo, and it was already late in the day—he would hit murderous traffic. He would go tomorrow morning and beard the doc in his den. If he was retired, that probably made him too old to be the Brokenhearts killer. Anyway, Smithback was pretty sure a kindly old shrink would be no match for him. He'd learn all there was to learn—and then just maybe publish the scoop of his career.

28

Aₛₛᵢₛₜₐₙₜ Dᵢᵣₑcₜₒᵣ ɪN Charge Walter Pickett stepped out of the elevator and into the humid warmth of the rooftop bar. Given the overall footprint of the ultra-luxe 1 Hotel, he'd expected this space to be large, noisy, and crowded with tourists. He was mistaken: the restaurant had closed for the night; the candlelit tables lined up across from the bar were only sparsely occupied; and beyond the low glass barrier at the building's edge the lights of Miami Beach, and the dark line of the Atlantic, spread out below.

Beyond the bar was a pool, lit, as was the rest of the roof, in muted blues. It was empty and surrounded by luxuriously padded deck chairs with individual tables and umbrellas. Here and there, discreetly placed tiki lights radiated a yellow-orange glow. Almost all of the deck chairs were unoccupied. Pickett walked three-quarters of the way around the pool before he came upon Pendergast.

The agent was relaxing, the chair placed in a reclining position. Pickett—a clotheshorse as far as his budget allowed—noticed that Pendergast had swapped out the black suit for one of pure white linen, and instead of the handmade English shoes he wore a pair of Italian slip-ons. His pale hair, and the very dark glasses he wore despite the late hour, seemed to reflect the blue-and-orange light coming from the pool and the lamps.

Pendergast saw him coming, put down a tiny glass of espresso, and sat up. "Sir," he said in an utterly neutral voice.

Pickett raised a hand, indicating that Pendergast should stay as he was. He, meanwhile, looked around, then perched on the edge of the adjoining deck chair.

Since he'd abruptly terminated the phone call with Coldmoon that morning, there had been no communication between Pickett and Pendergast. Pickett, of course, knew what had transpired after the call. And on the flight down, he'd done some thinking. A great deal of thinking.

"Had to catch a later flight," Pickett said by way of explanation.

"I was happy to wait up. Would you care for coffee—or a digestif?"

Pickett shook his head and Pendergast waved off the approaching waiter. "I presume you've brought my transfer orders."

Pickett patted his jacket pocket. "Coldmoon's, too."

"I must confess I've never been to Salt Lake City. I can't imagine how I've managed to miss it all these years."

Pickett didn't reply.

Pendergast took a sip of espresso. "May I see them? I assume they include the names of the agents who'll be replacing us. No doubt you'll want us to brief them." He held out his hand.

"In a moment," Pickett said. "I'd like to ask you a hypothetical question."

"My favorite kind."

"As you know, you're now off the case. But hypothetically: if I were to keep you on, what would your next move be?"

Pendergast appeared to consider this. "I would look into the, ah, client list of Miss Carpenter. She seems to have been a free-lance escort of the most enterprising caliber—I'm sure such a clever woman would have learned all kinds of secrets during her career."

"The Miami PD is already doing that—and you know it."

A brief pause. "Then I'd continue looking for commonalities among the three murdered women. All were killed at night, in high-traffic areas. Why would the killer take such chances? The care taken in the killings and the methodical nature of the graveside gifts would seem to place the killer at the far end of the organized-killer bell curve. That seems like fruitful ground for—what is the term?—traction."

Pickett stirred impatiently. "Goddamn it, Pendergast. I'm not a fool, so stop treating me like one. Those are all obvious lines of inquiry. I don't want to hear bullshit. I want to hear what *you* would look into—if *you* were given the chance."

The next pause was much longer. Then Pendergast took off his dark glasses, folded them, and slipped them into the pocket of his jacket. Now it was his pale eyes that reflected the pool. "Very well," he said. "It has always been my conviction that the old suicides, and the new murders, are fundamentally connected—beyond the obvious leaving of the gifts. Possibly even *historically* connected. The killer, despite his youth, may have a personal connection with these past suicides. At least one of which, we now know, has turned out to be a homicide. For these reasons I would put my main effort into investigating those earlier deaths. That's how you're most likely to track down this person—or persons."

Pickett frowned. "But the old suicides appear to have nothing in common, either—except that they were all from Miami."

"I repeat: Elise Baxter did not kill herself. She was murdered. A much closer look at the other two presumed suicides is in order."

Pickett sighed in exasperation. "That's assuming this assistant M.E. is correct—remember, the chief examiner was only partially involved in the autopsy."

"I have every reason to think she was correct. Further, I suspect that Flayley and Adler were also homicides."

"Flayley was just exhumed and autopsied, at your insistence—and the assistant M.E., whose opinion you seem so partial to, declared her death a suicide!"

"I'm aware of that. There is some kind of a slowdown in getting the autopsy records on Mary Adler, which, when available, might offer corroborating evidence. But I'm sure we're not here just to bandy words: you asked me what aspect of the case I would 'look into,' and I answered the question." Pendergast took another sip of his espresso. "So much for hypotheticals. What's more, this is fruitless speculation, as I am on my way to the Beehive State. Now, if you don't mind, I'd like to peruse my transfer orders."

Pickett sat quite still for perhaps sixty seconds. Then, slowly, he reached into his jacket and withdrew an envelope. Pendergast reached for it.

Grasping the envelope with both hands, Pickett tore it in two. Then he replaced the pieces in his jacket pocket.

"You have my permission to proceed along the lines you've just outlined," he said.

Pendergast's only reaction was the slight raising of one eyebrow. Sitting back, he withdrew his hand.

"Now I'd like you to listen to me very carefully, Special Agent Pendergast," Pickett said, clasping his hands. "I've gotten where I am because I believe in the system and its rules. I also have a good understanding of the psychology of motivation and reward. But I'm not so blinded by ego as to believe I can't still learn a thing or two. You're an iconoclast—and you enjoy being one. Your method of operating violates just about every principle I hold true, save for one—and that is arithmetic. You get results. Like pursuing this Baxter autopsy, when everyone thought it was a dead end."

Instead of responding, Pendergast simply finished his espresso.

"But getting results doesn't change the fact that your methods are unusual. With unconventional methods, there's no backstop against failure. What I mean is, those of us who follow the rules can feel secure even if we screw up. But if you break the rules, failure is magnified. And so here's what's going to happen. You and Coldmoon are going to stay here and finish this case—and do it your way. Naturally, I want to be kept informed of important advances. If you need help, let me know. Otherwise, I don't want to know about your going off piste. Keep things on the down low . . . *and get results.* I'll give you space to work, in exchange for one thing: if this case goes down in flames because of your methods, you're going to take the full rap. *Not* Coldmoon. *Not* me. And sure as hell *not* the New York Field Office. Make no mistake—I will hang you out to dry." He paused. "Deal?"

Pendergast gave a curt nod.

Pickett went on. "Another thing. No flying solo. This is a massive, sprawling case and you're going to need backup. You've met Commander Grove. He's there to get you whatever you need from Miami PD. This is a police department with some of the best resources in the country. They can get you the files and case data, they can throw a hundred cops at any problem you want solved, they can do surveillance, they can knock on doors, they can interview everyone on an entire city block if need be. You don't have to keep Grove in the loop, necessarily—but tell him what you need and he'll get it done."

"He seems a competent enough individual," Pendergast said.

"He's got a damn good reputation. And don't discount him because of the administrative position—he did more than his share of working the streets back in the day." There was a pause. "Are we clear, Agent Pendergast?"

"Completely, sir."

"Just remember: if things go south, it's on you—and you alone."

"That is how I always prefer it," said Pendergast.

Pickett held out a hand; Pendergast grasped it briefly; then Pickett rose, turned, and—navigating the perimeter of the shimmering blue pool—disappeared into the darkness of the rooftop bar.

29

CHARLOTTE FAUCHET LAY in bed at four o'clock in the morning, staring at the faint red glow on the ceiling cast by her digital alarm clock. A nightmare had woken her at two—she had been dissecting a cadaver, and the knife kept slipping until at last the cadaver sat up and berated her for incompetence. She had lain awake ever since, uneasy about the Flayley autopsy.

This wasn't like her—having nightmares, feeling uneasy. Thanks to that dirtbag of a boss Moberly, she'd developed a pretty thick skin. What Agent Pendergast—who seemed so nice—had done to the man was terrifying...yet perversely karmic. He seemed like the kind of avenging angel who would make an unshakable friend—or an implacable enemy.

Her mind wandered back to the dream. Clearly, the Baxter autopsy had shaken her confidence. She'd confirmed it was a homicide. But was she right? And what about Flayley—had she examined her hyoid bone thoroughly enough? As she reflected on that moment—the appearance of Moberly, the way he'd pushed her aside, his horrid slashing at the corpse's neck—she realized it had rattled her and, perhaps, broken her concentration. When she finished up the examination of the hyoid bone, she was flustered and hadn't given it her utmost attention. She might have missed something.

At four thirty, giving up on sleep, she finally got up, took a shower, downed a mug of coffee, got in her car, and headed to the morgue. The night was still soft: times like these were one of the reasons she was able to endure Miami, despite its glitter, traffic, crowds, and crime.

The morgue was quiet and shadowy as she entered, and when she turned on the lights she was briefly dazzled. Working quickly, she slid the cadaver out of its drawer and wheeled it into the operating theater. She mentally went through the forensic checklist. When she was sure all was ready, she brought the A/V system to life, explaining out loud what she was doing and why.

She wheeled the big stereo zoom microscope over the neck and started a new examination of the hyoid bone. The "body" of the bone, the center part, was clearly fractured—she had noted this in her original autopsy—either by Flayley's struggle at the end of the rope or by the short fall from the bridge. Nothing abnormal there. Now she turned her attention to the horns of the hyoid. The hyoid was one of the most unusual bones in the body, in that it didn't articulate with any others—it essentially floated between muscles and ligaments, providing an attachment for the tongue, the floor of the mouth, the epiglottis, and the pharynx. It was in the shape of a horseshoe, with a lesser and greater horn on each side. In Baxter, the horns had been symmetrically fractured by a push-choke, the right more than the left, suggesting that a right-handed person had wrapped both his hands around the neck and squeezed, the right thumb exerting the greater pressure. But here, the push-choke—assuming one occurred—had been too weak to fracture the bone. What she really should have done was order up an MRI, but that would have taken a lot of paperwork and time, not to mention raised a lot of questions.

She upped the magnification and started with the right horn, carefully removing the tiniest bits of tissue. She could see where Moberly's careless cutting had left grooves. Gently, scraping and brushing, she got the tip of the greater horn exposed and worked backward toward the lesser. It was a painstaking process, but by the time she reached the base of the horn she had found nothing. This was the bone that would have been broken by the killer; was it worth doing the same to the left horn?

She sighed, then proceeded. She couldn't feel secure until she had done everything she could.

About two-thirds of the way down the left horn, she stopped. Was that something? She upped the magnification one stop further and then saw it: the faintest crack on the inside of the bone. It was a greenstick fracture in which the bone had bent rather than broken, but—in this case—with enough force to cause a faint stress fracture that ran longitudinally along the length of the bone rather than across it. It was extremely subtle, almost invisible—so faint as to be beyond the reach of an ordinary digital camera. An MRI, however, would bring it into sharp relief.

She breathed out. Special Agent Pendergast had been right all along. He'd asked her to take a special look at the hyoid bone, and she had done so, seeing nothing. If Moberly hadn't come in, she might eventually have seen this fracture. But Moberly had pushed her aside and she'd lost focus... Then she shook her head. She couldn't blame Moberly: he might be a dick, but failing to identify the fracture was on her, and nobody else. She felt the blood going to her face at the thought of how she'd failed Agent Pendergast.

She straightened up, scolded herself for the self-pity, and went back to work. She was a scientist, and emotion should play no role. She finished cleaning and exposing the left horn. After describing everything she saw for the benefit of the recording, she carefully supported and protected the exposed bone with cotton pads and a covering, packed the cadaver back up, and rolled it into its refrigerated niche. Then she sat down at her desk to fill out the paperwork for the MRI.

It was strange how this homicide had not been as cleanly performed as Baxter's. The push-choke was weaker and had not killed the victim, only rendering her semiconscious. She didn't actually die until she was hung from the bridge, and a witness saw her dancing around a short while before finally succumbing. Odd, too, it was the left horn this time—not the right. Perhaps the killer was ambidextrous.

At any rate, this was vitally important information. She looked at her watch: seven. Pendergast would be awake—she figured him for an early riser. She opened a drawer and sorted through the pile of business cards she accumulated as part of her work. Finding Pendergast's, she took out her cell phone to call him, confess her earlier mistake, and offer him this new discovery.

30

Sᴍɪᴛʜʙᴀᴄᴋ ᴅʀᴀɪɴᴇᴅ ʜɪꜱ third espresso and grabbed a couple of granola bars for snacks on the drive along with a Zyrtec for the damn allergies, then went down to the garage. Starting up the Subaru and cranking the A/C, he took out his phone, typed in Bronner's address, and stuck the device in its dashboard holder. He eased into the street and set off, Siri giving him directions.

He had decided not to call Bronner ahead of time. It would be easy for the man to put him off on the phone, and then Smithback would have little recourse. Better to show up, slather on the charm, and talk his way in. He tried to imagine how Bill would have handled it. There were only a few vital questions he wanted answered—it should take ten minutes, tops. He hoped to hell Bronner wasn't getting feebleminded. He must have had a lot of patients in his day and it would be hard enough to remember Flayley and Baxter after eleven years, even with a sharp memory. He wondered if the old guy had seen their names in the papers.

He sensed his courage flagging and reminded himself he was following a lead nobody else had yet stumbled upon.

The morning rush-hour traffic around Miami was brutal as usual, but once he hit 826 it cleared up and became smooth sailing. He knew from experience to avoid Route 1 and its tourists as long as possible, instead paying the toll on the Reagan Turnpike. He finally picked up Route 1 in Florida City, and another half hour brought him past the Southern Glades and onto the beautiful causeway to Key Largo. His destination had sounded like a typical fancy address for that area: Buttonwood Lane, where no doubt every manicured house had its own gleaming boat slip. But when he finally arrived, he found it was anything but upscale: a shabby, midcentury-modern neighborhood of sad-looking dwellings, RVs, and crappy center-console boats decorated with FOR SALE signs.

Strange place for a psychiatrist to live, especially one who must still be getting a cut from the operation of his former clinic.

The house was at the end of Buttonwood Lane, right on the channel, and it was yet another surprise—a big, run-down dwelling with white stucco falling off in plates, terra-cotta roof tiles still askew from the last hurricane. It was buried in a riot of tropical vegetation that looked like it hadn't seen a pair of clippers in years. The house of a serial killer? Or just a creepy eccentric?

There was a wrought-iron gate across the driveway, white with streaks of orange rust. Smithback parked his car next to the gate, got out, and looked for an intercom or something, but there was nothing. The gate was locked.

What the hell kind of a gated house had no intercom or buzzer? Peering through the bars, he could just barely see a turquoise-colored truck in the driveway, hidden behind a cluster of bamboo. Someone must be home.

The street was quiet. He looked the fence up and down—no big deal. He grasped the bars, shimmied up, and swung over, landing lightly on the far side. He strode with as much confidence as he could muster up the driveway, past the truck, and to the front door. He would get only one shot at this, so it better be good.

He rang the doorbell. A long silence ensued—and then he heard the shuffle of slippers on a stone floor as someone made their way slowly to the door. A moment later it opened up.

Smithback had assumed Bronner would be some stooped, frail, white-haired guy in horn-rimmed glasses. He couldn't have been more wrong. The retired psychiatrist was massive, powerful, and not all that old—maybe sixty-five. His jaw was as big as a boar's and his hands were veined and hairy. As Bronner stared down at him, Smithback had the shivery sense that something wasn't quite right with him.

"Dr. Bronner?" he asked.

"How did you get in here?"

"I, ah, climbed over your fence."

At this Bronner's heavy-boned face darkened, but he said nothing.

"I'm the brother of a patient you treated years ago, who unfortunately committed suicide. Through no fault of your own, of course," he added hastily.

"Who?"

"A woman named Agatha Flayley."

A long silence. Smithback began to feel uneasy. He could see through the open door into a barren, unkempt house.

"Look, if this isn't a good time," he said, edging backward. "I mean, maybe you're busy—"

"Come in," Bronner said, stepping aside and opening the door further.

Smithback warily entered the house. It was as cheerless as a prison, but at least it had a view of the ocean beyond a button-wood border.

"Right on the beach," said Smithback. "Nice."

"Sit down."

Smithback sat on a ratty sofa.

"I remember Agatha," said Dr. Bronner slowly, taking a seat across from him, eyes on Smithback. "She came to see me—when was that? Thirteen, fourteen years ago."

"Do you remember the exact dates, by any chance?"

A faraway look. "Yes. Not precisely, but she was my patient for two years. In 2005 and 2006, I think. I don't have the medical records here, of course; they're back in the clinic. They're private, unless you have a signed HIPAA release."

"I don't. I'm not looking for that kind of information—just hoping to understand why she did it. I mean, the suicide surprised our whole family."

A steady look. "Funny, she never talked of any family."

God, this geezer had a mind like a steel trap. "Well, there was just me and my half brother. That's what I meant by family." Smithback swallowed, trying to project a serious but hopeful disposition.

"The suicide surprised me, too. She was certainly not the type, but then you can never be certain."

"One thing my brother and I were curious about was she had a good friend who saw you, too. Elise Baxter."

A slow nod. "Another suicide."

"You have a good memory."

"A psychiatrist never forgets his suicides." A long, serious, creepy look.

Smithback cleared his throat. "When did you see Baxter as a patient?"

"Just a few times. Late 2004, early 2005, maybe."

"Can I ask why she saw you? I mean, I'm curious what she and my sister might have had in common."

"She had a difficult mother. One of those parents who criticize constantly. But she didn't really need a psychiatrist for that. She needed a talk therapist, so I referred her out. Don't believe she ever followed through, though."

"They shared another joint friend. A person named Mary Adler. Did you ever see her, by any chance?"

A long silence. And then Bronner said, "No."

"Are you sure? Mary S. Adler of Hialeah?"

At this point Bronner stared at him long and hard. "What did you say your name was?"

"Smithback. Roger Smithback."

"Smithback. Not Flayley. Agatha was never married when she saw me."

Smithback swallowed. *Shit.*

"Okay, Smithback, what's your game?"

"No game, no game at all. Just a bereaved brother—"

"Cut that shit. I can read the papers. Mary Adler, Agatha Flayley, Elise Baxter. The Brokenhearts graves."

Smithback swallowed again, with more difficulty.

"You're no bereaved brother. You're a reporter—aren't you?"

Busted. Now what?

"That's right. You're a reporter and you're here *on false pretenses!*" Bronner suddenly roared, his knotted hands gripping the sides of his chair as he stood up, towering over Smithback.

"Um, yes. That's true." Smithback couldn't lie now. "I'm a reporter for the *Herald*, and I want to know why Flayley and Baxter were both your patients—and then, eleven years after their deaths, were chosen by Brokenhearts. Coincidence?"

Bronner advanced, clenching his fists, and Smithback abruptly lost his nerve and had to step back.

"What do you mean by this insinuation? You think I've got something to do with that business?"

"I'm not insinuating. I came in here in search of the truth."

"You're out to destroy my practice, you son of a bitch!"

"It has nothing to do with your practice. I'm going to publish this information—that the two victims were your patients—because it's in the public interest." Smithback tried hard to muster both courage and dignity, the effect spoiled by the fear squeaking in his voice. "I seek your comment on that fact, Doctor. *Is* it coincidence...or something else?"

"Here's my comment, you little shit!" Bronner balled up a massive fist and stepped forward. Even though Bronner had thirty years on the journalist, he was formidable, and Smithback, being a natural coward who'd always managed to talk his way out of dicey situations, skipped backward. "Just a moment, think about what you're doing, about how this is going to look—"

Bronner rushed toward him with a grunt. Smithback ducked a heavy swing and turned, scampering out the front door, the doctor in pursuit. He raced for the fence, Bronner behind. He leapt up just as the doctor seized his foot. Smithback gave a heave, losing one slip-on, and tumbled down the other side. He sprinted to his car—one foot shoeless—clambered in, gunned the engine, and tore off with a spray of sand. The last he saw was Bronner shaking the gate, face black with rage.

You bastard, he thought, *you can't threaten the press like that and get away with it.* He'd lost one of his shoes—a Vans Classic, sixty dollars a pair—and it didn't seem likely Bronner would give it back.

He glanced at the time on the dashboard display. Ten thirty—still plenty of time to get in a story. "Hey, Siri," he said as he drove, "look up Dr. Peterson Bronner." And then, as an afterthought, he added: "criminal record."

"Here's what I found on the web," the irritatingly pleasant voice replied. The first image that appeared on his phone's screen was a mug shot of the doctor, holding a sign up to his chest and standing against a cinder-block wall.

31

THE HEADQUARTERS OF the Miami Police Department was housed in a large, squat building that—with its tiers of smoked windows, angled up and out in cantilever style—reminded Coldmoon of an air traffic control tower. It was on Northwest Second Avenue, near the skyscrapers of downtown and not far from the city cemetery; he even recognized a few landmarks from their memorable dash to Agatha Flayley's tomb.

And that wasn't all he found memorable. Upon being picked up by Pendergast at his hotel, Coldmoon found his partner within a dented yellow cab whose interior odor, not to mention driver, were all too familiar. Pendergast, it seemed, had tracked down Axel and hired him as temporary chauffeur. "He knows the city," Pendergast had explained as they'd shot westward over the MacArthur Causeway. "And he seems to enjoy this new-found freedom to drive without the usual constraints. I admire a man who takes pride in his work."

Coldmoon—who was sick and tired of driving them around in the ludicrous Miami traffic—didn't complain.

After a suitably terrifying ride, the cab pulled up beside the entrance of the Miami HQ with a squeal of poorly maintained brakes. A mob of reporters, journalists, and camerapeople at the main double doors fell back at the sound, and Pendergast got out, Coldmoon following. Axel—Coldmoon still had no idea what his last name was—showed no intention of moving, but instead placed a small black wallet with a gold shield on the dashboard.

"What did you give him?" Coldmoon asked.

"A mere bauble," came the reply.

Sensing fresh meat, the crowd of reporters now closed back in on them. They pushed through, avoiding eye contact and ignoring shouted questions. One television journalist—a young woman with short blond hair, wide cheekbones, and an expensive-looking outfit—blocked Coldmoon's way and danced to one side and the other as he tried to pass. He recognized her from flipping channels in his hotel room: she was the investigative reporter for a local news channel. Someone-or-other Fleming—he couldn't remember her first name. Very attractive, but with eyes as bright as a rattlesnake's.

"Excuse me, sir!" the woman said, thrusting forward a microphone labeled with a garish 6 as Pendergast paused to look back. "*Sir!* What can you tell me about the latest victim? Can you confirm a serial killer's involved?"

Coldmoon removed his cap. "*H'ahíya wóglaka ye,*" he said. "*Owákahnige šni.*" And he stepped around her as tactfully as possible.

"What did you tell her?" Pendergast asked as they entered the building.

"Ms. Fleming? I said I couldn't understand and asked her to speak more slowly."

Pendergast clucked disapprovingly. "A lie is a lie, even in Lakota."

"On the reservation the elders had a saying—the only person worse than a liar is a hypocrite."

"My Cajun grandmother in New Orleans was fond of the same hoary proverb."

Pendergast walked over to a large front desk and said something in low tones to a uniformed officer. The cop pointed toward a nearby elevator bank. They showed their IDs, signed in, bypassed the metal detector, and headed for the elevators.

"We're going to what's known as the war room," said Pendergast. "It's where the MPD keep their electronic toys. It gives them access to the most up-to-date real-time information available, along with links to medical and criminological databases. I'm preparing a little worksite of our own, in a less conspicuous area, but this office will do for an initial confabulation. That liaison fellow, Commander Grove, promised to meet us there, along with Lieutenant Sandoval."

"You really think Pickett will live up to his promise and let us work without interference?"

"We haven't been packed off to Salt Lake City, have we?" They exited the elevator and made their way down a cluttered hallway. Coldmoon looked at his watch: 3:00 PM exactly.

The war room lived up to its name, bristling with computers and a huge glossy blackboard on casters. Coldmoon looked around. Some of the fluorescent bulbs behind their frosted ceiling panels were burned out, and one was flickering. There was a battered drip coffeemaker on a table in the far corner, surrounded by stacks of paper cups and cans of powdered milk. He could tell just by looking that the half-full pot had been sitting for only a few hours. Too fresh. Despite the high-tech equipment, this felt a lot more familiar than the sleek FBI headquarters in Miramar, where they'd been given the psych profile

by Dr. Mars. This place had a lived-in feel, a place where real police work was done, with scuff marks on the walls, a grumbling
HVAC system, and no windows. Coldmoon relaxed.

The center of the room was taken up by a rectangular table.
At one end sat Sandoval and Commander Grove. Sandoval's face
was studiously neutral, but the commander couldn't quite conceal his look of interest, even eagerness. And why not—this was
a spectacular investigation, one for the books.

"Gentlemen," Pendergast said, nodding at each in turn.
"Thanks to the work of Dr. Fauchet, we now know Flayley was
subjected to the same kind of push-choke strangulation that
killed Baxter. In short, these were homicides staged as suicides."
He turned to Sandoval. "Lieutenant, anything new to bring to
our attention?"

Sandoval stroked an imaginary mustache as his impassive
expression turned sour. "That damned newshound Smithback
is really riling people up. First he digs up the Brokenhearts
moniker, then just this morning he figures out that both Baxter
and Flayley saw the same shrink." He picked up his cell phone
and began reading aloud from an online article:

> While the police have declined to release the texts of the
> notes left on the graves, the grisly "gifts" themselves reveal
> a troubled person who, surprisingly, might not fit the mold
> of the classic psychopath—generally assumed to be with-
> out remorse or normal human feelings of compassion and
> empathy. One must ask: What do these "gifts" signify to
> the giver? Loss? Remorse? Repentance? Perhaps if the au-
> thorities would devote more time to looking into the psy-
> chology of Mister Brokenhearts, and asking themselves
> what terrible experiences must have happened to create an

individual with such a warped perspective, they might be able to find him—without further loss of life.

He replaced his phone on the desk in disgust. "We should have found that shrink ourselves, not learned it from a damned newspaper. Just like we should have leaned harder on a possible link between the old suicides and the new murders. That's on us."

"At least that reporter doesn't know the 'old suicides' *weren't* suicides," Coldmoon said.

Sandoval nodded. Then he pushed a small remote control on the desk, and the large black rectangle at the far end of the room came to life. Coldmoon realized that it was not a blackboard after all, but an ultra-high-resolution monitor. The screen split into three windows displaying head shots: Baxter, Flayley, and Adler.

"I find it curious," Pendergast said, "that while all of these supposed suicides lived in Greater Miami, they were killed hundreds of miles apart. And yet the recent Brokenhearts murders all took place in Miami Beach."

"You think that's relevant?" Sandoval asked.

"I haven't the faintest idea."

Sandoval turned to Grove. "Anything yet on the Adler autopsy files, Commander?"

"We finally broke the logjam," Grove said. "Our team located her files and morgue photographs. I'll be getting them within the hour. She was apparently a follower of a country music group, the Fat Palmettos, and she traveled up to North Carolina from Hialeah for a concert that never took place—the lead guitarist sprained a thumb."

"The Fat Palmettos," Coldmoon said.

"They disbanded several years ago."

"We'll check on them anyway," said Sandoval. "Meanwhile, our teams here in Miami Beach are interviewing her remaining family, former co-workers, the rest. Nothing of note so far."

"Any developments on Misty Carpenter and her unusual business?" Coldmoon asked.

"We've decrypted her client list," said Sandoval, "and started interviews. Once again, it looks like she was simply a target of opportunity."

"Mmmm," Pendergast murmured. He looked away a moment, his eyes narrowing. Then he glanced again at Sandoval. "Thank you very much, Lieutenant. This has been extremely helpful."

"Sure," Sandoval said, gathering his stuff together.

No questions, no second-guessing, no nothing—just pure co-operation. Coldmoon had to admit: Pickett's word seemed good.

"Commander Grove," Pendergast said, "now that we have a clearer sense of what we're looking for, I was hoping the research and external relations departments of the Miami PD—which I understand are your jurisdiction—could cast a net for us. Specifically, a search for deaths, declared as suicides, that match the MO of Baxter, Flayley, and Adler. It's true we haven't yet gotten confirmation on Adler, but I think it's worth searching for additional suicides possibly tricked out to look like murder—don't you?"

"I do—very good idea." Grove began jotting notes in a small, leather-bound notebook.

"It will be a rather wide net, and I'm afraid your people will have a lot of work on their hands. You'll need to search for suicides matching the following characteristics: female, aged twenty to forty, who resided in Greater Miami but died out of state, hung with a knotted bedsheet, and leaving no suicide note. If any autopsies resulted in a conclusion of murder, or even suspicion of it, include those as well. For the time being, to make the search more manageable, you might limit things to states east of the Mississippi."

"Got it," Grove said, still writing. "And the time interval?"

"January 2006 to January 2008."

Coldmoon glanced at Pendergast. With such broad parameters, he figured they'd probably get a list as long as the phone book. Thank God they had Grove and his ability to marshal the data-gathering resources of the Miami PD.

Grove stood up. "If there's nothing else, gentlemen, I'll get right on it."

"We're greatly indebted to you for this assistance, Commander," Pendergast said.

"Think nothing of it. Maybe you can give me a tour of Twenty-Six Federal Plaza next time I'm in New York."

"It would be my pleasure." And Pendergast turned away as Grove followed Lieutenant Sandoval out of the war room and down the corridor.

32

Sмітнваск нар just gotten into the newsroom and was settling into his cubicle for the morning when the pool secretary, Maurice, came up to him with a crate of mail.

"A bunch of letters for you," he said.

"Can't someone open them up and see what they are? I've got research to do."

"We did open them up. Six are supposedly from Mister Brokenhearts himself. Mr. Kraski has those in his office and wants to see you *tout de suite*."

Smithback groaned as he stood up and threaded his way through the cubicles to the editor's office. Kraski was a big guy in a sweaty shirt and tie—no jacket—with a flat-top crew cut that had gone out of style in 1955. He looked like he'd studied the textbook on being a tough, foulmouthed newspaper editor. The only thing he lacked was the cigarette hanging off the lip. Underneath, of course, he was the sweetest guy in the world— a cliché right out of *The Front Page*.

"Where the hell have you been?" Kraski said by way of greeting.

"Hey, boss, it's nine thirty. And that was quite a scoop I got yesterday, with the shrink story. I mean, two of the dead women had been *seeing* him! And the bastard tried to attack me when I asked him about it. I ran a background check and found the guy assaulted his wife during a divorce five years ago—he had to take anger management classes. That's why they eased him out of his practice. I tell you, the man *looks* like a serial killer."

"Maybe." Kraski waved his hand. "Then how do you explain what's right here on my desk: six letters to you from Mister Brokenhearts?"

"They're bullshit, of course."

"You think so? Take a look." He pushed them over. Five of them were on cheap paper, with strange handwriting, one in crayon. The sixth letter was in an expensive, creamy envelope.

He pulled a letter out at random.

Hey Smithback, I'm Mister Brokenharts and I'm going to rip your fucken balls off and...

It went on in that vein, replete with misspellings and grammatical abominations. He pulled out another.

Dear Roger Smitback, I am Mister Brokenhearts I got two women hostate they are at 333 Ocean Way Drive Allmeda you better come now or I gong kill them...

He pushed that one aside as well and took up the creamy envelope. He slid out the letter and unfolded it. It was written in an elegant cursive hand, each letter carefully formed. Smithback began to read, a chill forming along his spine.

Dear Roger,

You, perhaps, understand. Their deaths cry out for justice. Hers most of all. Until she is at rest, I cannot rest. She was my reason for life, and why I must survive. Do you understand? I must atone. If you cannot help me do so, I will have to continue on my own—and this will not end well.

Yours truly,
Mister Brokenhearts

"Jesus." He looked up at Kraski. "This letter...it might be the real deal."

"My thoughts exactly."

"We've got to bring this to the police—right?"

"Sure, sure. Thing is, we don't really *know* it's Brokenhearts. I mean, there's five other letters here—and that's just today's mail. On top of this psycho shrink of yours." He stabbed at the envelope with his finger. "This is *your* story. Get to work. As soon as your piece goes live—say, two hours from now?—we'll turn all six over to the police."

Smithback took the letter and envelope. "Okay."

"Get a sample of that shrink's handwriting. Maybe we can figure out whether it's the same guy. But we need to fact-check the shit out of your piece, so be careful. Only sourced, on-the-record stuff. You have a tendency to opinionate. Don't."

"Yes, sir."

"Now get your ass going."

Smithback carried the letters back to his desk, shoved the crate with the others away with his foot, and got to work. The first thing he did was read the letter again, and he was struck by a phrase that stood out from the rest. *She was my reason for life, and why I must survive.* He googled it and found it was an altered quotation from the novel *Atonement* by British novelist Ian McEwan. Juicy. Very juicy. He'd have to put that in.

A letter from Brokenhearts, addressed to him personally. And a troubled shrink with not one but two links to the case. Game theorists speculated that evolution was a direct result of successful outcomes. If that was true, he was quickly evolving into a star homicide reporter.

He began to write, fingers flying over the keyboard.

33

COLDMOON LOOKED AROUND the room, hands on his hips, lips pursed. It felt like he'd stepped back in time, or perhaps fallen into the set of the movie *Key Largo*, with the ceiling fans, the potted palm in the corner, the big wicker chairs with the round backs, the beadboard walls, the jute rugs...and the stifling heat. In the middle of the huge room was an ornate Victorian table surrounded by chairs and littered with documents, files, and photographs—nary a computer. Behind it, the busy, faded wallpaper pattern on the rear wall was disturbed by two corkboards and a series of large maps. It was hard to believe an old, decaying place like this could still exist on the edge of Little Havana. The distant noise of rush-hour traffic on the Dolphin Expressway filtered through the windows. The fans turned slowly, stirring the dead air, and the late-afternoon sun came in through the louvered windows, striping one wall with bars of light.

Pendergast was seated in one of the wicker chairs in his white linen suit, his fingers tented, an evidence box on the table beside him. In another corner Coldmoon saw the cabdriver Axel lounging on a couch, cleaning his nails with a switchblade.

"Come in, Agent Coldmoon, and make yourself at home."

Coldmoon entered.

"I was fortunate to find this place," Pendergast said, "midway between the Miami FBI Miramar building and Miami PD. A most convenient location, which should cut travel time considerably—should the need arise. Centrally located to all the relevant places in our investigation—and away from the tourist traffic that has been the bane of our existence."

Coldmoon walked to the window and opened the jalousie blinds, trying to get a breath of fresh air, instead getting a smoky noseful of *pollo de la plancha.*

He turned. "Say, think we can fire up the A/C?"

"There is no air-conditioning," said Pendergast. "I am sorry, it gives me the catarrh. I was fortunate that an old and dear friend was able to loan me this historic space, even if it lacks some amenities."

Coldmoon began rolling up the sleeves of his denim work shirt. "Historic?"

"It is where John Huston wrote the screenplay for *The Treasure of the Sierra Madre*. At this very table, in fact."

"Right."

A buzzer high up on one wall rang once, then twice, its bell muffled by dust. Pendergast looked over. "Axel, would you mind letting them in?"

Sullenly, Axel folded his knife, got to his feet, and shuffled toward the door leading to the stairwell. Coldmoon thought him an odd choice for a chauffeur—he came and went as he pleased and, though clearly a skilled wheelman, was seemingly indifferent to the safety of himself and his passengers, and with an unpleasant personality to boot. Still, he thought he understood why Pendergast had engaged him: the man was streetwise, and he had that kind of trustworthiness that could only be won from somebody who prized cash above all else. He clearly distrusted law enforcement: there was no chance Pickett or anyone else would hear about their movements through Axel.

Coldmoon heard a brief murmur of conversation, ascending steps, and then Dr. Fauchet appeared in the doorway, Commander Grove behind her. They glanced around in obvious surprise. Axel was not with them—apparently, he'd taken the opportunity to leave on one of his mysterious private duties.

"Dr. Fauchet. Commander Grove. Welcome. Please have a seat." Pendergast indicated the table. "May I get you anything to drink? Evian? Pellegrino?"

"What is this place?" Grove asked.

"My own little refuge," said Pendergast. "Call it a meditative retreat."

The two shook their heads as they sat down at the table. Fauchet dumped a large armload of files on the antique tabletop as casually as if it had been purchased at Ikea, while Grove cleared an area and set down his briefcase.

"Commander Grove," Pendergast said, turning toward the man. "I believe you have news for us."

Grove pulled out his ever-present notebook. It amazed Coldmoon that the man could carry so much information in something so small. Half of it, he figured, must remain in his head.

"I had to push my people pretty hard the last twenty-four hours. The research and analysis teams cross-correlated ViCAP searches with records from departments of public health, as well as both state and local police agencies, up and down the East Coast. And naturally the local databases had proprietary methods of searching and indexing, not to mention the usual misfilings and false positives that slow everything down." He waved a dismissive hand at these annoyances. "In any case, out of several thousand suicides we ultimately found eighteen that matched the pattern: the right age, date, location, manner of asphyxiation, probable cause of death. I forwarded the autopsy files and police reports to Dr. Fauchet, who will fill you in on her findings."

Following this admirably brief introduction, Dr. Fauchet took the ball. "I should start by telling you that, based on the autopsy photographs Miami PD finally pried out of the Rocky Mount coroner's department, I was able to confirm Mary Adler was killed in a manner similar to Elise Baxter and Agatha Flayley: via a push-choke that, in her case, fractured the right wing of the hyoid, leaving the left wing intact. Clearly murder, well concealed but indisputable. In addition, the body of the hyoid itself was partially fractured, most likely in a staged hanging that took place after death.

"Of the eighteen suicides, I was able to eliminate fifteen for various reasons. They were obvious suicides, and the kind of trauma evident from the autopsy photographs and coroners' notes did not match our three victims. The sixteenth I eliminated because, although one wing of her hyoid bone had been broken, when I looked deeper into the case I found this was because the banister from which she hanged herself collapsed, causing significant injury to the maxillary bones as well as the neck itself." She paused. "On the other hand, the remaining two women displayed precisely the MO we're looking for: fracturing of at least one wing of the hyoid, with the right wing more severely depressed than the left, followed by postmortem hanging with a knotted bedsheet."

"You're convinced they were homicides, staged by our killer to look like suicides?" Pendergast asked.

"I'm convinced they were homicides staged as suicides," Fauchet said. "As to who did it, that's your responsibility, Agent Pendergast." This riposte was accompanied by a smile as she opened her briefcase and took out two thin manila folders, which she passed across the table to Pendergast and Coldmoon.

"Laurie Winters and Jasmine Oriol," she continued. "The former found dead in Bethesda, Maryland, and the latter in Savannah, Georgia, within four months of each other. Both single, both younger than forty, both from the Miami area, neither leaving a suicide note. One away on a business trip, the other a freelance photographer on assignment. And both, as you'll see, with the same fracture of the greater horns of the hyoid. Note that in the case of Winters, only the right horn was fractured; both of Oriol's horns were fractured. I've noted this on the X-rays. In the defense of the original medical examiners, however, I should point out that, externally, the necks of both victims were badly abraded—although not to the extent of Flayley—and in the case of Oriol, the cartilaginous material of the larynx was crushed, as well."

As Fauchet explained, Coldmoon paged through the photos. There were a few color shots of the suicide scenes; some close-ups of the victims' necks before and after dissection; and the X-rays Fauchet had mentioned. The fractures had been marked with circles, but he nevertheless had to look closely to see the hairline breaks. It was as Fauchet said: under the circumstances, you'd have to be a fairly paranoid M.E. to, quite literally, see the skull beneath the skin.

"So these two newly discovered victims appear to have been killed by a right-handed man," Pendergast said. "Along with Elise Baxter and Mary Adler."

"Yes. In all four cases, one or both wings of the hyoid were fractured, with the right wing invariably suffering more trauma than the left."

"Not with Agatha Flayley, however. You told us that, in your second examination of her corpse, you noticed the left wing of the hyoid had a greenstick fracture—but not the right."

"That's true," Fauchet said.

"And then there was my friend Ianetti, the document examiner," Grove piped up. "He said the two notes he examined were the work of a left-handed individual—which corresponds to the way the throats of the recent victims are believed to have been cut: from behind, right to left."

There was a moment of silence. Then Pendergast shifted in his chair. "Well, what's a serial killing without riddles? In any case, excellent work, Dr. Fauchet. Thanks to you and Commander Grove, we now have five long-dead victims on which to base our investigation." He paused. "One additional question. You've made it clear how difficult it is to classify these as murder instead of suicide, requiring a surgical or radiological examination. What about from a *tactile* perspective?"

Dr. Fauchet frowned. She seemed a little deflated by Pendergast's observation about the apparent left-handedness of the Flayley killer. "I'm not sure I understand."

"These women were strangled by a strong set of hands. The ligature marks, the supposed self-asphyxiation, happened later. If you were to touch, palpate, these necks directly with your fingers—ignoring the visual evidence of the abrasions and contusions—would the damage to the horns of the hyoid wings *feel* different from, say, the damage that a suicide by hanging would normally cause?"

"That's never occurred to me before. I...well, I suppose it would. You might even feel the fracturing of the bone with your hands around the neck—a sort of click, I would think. Why do you ask?"

"I just wondered if the killer was unaware—or *well* aware—that he was leaving us this clue."

Now Grove spoke. "I've already liaised with Lieutenant Sandoval about obtaining backgrounds on Winters and Oriol. Dr. Fauchet, if you could please assemble all relevant data on the five autopsies—the two you performed, and the three whose results you've analyzed—that would be very helpful."

"Already in process," Fauchet said.

"There's something else," Pendergast said. "Commander, I think Miami PD should put the Winters and Oriol graves under surveillance."

There was an uncomfortable silence. Grove cleared his throat. "Yes. I see the logic in that. God forbid, but if he kills again, we may just catch him in the act of, ah, *decorating* one of those graves. I hope it doesn't come to that."

"Hold on," said Coldmoon. "Wouldn't it be better to get word out that we've identified two more homicide/suicides, Winters and Oriol? It might just stop this guy from sacrificing another woman, knowing we're watching their graves!"

"The sad truth is," said Pendergast, "with such a large data set to work from, it's possible that other murder/suicides slipped through Commander Grove's net. What I mean is, even if these two graves don't receive presents, there may be others that will."

He let this grim idea hang in the air for a moment. "Nevertheless, in the hope of forestalling that, I think the time has come to communicate directly with Mister Brokenhearts."

"What?" Coldmoon asked. "How, exactly?"

"He now has a pen pal."

"You don't mean that reporter, Smithback?" Grove said. "You can't trust him. We're already checking out this psychiatrist he wrote about. Why throw free publicity his way? God knows, he's got half the city in a panic already."

"That persiflage is merely clouding the central issue," Pendergast said. "Which is this: Brokenhearts reached out to Smithback." And with this he removed the top from an evidence box; reached in and removed some latex gloves, which he pulled on; and then withdrew five letters of varying sizes, their envelopes ripped open, and arranged them on the table. Lastly, he withdrew another letter, without an envelope, its single page sandwiched between layers of glass.

"These are six letters Smithback received this morning," he said. "Five of them are from cranks. The sixth one—the one he quotes in his most recent article—is the genuine item. Our friend Mr. Ianetti, the forensic document examiner, has verified that the paper, ink, and handwriting are the same—not to mention the tone and style of the letter, which includes a literary allusion. This is Mister Brokenhearts speaking to Roger Smithback. Is it just the letter of a sick individual, seeking attention? I don't think so. After all, he's written letters before—and they were private letters, left on tombs, not delivered to newspapers. I think that Smithback's article may have inadvertently touched a chord in Brokenhearts. He didn't foam at the mouth about what a psychopath Brokenhearts was, like the rest of the news media. And this is Mister Brokenhearts's response." He leaned over the sandwich of glass. *"I must atone. If you cannot help me do so, I will have to continue on my own."* He sat back and looked around. "You will note that, if he'd stayed true to his pattern, Brokenhearts would have killed again last night. Smithback just might have given him a moment of pause—and bought time.

But make no mistake: he's not only asking for help—he's making a promise. If we don't find him—or find some way to help him—he will kill again. And soon."

The table fell into silence. After a moment, Pendergast looked at Grove and Fauchet in turn. "Thank you so much for your help. It's late, and I know you must both be very busy, so I won't keep you any longer."

Coldmoon waited while the two left. Then he turned to Pendergast. "You're not really going to use Smithback to communicate with Brokenhearts?" he asked. "I didn't want to say this in front of the others, but I think it's a terrible idea."

Pendergast smiled. "It's true I said Mr. Smithback has a pen pal, but I said nothing about speaking to Brokenhearts through him. Perhaps, growing up, you heard the aphorism 'It takes a thousand voices to tell one story.' No—this story will be told a different way, with different voices." He pulled out his phone, dialed a number. "Hello. Is this WSUN 6, South Florida's news channel? Excellent. I'd like the office of Ms. Fleming, please. That's right, Carey Fleming. Thank you."

34

THE STUDIOS OF WSUN-TV were not in downtown Miami, as Coldmoon expected. Instead, they were located out in the sticks, in the distant southwestern suburb of Kendale Lakes, sandwiched between a thirty-six-hole golf course and the Miami Executive Airport. Even with Axel at the wheel, it had taken over forty minutes to get there.

Coldmoon got out of the taxi and into a parking lot surrounding a long, low building that bristled with satellite dishes and radio towers. A line of news vans, their roofs covered with smaller versions of the same electronic toys, stood nearby, parked for the night. He yawned, stretched, and massaged the small of his back. In the distance, beyond a rank of single-level houses with pool cages and identical tiled roofs, he could see an unending line of greenish-brown wetlands. In the short time he'd been in southern Florida, he'd learned that it seemed to have four distinct habitats: coastal boulevards for the über-rich; gated subdivisions for affluent retirees; bleak neighborhoods out of *Grand Theft Auto*—and swamp.

Commander Grove was sitting in the visitors' waiting area

just inside the entrance, and he rose from his chair as they pushed their way through the glass doors into the artificial chill.

"You're just in time," he said, shaking their hands in turn. "I was afraid you might have gotten lost." He turned to Pendergast. "Your segment is next. I'll get the assistant producer." And he hurried off down a hallway.

"He seems familiar with the place," Coldmoon said as they signed in at the reception desk.

"Given that his duties include community relations, it may well be his home away from home," Pendergast replied.

Grove immediately returned, followed by a brisk young woman with a clipboard. "My name's Natalie," she told them as she shook their hands. "Thanks for reaching out to us last night. Which one of you is Agent Pendergast?"

Pendergast gave a slight bow.

"Great. Have you been on live television before, in a studio setting?"

"I have not." Pendergast's expression—as it had been during the entire drive out—remained neutral. Coldmoon knew he'd spoken to Pickett earlier in the day, but the substance of the conversation had not been shared with him.

"That's just fine," the young woman said, leading them away from reception and down a long, unfurnished corridor. "Ms. Fleming will take the lead in asking the questions. She's a great host, really nice, and with her experience in Philadelphia and Hartford we were lucky to get her. Your segment starts in ten minutes." They passed a window; glancing in, Coldmoon saw two ghostly faces and a dark room full of monitors, mixers, and other video and sound equipment.

They paused in an intersection while Natalie took a second to inspect Pendergast more closely. "Hmmm. Well, we can't do anything about the black suit, but otherwise I don't see many is-sues. Let's just run you past makeup, then we'll get you wired up and do a sound check."

Natalie ushered Coldmoon and Grove into what Coldmoon assumed must be the green room, then she took Pendergast far-ther down the hall, still speaking to him as reassuringly as if he were about to undergo an operation.

Coldmoon looked around the green room. There were couches, overstuffed chairs, a table with fruit and cheese plat-ters, and a small glass-fronted refrigerator filled with bottles of water and diet soda. The only studio he'd ever been in was a radio station outside of Rapid City, and it had consisted of two rooms and a toilet. This place—with its whispered ventila-tion, high-tech equipment, and free food—was a revelation. He helped himself to a bottle of water and took a seat.

Grove sat down beside him. The normally phlegmatic com-mander had an eager air about him; Coldmoon almost expected the man to rub his hands together with glee. "This is perfect," he said. "I was actually quite relieved when Pendergast called this morning to say he'd agreed to an interview with WSUN. Not only agreed, but *suggested* it. Its market penetration is the best in Miami-Dade, and the viewing demographics are ideal."

"Nice that it could be arranged so quickly," Coldmoon replied, cracking the top of the water bottle. "I understand you helped with that."

"Carey and I are old friends." Grove reached over and grabbed a slice of gouda from the table. "And this is the perfect opportunity to reassure the public. But I'm a little bit unclear as to what he's planning to say. He implied it had something to do with what that reporter, Smithback, has been writing about."

"Sorry," Coldmoon said. "I just don't know."

"I'm sure your partner means well, but these newspaper reporters—they'll twist anything to sell more copies." Grove snagged another piece of cheese. "At least we can count on Carey to give things the right spin. She's a class act, a real pro. And calming the waters a little will help folks sleep easier until we lock this guy up."

There were footfalls in the hallway, and then Natalie reappeared with Pendergast still in tow. The agent did not look pleased. They had put some kind of orange foundation on his face—probably to keep his pallor from appearing truly corpselike under the bright studio lights—but here, in normal lighting, he looked like a wax doll.

"Okay." Natalie checked her watch. "Three minutes. Let's go to Studio B and get you wired up."

They started down another neutral hallway, Grove and Coldmoon bringing up the rear. Pendergast was still silent.

"A little case of nerves?" Grove asked him. "No, I guess not—working in New York, you must have conducted more than your share of press conferences. Anyway, Carey's not going to throw you any hardballs. Everyone wants the same thing here—reassurance."

Grove continued his sporadic coaching as they went through one set of double doors, down a short corridor, through another set of doors—and suddenly they were in Studio B: a large, warehouse-like space with cables snaking all over the concrete floor, people standing around the periphery, and a semicircle of three cameras facing a small set dressed to look like a living room, with a backdrop of the Miami Beach shoreline behind it. Coldmoon looked around in surprise. It was so fake—just partial walls and no ceiling, nothing but black drapes and cinderblock walls surrounding it, and a flooring of engineered wood that ended mere feet away from the set dressing—that he found it hard to believe any viewer would buy the illusion. There was a desk with silk flowers, some potted palms, and two plush director's chairs placed on either side of a glass table. A woman sat in one of them, and Coldmoon recognized her as the person who'd buttonholed him on the way into Miami Police headquarters. A tiny army of cosmeticians and sound engineers surrounded her. A man holding a two-way radio stood back between the hooded cameras, gazing with a watchful air; Coldmoon figured he must be the producer, or director, or whatever. The woman in the chair appeared to be in a fussy mood, muttering at the people swarming around her and even slapping away the hand of one woman holding a touch-up brush. Meanwhile, Pendergast had been shown to his seat and was having a microphone threaded up beneath the back of his jacket and pinned to his lapel.

"One minute," called a voice from the darkness behind the cameras. The lighting around the set, already bright, went up a notch. Several cameras on dollies adjusted their positions.

"You gentlemen please stand there," Natalie said in a low voice to Coldmoon and Grove. "We go live in a minute." She pointed her clipboard toward a sheltered spot that allowed views of both the set itself and monitors displaying live feeds.

"Thirty seconds!" came the disembodied voice. Now the sycophants vanished from the stage and the newswoman—her face suddenly lighting up with a brilliant, welcoming smile—turned to Pendergast. They engaged in some back-and-forth Coldmoon couldn't make out. Then the producer pointed at them with an exaggerated gesture; the monitors stopped displaying advertisements and test patterns and focused on the set; and out of nowhere came a bit of calypso-based theme music.

"Welcome back to *News 6 at Seven*," the woman chirped, "Miami's number one source for everything *you* need to know. I'm Carey Fleming. As I mentioned at the top of the show, we're lucky enough to have as our next guest a highly decorated member of the FBI, Special Agent Aloy—" to Coldmoon's amusement, she stumbled over Pendergast's first name— "Pendergast. He's the lead agent in the FBI's investigation of the Mister Brokenhearts murders, and he's here today to bring us the exclusive, latest developments in the case—as well as what we, the public, should know about this monster."

Fleming turned her attention from the cue light to her guest, putting on a serious face. Two of the cameras swiveled obligingly in Pendergast's direction. "Agent Pendergast, thank you and welcome."

Pendergast nodded in return.

"I understand you're based in New York. I hope you're enjoying our beautiful city, despite your unfortunate reason for coming."

"Miami is indeed a most delightful place."

A gratified smile. "But perhaps it's not your first visit. After all, I can tell from your accent that you're not from, as we say, up north."

"That is correct. I grew up in New Orleans."

"How nice." Fleming glanced at a small teleprompter set low into the wooden floor that, Coldmoon assumed, displayed notes for the interview. "What can you tell us about progress in the case? Especially since this third brutal killing."

"Nothing," Pendergast replied.

Coldmoon felt Grove stir restlessly in the darkness beside him.

If Fleming was surprised by this reply, she concealed it well. "Do you mean nothing new has been discovered since the killer's letter appeared in the newspaper?"

"I beg your pardon, Ms. Fleming, but your question was whether there was anything I could tell *you*."

"Ah." The woman nodded knowingly, with a wink at the camera. "You mean, there are a number of aspects—developments—you're not at liberty to share with the public."

"That is correct."

"Can you tell us, then, if you're satisfied with progress in the case?"

"I am rarely satisfied. We have, however, identified certain avenues of investigation."

Fleming was game—Coldmoon had to give her that—and seemed skilled in handling recalcitrant guests. "I'm sure that will ease the minds of our viewers. While I realize there is probably a lot you can't tell us—" Fleming leaned in a little conspiratorially— "could you at least let us know if you're close to catching this monster?"

"Alas, that is something I can't predict. However, there is one favor I'd like to ask you."

"Of course."

"Please stop referring to him as a monster."

Coldmoon heard Grove draw in his breath sharply.

The woman's smile froze on her face. "I'm sorry if you disagree with the characterization. Isn't it true this person has brutally murdered three innocent women?"

"That is true, yes."

"And if that isn't enough, hasn't he cut out their hearts and used them to decorate the graves of suicide victims—bringing even more grief to their families than they've suffered already?"

"Yes."

"Then, Agent Pendergast, in what way is this, this *creature* not a monster?"

"*Monster* has connotations of evil. Of taking pleasure in cruelty. Of a psychopathic lack of guilt or remorse."

"Yes, but—"

"And I don't think that's a correct characterization of Mister Brokenhearts at all. He has killed, without doubt—but not for the sake of killing."

"What do you mean?"

"He took no pleasure in it. In fact, evidence indicates the reason he cut his victims' throats was to ensure their deaths were as quick and painless as possible. Remorse, and not the lack of it, is *precisely* what these murders are about."

"I'm not sure our viewers are going to understand. Could you explain?"

Pendergast rotated his gaze from the news anchor to the nearest camera. Still speaking, he rose from his chair.

"In fact," he said, "the very reason I'm here is to speak to Mister Brokenhearts. Face-to-face."

"Agent Pendergast—" Carey Fleming began, but Pendergast paid no heed. His attention was now focused intently on the camera.

"Mister Brokenhearts, I know you're there, watching and listening," Pendergast said as he slowly walked toward the camera, its operator dollying back slightly as he approached. "I know you're not far away—not far away at all."

"Son of a bitch," Coldmoon heard Grove mutter under his breath. "What the heck is he *doing?*"

Pendergast went on, a gentle, honeyed voice filling the studio. "You're not a monster. You're a person who has been harmed, perhaps even brutalized."

On a monitor, Coldmoon could see Pendergast approaching the camera until his head and shoulders filled the frame. "I know you've had a terrible life; that you've been hurt; that you haven't had the guidance we all need to tell right from wrong."

Coldmoon, fixated, saw Fleming motioning frantically to the producer while the camera was locked on Pendergast's close-up. *This is live,* she was mouthing with an exaggerated chopping motion; *this is live.* But the producer gestured for the cameras to keep rolling. Coldmoon realized that this was great footage, and the producer obviously knew it.

"I can't believe they're airing this," Grove whispered in dismay. "And live, no less!"

Pendergast focused intently on the lens as the camera operator tightened the shot. "It's because you never had that kind of guidance that I'm reaching out to you now. While it's my job to stop you, I want you to know one thing: I'm not your enemy. I want to help you. You're intelligent; when I tell you that what you are doing is profoundly wrong, I believe you will listen. I understand your need to atone. But you have to find another way. Trust me, listen to me: you must find another way."

Pendergast paused. The producer spoke into his radio, gesturing sharply to keep the cameras on Pendergast and not cut away to Fleming, who had stopped her gesturing and was now staring at Pendergast, realizing the agent had taken over her set. It amazed Coldmoon how utterly mesmerizing his partner had suddenly become. The man surely had Miami in thrall.

"*You* have the power, to act or not act. Use that power. Ponder what I've said. Write to me, talk to me, if I can help. But above all, remember: *you have to find another way.*"

Pendergast gave the camera a lingering glance. Then he stepped back and turned away. As he did so, the cameras panned back and the producer pointed at Fleming.

She recovered instantly, putting on a serious face, as if the entire episode had been scripted. "And that, ladies and gentlemen, was Special Agent Pendergast, speaking directly to the serial killer calling himself Mister Brokenhearts. Let us hope and pray he is watching."

The producer cut to a commercial and could hardly contain his expression of glee, while Coldmoon saw Carey Fleming give Pendergast a baleful glare as he continued to walk off the set. As she did so, Coldmoon felt his phone buzz in his pocket. He pulled it out and saw, without surprise, that it was ADC Pickett.

35

Hᴇ sᴀᴛ ᴏɴ the floor of the darkened house, the images from the old thirty-two-inch Trinitron throwing jerky patterns on the bare walls. The commercials on the screen unspooled in antic pantomime—he'd managed to mute the sound with the remote, but beyond that he was unable to move. He felt paralyzed.

It was just chance he'd stumbled upon the program. And there was that FBI man—strange, black-clad, but pale as death itself—standing in front of the camera, talking to him. To *him*.

I know you're there, watching and listening.

He stared at the screen in such astonishment he could hardly focus on it. No one had ever spoken to him like that. Even when he was very young, in the good times before the Journey, he did not remember such talk, such sympathy, such kindly understanding.

I know you've had a terrible life; that you haven't had the guidance we all need to tell right from wrong.

But he did know right from wrong. He *did*. After all, it was because he knew that he was Atoning. That was the point of the preparation, and the Action. How could this man understand him...yet not understand that?

While it's my job to stop you, I want you to know one thing: I'm not your enemy.

Suddenly, regaining control of his limbs, he hurled the remote control at the screen. It bounced off in pieces and fell to the floor. He looked around for a moment in confusion and misery—at the dust heaped in the corners, the peeling wallpaper, the front door with its two cracked panes, the owl-patterned outside light with its busted bulb...and then suddenly he burst out crying. He had not cried in a dozen years but now he wailed, falling prostrate to the floor, writhing back and forth, grinding his teeth and pounding his fists against the old wooden planks, shrieking as if somehow sound alone could wrench the demons from him, roll back the years, undo the terrible, unspeakable Journey.

But the demons remained, and eventually the shrieks subsided: first to weeping, then racking sobs, then—at last—nothing. He lay on the floor, body aching, spent.

While it's my job to stop you, I'm not your enemy.

He let the emotion drain from him, breathing now without hurry, letting his humbleness renew itself, bit by bit, in the darkness of the room. He ran through his senses, one by one, ending with sound. All was quiet, save for the background hum that never fully went away.

The weakness he had just demonstrated was as expected. Despite that weakness, he knew his duty and he still had the power to make things right.

Now he had something new to prepare for.

It's my job to stop you.

It's my job to stop you.

Slowly, slowly, he rose from the floor. He felt the ground firm beneath his feet, and his resolve did not waver. He glanced around the shadowy room, lit only by the muted television.

That man, clad in black like a judge, reaching out to him like that: Who was he? Was he really just an FBI agent? Or an avenging angel—or the Grand Inquisitor?

He did not know. What he *did* know was that there was still crucial work to be done—and so much depended on him.

Now he strode with purpose toward the only furniture in the room: a scuffed card table and a single folding chair. He sat down, pulling the seat up to the table. On the black vinyl tabletop lay three bundles of soft felt cloth.

He stared at the bundles as his heart returned to its normal rhythm. Reaching for the left-hand bundle, he opened it, revealing an old carborundum—silicon carbide—whetstone; a tin of theatrical makeup in matte black; and a battered can of light-grade mineral oil. The stone, which was of a quality no longer available, had two different sides: four thousand grit and eight thousand grit. Since he never let his friends get dull, there was no need for a rougher stone.

Now he moved to the other two bundles, which he opened far more carefully. Archy slept in the first; Mehitabel in the second. He did not want to wake them too rudely.

Just seeing them in the warm, flickering glow of the television helped remind him of his tragic obligations. *So much depends...*

Taking hold of the sharpening stone, he placed it before him, finer-side down, then lubricated the four-thousand-grit side with a few drops of oil. He knew water was now more commonly used, but old ways—like old friends—were what he preferred. With two fingers, he rubbed the oil into the stone until it gave off a dull shine. He wiped his fingers carefully on the leg of his black jeans for sixty seconds. Only then did he pick up Mehitabel; place her blade at a precise fifteen-degree angle against the stone; and then—almost reluctantly, without joy—begin to hone her in long, deliberate strokes.

36

THE LETTERS ARRIVING for Smithback had now swelled to three crates, stacked up in his cubicle. This epistolary flood had proved an unexpected boon. Of course, virtually all of them so far—aside from the genuine one from Brokenhearts himself— were from cranks, psychics, crazies, poisonous neighbors, clairvoyants, estranged husbands and wives, and other messed-up people...but they were nevertheless a gold mine of stories. Smithback had been writing nonstop on the case since the story he'd broken roughly a week before.

There was, for example, the piece about the psychic who broke into the Flayley mausoleum with a spirit pendulum and Ouija board, claiming to be in communication with the dead. And there was the Iron John Men's poetry group meeting that was "swatted" by a radical feminist. And the luckless heart surgeon who, subjected to a conspiracy theory that went viral, had arrived at his hospital the previous morning to find a mob awaiting him.

On top of that, Pendergast's surprise appearance on television the night before, instead of calming things down, had electrified the city. Half of Miami was furious at the apparently sympathetic tone the agent had expressed in his impromptu appeal, while the other half was enraged at the authorities for not having caught Mister Brokenhearts. It was all anyone could talk about.

Amid this cacophony, the only one who had suddenly gone quiet was Brokenhearts himself. There had been no more killings, no more letters—nothing.

Smithback was riding high. Except for the damn Bronner lead. What seemed so promising had gone nowhere. Baxter and Flayley had been his patients—but not Adler, the other suicide victim. After his article, the police had launched an investigation, but Smithback learned from his cop informant that Bronner had ironclad alibis for the nights in question. It appeared to be coincidence: Bronner was simply a wife-beating alcoholic asshole with anger management problems, not a serial killer.

But despite that setback, the rest was gravy. Smithback still had hundreds of letters to open, and God alone knew what juicy stuff and bizarre confessions might surface. He was delivering the goods and Kraski was leaving him alone. It was indeed a gold mine of entertaining stories—and Smithback was going to mine it for all it was worth.

37

COLDMOON LOOKED MOROSELY out the louvered window of what he'd started calling Pendergast's safe house on the outskirts of Little Havana. Traffic was moving sluggishly through the soupy air, and as he watched, Axel's taxi pulled away from the curb and joined the flow, headed off on yet another mysterious errand. It was not quite eleven in the morning, and already the sun was flaring off the car windows and bare metal shopfronts, filling the air with a blinding heat and light.

Growing up in South Dakota, Coldmoon had loved the hot, dry summers. But Miami was a different beast entirely. Here it was, just turning April, and already every day seemed hotter than the last. It was so damn humid that your body, in a futile effort to cool down, would get drenched with sweat that wouldn't evaporate. And the sun didn't come at you gently, like it did in the northern latitudes, but hammered straight down on you mercilessly, like a white-hot frying pan over the head.

He turned from the window. Pendergast was sitting at the table, holding a gold chain of some sort, to which was affixed a medallion of what appeared to be a saint. Coldmoon had noticed it in the agent's hands when he'd been lying on Elise Baxter's bed in that Maine lodge. Pendergast never said where he got it, or why he carried it, but he seemed to bring it out and contemplate it at the strangest times—like now.

He heard the closing of the front door, and a moment later, Dr. Fauchet appeared in the doorway with another armload of files. She was dressed in a crisp yellow dress, and she nodded a greeting to Coldmoon and then bestowed a radiant smile on Pendergast. How the hell did these Floridians manage to get through a morning, let alone an entire day, without wilting?

Grove came into view in the doorway behind her and the two stepped into the shadowy room. "Morning," Grove said to Coldmoon and slapped his briefcase on the table, taking a seat.

Coldmoon noticed the commander's tone was a trifle formal, not quite his usual avuncular self. Perhaps he was still stewing about the way Pendergast had hijacked last night's television interview—even though afterward Pendergast had explained his rationale to Grove, with Pickett listening in on speakerphone. To Coldmoon, his partner's arguments made sense. Given Brokenhearts's psychological profile and his outreach to Smithback, Pendergast believed he could be influenced by a direct appeal. And maybe it had actually worked: there hadn't been any killings since Carpenter—at least, not yet. Coldmoon's gut feeling was that what Grove really minded was being kept in the dark. After all, he was the ranking local officer and he'd been unfailingly helpful in putting the resources of the Miami PD to work on their behalf. It had been a little unsporting of Pendergast to spring that sudden public appeal on him without warning.

Nevertheless, the commander walked over and greeted Pendergast cordially, shaking his hand. "I got your message," he said, taking a seat at the table. "I understand you have some more work for us."

"I'm afraid so. But first, I have something I would like to show you—to get your thoughts."

Nice damage control, Coldmoon thought.

Pendergast glanced over at the medical examiner. "Dr. Fauchet. I didn't expect to see you, but I must say it's a pleasure."

"I caught a ride with Commander Grove," she said. "I hope you don't mind."

"Not in the least—in fact, it's fortuitous. Though I fear I might be keeping you from your work."

"I'm on vacation."

Pendergast raised his eyebrows. "Indeed?"

"Yes. Not that I'm going anywhere special," she added quickly.

Coldmoon listened to this exchange. Fauchet—the clipped, efficient young medical examiner—using a vacation day to check on the progress of a criminal case? She seemed oddly self-conscious. If he didn't know better, he'd have guessed the woman had a crush on someone. Maybe himself? He glanced over and saw her gazing at Pendergast. Nope, wasn't him.

"I'd value your thoughts as well," he told Fauchet, to her evident pleasure and confusion.

He rose to his feet and strolled over to the rear wall, where the two large corkboards now held three-by-five cards, blue string, and photographs. The one on the left contained the index cards for each of the three recent homicides, arranged chronologically in a column. The other corkboard held one card for each of the suicide/homicides Brokenhearts had visited, along with photos of the victims, brief biographies, and photocopies of his notes to them. A series of parallel blue lines linked each recent Miami

killing to the card representing the grave to which it corre-
sponded. Below the three right-hand cards were two others, one
for Laurie Winters and another for Jasmine Oriol.

Pendergast glanced about the table. "There comes a moment
when every investigation reaches a tipping point. Thanks to
your efforts—" he nodded at Fauchet and Grove— "I believe
we've reached that point."

This rather dramatic announcement caused the tension in
the dead air of the room to ratchet up.

He moved toward the corkboards, pulling a gold pen from his
pocket as he did so.

"Let us start with the three current homicides: Felice Montera, Jenny Rosen, and Louisa May Abernathy, aka Misty Carpenter." As he spoke, he touched his pen to each of the index
cards. "They are linked to three eleven-year-old suicides: Elise
Baxter, Agatha Flayley, and Mary Adler." More touchings of the
pen. "I have always believed that these homicides dressed up as
suicides are crucial to understanding the new murders."

Homicide	Date	Suicide/ Homicide	Date	Location
Felice Montera	3/19/18	Elise Baxter	11/06	Katahdin, ME
Jenny Rosen	3/22/18	Agatha Flayley	3/07	Ithaca, NY
L. M. Abernathy	3/25/18	Mary Adler	7/06	Rocky Mount, NC
		Laurie Winters	9/06	Bethesda, MD
		Jasmine Oriol	5/06	Savannah, GA

"But how?" Commander Grove asked. "I mean, they're all over the map."

"But are they?" Pendergast said. "The main investigative thrust has been naturally focused on the recent murders in Miami Beach—in order to find and stop the killer. The older killings have been evidence, used to flesh out the impetus that's driving the current-day killer. Why put *this* heart on *this* grave? What connection does, say, Felice Montera have to Elise Baxter, or Jenny Rosen to Agatha Flayley?"

Pendergast looked around the table. "And therein lies a logical flaw. The investigation has focused on the relation between the new killings and the old—when in fact there is no relationship. Instead, we should concern ourselves with the internal relation that exists among *the eleven-year-old murders themselves.*"

He walked past the corkboards to the maps, stopping at a large one of Greater Miami, on which all the relevant locations had been marked. He turned to Fauchet. "What does this map resemble, Dr. Fauchet? Besides the obvious, I mean."

She paused before answering. "A...well, a pincushion."

"Precisely! It's *busy* with pushpins. Different locations and different colors: red for the new murder sites, green for their domiciles, blue for the graveyards, yellow for the residences of the old murder/suicides. Not to mention orange for Winters and Oriol, who thankfully have not been paired with contemporary murders." He waved at the map. "Does anyone see any pattern? Any relevance? Any clue to what agenda Mister Brokenhearts— whom we know to be an intelligent, organized killer—might have been pursuing?"

Silence all around.

"Understandably not. Because I believe the pattern lies elsewhere—with those who were murdered eleven years ago."

He pointed at the right-hand corkboard. "Baxter, Flayley, Adler, Winters, and Oriol."

Fauchet frowned. "But they seem even more random. As Commander Grove said, they're literally all over the map."

"They seem random because we've been operating on a false assumption. We've been preoccupied with their connection to Mister Brokenhearts, and whether those decade-old deaths were suicides or homicides. Nobody stopped to examine one basic point of evidence: the dates those women died."

Now Pendergast moved to another, even larger map: of the eastern seaboard of the United States. He grabbed a handful of black pushpins from a nearby tray. "Let's examine them, not in the order the hearts were left on their graves, but in the order *that they were killed.*" He began fixing the pins into position. "Jasmine Oriol, who died eleven years and ten months ago just south of Savannah, Georgia. Mary Adler, who died eleven years and eight months ago in Rocky Mount, North Carolina. Laurie Winters, eleven years and six months ago, just north of DC in Bethesda, Maryland. And Elise Baxter, who died in Katahdin, Maine—almost exactly eleven years and four months ago." He stepped aside.

"My God," Grove said, staring at the map, mouth agape. "It's a trail. The killer left a goddamned *trail!*"

"Right to the Canadian border," said Coldmoon, wondering when Pendergast had figured this out. "With each murder exactly two months apart."

"There's something else interesting about these murders," Pendergast said. He placed his finger beside the southernmost pushpin—Oriol—then slid it slowly up to the northernmost: Baxter.

"All the deaths took place along I-95," said Coldmoon.

Pendergast nodded. "Not only that, but they're roughly equidistant from each other." He paused. "So what do we have? Killings done in the same way: strangulation fashioned to look like suicide. Killings separated from each other by equivalent degrees of space and time. Killings that follow an obvious route: mile for mile, from one end to the other, Interstate 95 is the most heavily traveled road in America."

He turned toward the group at the table. "I submit to you that, when viewed in such a manner, this series of crimes is almost painful in its regularity. This killer—or killers—was following a careful plan. A deliberate plan. It's almost as if he *wanted* law enforcement to notice the pattern."

"But you've forgotten one," Coldmoon said.

Something almost like a smile flitted across Pendergast's face. "Not forgotten, Agent Coldmoon—just withheld for the moment." He picked up one more pushpin, pressed it into the map. "Agatha Flayley, the last of the suicide/murders: killed in Ithaca, New York, just eleven years ago. Two hundred miles from I-95. And with a different MO." And with this he, too, took a seat at the table.

There was silence for a moment.

"I don't understand," Grove said. "You just laid out a flawless pattern—and then, with this Flayley killing, turned it on its head."

"I'd phrase it differently, Commander. It's quite possible Agent Coldmoon has the perfect Lakota aphorism for this situation, but I hope he'll permit me to quote a Latin one instead: *exceptio probat regulam in casibus non exceptis.* The exception that proves the rule. This last of the old murders *is* different from the others—but it's that very difference I find most telling." He clasped his hands on the table and leaned forward. "Consider: It takes place out of sequence—four months after Baxter's death.

All the other strangulations were two months apart. The MO is different. Even though Flayley was strangled, it was done with less force—so much less that she was still alive when she was thrown from the bridge. That, too, is different. The others were all hanged in bedrooms or bathrooms, but Flayley was thrown off a bridge, in a public place."

He paused, and then said: "In the other killings, greater force was brought to bear on the right horn of the hyoid bone, suggesting a right-handed individual. In the Flayley case, the *left* wing of the hyoid was slightly fractured." He paused. "A slightly weaker, left-handed individual, perhaps?" Now Pendergast let his chin rest lightly on his tented fingers as he looked from Coldmoon, to Grove, to Fauchet, almost impishly. When his gaze met Fauchet's, he winked.

"A partner!" Fauchet and Coldmoon said simultaneously.

"Indeed," Pendergast said. "Although I think the word *apprentice* might be more apt."

"That handwriting guy, Ianetti, said the person who wrote the notes was left-handed," Coldmoon added.

"Yes—yes, he did." Grove, who'd seemed lost in thought during this exchange, suddenly straightened up. "Same with the throat slashings. It all fits."

"It might explain not only why this killing was different—but why it was the last of its kind."

"How do you figure that?" Coldmoon asked. Fascinating or not, he was a little annoyed at this Yoda-like line of questioning. Why hadn't Pendergast shared these revelations with him earlier?

"Up until Ithaca, the murders had been growing increasingly efficient. The killer was gaining experience, perfecting his technique. But Flayley was different: her strangling was botched, a kind of *homicidus interruptus*, and the act of throwing her off a bridge—with the potential for witnesses—hints almost of desperation. And it suggests other things as well: youthful impulsiveness, drama, the desire to impress."

"So this apprentice had been an onlooker, so to speak," Grove said. "And Flayley was a chance for him to 'make his bones.' But not having the experience or stomach for the job, he made a hash of it."

Pendergast raised his chin from his fingertips. "The mixed metaphor notwithstanding, that seems likely. But there are still other points of interest about this particular killing."

"It's nowhere near I-95," Fauchet said.

"Correct. In other words, we have a second killer—a squeamish apprentice—who takes his first killing in a new direction and almost botches it. Still, there's a similarity: he also does his one and only killing near a major traffic artery."

Coldmoon looked once more at the map. "I-81."

Pendergast nodded.

"So they were swinging back south again?" Fauchet asked.

"It seems so. And now that we know the route the killers took, let us traverse it one more time—*in reverse.*"

Coldmoon turned back to the map, and—suddenly—saw where Pendergast was going with all this; how everything fell neatly into place. "Florida," he said in a low voice. "They must have *started* in Florida."

"I'm sorry," Fauchet said. "I don't get it. We haven't found a killing with this MO in Florida."

"My dear Dr. Fauchet, that's because we haven't *looked* in Florida. Commander Grove was asked to search for possible suicide-killings *outside* Florida. Perhaps the first homicide—victim zero, if you will—happened right here in Miami, two months before the one in Savannah. The distance fits. And if the time fits as well, it would have happened twelve years ago almost to the day."

Coldmoon was thinking fast. "The killer—killers—headed north from Florida," he said. "Following a precise schedule. They looped around after reaching Maine, killed again in Ithaca—then the killings stopped. Why?"

"An excellent question. Why do *you* think?" Pendergast asked.

"Well, a few possibilities. One: they were caught and imprisoned on some other charge. Two: one or both were killed or incapacitated. Or three: the apprentice refused to continue." He paused.

"Refused to continue," Pendergast murmured. "Was he, perhaps, horrified at what he'd done—or been forced to do? Could he escape his guilt? Did he, perhaps, grow up to become—"

"Brokenhearts!" Coldmoon snapped his fingers. "*Brokenhearts* was the apprentice." Then another idea occurred to him—a horrifying one. "If that Mars profile of the killer is correct, and he can't be more than twenty-five, then he must've been little more than a kid when he was forced to take this road trip. Maybe the killing stopped because...because *the apprentice killed his master*."

There was a silence.

"But we're still left with the question of motive," Pendergast said. "What precipitated the original killing spree? I believe the answer lies right here in Miami—that is, if we can identify victim zero; the one that started them all." He turned to Grove. "I am hoping you, Commander, will deploy your teams to find that first murder for us. In that homicide lie the answers we seek—what started this murderous journey and who were the two killers? That will lead us to Brokenhearts."

"I'm on it," Grove said. "We'll put the entire division on this one. I promise you an answer in twenty-four hours or less. Dr.

Fauchet? If we get any potential hits, I may need your help with the forensics."

"Call anytime. As I said, I'm taking some vacation days but I'm always on call."

Even as she spoke, Grove was rising from his chair and walking halfway to the door. For a gracefully aging man, he could move with remarkable speed. And with one quick glance at Pendergast, Fauchet disappeared out the door after Grove.

Once the echo of their footsteps died away, relative silence settled over the loft. Then Coldmoon looked at Pendergast. "You figured all this out...and didn't tell me?"

"I wasn't sure. In fact, I'm still not. It is a lovely theory, I admit, but it's still just that: a theory. We need to find that first killing in Miami."

"I'll bet you've been suspecting something like this for a while. How long—as far back as Ithaca?"

"Agent Coldmoon, these realizations don't switch on like a lightbulb. That's for mystery novels. Rather, they develop slowly, beneath the surface—like a subcutaneous abscess."

"Nice metaphor." Coldmoon heaved a sigh and shook his head in bemusement. Then he reached into the back pocket of his jeans and pulled out his thermos. *"Atanikili,"* he said.

The agent bowed slightly. *"Philámayaye."*

Coldmoon raised his eyebrows in surprise. "You've been boning up."

"It seemed a good idea, under the circumstances."

"Never hurts to learn new things."

"True."

"Or *try* new things."

There was a pause while Pendergast peered at the thermos. "Perhaps."

Coldmoon pried off the top, unscrewed the inner lid, and poured a generous measure of tarry black liquid into the red cup. A smell like burnt rubber—one he loved more than almost anything else—filled the room. He held the cup out to Pendergast. "Coffee, partner?"

Another, longer pause. Then Pendergast accepted the cup; took a small, tentative sip. "The floral bouquet of poison sumac blooms first on the palate," he announced. "Followed by notes of diesel oil and a long finish of battery acid." And he handed the cup back.

"Exactly the way I like it," said Coldmoon, closing his eyes contentedly and downing the lukewarm beverage in a single gulp.

38

THE NEXT MORNING at six thirty, Coldmoon woke from a sound sleep to the chirping of his phone. Grumbling to himself, he answered.

"Agent Coldmoon? It's Grove. I haven't been able to reach Pendergast."

"What a shock," said Coldmoon.

"I've had teams working on the search since yesterday's meeting," Grove said. "They've been at it all night. We're focusing on Miami-Dade, but just to be safe we're not discounting any county in South Florida."

"Sounds good," Coldmoon said, trying to keep the sleep out of his voice. "Got anything?"

"They're about two-thirds of the way through, and so far we've gotten three possible hits. *Possible* is the operative word, so I didn't want to disturb Dr. Fauchet's vacation at this hour. Still, I didn't think I should wait any longer, so I'm having a uniform bring them over to your partner's, ah, makeshift office for you to look at. They should be there within the half hour. He'll wait there until you arrive."

"Thank you, Commander."

"Sure thing," Grove said with a laugh. "Feels kind of good to boss people around again. We should be finished by late afternoon, and I'll bring over any more files myself—if we find any. Meanwhile, I'll be out chasing down leads. Nothing like throwing around the title *commander* to cut through bureaucratic red tape in some backwater police department."

Although Coldmoon had been initially dismissive of the seemingly desk-bound Grove, he had to admit the man was capable of efficient work—and he wasn't afraid to roll up his sleeves, either.

After he hung up with Grove, Coldmoon called Pendergast—who answered his call immediately—and told him the news. He then went into his kitchenette to make a desperately needed cup of coffee before he could function. He poured more grounds into a coffeepot that had spent two days on the warmer, then showered and dressed. Gulping one cup, he filled his thermos with the rest, got into the Mustang, and headed for the "office." He arrived at the same time as the uniformed cop, grabbed the bulky envelope handed to him, and carried it inside. He found Pendergast already there in the shadowy interior, examining the wall of maps, face pale.

He pivoted as he heard Coldmoon enter. "Ah," he said, seeing the envelope with its Miami PD stamp in Coldmoon's hand. "Let us see what the good commander's teams have dug up."

Coldmoon tore open the envelope. Inside were three case files, battered, dog-eared, and smelling of dust and yellowing paper. He laid them out on the table.

"Should we have Fauchet join us?" he asked.

"Undoubtedly. But let's go through these first and contact her when we actually require her expertise. She's technically on vacation, after all. Grove promised you any more files by the end of the day—perhaps she can examine them all at once."

Coldmoon took a seat at the table, and Pendergast did the same. He took one of the files for himself, slid another toward Coldmoon, and put the third to one side.

"Good hunting," Pendergast told him. "Or, as a friend of mine in the NYPD might say: knock yourself out."

Coldmoon poured some coffee from the thermos, noticing as he did so that Pendergast edged away from him. He flipped open his file and began paging through the contents. They detailed the short, sad history of one Carmen Rosario, who'd been found hanging from a closet rod in her El Portal apartment. The CSU photos showed a scene he was now all too familiar with: a strangled victim, her once-attractive face mottled and bulging, eyes staring, tongue protruding like a fat cigar. She was thirty-two, divorced, no children, and had worked as a waitress until a few weeks before her death. She had a history of drug abuse and alcoholism. Her mother had died of cancer two months before.

He next turned to the M.E.'s report and leafed through it. He glanced up to see Pendergast looking across the table at him. "Anything of note?"

"Looks like a genuine suicide to me. Drugs, alcohol, dysfunction."

"Is there a toxicology report?" Pendergast asked.

"Traces of alcohol and opioids in her system, but not enough to kill her."

"No—just enough for her to overcome her inhibitions and do something rash."

"The pattern of bruises is consistent with hanging by a knotted bedsheet. The M.E. noted the hyoid bone was fractured in

the center. Conclusion: suicide by ligature strangulation. No evidence of a choke hold."

"And the X-rays?"

Coldmoon detached them from the rest of the report and
held them up to the light. "I only notice the one central fracture.
But you know, these could just as well be X-rays of beaded sad-
dle blankets for all I can see in them."

He slid them over and Pendergast picked them up and stared,
then laid them down. "It seems unlikely she's a candidate."

Coldmoon closed the file. "What about your file?"

"I'm not quite sure why Grove's team flagged it. Samantha
Kazunov, a twenty-three-year-old woman from South Miami
Heights. Found in bed, a knotted sheet around her neck fixed
to one of the bedposts. The case was initially flagged as a possible homicide, because evidence indicated another person had
been at the scene. That other person turned herself in to the
police the next day. In her statement, she said she was the dead
woman's lover and that she had died of accidental autoerotic
asphyxia. This was supported by the position of the body and
other factors. The lover had been in the bedroom, acting as
'spotter' to make sure Kazunov didn't take things too far—
which she unfortunately did."

"Stroke 'n' choke," Coldmoon said. "The deceased was a
gasper."

Pendergast closed his eyes. "Agent Coldmoon, there are certain expressions so vulgar one can only wish them unheard."

"Sorry."

Pendergast opened his eyes. "She evidently tried to save
Kazunov. In any case: neither suicide nor homicide. Erotic asphyxia is more common among men than women; however, it
is seen in both sexes. Since we know Mister Brokenhearts must

be male, I think we can safely rule out Kazunov's ex-lover as a suspect. We can turn both these files over to Dr. Fauchet for a closer look, but I sincerely doubt they are the victim zero we are looking for." Pendergast closed the file and laid it on top of Carmen Rosario's.

Together, they looked at the lone unexamined file on the table.

Pendergast gestured. "Shall we?"

Coldmoon opened the slim, olive-colored file.

"Lydia Vance," Pendergast read off. He picked up the summary sheet. "Resident of Westchester. Thirty-one, married to John Vance, staff sergeant in the marines. It was he who found the body." He scanned the pages. "She was found hanging from a showerhead with a knotted bedsheet around her neck almost exactly twelve years ago. No suicide note."

"Any other family?"

Pendergast paged through the file. "No parents, siblings, or children listed."

Coldmoon was typing the name into the nearby computer. "John Vance...I get a whole lot of hits for John Vances in Florida, but none that match that address. Is there an autopsy in the file?"

Pendergast pulled out an official-looking document with additional pages stapled to it. "According to the M.E., suicide by asphyxiation." He glanced over the document, removed a single X-ray, and held it up to the light.

Coldmoon leaned in closer and looked at it with Pendergast.

"Simple fracture of the central hyoid body," Pendergast said. "No evident damage to the horns or evidence of a push-choke." He dropped the X-ray back on the file and scanned the next set of pages.

"What about her husband, the marine?" Coldmoon asked. "The one who found her?"

Pendergast flipped back through the pages. "The man had just completed two tours of duty. The first was in Iraq, which ended prematurely when he was injured by an IED. That resulted in his being transferred to Okinawa for the second tour, where he was assigned to law enforcement with the USMC military police. He returned via military transport to Miami, went straight to his apartment, only to find his wife dead. She'd strangled herself while he was over the Pacific."

A brief silence descended.

Coldmoon exhaled. "Can you imagine? Just back from serving your country—not one, but two tours—and that's your welcome home." A pause. "What's the rest?"

Pendergast removed another set of pages and began glancing through them. "It would appear that the husband, John Vance, did not accept that his wife committed suicide. He'd spent some time in the criminal investigation division of the military police, and he insisted her death was murder, staged to look like suicide."

"No shit. Does it say why he thought that?"

Pendergast read some more. "He was insistent about it, writing letters to the police, visiting Miami PD numerous times. His wife, he says, was not depressed, never showed suicidal tendencies, did not drink or take drugs, and was allegedly looking forward to his return. The case stayed open longer than usual—probably as a courtesy, given he was a returning vet. But Miami PD refused to change the determination of death, saying the autopsy and forensic evidence pointed overwhelmingly to suicide."

Coldmoon looked at the final set of pages Pendergast was holding: dog-eared, dirty at the edges, and covered with handwritten notes, sheet after sheet on Miami PD letterhead. The man's wife killed herself just before he was expected home from his tour of duty. Why would she have done such a thing...unless she couldn't bear the idea of living with him again? Or unless she was really murdered?

"Vance didn't have any hard evidence it was a homicide?"

"Not that I can see. He was, however, MP."

"That gives him some cred."

"It would seem so."

"So what happened to him?" Coldmoon asked.

"He continued to press the Miami PD. There's quite a lot of activity in the file. It seems he grew embittered. There's a note by a police psychologist here, saying Vance couldn't accept the truth. He finally moved out of the city, to a hunting camp that had been in his family for decades."

"And that's it?"

"Not quite." Pendergast turned over a newer-looking piece of paper, clipped to the final set. "He continued to importune Miami PD, insisting he had new information about the 'murder' of his wife. Just two years ago, Miami finally sent somebody out to the camp for a follow-up interview." He flipped up the sheet. "Here's the report."

"What does it say?"

"Nothing new. Vance was still insisting it was murder, but offered no new evidence. The officer states that his health was deteriorating and he was barely ambulatory." He passed these last sheets to Coldmoon. "It seems this last interview was an attempt to get the man to shut up. Apparently it worked, as that's the latest document in the file."

"Two years ago," Coldmoon repeated. "And he *still* believed she was murdered."

Pendergast nodded.

"Hanged with a knotted bedsheet. No suicide note. The location's right. The time frame is right. MP husband felt sure she was murdered. You know, I think there's a chance she might be our victim zero."

"May I point out this is not the first person we've encountered who believed their loved one did not commit suicide?"

"You mean the Baxters. And we proved them right."

"True. But in this case, unless I'm missing something, there's absolutely no X-ray evidence she was killed by a choke hold."

Coldmoon paged through the most recent report. "If there's even a chance this *is* victim zero, maybe we should follow it up. Ask this guy Vance why he's still so convinced she was murdered."

"What will he say to us that he didn't already say to the police?"

"Take a look at this interview," Coldmoon said, holding up the sheet and then tossing it back to Pendergast. "It's all pro forma. The cops just asked a few dumb questions. I think we ought to go talk to the old coot. We have time to kill. Grove's not going to bring over any more files until late in the afternoon."

Pendergast looked at him.

"Do you disagree?"

"Not at all. I have little interest in waiting around for news that Brokenhearts has killed again. I merely ask these rhetorical questions because—without our friend Axel at hand—you'll have to drive."

"Oh. Shit." Coldmoon had forgotten about that. "What was that place again?"

"A small town with the charming name of Canepatch. About sixty miles west of here."

"Canepatch. Figures." Coldmoon stood up. "We can get there and back in three hours, tops. No point in sitting here waiting. After all, it can't be any hotter there than it is here."

"That remains to be seen," said Pendergast, who—returning the scattered sheets to the folder and picking it up—rose and walked toward the door.

39

In her windowless office next to the morgue, feeling a little guilty for what she was about to do, Charlotte Fauchet once again opened the accordion file marked LAURIE WINTERS. She had already thoroughly reviewed the file, along with Jasmine Oriol's: but then, of course, she'd had her medical examiner hat on. For a second time, she'd had trouble sleeping the night before. Certain items in the nonmedical part of the files had gotten her thinking. Maybe it was those sessions with Pendergast and Coldmoon in the "safe house," which had given her firsthand insight into the investigative aspects of catching a killer. Maybe detective work was rubbing off on her. In any case, now that she was on vacation—and with no real plans to speak of—she'd decided to drop by the office in the morning to examine the files more thoroughly.

Fauchet began laying out photos of the autopsy. Winters had been found hanging from a rod in a closet at a roadside motel outside of Bethesda. The autopsy had been performed by the local medical examiner, who was also—for a change—an experienced forensic pathologist. As she looked over the photos one by one, she was impressed by the level of technique and clean workmanship.

The problem was, despite the M.E.'s credentials, he seemed to have approached the autopsy without the slightest doubt regarding the police conclusion—that it was an open-and-shut suicide. That lack of skepticism prevented him from asking a question: how did an incomplete hanging like this fracture a *wing* of the hyoid bone, but not the *body* of the bone? Funny how all the surgical precision in the world didn't matter if the mind was already made up. It reminded her of the earlier cases, where the certitude of the police and the subtlety of the evidence had, it seemed, sometimes helped lead M.E.'s to predetermined conclusions.

Interesting.

She turned to the police report of the "suicide." Winters, twenty-four, had been driving up I-95 on a freelance photography assignment—to photograph her cousin's wedding in Massachusetts. She had reached the Wildwood Manor Motel off the 495 bypass and checked in around eight o'clock. A cleaning lady found the body the following day, hours after checkout time.

The investigating officer, Sergeant Sweetser, was a professional who'd been quite thorough in his investigation. He'd copied from the motel's register the names, car makes, and license plate numbers of the previous night's fellow guests, along with brief descriptions of each occupant given to him by the manager.

Fauchet flipped through the interviews. There was nothing of interest. Nobody had seen or heard anything out of the ordinary, and all had accounted for themselves in normal, unsuspicious ways. Winters had had no visitors that anyone had noticed. And the night manager insisted *he* would have noticed, because anyone arriving or leaving by car would have to pass by his office.

Using Google street view, Fauchet looked at the façade of the motel, which still existed. It was along the highway, outside of town and not easily accessible on foot. That meant the killers were probably staying at the motel themselves.

Good old Sergeant Sweetser had interviewed six guests, but the rest had already checked out by the time the police arrived. It seemed likely to Fauchet the killers would have left early that morning; why hang around and get caught up in an investigation? So the killers would not have been among those interviewed. That was another important clue.

As she skimmed the list of license plates, she saw there was another Florida plate, on a 1997 Mercury Tracer wagon with the number JW24-99X. If the killer was from Florida, as Pendergast had implied in yesterday afternoon's meeting, this could be another clue. And it made sense: if the killers were traveling up I-95 hunting for victims from Florida, it would be easy enough to cruise through a motel parking lot, looking for Florida plates.

According to Sweetser's report, the motel register said the Tracer belonged to a man by the name of George Lehigh. The second occupant of the room was listed as his son, Travis.

Father and son. Master—and apprentice?

She felt a creeping chill. They were not among those guests who'd been interviewed. But Sweetser had obtained a description from the manager. She turned to it and was disappointed to find it perfunctory—both with brown hair, average height, average build, no distinguishing characteristics—except both father and son were wearing Marlins baseball caps. The son, Travis, "looked to be in his midteens."

Fauchet put down the report and thought for a moment. Was *Lehigh* their real name? Almost certainly they would be traveling under false identities. It didn't look like Sweetser had run any license plates—not surprising, given the supposed suicide. But surely there would be a record in some database, somewhere, of who was registered to that plate eleven years ago.

She took out Pendergast's business card and started dialing the cell number. Then she stopped and laid down her phone. She shouldn't go off half-cocked. After all, these potential clues were intriguing, but they were just that: *potential* clues. If she was freelancing, the least she should do was follow through the way Pendergast would: examine both files, dot her *i*'s and cross her *t*'s. After all, the Miami PD, whose job it was to examine such things, would know what to look for.

But wouldn't it be wonderful, she thought, if she could deliver to Pendergast the identity of Brokenhearts on a silver platter...just like that?

She put away the Winters folder and turned to the accordion file labeled JASMINE ORIOL.

40

I FIGURE THERE'S a pretty good chance we'll get shot out here," said Coldmoon, with a mirthless laugh, as they passed by a shabby trailer with five skeletonized cars out front, surrounded by bedraggled palmettos. "These crackers aren't likely to pass up the chance to try and jack a Shelby."

"Perhaps not," said Pendergast. He'd been paging through the Vance file again, and now he slipped it into the pocket of the passenger door. "But if it eases your mind, I'd lay odds you could outrun them."

Coldmoon downshifted the confiscated drugmobile as they approached a sharp turn. Beyond the smoked windows, the landscape whizzed past—stands of tall marsh grass, clusters of dense vegetation and trees, an occasional trailer or abandoned roadside attraction. And always, running everywhere, channels of lazy brown water, with the occasional alligator basking in the sun.

The first half hour had been the usual snarl of Miami traffic. But as they continued west, past the racetracks and par-three golf courses and trailer parks, he did his best to relax, forget he'd been the one to suggest this boring field trip, and enjoy the ride.

The initial section of road was familiar from his drive to Cape Coral, anyway, and as that little jaunt taught him, the layout of Florida was bizarre: millions of people pressed against the coasts like ants, and in the middle nothing but lakes, orange groves, cattle ranches, and—of course—swamps.

After they made the turn, Okeechobee Road ran arrow-straight through the flat landscape, the asphalt shimmering in the heat, mirages coming and going on the road surface. They entered an area of wetlands, with tall trees rising upward, bulbous root systems extending into the water like a tangle of snakes. They passed a large family of basking alligators, lying in the muck along the verge, black and oily and gleaming in the patchy sun, slitty eyes open. Some were even lying on top of others. Didn't the bastards ever shut their eyes? Coldmoon shuddered. God, he hated the look of those creatures—and all of a sudden they seemed to be everywhere, roughly corresponding to the abrupt drop-off in human habitation. He had no idea Florida had so many. They were like giant snakes with legs. He wondered why alligator leather was so expensive, when all you had to do was come to the bayous of South Florida and pick off as many as you liked.

"Our turnoff should be in about five miles," Pendergast said.

Coldmoon checked his iPhone. Thank God it still had a couple of bars—the last time they drove out of town, he'd lost cell reception almost immediately. "Four point four miles to be exact," Pendergast continued. "Then another ten to Paradise Landing and three more to Canepatch."

"Great." Coldmoon, eager to get the interview over with, accelerated again, this time to ninety. The chopped-down Mustang seemed to prefer high rates of speed: the engine settled down to a mild roar, and the laminar airflow kept them low and steady on the road. The biggest indication of speed was the insects now peppering the windshield like hail, once in a while a particularly large specimen leaving a huge yellow splat.

The turnoff came before he expected it. There was no sign, but it was the only one around. He braked smoothly and hard, swinging the Shelby onto the side road. It began as potholed blacktop, but within a few miles turned into a white lane of crushed oyster shells. The trailers and rusting hulks of engines they'd seen before were gone. Instead, they were now passing stands of brackish water, saw grass marshes, and tall, strange-looking plants.

"Is this the Everglades?" Coldmoon asked.

"I imagine we entered the preserve when we left the state highway."

He looked around. "Can you imagine the drive this guy must make to buy beer?"

"Even longer, I would imagine, for a decent Bordeaux."

Coldmoon was used to emptiness, but it was the emptiness of the South Dakota prairie. This kind of desolation felt strangely claustrophobic, as if he was hemmed in by the tropical growth that grew wilder with each mile they went. "Why would anyone live out here?" he muttered.

"Here we have a man," Pendergast said, "who was sure his wife was brutally murdered. Rightly or wrongly, he was convinced it wasn't suicide, but he couldn't make anyone else believe him, especially law enforcement. He was dismissed, ignored, humored as if he was crazy. An experience like that can break a man. It's no surprise he decided to retire from humanity."

"Okay," Coldmoon said. "But that was twelve years ago. You think Vance's still there—or even alive?"

"He was as of two years ago. We shall find out soon enough."

"Yeah. But did you ever see the movie *Deliverance*?"

"No."

"Well, all I can say is, if I start hearing any banjos, I'm turning the hell around."

Behind them, the car was sending up a corkscrew of white dust. As the road deteriorated, Coldmoon slowed. The wild vegetation gave way to vast, tall grass, so high it felt like they were traveling in a green ditch. After another mile, a dark cypress forest loomed up. It seemed to go on forever, growing darker and darker until they found themselves in a gloomy swamp, the elevated dirt road running among the massive trunks of cypress trees and a thick, brushy understory. The greasy gleam of alligators could be seen again, here and there, in the rare patches of sun.

"Another mile and a half to Paradise Landing," said Coldmoon, checking his phone. The two bars had dropped to one. After a few more minutes, sunlight could be seen through the cover of trees; then the road made a turn and ran alongside a broad canal. The forest opened up, exposing a burnt-green landscape with several sagging docks extending into the water, a shuttered convenience store, and a couple of rusted gas pumps under a metal awning. Beyond the docks, Coldmoon could see parallel lanes of a once-paved boulevard, with streetlights and rows of half-built homes looming up: concrete shells abandoned before completion. At the close end of the boulevard lay a few kayaks of faded fiberglass, flung together and of questionable seaworthiness. A peeling sign read, WELCOME TO PARADISE LANDING.

Coldmoon brought the Shelby to a stop and they stepped out. He looked warily for alligators, but if any were around they'd submerged themselves in the canal. A pair of egrets took off from the dock posts.

"Looks like one of those failed Florida developments you read about." Coldmoon glanced again at his phone. "We're still three miles from Canepatch. But the road seems to end here."

Pendergast said nothing, just gazed ahead at the brown waterway with distant eyes.

"After you, kemosabe."

Pendergast, still without answering, walked down to the dock. Coldmoon followed. A small aluminum airboat, not nearly as old as its surroundings, was tied up to one of the moorings.

"Evidently, someone still uses this place," Pendergast said. He leaned over and examined the boat. "And the keys are in the ignition. How convenient."

"You're going to steal it," Coldmoon said.

"We have the right to *requisition* it," Pendergast said. "But that won't be necessary." He nodded at a crooked wooden sign, on which had been painted:

AIRBOAT FOR RENT. $10/HR $50/DAY.
TANK OF GAS $20.

"Awfully trusting out here," Coldmoon said.

"I doubt anyone would come all this way just to hijack such a specialized form of watercraft."

Coldmoon shouted out a greeting—once, twice—but there was no reply except for the buzz of insects.

Pendergast reached into his black suit—Coldmoon had long since stopped wondering how the man could stand wearing it in all the heat and humidity—slipped out a money clip, removed a hundred-dollar bill, and speared it to a rusty nail sticking out of the sign. He gestured toward the boat. "Be my guest."

41

Fᴀᴜᴄʜᴇᴛ, ʜᴀᴠɪɴɢ ᴀʟʀᴇᴀᴅʏ seen the file on Jasmine Oriol, knew it was much sketchier than Laurie Winters's. Oriol had been found in a motel outside Savannah, Georgia. The case had been handled not by a medical examiner, but by an elected county coroner without an MD, who in turn farmed out the autopsy to an intern at the local hospital. This might very well have been his first real autopsy, and it was a piece of work. The forensic photographs were amateurish and underexposed. The report that accompanied them was almost useless. No photographs of the hyoid bone were sharp enough to show anything useful. The toxicology report indicated that, as with Winters, there were no drugs or alcohol in her system—and that was about it. Shaking her head, Fauchet gathered up the photos and returned them to the file along with the coroner's report. Short of an exhumation, she'd have to take the report of the broken hyoid wings on faith. But again, it was the nonmedical aspects of the crime that now intrigued her—especially the possibility of the investigating cop having, as in the case of Laurie Winters, made a record of license plates.

She flipped open the police reports. Jasmine Oriol had been on her way from Miami to visit her fiancé in New York City, where he was in medical school. This was the first night of her cross-country trip. Florida was a long-ass state, and maybe Jasmine had gotten a late start—in any case, she hadn't made it far.

Much to Fauchet's disappointment, the investigating officer had not copied the motel register, or listed the other guests and their license plate numbers. At least there was an interview with the motel manager, a man named Wheaton, who had been eager to help to the point of volubility: the transcribed interview ran to four single-spaced pages.

Fauchet began reading. Oriol, the manager said, had arrived around six o'clock, asked for a restaurant recommendation, then gone to a diner across the street. Wheaton saw her returning around seven thirty. She stopped in again at the front desk at eight and asked for a hair dryer to use the next morning. The manager didn't notice anything out of the ordinary—she seemed cheerful and had talked in passing about her fiancé.

The next morning, he was surprised when she slept in: he thought she'd be eager to be on her way. But he didn't bother her until noon, when he finally sent the maid around. He heard screams, came running, and saw the woman hanging from the ceiling fan, having kicked over a chair underneath her. From this point, the manager went on and on, bemoaning the tragedy and its effect on business, saying that nothing like this had ever happened before, why would she ask for a hair dryer before killing herself, this was a respectable place, and so forth almost interminably until the interviewing officer gently but skillfully ended the interview.

But it was a good question: why ask for a hair dryer to use the next morning and then go hang yourself? Spontaneous suicides, Fauchet knew from medical school, almost always involved drugs or alcohol. But her toxicology report was clean.

There was a file of the maid's interview, just half a sheet. She read through it and found it a hysterical, babbling mess.

Fauchet sat back, lips pursed. If only the police officer had thought to copy the motel register listing the car makes and license plates, she would know whether the same Mercury Tracer with the Florida plates had been at that motel. She wondered if the motel still existed; a quick Google check indicated it was gone.

She went back through the folders for the other three murders, which still sat on a corner of her desk: Baxter, Flayley, Adler. In no case was there a police officer as thorough as in Bethesda; there were no lists of car models or license plates. Then again, why should there be? All three murders were thought to be suicides.

But she still had the Florida plate number from the motel where Winters was killed. Okay, now it was time to call Pendergast. He could run that plate in ten seconds.

She dialed his number and was immediately directed to voice mail. She tried Coldmoon and the same thing happened. She then dialed the Miami FBI number and, after a lot of being bounced around, learned that the precise location of Agents Pendergast and Coldmoon was unknown, but it was believed they were out in the field.

She set down her phone. She had a brother, Morris, with the Florida Highway Patrol out of Jacksonville. Maybe he could see whom the plate belonged to. She picked up the phone and dialed his number.

"Hello, Sis," came the deep voice.

Fauchet exhaled with relief. She explained what she wanted

and why. There was a long silence, and then Morris said: "Sis? Let those FBI guys deal with it."

"Listen, Morris—"

"I know you were really into *Harriet the Spy* as a kid. But you're an M.E., not a detective."

She felt crestfallen. "I can't get hold of the 'FBI guys.'"

"Call Miami Homicide, then."

She didn't want them to have the collar; Pendergast was the one who'd put the critical pieces together. "Can't you just give me a name? There's a serial killer out there, and he might kill again at any moment."

"All the more reason you should leave this to the professionals." A long sigh. "I love you, Sis, but sorry. They flag those kinds of checks these days—you wouldn't want me to get fired, right?"

She didn't answer, waiting him out.

"You know," he said finally, almost reluctantly, "under the Florida open government act, everyone now has access to a section of the MVD database. You can't run a plate, but you can check on citations, accidents, DUI, fraud, criminal stuff."

Fauchet thanked him and said goodbye. Then she put down the phone and ruminated.

The killings ceased after Ithaca. Pendergast had speculated that the murders might have stopped because the killer, or killers, died. And Coldmoon had taken the speculation further, wondering if maybe the apprentice had killed the master. That was possible, of course. It was also just as possible something else happened: some sort of accident—like a *car* accident—ended the killing spree.

Okay. It was a long shot, but worth a try—to see if the license plate from the Bethesda motel had been involved in an accident in the weeks following the Ithaca murder.

She logged into the morgue's computer system and moused her way through the labyrinth of governmental menus until she reached the MVD. A minute of poking around brought her to a database search page, where she typed in the license plate number and the date parameters of her query.

Bingo.

A 1997 Mercury Tracer wagon, Florida license plate JW24-99X, was involved in a fatal accident on I-81 south of Scranton, Pennsylvania, in March 2007...just one week after the Ithaca killing.

Fauchet quickly searched the internet and brought up a local newspaper article about the accident. It was brief: the vehicle had gone off the highway, hit a guardrail, and rolled. The car's registered owner, a man named John Bluth Vance, had been killed in the resulting crush of metal. His fourteen-year-old son, Ronald, had been taken to the hospital with serious injuries. The cause of the accident was "under investigation."

And that was it. There were no subsequent articles about Vance's death, the accident, or his son's movements. It was as if Ronald Vance simply vanished—that is, if the accident hadn't ultimately killed him.

Fauchet felt her heart pounding. This could be it. Admittedly, the evidence was thin—she'd only matched the car to the site of one killing—but the date and place of the accident matched with the sudden cessation of homicides...as outlined by Pendergast.

The killings stopped after Ithaca because of the fatal accident—which ended the brutal road trip. That wasn't all. They—a father-and-son team—had been traveling under assumed names. They drove a car with Florida plates. And they had stayed at the same motel as Laurie Winters on the night she was killed.

The son, Ronald Vance—alias Travis Lehigh—would now be twenty-four, maybe twenty-five. If she was right, this fourteen-year-old boy had been forced to participate in a series of horrific murders that—as Pendergast hypothesized—culminated in his committing the final murder at Ithaca himself, shortly before his father was killed in a car accident.

On a hunch, she did a meta-search of the medical databases at her disposal. Nothing showed up on a sweep of the Miami area, or for the state of Florida, either. But when she did a nationwide search, she learned that a Ronald Vance, aged twenty-four, had been released from the King of Prussia Subacute Care Center in September of last year. Digging deeper, she found Vance had been transferred to the center from Powder Valley State Hospital outside of Allentown, nine months before.

Powder Valley Hospital, she quickly discovered, specialized in long-term rehabilitation of neurologic trauma. And like King of Prussia, it wasn't far from Scranton. If Ronald Vance had been admitted to Powder Valley *as a minor*, the records would be sealed. That's why she could only see the recent transfer and release dates.

No wonder the guy was so utterly messed up: he'd been dragged on a monstrous road trip by his father, then gravely injured in a car accident. And that accident resulted in some kind of head injury that took him a decade to recover from. *Assuming he recovered* . . . what if he'd developed a psychosis that, to those caring for him, appeared to present itself as trauma instead?

It all made sense. *Ronald Vance was Brokenhearts.* He'd been released from the subacute care center less than seven months ago—half a year before the new murders started up. Now he was trying to atone for those previous murders—by killing more people! There was a motive here, even if it was insane.

She took a deep breath. Admittedly, there was more due diligence to be done. But this felt right.

This felt huge.

Fauchet turned to a people-search app on her phone and typed in "Ronald Vance, Miami." It took her less than ten seconds to get a hit.

Name:
Ronald C. Vance
Age:
24
Address:
203 Tarpon Court
Golden Glades, FL 33169

Holy shit: there it was. So he *had* come home!

Golden Glades—where was that again? She pulled up her keyboard and typed in the address, and a map of the endless Miami sprawl appeared on her screen. *There*: abutting North Miami Beach, only a few miles from Pendergast's safe house. And not too far from the site where the first heart was left.

A half-hour drive. Maybe less, if the traffic cooperated.

Once again she tried to call Pendergast and Coldmoon, but the calls still went straight to voice mail.

She went over the train of logic again, slowly. Was it actually possible she was right? Could Ronald Vance be Mister Brokenhearts—and could he really be living just a short drive away?

She stared at the screen and the map it displayed, with the little red arrow blinking just above the street named Tarpon Court.

42

Up close, the airboat was even smaller than it had looked from a distance. The bow swept upward, like a World War II landing craft. There were two seats, one behind the other, both on stilts. The big prop at the rear was attached to a ninety-horsepower Lycoming engine and enclosed in a wire cage. Cold-moon rapped on the gas tank: full.

Pendergast turned to him. "Have you ever driven one of these?"

"No," said Coldmoon.

"In that case, no time like the present. Care to take the helm?"

"I'd rather not. I, um, don't like water."

He felt Pendergast's amused gaze on him. "I'm not overfond of the substance myself, at least in large, stagnant, miasmic bodies. But if you don't mind, I'd prefer to function as guide and lookout."

"Let me guess. If I object again, you'll remind me whose idea it was to interview John B. Vance." Coldmoon got into the boat and, muttering to himself in Lakota, stepped up to the wheel, then cast an eye over the helm. Everything looked pretty simple: a key, a choke, and a combined throttle and gearshift with neutral, forward, and reverse. And there was a little stopcock on what was obviously the fuel line. He sat down in the front seat, opened the stopcock, set the throttle to neutral, pulled out the choke, and turned the key. The engine fired up almost immediately.

"Ready to cast off?" asked Pendergast.

"Do I have a choice?"

Pendergast untied the boat, climbed aboard, and gave them a push away from the dock with a wing-tip shoe.

When Coldmoon eased the throttle forward, the propeller engaged with a whir of wind, and the flat-bottomed boat surged forward. Coldmoon cautiously steered it into the main channel. Pendergast, meanwhile, had reached into his jacket pocket and brought out a map, folded into a remarkably small size. *No wonder he wanted to be guide*, Coldmoon thought, wondering whether Pendergast had purchased his seemingly bottomless suit jacket from a magician's supply store.

"Canepatch is almost exactly three miles to the southwest of us," he said.

Coldmoon pulled out his phone to check the GPS. "Zero bars. Figures."

"That is why we have *this*." Pendergast opened the map with a whip-like motion, and it extended to an alarming size. "Set a course for two hundred ten degrees."

"How the hell do I do that? I've never driven a boat before. My preferred mode of travel is a horse, and they aren't usually equipped with GPS."

Pendergast pointed at a small compass, set into a bulb on the helm. "Turn the boat until it is pointing toward two ten. Then go straight."

"I knew that." He steered the boat around until it was pointing in the right direction. There were many channels among the cypresses, and the direction they headed was fairly open.

"What is our speed?" Pendergast asked.

"Um, eight miles per hour."

"Barring any obstructions or delays, we should reach Canepatch in twenty minutes."

The water was smooth, and the movement of the boat produced a refreshing breeze. It was loud as hell, though—even louder than the Shelby. Weaving among the big trees, Coldmoon tried to keep the boat headed in the direction indicated by the compass. Once in a while they passed a hummock of mud, where there was invariably an alligator or two. Another time, he was sure he saw a snake winding through the water.

They continued on through the mangroves, the noise of the engine making conversation all but impossible. Strange trees came together overhead in an exotic canopy that threw the bayou into semi-darkness. Coldmoon found it impossible to imagine anyone would live out here. In fact, the farther they went, the more certain he felt that nobody did. The rented airboat must be for fishermen or the like. The old guy had either died or returned to civilization—who could live out here for a decade without going crazy?

"And here we are," said Pendergast. Ahead, in the gloomy shade, Coldmoon could see a dock sticking into the water. Beyond, solid land rose up, and the cypress trees gave way to a forest of oaks above a thick carpet of ferns.

As Coldmoon slowed alongside the dock, he could see, looming through the trees, a large old wooden house on a rise, with a wraparound veranda. It was remarkably shabby, and yet hinted at current habitation. Coldmoon wasn't sure why he believed this: there was no hum of a generator, no curl of smoke from a chimney, no satellite mini-dish on the roof of the structure. From the look of things, it might be squatters.

He clumsily brought the boat in, bumping hard against the dock. Pendergast jumped out and tied it to a post as Coldmoon killed the engine.

"So much for the element of surprise," Coldmoon said, jerking a thumb toward the huge propellers slowing in the cage behind them.

Pendergast glanced at Coldmoon. "I would not care to surprise the kind of person who chose to live out here."

Coldmoon patted his jacket where his sidearm was. "As in, some crazy old geezer who'd shoot first and ask questions afterward?"

"Precisely."

"I suppose that's why you'll ask me to go first."

They stood on the dock, peering at the house. A narrow, sandy trail led from the small clearing, through ferns, across a wooden bridge, and up the hill. There was a makeshift sign on the bridge he couldn't read.

Pendergast cupped his hands. "Halloo!"

Silence.

"There's no boat at the dock," said Coldmoon. "Maybe no one's home."

"Halloo!" Pendergast called again. "John Vance?"

A faint, unintelligible voice filtered back down. Coldmoon squinted up at the house again, but nobody was visible.

"Let's go." They advanced along the trail and approached the bridge, where the crudely lettered sign read:

DANGER!!
DO NOT PROCEED!

Pendergast paused to call out again. "FBI!" he said. "We'd like to come up and ask a few questions!"

The voice responded: high-pitched and urgent, still unintelligible.

Coldmoon took another look at the sign. The trail forked here, one path leading over the bridge—which indeed looked rotting and dangerous—and the other winding its way around through the ferns.

Another call from above.

"Was that a cry for help?" Coldmoon asked.

"It sounded like it."

"Mr. Vance?" Coldmoon shouted. "Do you need help?" He turned away from the bridge and walked down the sandy path.

"Thank God," came a weak voice. "Help me—cut myself with a chain saw!"

The voice seemed to be coming from the house, but it was hard to pinpoint with all the trees. Coldmoon squinted into the dim tangle of vegetation. "Shit, I see him! A white-haired guy, lying on the veranda!"

"Please help!" came the voice, already growing weaker. "Help!"

"Jesus." Coldmoon began walking faster down the path.

"Hold on," said Pendergast, reaching for him.

"*Hurry, I'm bleeding to death!*"

Coldmoon shrugged off Pendergast's hand and broke into a jog.

"Wait!" Pendergast cried. "We *don't know*—"

But he never finished his sentence, and for Coldmoon it was almost surreal: the way the ferns underfoot simply opened up, the ground fell away, and then they both dropped with surprising speed into a dark chasm.

43

THE NEIGHBORHOOD OF Golden Glades was laid out in a grid of ranch houses, surrounded by unkempt lawns and patches of sand. Bedraggled fan palms broke up the monotonous march of homes. The streets were lined with bins, green for garbage and blue for recycling—evidently, it was trash day.

Fauchet had decided to drive by the house—that was all—to see if someone was home. There was no harm in that—certainly no danger. Drive by, check it out, then report what she found to Pendergast. Assuming, that is, she could ever reach his cell phone.

She turned into Tarpon Court, a curving asphalt road that seemed less prosperous than its neighbors. A few of the houses were boarded up, and some others had colorful graffiti sprayed on the façades. The numbers to her left reeled off: 119, 127, 165, 201. Finally, there it was: 203.

She slowed the car. The house, of faded yellow stucco with white trim, was set back from the street, and it looked even shabbier than the rest. A half-dead oak blocked the picture window in front, and a rusting lawn mower sat beside it, sprouting weeds. The patchy St. Augustine grass of the front yard was at least a foot tall, matted down by recent rains. The driveway was webbed with cracks, and an old newspaper sat in the baking sun, in front of a garage door with peeling panels of fake wood.

She cruised by as slowly as she dared, then continued to the end of the block, preparing to circle around. Out of sight of the house, she pulled over briefly to try Pendergast again. Nothing.

Continuing on around the block, she started working up a story in her head in case she was stopped by a nosy neighbor. *I'm looking for my aunt's house. Reba Jones.* She figured the likelihood of anyone questioning her was slim, especially considering she was driving a late-model Lexus. Or perhaps that would look even more suspicious in a neighborhood like this. But whatever the case, the more she thought about it, "looking for my aunt's house" sounded lame. She needed something better.

Rounding the last corner, she reentered Tarpon Court. What if Brokenhearts was out stalking another victim? Or what if he'd already fled, leaving a house full of evidence? It was true he had suddenly gone quiet. Her brother's cautionary words echoed in her mind: *Leave this to the professionals.* Well, she *was* a professional. She was a forensic pathologist with a medical degree, and a detective to boot—at least, with human bodies. She'd even figured out Brokenhearts's identity and address. Anyway, she thought she had.

She approached the house a second time. This would be her last pass. Circling the block three times would be out of the question, so whatever she found, it had to be now.

Or maybe...just maybe...she should stop and ring the bell.

On what pretense? Remembering something, she glanced into the backseat—and sure enough, like a gift from God, there were the Jehovah's Witness pamphlets that had been thrust at her in the parking lot by some well-meaning soul as she was leaving work two days before. Perfect.

Drawing on her courage and thinking of Pendergast's reaction—and Dr. Moberly's mortification—if she brought in this unbelievable breakthrough on a silver platter, she boldly drove into the driveway of 203 Tarpon Court, snatched up the pamphlets, exited the car before she could change her mind, then strode up to the door and pushed the doorbell.

No sound.

The door looked as decrepit as the rest of the house, with an overhead light stamped in an owl design and two small, cracked windows beneath its upper edge. Putting her ear to it, she pushed the rusty doorbell again. Still no sound—the mechanism must be broken.

She knocked. And waited. Then knocked again, more boldly, chips of paint falling from the humidity-swollen door.

She could hear no movement in the house, no sound, nothing. The place gave all appearances of being empty. What now? The blinds were carefully drawn, their edges stained with mildew. She could see nothing inside.

What the hell. Pamphlets in hand, she picked her way through the tall, moist grass and walked around the house. Arriving at the back door, she paused. From here, she was out of view of the houses on either side. Should she knock? If he answered, how would she explain her presence at the back door? Really, this was stupid. She took a step backward, then another.

On the other hand, the man wouldn't dare do anything to her—not in his own home. That just wasn't his MO. If it was indeed Brokenhearts.

It *was* Brokenhearts. Wasn't it?

Leave this to the professionals.

That did it. She took a breath, stepped forward again, raised her hand, paused a moment, and then knocked loudly on the back door. Under the pressure of her knuckles, the door—unlocked—creaked open an inch. She couldn't help herself and leaned in close, peering through the crack. Just beyond, in the mudroom, hanging on a coat hook, was an old Marlins baseball cap.

44

Iᴛ ᴡᴀs ʟɪᴋᴇ being swallowed by Mother Earth herself, with a sudden groaning of soil and jumble of ferns and rush of damp wind. Coldmoon tumbled, his fall arrested when something like a steel cable suddenly grabbed him as the storm of dirt began to subside. Coughing, choking, he spat sand from his mouth and realized it was Pendergast who had stopped his fall, holding him by the arm on a steep slope of sand and earth, which descended into a deep, swirling pool of muck.

With his other hand, Pendergast was gripping a thick root. "Dig in," he said. "Find a purchase."

With his free hand, Coldmoon scrabbled against the shifting wall of earth, grabbing another root, his feet managing to locate something to balance on. As the rumbling subsided, the collapsing hole seemed to stabilize, its edges still folding in, dropping ferns on them as they clung to the steep slope.

"Earthquake?" Coldmoon gasped.

"Sinkhole," Pendergast replied.

With a remarkable display of strength, he was able to reach

up and grab a higher root. The sandy dirt continued to crumble away around the perimeter.

Coldmoon followed Pendergast's example and found another root of his own. He pushed with his feet, ensuring he had a good purchase.

"I can climb," he said, and Pendergast released him.

The slope was steep but not vertical, with many exposed roots, and Coldmoon used them as hand- and footholds, the soil cascading down on his head and getting in his eyes and mouth, sometimes forcing him back down a step. The sinkhole might have stabilized, but it was nevertheless like trying to climb up an ever-shifting sand pile: a few feet up, then almost as many back down again, as the sandy flanks cracked, crumbled, then fell away. Nevertheless, it was only minutes before Pendergast reached the lip of the hole, Coldmoon close behind, gasping and spitting out sand and dirt. As his head and shoulders cleared ground level, he could see the broken ferns littering the trail now dangling over the far edge of the sinkhole and, in the distance beyond, the dilapidated lodge. The elderly figure on the veranda was still struggling to rise. "Help!" the figure cried again.

A sudden, sharp crack rang through the air. Simultaneously, Coldmoon felt a blow, as if he'd been punched in the back with enormous force. With vast surprise, he realized he'd been shot. There was no pain, but he suddenly lost all strength; his hands released and he felt himself tumbling backward. Seconds later he landed in dark stagnant water that immediately closed over him, and all went black.

45

Pᴇɴᴅᴇʀɢᴀsᴛ sᴡᴜɴɢ ʜɪs arm down to grab Coldmoon again, but the agent, shot in the back, was already out of reach. Clinging to a root near the top of the hole, he saw Coldmoon hit the water below and instantly vanish into the swirling murk.

A second shot rang out and he felt a massive thud strike the dirt beside his head. With a mighty heave he pulled himself up and out and rolled over into the cover of the ferns. As he did so, a third shot boomed out, the round snipping the greenery above his head as he dove behind a live oak. It was clear the shots were coming from somewhere inside the lodge, most likely the second floor. Even as he searched its façade, trying to locate the shooter, another shot rang out—and the head of the man crawling on the veranda disappeared in a gout of red and gray.

Pendergast pulled out his Les Baer—at the same time realizing he'd lost his backup Glock in the collapse—and waited behind the tree. He counted to eight and then peered around for a moment before ducking back. All was now quiet. He could not see the shooter. Coldmoon remained at the bottom of the sinkhole, shot. Taking another quick look from behind the tree, Pendergast fired two rounds at the house, then slipped through the cover of ferns to get a glimpse into the sinkhole. He could see nothing but ribbons of sand and dirt slipping downward as the edges of the hole continued to crumble. No sound from Coldmoon.

Anticipating another shot, he threw himself back toward the cover of the old oak, its knuckled branches twisted into gnarly, arthritic shapes. As he did so he heard another shot, this one so close it tore the shoulder pad from his jacket. But he managed to make out a flash of fire from an upper dormer window of the house; after killing the man on the veranda, the shooter had apparently gained elevation to get a better angle of fire. The man must have a scoped rifle, and clearly knew how to use it.

Leaning against the tree, breathing hard, Pendergast considered his situation. As he did so, he heard two more shots and wondered briefly what the man was shooting at—until he heard the dull crump of an explosion and saw a pillar of fire rising from the direction of the dock. The shooter had just destroyed their airboat.

It was obvious they'd walked into a trap. But how was that possible? Who had known they were coming here? They hadn't even known of this location until that morning. Pendergast's mind raced. The shooter had arranged this ambush in advance. That meant they hadn't been followed: it could only be a person who knew they'd be examining the file on the Vance suicide / murder. That person would know they'd see Vance's address. From there, it wasn't much of a stretch to guess they'd want to interview the man.

There was another possibility, of course: that John Vance was, in fact, Mister Brokenhearts—and they had surprised him in his lair. But in that case, who was the elderly man lying dead on the porch?

Pendergast understood that he had only seconds to decide on a course of action. Movement in any direction would expose him to fire. The shooter was roughly a hundred yards away, which meant he was out of reach of Pendergast's 1911 save for the luckiest of shots. And in an exchange of gunfire, he would be dead before he got lucky.

To equalize the contest, Pendergast had to get closer, get the shooter within range of his own firearm. And he had to do it fast.

He burst from the cover of the tree, heading toward the house. Another shot rang out and he threw himself down behind another tree. Between him and the house there was now only open ground. He'd have to circle the lodge and come in from the back, where the cover was denser.

But this was what the shooter would expect.

Drawing on his past experience as a hunter of big game, Pendergast decided he should follow the example of the Cape buffalo: flee, drawing the shooter out of the house in pursuit, then circle back around and take him from behind.

The island was quite narrow. In order to circle to the back, he would have to enter the water.

Moving fast, he rolled out from cover and, aiming a suppressing shot at the dormer window, zigzagged back down the path, ducking from tree to tree. Shots rang out; he returned fire even as he felt a hard tug at his thigh just before making the final turn toward the dock. The airboat was burning, sending up a plume of black smoke that had the advantage of forming a field of cover. He took a second to examine his wound—flesh only, no bone or arteries involved. Sliding into the water—feeling its sting where the bullet had nicked his thigh—he kept low. The water was shallow, and the bottom mud too thick to allow him to move fast. Another shot rang through the trees as he worked his way to the end of the dock, the mud sucking at his feet, almost fatally slowing him down.

At the far end of the dock, he took cover behind the furiously burning boat. Keeping it between him and the house, he waded farther out into the swamp to where the water was deep enough to immerse himself. He moved laterally, sinking deeper, using cypress roots as cover, staying low, his head just out of water.

Movement; a swirl of water; and then, with a sharp glance to the right, Pendergast caught a glimpse of the nostrils and eyes of an alligator, sinking out of sight. The surface still rippled with underwater movement, however, and the ripples were coming straight at him.

Pendergast kicked up and away from the mucky bottom and lashed out with his foot, making contact with the creature. It erupted from the water with terrifying speed, reptilian eyes fixed on him, long uneven lines of teeth gleaming as its mouth gaped wide, and Pendergast fired directly into the gullet, the round blowing off the back of its head. It fell backward into the water, thrashing in frantic death throes.

Another shot came from the house, a gout of water spurting up to his left.

Pendergast sank back down into the water and moved as quickly as he could, holding his breath and crawling along the bottom, eyes open, another round zipping past him and leaving a trail of bubbles. He took cover behind a cypress. At two hundred yards, the lodge did not have a direct view of the dock, but Pendergast's thrashings would have been clearly heard and it was sheer luck he hadn't been hit. His only choice was to move in a straight line, keeping the trees between him and the house, and increase his distance from the shooter.

As he looked around, he saw another pair of eyes peek up from the brown water, and then another. A commotion began near the end of the dock: it was the gator he'd shot, being torn apart by its compatriots.

The water got deeper, and soon he could swim freely underneath the surface. Grabbing the extra clip from his jacket and then letting the jacket go, he took a bearing toward the next tree, held his breath, and ducked under, swimming hard, eyes open in the muddy water. More distance, more intervening trees.

The shots had now ceased; he was finally too deep in the trees and too far away for the shooter to waste rounds. But even as he caught his breath, he saw the ripple of another alligator coming at him, moving fast below the surface. He braced himself, thrust the muzzle of the gun underwater—and when he felt it make contact, pulled the trigger. The kick of the underwater shot almost tore the gun out of his hands, but it did the job: the reptile jerked sideways, coming up out of the water, its lower jaw partially torn away, and then it fell back, sinking in a cloud of blood.

Keeping to the water, Pendergast began working his way around the island, circling at a distance. On the far side, a tongue of land extended out into the swamp, forming a sort of lagoon, at the head of which was a small cluster of ruined buildings. The peninsula was covered with slash pines, cattails, and strangler figs—thick brush that made for excellent cover. He worked his way toward the spit of land, keeping his head barely above water, alert for not only alligators but Florida panthers as well—common in the Everglades. No shots came: the shooter must have lost track of his location.

He crawled to a muddy embankment thick with mangroves. Keeping low, he made his way along the edge of the water until he reached the tongue of land. He had to keep moving; keep his adversary guessing. Leaving the water, he scurried through the understory at a crouch, staying in the thickest areas, careful not to make any noise or disturb the vegetation more than absolutely necessary. He could just glimpse the ancient lodge from time to time through the cypress trees. Finally, the ruined structures came into view—metal sheds on stilts over the water; a corrugated boathouse; a mudbank covered with rotting fifty-five-gallon drums and abandoned equipment; a pair of decaying hoists; and the hull of an old wooden barge. And lying everywhere on the mudbank were dozens and dozens of fat alligators, crowded into the patches of sun, their armored backs glistening. They seemed to be asleep, but Pendergast knew that was merely a hunting strategy: they were alert and waiting for prey.

His silvery eyes took it all in, along with the lines of posts in the water and rotten metal mesh that had once served as breeding cages. It was clearly an abandoned alligator farm. The ruins offered numerous hiding places and ambush points: an ideal spot for a man with a handgun facing off against one with a rifle. He paused in a cattail thicket, taking stock. If he could reach the cover of those sheds, he could change the rules of engagement. Everything depended on whether or not the shooter had truly lost track of his location—or was biding his time.

Bursting from cover, ignoring the pain in his wounded leg, he sprinted across the open area toward the closest shed. Instantly, flashes of gunfire erupted from one of the ruined structures ahead, and Pendergast threw himself down, rounds thudding into the earth on all sides. Crawling frantically, he retreated to a muddy ditch, bullets humming, then worked his way back to the embankment and slid into the water, pausing just long enough to take a quick shot at the dark maw of the shed where the rounds had come from.

The shooter had not lost track of his location. In fact, he'd anticipated what Pendergast would do and moved from his sniper's nest to an ambush point in the old alligator farm.

Using the embankment as protection, Pendergast moved through the water and came around a turn in the shore, where a fallen cypress lay. Just above and beyond would be the shed where the shooter had fired from. With exceeding caution, he raised his head and peered through the ferns. He saw movement between the sheds: the brief flicker of a person running. He raised his gun, but it was too long a shot and it would only give away his position. He noticed that the man had moved to a central point among the ruined sheds. Evidently, he was determined that Pendergast not reach any part of that area. He was clearly a man who knew the layout of the island. And every tactical move he'd made so far indicated a military or law enforcement background. Such as John Vance had.

From his vantage point, Pendergast could see no way forward. The only option was to go back out into the water, using the fallen cypress as coverage, and circle farther around, looking for another approach. He had now taken the measure of his adversary, and the odds weren't favorable. The shooter knew Pendergast would come to him; he knew time was on his side. As long as there was a possibility, no matter how remote, that Coldmoon was still alive, he had to deal with the shooter and get back to the sinkhole. The man with the rifle knew that as well as he did.

He inched along the fallen tree, careful not to make ripples in the glassy sheet of water. At the end of the trunk, he peered around.

The only way to determine the current location of the shooter would be to encourage him to shoot. Which meant showing himself. Pendergast was now fairly sure, from the sound and the character of the rifle, that the man was firing a scoped Winchester 94, .30-30. It was a decent hunting rifle but not, by any means, a tactical combat weapon.

Still working his way through the water, watching carefully for alligators and water snakes, he made for a particularly dense stand of trees. Using them as cover, he slid closer to the jumble of buildings, crawling along the bottom and keeping his head under water as much as possible. This was made a little easier by a line of underwater fence posts connected by wire mesh.

He worked his way from three hundred yards to two hundred before the next shot came, this time whacking splinters off a tree trunk beside his head. That was useful information; he now knew the man had changed position into the main shed over the water and was firing at him from the darkness of an open door.

Creeping forward with utmost caution, he closed in another fifty yards. The sliding doors of the shed were halfway open. Pendergast could not see where the shooter was positioned within the well of darkness beyond—and could only locate him by precipitating a shot, with its attendant muzzle flash. Even then, the target was still too far away for his sidearm to be effective. He had to get within fifty yards to be reasonably sure of a hit. The problem was, at fifty yards, with his 1911 up against a Winchester, he would be a dead man.

The logic of the situation was dismayingly simple. He could not leave the island as long as there was a possibility Coldmoon was still alive. Even if he tried to swim away into the swamp, he was certain the shooter, whoever he was, had a second boat somewhere—probably inside the boathouse or one of the nearby sheds—which he would use to chase him down. Besides, if he tried that, chances were the alligators would get him long before a rifle did. He had no choice but to get the shooter, here and now.

From the darkness of the sliding doors, something was flung out, landing a second or two later in the water. At first, Pendergast could not make out what it was. But the alligators sprawled along the bank did, and in a flash they were in the water, a sudden boiling around the spot where the thing had landed: thrashing and struggling, with whipping of tails and snapping of jaws.

They were fighting over a piece of meat.

Another piece was flung out with a splash, generating another feeding frenzy as more of the brutes spilled into the water. When the third toss came, Pendergast fired into the darkness of the shed, only to draw return fire that drove him back behind another massive cypress stump.

This was a new strategy. There must be a hundred animals in the water now. The pieces of meat had been consumed and the reptiles were spreading out, aroused from their torpor and eager for more. He could see the ripples and swirls on the surface, the dimpled water indicating movement below. Some of the ripples were coming toward him. He moved behind the stump, a mass of roots ending in a twisted knot of wood. There he hunkered down, hoping the hungry beasts would not notice him or the blood seeping from his bullet wound. If he tried to flee the approaching hordes, his movement in the water would only attract them.

He ejected the empty magazine and slapped in the spare.

And then he pressed himself against the stump, working his legs into the root bundle and remaining perfectly still. He could see the blurry outline of the gators, moving back and forth like giant eels. A head emerged, just the nostrils and eyes, and then another head, until they seemed to be everywhere, peering hungrily about.

He remained pressed against the trunk, a shooter on the far side and alligators all around.

46

Pendergast saw the swirl of water and felt the thing brush past his legs just seconds before it paused to attack. He grabbed a knob on the cypress root bundle and hauled himself out of the water just as the alligator lunged. It caught the toe of his shoe but, unable to hold on, slipped back into the water. Another brute lunged upward, jaws closing like a steel trap. Pendergast pulled himself farther out of the water, trying to avoid the snapping jaws while still remaining in cover. Yet another gator lunged up and he shot it point-blank in the throat. It fell back, thrashing, eyes still open, black blood spreading in the dark water. Below him, the water swirled as additional alligators jockeyed for position. If he crept any higher up the side of the stump, he would expose himself to the shooter, but by staying put he could not avoid the reach of the alligators. He shot another that erupted from the water to grab his leg, then another: an unavoidable waste of ammunition as well as being a losing strategy, as the shot animals only added more meat to a feeding frenzy. The frantic thrashing spread further as the living gators tore into the dying ones, strewing entrails and body parts in the water. Pendergast, precariously clinging to the tangle of roots, knew he couldn't shoot them all. He couldn't climb higher; he couldn't descend.

As he considered his situation, he heard a roar, recognizing it a second later as the sound of an airboat engine starting up. Peering around the edge of the tree, he saw the craft emerge from the darkness of a far shed, a figure at the helm. It circled through the trees and he fired at it once, even though it was far out of range and moving fast.

Pendergast tried to move around the side of the stump, but a gator tore at his damaged shoe, almost ripping it off. As the boat circled he became fully exposed to it, unable to move, unable to take cover.

The boat slowed and came to rest across the clear patch of water. Its pilot was in shade, two hundred yards out.

Despite the fact the man was well out of range, Pendergast took careful aim, squeezed the trigger. A jet of water went up ten yards in front, wide of the craft.

"Agent Pendergast," a voice came over the water. "All you're doing is wasting bullets and attracting more alligators."

Pendergast recognized, to his enormous surprise, the voice of Commander Grove, the external affairs liaison from Miami PD.

"That's a fancy sidearm you're packing, but it can't work miracles." Grove paused. "Go ahead, anyway. Give it your best shot." The outline of a figure spread his arms, holding the rifle aside.

Pendergast aimed for the boat's engine and squeezed off his last two shots, spacing them apart long enough to make a correction on the second. A gout of water popped up a dozen feet to the right; the second, much closer at three feet. But not close enough. He fired again, but the hammer fell on an empty chamber, as he knew it would.

"Impressive shooting, under the circumstances. Still, you're an optimist, and in this crazy world, optimists die." The boat engine revved up and the airboat crept toward him. "I saw you lose your backup weapon through the scope, and I'm counting on your not having a third magazine for the 1911. Those seven-shot clips are heavy and I never knew an FBI agent to carry more than one spare. I mean, if you can't do the job with fifteen rounds, that's pretty sad. What kind of agent would carry a third magazine?" Grove laughed.

As the man spoke, Pendergast was assembling the missing pieces—the *real* missing pieces—of the puzzle. The picture they formed was depressing indeed. He briefly contemplated his options—either launch himself into the sea of alligators or wait to be shot. The water was still teeming with the agitated reptiles; another lunged up at him, and Pendergast smacked its snout with the butt of his empty gun. There was no longer any possibility of, or any point in, trying to remain in cover.

"Keep your hands away from your body and in sight at all times," Grove ordered curtly.

The airboat eased closer. Grove, at the helm, kept one hand on the wheel with the other aiming the rifle. "You FBI assholes come down here like you're manna from heaven. I wonder if you have any clue as to what's really going on."

"I do now," said Pendergast.

Grove eased the boat within twenty feet and cut the throttle, taking up the rifle in both hands and holding it steady on Pendergast.

"I wonder if *you* understand," Pendergast added.

Grove laughed. "I've got it about 90 percent figured out—

thanks to you and Coldmoon. Anyway, with you two dead I'll have time to piece together the rest and clean it all up. Unless, of course, you'd like to pass on a few pointers. You know, to help me out."

"I'd rather you satisfied my own curiosity first," Pendergast said. "I'm assuming it was you who doctored the Vance file to lure us out here?"

Grove's upper lip twitched with a note of self-satisfaction. "You should pin a medal on me for figuring out it was John Vance who set all this into motion. It wasn't until the second note had been placed on a grave that I started to wonder. Of course, as a police 'liaison' it was a breeze to insert myself into a case involving the FBI—just as a way of keeping tabs on things. And then, with the third note, I knew all this was more than coincidence. When I did some digging and learned Vance was dead, killed in a car accident, I was surprised as hell. But I quickly realized there was only one other possibility." He shook his head. "Who'd have expected that hangdog little Vance punk would grow up to become a serial killer?"

"If John Vance was dead, you must have pulled his death notice from the file. And added a fictitious interview with him— one that would lead us directly to Canepatch. Where you'd be waiting."

"Pretty fast footwork, right—pulling his son from the file so you wouldn't get suspicious, and adding that fake two-year-old interview report? I figured you'd want to talk to Vance."

"And he would have wanted to talk to you. After all, you did kill his wife. Correct?"

"You're smarter than the average bear. But just so you know, it was an accident."

"I assume you were having an affair with her. The husband

was returning from a tour of duty; she threatened to confess to him; and you killed her to silence her and preserve your career. Being a cop, you knew what to do to make it look like a suicide."

"I *said* it was an *accident*."

"Of course it was. As a self-professed former homicide detective, I'm sure you've heard that many times." Pendergast's voice suddenly launched into a high-pitched, sniveling whine. "*It was just an accident.*"

The satisfied smirk left Grove's face. "Fuck you—"

"But Lydia's husband, being former military police, sensed it was murder. He didn't have any hard evidence; he just *knew*. He couldn't convince the Miami PD of that—thanks no doubt to your behind-the-scenes manipulation of the investigation. Such as substituting her potentially damning X-rays with those of another, unrelated suicide victim."

Grove just glared at him.

"Clever of you, though, to leave Vance's hounding of the police—*real* hounding, by a man convinced his wife had been murdered—in the file. That added to its verisimilitude."

"I'm glad you're coming around. Anyway, Vance's long gone. With you and Coldmoon out of the way, that just leaves Mister Brokenhearts. As soon as I'm finished here, I'm going to do the world a solid by smoking his ass."

"How good of you—considering you created him in the first place."

"Bullshit!"

"Hardly. You're the one responsible for this entire chain of killings. In fact, you've been the *primum mobile* all along. The only difference is that, now, you know it. How many murders, exactly, can be laid at your doorstep? Let's add them up: Lydia Vance, Jasmine Oriol, Laurie Winters, Mary Adler, Elise Baxter,

Agatha Flayley—and that's not even counting the women slaughtered by Brokenhearts: Felice Montera, Jenny—"

"I keep telling you, no *way* am I responsible. Lydia was going to shoot off her mouth, and I was just trying to reason with her, but things got physical and, well—"

Again, the shrill, crybaby voice erupted from Pendergast. *"I was just trying to reason with her, but things got physical and, well . . . I strangled her."*

"Shut your fucking mouth."

"Contrary to your pusillanimous rationalizations, these murders are all a direct result of your actions, Commander—and you can't fool yourself into denying it. Nine cruel, needless, senseless murders."

"I've heard enough." Grove raised the rifle and took aim. Pendergast noted, with detached resignation, the slow squeeze of the trigger finger. He tensed his muscles, ready to leap into the swirling water, knowing it would be a useless gesture.

Still, any gesture was better than none at all.

47

As PENDERGAST STEELED himself for the final leap, he heard a noise, a *chunk*, come from the direction of the boat. Grove's head snapped forward as if he'd been slapped from behind. His rifle jerked up and went off, the round going wild. Grove's expression turned to one of pure astonishment. Then he did a pirouette that was almost graceful, his body turning to reveal the handle of a hatchet, blade buried in the back of his skull. He remained still for a moment, then toppled headfirst into the water.

The splash of Grove's body, and the sudden introduction of fresh blood and brains, generated another frenzied boiling of water. A dozen alligators converged, jaws snapping, tails whipping, seizing the body on all sides and shaking it back and forth.

And now Pendergast saw a battered kayak glide up behind the airboat. A young man was paddling it, lean and muscled, with closely trimmed hair and a grin that seemed permanently stamped on his scarred, crooked face. He wore a T-shirt that said, BECAUSE IT IS BITTER. He raised an arm in a tentative greeting, a very red tongue exposed behind cemetery teeth. "Agent Pendergast? It's me."

"Mister Brokenhearts," Pendergast said.

He watched as the young man, trembling slightly, boarded the idling airboat and brought it through the mass of alligators and over to the stump. Pendergast stepped aboard. The youth spat into the water at the pack of tearing, twisting, snapping alligators. A long filleting knife, its razor-sharp blade blackened, was now in one hand.

"So that's the man who killed my mother. I should've known it was a cop. I've been following you, you know, since I saw you on TV—"

"I know," Pendergast interrupted, taking the helm. "We'll talk about it later. Right now, we have to go."

"No. No, I can't leave Archy behind."

"There's no time."

The grip on the knife grew tighter, the knuckles whitening. "But Archy...not *with those gators*...!"

Pendergast turned and fixed the youth with a look. "By stopping that man, you saved a life. *My* life. Now you have a chance to save a second. My partner's on that island. He's been shot. We need to get to him."

The youth stared at him, red-rimmed eyes wide. "I don't care. My mother's dead. Nothing—none of *them*—brought her back. 'Death has a hundred hands and walks by a thousand ways.'"

"Don't take refuge in literature. That's cowardly, and you're not a coward. This is the real world—where real people live, hurt, and die."

"Yes. And violence is the only answer."

"Has violence worked for you? Have you atoned yet? Do you feel healed?" He lowered his voice. "Trust me, I *know* about violence."

Brokenhearts stared, his misshapen face twisted with emotion.

"Did violence bring your mother back—no matter how many times your father tried? And what did violence do to you? Violence is an answer—but it's the *last* answer."

A keening sound of despair came from the man's lips.

"Feel the pain in others you have caused, through violence. Feel the loss—the terror and sorrow. *That's* the beginning of atonement." He lowered his voice. "I sensed you were shadowing me. At least, I hoped you were. And now we're face-to-face. The rest is up to you." He held out his hand. "First, the knife."

For a moment, the youth was motionless. Then he extended his hand and Pendergast gently took away the knife. Pocketing it, Pendergast turned immediately and pushed the throttle down, the airboat lurching forward with a roar, and he aimed it down the channel toward the landing, running it up onto the mud, then leaping out and crashing through the understory, heading for the sinkhole. Sixty more seconds and he arrived at the yawning pit—and there was Coldmoon at the bottom, weakly holding on to an exposed root, barely conscious and hardly able to keep his head above water. Several agitated water moccasins swam in the bloody, murky water around him.

"Hold on!" Pendergast seized a root and swung into the pit, scrambling down from handhold to handhold as fast as he could. When he reached the bottom he kicked off, ignoring the snakes, and in two strokes reached Coldmoon. Grasping him around the chest, keeping his head above water, he pushed his way back to the side of the sinkhole. When he looked up, he saw Mister Brokenhearts's face at the edge of the pit, peering down, expressionless.

Grasping a root, Pendergast tightened his hold on Coldmoon and began hauling him up the slick, muddy slope, finding fresh hand- and footholds, every muscle straining. Another step, another haul, another clenched root. At the extreme end of exhaustion, he approached the top.

"Give me a hand," he gasped.

Mister Brokenhearts stared down, his face distorted with indecision. He looked to one side, and then the other, as if he might run. The airboat was at the dock. It was a perfect opportunity to escape.

"You could run," Pendergast said as he struggled. "But you won't—at least, not if you truly do want to atone."

Brokenhearts reached down and grabbed Coldmoon's arm with one hand, Pendergast's with the other, and hauled back, helping drag both up and over the edge. Coldmoon lay on his back among the crushed ferns, unconscious now. Pendergast took his pulse, checked his airway, and gave him a rapid examination. He was shot, possibly snakebitten, suffering respiratory impairment due to water in the lungs. Pendergast rolled him on his side and slapped his back, shaking him hard. Coldmoon coughed, water and blood running out of his mouth. He wheezed loudly; Pendergast guessed a collapsed lung—at the minimum.

"Help me get him to the boat."

Brokenhearts assisted as Pendergast half dragged, half carried his partner to the airboat. Laying him on the rear seat, he used a life preserver as a pillow and covered him with a boat tarp. Then he grabbed the helm and revved up the engine. "Push us off."

Brokenhearts pushed the boat away from the mud and hopped back in, finding a spot in the bow, while Pendergast swung the wheel around and headed back toward Paradise Landing at high speed, weaving frantically through the cypresses and saw grass, throwing up a massive wake and doing his best not to tear out the bottom of the craft on submerged mangrove roots.

Arriving at the dock, he leapt off and ran to the Mustang, pulled open the door, grabbed the radio mike, and called in an "agent down" message, giving coordinates. This accomplished, he went back to the boat and bent down over Coldmoon, giving him a more thorough examination. The man was barely alive, with a fast, thready heartbeat, but still breathing. His skin was cold and clammy. The bullet wound was bleeding, but not badly—most of the bleeding would be internal. Better not to disturb him further, but rather leave him in place until the paramedics arrived.

"Can...can I help more?" asked Brokenhearts.

"Yes." Pendergast reached for Coldmoon's belt, unclipped a pair of handcuffs, and tossed them over. "Put those on. You're under arrest."

The young man fumbled with the cuffs for a moment before figuring out how to lock them around his wrists. "I'm sorry," he said, the words abruptly beginning to spill out. "I know you understand. You said so on that television show, when you told people I wasn't a monster. But even *you* can't fathom the depth of my sorrow. I mean, what you said back there—about violence, about atonement." The sudden flow stopped for a moment. "I can't put my grief into words. I've tried, but I can't. Stephen Crane did, though. I could read you—"

"Later," Pendergast said quietly. He tucked the tarp more tightly around Coldmoon as the faint sound of an approaching helicopter reached them from beyond the trees.

48

PENDERGAST WATCHED THE medevac chopper rise into the air above Paradise Landing, carrying his comatose partner to the University of Miami Hospital. The chopper was departing, but the rest of the cavalry would be here soon enough. A temporary silence descended over the shabby docks as he led Brokenhearts to the Mustang and put him in the backseat. The young man paused to ask if he could retrieve some object from his own vehicle, which was hidden in the grass just off the dirt road. The object turned out to be a book of poems. Brokenhearts got into the backseat, mumbling to himself, over and over, rocking back and forth, the book clutched in his cuffed hands. Pendergast recognized the mumbling as verse.

In the desert
I saw a creature, naked, bestial,

Pendergast slipped behind the wheel, turned on the LED emergency dash lights, and started the car with a roar. He backed it around and, with a spray of dirt, accelerated down the dusty road, putting on the siren. Reaching the paved asphalt, he pressed the pedal down and pushed the Shelby to over a hundred miles an hour. It shot along the road, walls of vegetation flashing by in a blur of green.

Who, squatting upon the ground,
Held his heart in his hands,
And ate of it.

In the distance, Pendergast could see flashing lights coming toward him; the Miami Homicide flying squad, on their way to Canepatch for evidence collection and to recover whatever remained of the body of Commander Grove—if anything. Pendergast checked in with them by radio as they flashed by: squad cars, Crime Scene Unit vans, sirens Doppler-shifting down as he blew by.

Ten minutes later his radio buzzed; he pulled it down and listened. The dispatcher told him that Coldmoon had arrived at U Miami and was heading into surgery. His condition was critical.

I said, "Is it good, friend?"

The road merged onto Tamiami Trail and Pendergast passed more police cruisers. The Shelby was now traveling at 120 miles per hour, Pendergast's silvery eyes looking far ahead, his mind focused only on speed and the long straight road. In the back-seat, Mister Brokenhearts kept up his monotonic recital.

"It is bitter—bitter," he answered;

The radio hissed again and he pulled it down. "Pendergast here."

"Lieutenant Sandoval. Have I got it right that you're bringing in Brokenhearts?"

"Yes."

"We're liaising with the FBI. You're to bring him straight to the FBI HQ."

"Understood. And Coldmoon?"

"In surgery. I'm sorry—they doubt they can save him. That son of a bitch Grove, hard to believe…"

Pendergast hung up the radio and pressed the accelerator further, the Shelby's speedometer inching toward 130.

He shot past a succession of shabby roadside attractions, siren wailing, cars pulling off on both sides to make way. In the backseat, Brokenhearts continued to rock slowly and mutter. Now more cars were appearing as he approached the western suburbs. He slowed to 100, then 90. Passing the Everglades boundary, he entered the suburb of Tamiami, then Sweetwater, where he was forced to a crawl by heavy traffic.

"But I like it

"Because it is bitter,

They inched through traffic until he reached the Reagan Turnpike, where he headed north. In another twenty minutes he joined I-75 as far as the exit to FBI headquarters. As he passed through the gates, he was met by two cars and a van. Swinging around to the processing bay in the back, he was met by a mass of agents, Miami police, squad cars, and vans. He pulled to a stop as half a dozen people surrounded the car and opened the doors, removing Brokenhearts, who submitted meekly.

Sandoval came over, grasped Pendergast's arm, and helped him out of the car. Agents, support staff, MPD brass—everyone was there. Brokenhearts stood in the hot glare of the sun, hands clasping the book, head bowed.

"Agent Pendergast, allow me to congratulate you," said Lieutenant Sandoval. Brokenhearts's handcuffs were now being reinforced with leg irons. "If I may ask—who the hell is he? I mean, his real name."

"His name is Vance." Pendergast looked around. "Get me on a helicopter for U Miami Hospital."

Nearby agents began shouting orders and gesturing. Brokenhearts, now in chains, was being led away. As he passed Pendergast, he glanced over and muttered one final line:

"And because it is my heart."

The FBI chopper took Pendergast from HQ to the helipad on the roof of U Miami, where he was met with more agents from the Miami Field Office and several MPD detectives. Speaking to no one, he sprinted as fast as his wounded leg allowed from the helicopter, past the group, and into the building, bypassing the elevator and taking the stairs two at a time until he reached the main surgical floor. He arrived at a small waiting area outside the surgical bay, guarded by a pair of FBI agents.

"Coldmoon," he said. "How is he?"

"We'll get a doctor to talk to you, Agent Pendergast."

Pendergast nodded. Then he began pacing the small waiting area, the only sound the faint whisper of his footfalls echoing off the linoleum floor.

Finally a doctor came out, still in scrubs, blood smeared on her gown. "Mr. Pendergast? I'm Dr. Webern." She did not offer her hand.

"Doctor. How is he?"

She hesitated. "Well, he's a tough customer. But his condition is extremely critical."

"His odds?"

"I wouldn't want to speculate. The bullet went through the lungs and expanded into a pretty massive thoracic wound. He's lost a lot of blood, and the water moccasin bite made it worse, as the venom triggers coagulopathy. It's amazing he survived at all. But we've got a team of eight surgeons and fourteen support staff working for him, and believe me, they're some of the best in the world."

Pendergast nodded silently.

"Can I get you a counselor or clergy?"

"No, thank you."

She frowned. "Are you going to be all right, Agent Pendergast? Waiting here by yourself? Your leg is bleeding."

"I'll be fine."

"Then if you'll excuse me, I'm needed back in the OR."

"Of course."

The doctor gave him a faint smile, replaced the mask on her face, and turned away, disappearing back into the operating suite.

49

IT ONLY TOOK seventy-two hours for the med/surg nurses to grow heartily sick of him.

Coldmoon had first woken up in post-op. Initially, he'd thought he was still asleep, in some nightmare of green walls and bright ceilings and masked beings hovering around. Then he fell asleep again. The next time he woke, he realized it hadn't been a dream, after all, and now he was in what looked like the recovery bay of a hospital ICU. Doctors would come by, peer down at him, then consult with colleagues in low tones; nurses would check his vitals, stick a needle into the injection port of his IV catheter—and he'd fall asleep again. Soft beeping and buzzing and whisperings of machinery filled the silences. This seemed to go on forever, sleeping and waking, sleeping and waking, but he later realized it couldn't have been more than twenty-four hours.

Finally, he woke up in a private room on a step-down floor. He was hungry and thirsty and, for the first time, in pain. They fed him—after a fashion—and he was ministered to by more doctors. They assured him he was going to pull through. Later, they explained he'd been very lucky, given the caliber of the gun and the location of his wound. By this point, two more days had gone by and he'd recovered sufficiently to complain about the coffee. It was maddening. They would only bring him de-caffeinated beverages. Worse, he was unable to explain how to brew it the proper way. There was a drip machine in the med staff's break room, but just when he'd convinced one nurse to leave the pot on the warmer, there'd be a shift change, and the staff coming on duty would throw out the stale coffee and brew a new pot. If he complained, they'd just sedate him and he'd drift back to sleep.

He stared out the window, seeing majestic royal palms and the clear blue sky of early April. At this rate, he might never re-cover.

The door opened and, instead of a nurse, in walked three slightly blurry figures. Coldmoon turned to see them better, wincing slightly at the pain. The first, he realized after a moment, was his boss, ADC Walter Pickett. Beside him, wearing one of her trademark pastel dresses, was Dr. Fauchet. Behind them, a black shadow approached, ultimately resolving itself into the form of Agent Pendergast. They all looked down at him.

Coldmoon swallowed painfully. "About time you showed up."

"I've been here before," Pickett said. "You were just too high on painkillers to remember."

"They wouldn't let me in until now," Fauchet said. "Just imagine—and me, a doctor."

Pendergast said nothing. And yet, somehow, Coldmoon felt he'd seen the man more than once over the last few days—that pale face and black suit hovering over his bed, pale eyes full of concern.

One of the nurses, Estrellita, came in with a cup of coffee on a plastic tray. She set it down and turned to leave, but Coldmoon objected. With an effort, he reached over, sipped the lukewarm beverage.

"Too fresh," he said, handing it to her. "Bring it back once it's sat another few hours."

The nurse glared at him with what he hoped was feigned annoyance. Then she turned toward Pickett. "Anything you can do to get this one's discharge expedited would be appreciated."

As she left, Pickett came closer and gently grasped Coldmoon's hand. "Think you're going to remember what I say this time?"

"I'll try."

"You're going to be fine. The wounds are healing, you've recovered from the shock and loss of blood, and there's no sign of infection. Just as important, you're a hero. You're going to get the FBI Star."

"I am?" Coldmoon asked.

"Oh yes," Pickett said.

"Funny, I don't remember being a hero. I don't remember much of anything. We were headed toward that broken-down lodge, and then the bottom fell out."

"One could say that." It was Pendergast who spoke.

"Speaking of heroes," Pickett went on, "Pendergast here saved your skin *and* brought in Brokenhearts. Must have been some kind of first—him bringing in a perp alive, I mean. We considered him for the Medal of Valor, but then I saw he'd already been awarded it twice. No point swelling his head any more than it already is."

Was he joking? Apparently not: Pickett's tone was affable enough, and there was a faint twitch to his lips that was probably the closest thing he could manage to a smile. Coldmoon tried to sit up in bed a little, thought better of it, and lay back.

He couldn't seem to clear his head, and weariness was never far away. "So. Is someone going to tell me what happened?"

"The details can wait," Pickett went on. "The important thing is, Brokenhearts is in custody."

"So who was he?"

This time it was Pendergast who answered. "Ronald Vance. Son of John Vance—the man we'd gone out to Canepatch to interview."

"Was John Vance the old man on the porch?"

"No. That was a local man who rented airboats—may he rest in peace."

"Ronald Vance," Coldmoon repeated after a moment. "And is that where he lived? Canepatch?"

"No," said Dr. Fauchet. "That was an abandoned alligator farm once owned by the grandparents of... well, that's not important. Anyway, Brokenhearts himself lived in Golden Glades. Tarpon Court."

"Where's that?"

"About a dozen miles from here. Ugly old house, too." She beamed with ill-concealed pride. "I was the one who discovered the address. *And* the house."

"You didn't go out there?" Coldmoon asked.

The M.E. nodded.

"And you walked right in? To Brokenhearts's place?"

"Hell, no! I knocked on both the front and back doors. Nobody answered, and y'all weren't picking up your cell phones, so I left. You think I'd walk right into a serial killer's house, all by myself, with no backup? What do you think I am—crazy?"

Another nurse came in. "Mr. Coldmoon needs his rest," she informed the room in general.

"Caffeine," Coldmoon said. "Caffeine is what I need."

"You already refused a nice fresh cup of coffee, sugar."

Coldmoon tried to glare at her, with little success. Talking was making his throat hurt. "Give. Me. Real. Coffee."

The nurse shook her head. "Armstrong Coldmoon, I keep telling you the only way you're going to get your kind of coffee is to walk out the front door and then make it yourself."

There was a silence.

"Armstrong?" Pendergast repeated.

"What about it?"

"That's your Christian name?"

"I don't know what's so Christian about it, but it's my first name, yes." This was followed by another silence Coldmoon eventually realized he was expected to break. "My great-great-grandfather killed Custer. Helped, anyway. In Lakota, you sometimes take the name of a vanquished enemy. So *Armstrong* has been a name in my family ever since."

"Mr. Coldmoon needs his—" the nurse began again, but at this Fauchet linked arms with the woman and gently but firmly led her out of the room, peppering her with questions about Coldmoon's medications. The three men watched as Fauchet closed the door.

"In any case," Pickett said, turning back and stiffening his spine as if to make a formal announcement, "now is as good a time as any to let you know there's an opening in Washington for an executive assistant director of the National Security Branch, and I've been offered the position. Closing this case obviously played a part in that offer." He cleared his throat. "I may be a demanding supervisor, but I also give credit where credit is due. And so, Agent Coldmoon, you should know that—in addition to the FBI Star—I'm initiating the paperwork to promote you to senior special agent."

Coldmoon didn't know how to answer. "Thank you, sir."

But Pickett was already turning to Pendergast. "Agent Pendergast. As I've mentioned, you deserve a large share of the credit here. I suppose I could promote you to supervisory special agent, but I doubt you'd want to be burdened by the managerial duties."

Pendergast bowed slightly. "Quite true."

Pickett glanced at his watch. "So before I go, is there anything else I could do for you? Professionally, I mean?"

"As a matter of fact, there is. You recall the recent agreement we made at that rooftop bar, regarding the details of my, ah, operational parameters?"

A cloud passed across Pickett's face before he could stop it. "Of course. And I'll make sure my successor at the New York Field Office continues to honor your unorthodox methods—assuming, of course, you maintain your impressive closure rate."

"I shall make every effort." Pendergast indicated his thanks with a nod. "That leaves just one other matter—the nature of my work environment. Specifically, with regard to a partner." His face, pale at the best of times, was now like marble. "As you no doubt remember, I initially opposed the idea of working with Agent Coldmoon. However, I…" He seemed to be uncharacteristically stumbling. "It should be noted—"

"Um, one other thing," Coldmoon interrupted. "As part of my promotion, I mean."

The other two turned to look at him.

"I'd rather you find me another partner, sir. Going forward, I mean."

Pickett raised his eyebrows.

"No offense to Agent Pendergast. But I'm not sure our investigative methods are entirely, entirely…in sync." Christ, he was tired. "I mean…" He waved an enervated hand over his prostrate body.

"No offense taken," Pendergast said quickly, gliding in before Pickett could speak. "After all, it would hardly be fair—given what's happened to other agents I've worked with in the past. Agent Coldmoon's current condition speaks for itself. I believe there is a story going around the Bureau to the effect that to partner with me would be a fatal enterprise. That I am a sort of Jonah on the FBI's vessel, as it were. An unfortunate rumor, but one I find hard to dispel."

Pickett looked from Pendergast to Coldmoon and back again, unable to completely keep his features free of suspicion. "Very well," he said. "If that's your formal request, Agent Coldmoon."

At that moment the nurse barged back in. The expression on her face showed she meant business this time. "Out. All of you."

"Yes, of course," said Pickett hastily. "Agent Coldmoon, you'll be hearing from me. Get back on your feet soon."

Pendergast turned to follow him out. At the last moment, he glanced back. "Thank you," he said. "*Armstrong.*"

"You owe me," Coldmoon whispered as weariness overwhelmed him. "Big time."

50

Roger Smithback sat at his desk, fingers motionless on the keyboard. His office had been cleared of the heavy crates full of letters—all pointless now, with the real Brokenhearts caught just a week ago, and Miami getting back to normal... or as normal as it ever got.

The thing was, Smithback ruminated, the murders didn't *feel* solved to him. Oh, he'd heard the explanations—the police had doled them out to the press like a party line, which it probably was—but there were still questions that remained unanswered. In fact, there were whole pieces missing: exactly what triggered it all, why the hearts had been left on those particular graves... even who, precisely, was guilty of what. He'd asked these questions, of course, but had been stonewalled by the fact that Mister Brokenhearts, aka Ronald Vance, was a very sick individual who was under lockdown, being questioned by psychiatrists and psychologists, and that his motives could not now be revealed by the police—if he had any intelligible motives at all. The same went for this Commander Grove who'd died in an Everglades shootout: although his role in triggering the killings had been alluded to, the police tended to close ranks around their own, even the rotten apples, and nobody would answer his questions.

Which was bad news for him. He'd gotten some serious visibility on this story early on. In return, the whole damn city expected he would ultimately deliver the goods—and he couldn't. He didn't have any more information than the rest of the crime beat reporters. Interest in the crazy letters he'd been receiving had waned. The news cycle was moving on and the Brokenhearts case was on its way from the front burner to the back; the wounded FBI agent at the heart of the case would soon be released from the hospital; and Kraski, his editor at the *Herald*, wanted to shift him back to the vice beat. In fact, Kraski had only allowed him this final story on the murders—a kind of editorializing summing-up—after some serious pestering on Smithback's part.

He stared at what he'd written thirty minutes ago, and hadn't been able to add to since.

Until such time as the psychological specialists from the Miami PD and FBI are able to complete their evaluation of Brokenhearts, now revealed as Ronald Vance, we may never understand the motivations that led to his murderous rampage. We may never know what Vance was "atoning" for and why he felt such a burning need to do so.

What we do know is that Ronald's father, John, led his son on a homicidal journey that spanned the East Coast 11 years ago. But that revelation leads only to more questions. What was the trigger that set them on this path of murder? What precisely was the relationship of this father-and-son killing team? Why did the murders staged as "suicides" stop when they did—and why did the son, Ronald, wait so long to start killing again? Why the hearts on the graves? In sum: What exactly is the link between the fake suicides 11 years ago and the Brokenhearts killings today? And exactly how did the death of Miami PD Commander Gordon Grove fit into this picture of violence?

Henry Miller wrote that "until we accept the fact that life itself is founded in mystery, we shall learn nothing." Perhaps all we can do, then, is accept the fact that this tragedy happened, and hope that—with such acceptance— understanding will eventually follow.

"Really, must you quote Henry Miller?" came a dulcet, languorous voice from over his shoulder. "You're setting a bad literary example for the *Herald*—and these days, newspapers need all the help they can get."

Smithback wheeled around to see Agent Pendergast standing over him. He'd come up behind the journalist so silently, Smithback had no idea how long he'd been standing there. "Jesus, you almost gave me a heart attack."

"I frequently have that effect on people." Pendergast looked around at the half-empty newsroom, then took a seat, folded one black-clad knee over the other, and regarded the journalist impassively. "Your brother would have finished that piece by now."

"That's probably true. But then, Bill wasn't one to let facts stand in the way of a good story."

"Of what facts, in particular, are you unsure?"

Smithback regarded the FBI agent through slightly narrowed eyes. He hadn't seen Pendergast in maybe two weeks. What was he up to? "Are you kidding? I mean, where do I start?

When is Brokenhearts going to explain just what the hell he was doing?"

"He's already done all the explaining we can hope for. He's confessed to having committed the three recent murders in Miami, as well as being involved in the old murder/suicides. He killed Commander Grove, too."

"Why? What did Grove do to him?" He paused, thinking. "Did Grove...have something to do with his mother's death?"

More silence.

"Wait, did Grove kill his mother, Lydia, twelve years ago? Right before the father returned from a tour of duty?"

Pendergast only smiled.

"I get it. The father was going to mess up their little love nest. Probably an argument escalated. Right?"

"You could call it a reasonable assumption."

"Vance intuited that his wife's death was murder, made to look like suicide. But the cops didn't buy it. Grove must have done all he could to keep a lid on the investigation."

"Keep going."

"So: why then did Ronald's father stage all these killings of women, dressed up like suicides?"

"Why, indeed? What did the murders have in common?"

"They were all killed the same way as Lydia Vance—murder made to look like suicide by hanging with a knotted cord."

"What else?"

"They all came from Florida."

Pendergast folded his arms and fixed Smithback with pale eyes, waiting.

"One thing the cops did say was that John Vance's first tour in the Gulf was cut short by a TBI from a roadside bomb. That's why he was an MP his second tour. When he came home and found his wife dead, and the cops ignored him, he went nuts. He started killing Miami women in other parts of the country, exactly the way his wife was killed. A murderous road trip, with his kid riding shotgun."

A slow nod. "To what purpose?"

Smithback scratched one cheek thoughtfully. "Maybe... maybe he was planning to eventually confess what he'd done and humiliate the Miami PD by exposing their incompetence. But then why drive all over the damn place? Why not stage the killings here in Florida?"

"Give the man some credit. He may have felt a perverse, vengeful need to show up the Miami police, but he didn't want to make it too easy—so easy that, say, he might get caught before he was finished."

"That makes sense. Killing as catharsis. And when he was satisfied, he'd have found some suitably gratifying way to drag the Miami PD through the mud for not seeing the pattern. Except his plans were cut short by the fatal car accident."

"Not bad. That might get you a C in journalism class. But you aren't answering the questions you raise in your own article: what was the *dynamic* between father and son?"

Smithback paused. "The cops said the son, Mister Brokenhearts, confessed to the last murder, the one in Ithaca off the bridge. Apparently, his father had told him it was time to step up, be a man."

"Do you think he wanted to do that?"

A longer pause. "No."

"So follow that thread to its end. *Why* did the murders stop?"

"I just said. Because of the car crash a week later."

Pendergast gave him that silvery look again.

"Wait a minute. You don't think—you're not saying that crash was deliberate? That Ronald couldn't take it anymore and wanted it to stop...and tried to kill the two of them *himself*? But he wasn't even old enough to drive!"

Pendergast said nothing.

"It wouldn't matter—he was old enough to reach over and grab the wheel at the right moment." Smithback was thinking fast now. "His dad was killed in the crash...*but he wasn't*. Bad enough that his mother had been murdered. He hadn't wanted to kill those innocent women. But he was young. Young, confused, and mentally ill. *And* he was injured in the crash—badly injured."

"Head trauma. On a related note, you might find his father's obituary quite enlightening. Not the one that ran in the Scranton newspaper, but the one from the *Greater Pittston Eagle*, a locale closer to the actual crash. It's not so much an obituary, really, as an article covering the accident. It's quite graphic in its attention to detail. John Vance died as a result of being impaled on the steering column. Apparently, the man's rib cage was crushed and the steering assembly pierced his heart. The son was trapped in the mangled car with his dead father for over forty minutes until he was freed by the Jaws of Life."

"Oh God," Smithback said. He was shocked...but still thinking fast. "So he would have been hospitalized—hospitalized *and* institutionalized—until he reached adulthood. The doctors probably considered his ravings, if there were any, a side effect of TBI. But all that time he was actually tortured by what he'd done. Hence the need to atone. Right?"

"Close enough. You published his letter yourself: *Their deaths cry out for justice. Hers most of all. She was my reason for life. I must atone.* I'd say you just raised your grade to a B, Mr. Smithback."

Smithback barely heard him. "And all these years, Grove

thought he'd gotten away with the murder of his lover. He didn't realize John Vance, her husband, had gone on a killing spree afterward. They were all recorded as suicides. How would Grove know? Now, coasting to retirement as a police liaison or whatever, he wouldn't have gotten concerned about a bunch of new murders. *Until* he realized the new killings were linked to the old ones—which, because they imitated his killing of Lydia Vance, might in turn lead to her... and from there to him."

The agent gave a slow nod of affirmation.

"This is pure gold. Can I quote you—on the record?"

"Quote what, exactly? I've only asked questions."

"I need a source."

"In that case, you'll have to content yourself with calling it 'a deep background source in law enforcement.'"

"I can live with that." Smithback began turning toward his keyboard, then paused. "But why would Brokenhearts think killing more people could help atone for the old murders?"

"Only Ronald Vance can answer that—assuming even he knows the answer. Who can guess what went on in that damaged, tormented mind during these ten years of hospitalization? But one thing is clear: he didn't want his recent victims to suffer more than necessary. Hence the quick killing cuts with a sharp knife. His only interest was in retrieving the... gifts."

"Right." Smithback returned his fingers to the keyboard, then stopped once again. "Um, please don't take this the wrong way, but—why are you helping me?"

Pendergast adjusted the already perfect cuffs of his shirt. "I'm from New Orleans, and we tend to be a superstitious lot. Your brother Bill was a friend of mine. I have a strong sense that— if I didn't help you with this story—his shade might disturb my peace."

"Huh. You're probably right." And Smithback began typing quickly, getting it all down. After a minute, the typing slowed. "Hey. One other thing. That doesn't explain how Commander Grove managed to lure you two out into—"

But when he turned around, all he saw was the half-empty newsroom, his fellow workers hunched over their own screens. It was as if Pendergast had never been there at all.